PRAISE FOR KEND

D0400284

"In Elliot's latest gripping novel the mystery and suspense are top-notch, and the romance embedded within will quench love story junkies' thirst, too. The author's eye for detail makes this one play out more like a movie rather than a book. It can easily be read as a standalone but is obviously much better if the prior three are digested first."

—*Romantic Times Book Reviews* on *Targeted*, 4 stars

"Elliot's latest addition to her thrilling, edge-of-your-seat series, Bone Secrets, will scare the crap out of you, yet allow you to swoon over the building romantic setting, which provides quite the picturesque backdrop. Her novel contains thrills, chills, snow and . . . hey, you never know! The surprises and cliffhangers are satisfying, yet edgy enough to keep you feverishly flipping the pages."

—*Romantic Times Book Reviews* on *Known*, 4 stars

"Elliot's best work to date. The author's talent is evident in the characters' wit and smart dialogue. . . . One wouldn't necessarily think a psychological thriller and romance would mesh together well, but Elliot knows what she's doing when she turns readers' minds inside out and then softens the blow with an unforgettable love story."

—*Romantic Times Book Reviews* on *Vanished*, 4½ stars, Top Pick

"Kendra Elliot does it again! Filled with twists, turns, and spine-tingling details, *Alone* is an impressive addition to the Bone Secrets series."

—Laura Griffin, *New York Times* bestselling author

"Elliot once again proves to be a genius in the genre with her third heart-pounding novel in the Bone Secrets collection. The author knows romance and suspense, reeling readers in instantaneously and wowing them with an extremely surprising finish . . . Elliot's best by a mile!"
—*Romantic Times Book Reviews* on *Buried*, 4½ stars, Top Pick (HOT)

"Make room on your keeper shelf! *Hidden* has it all: intricate plotting, engaging characters, a truly twisted villain. I can't wait to see what Kendra Elliot dishes up next!"
—Karen Rose, *New York Times* bestselling author

A
MERCIFUL
TRUTH

ALSO BY KENDRA ELLIOT

MERCY KILPATRICK NOVELS

A Merciful Death

BONE SECRETS NOVELS

Hidden

Chilled

Buried

Alone

Known

BONE SECRETS NOVELLAS

Veiled

CALLAHAN & MCLANE NOVELS
PART OF THE BONE SECRETS WORLD

Vanished

Bridged

Spiraled

Targeted

ROGUE RIVER NOVELLAS

On Her Father's Grave (Rogue River)

Her Grave Secrets (Rogue River)

Dead in Her Tracks (Rogue Winter)

Death and Her Devotion (Rogue Vows)

A
MERCIFUL
TRUTH

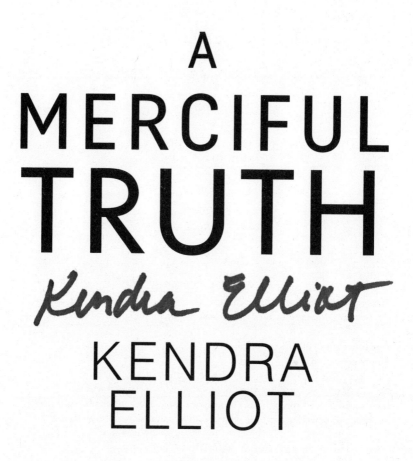

KENDRA
ELLIOT

Montlake
Romance

This is a work of fiction. Names, characters, organizations, places, events, and incidents are either products of the author's imagination or are used fictitiously.

Text copyright © 2017 Kendra Elliot
All rights reserved.

No part of this book may be reproduced, or stored in a retrieval system, or transmitted in any form or by any means, electronic, mechanical, photocopying, recording, or otherwise, without express written permission of the publisher.

Published by Montlake Romance, Seattle

www.apub.com

Amazon, the Amazon logo, and Montlake Romance are trademarks of Amazon.com, Inc., or its affiliates.

ISBN-13: 9781477848296
ISBN-10: 1477848290

Cover design by Eileen Carey

Printed in the United States of America

For Amelia.
Everything is within your power.

ONE

Police Chief Truman Daly slammed the door of his Tahoe and raised a hand to protect his face from the heat of the fire. He took a half step back, bumping into his vehicle. Flames had engulfed the old barn and were stretched high against the night's black sky.

A total loss.

He'd believed he'd parked a safe distance from the fire, but the toasting of his cheeks caused second thoughts.

He pulled down on the brim of his cowboy hat to cover his face, ignored the flooding memories of a past deadly fire, and jogged toward the two Deschutes County sheriff patrol vehicles that'd arrived before him. The two deputies stood behind their cars, talking on their radios, eyeing the towering flames.

There was nothing they could do. A faint siren sounded in the distance, but Truman knew the fire department was too late. Its goal would be to keep the fire from spreading to the woods and neighboring ranches.

"Hey, Chief," one of the deputies shouted over the roar of the fire as he approached.

Truman recognized the older deputy. *Ralph something.* He didn't know the other one.

"Did you see anyone here?" Truman asked, knowing there was no way to check inside the barn.

"No one," said Ralph. "We've been here fifteen seconds, and there was no chance in hell we'd try to look inside." The young deputy next to him nodded emphatically.

"Let's walk the perimeter," said Truman.

"You go around to the right, and we'll head left," suggested Ralph.

Truman nodded and headed around toward the back of the burning barn, putting plenty of space between himself and the hot inferno and welcoming the crisp November air. *The fire has gotten bigger in the few seconds I've been here.* In the last two weeks, three other fires had popped up around his small town of Eagle's Nest in Central Oregon. He and the fire department hadn't caught the serial arsonist, and none of the previous arsons had been on the scale of this one. The first had been an abandoned car. Then someone's trash. The last had been a small shed.

He's escalating.

Sweat ran down his back, and it wasn't solely from the fire. *I hate fires.* He jogged through the sagebrush and rocks, the ground well lit as he scanned for any signs of victims or a possible fire starter. Ponderosa pines towered about fifty yards away, and Truman was thankful to see the immediate area around the barn was clear of fuel for the fire. At one time there'd been a few small holding pens, but nearly all the fence rails had collapsed and rotted away. He doubted the old barn had been used in the last decade.

This fourth fire was several miles outside his city's limits, but as soon as he'd received word about it, he'd rolled out of bed and gotten dressed. The arsonist had pissed him off, and Truman now took every fire personally. Truman could imagine the asshole's glee as he sent police and fire crews scrambling to put out his handiwork.

One of these times, he's going to hurt someone.

The fire engine sirens grew louder, and two gunshots cracked over the sounds of the flames.

Truman dropped to his stomach and rolled behind a rock, his weapon in hand. *Who's shooting?* He froze and listened, trying to hear past the roar in his ears.

Two more shots.

Was that a scream?

His heart pounding, he called 911, reported shots fired, and advised the dispatcher to immediately let the approaching fire trucks know. He ended the call and slowly moved out of his hiding place behind the rock, his eyes peeled for the shooter. *Who fired?*

Eagle's Nest officers had never found anyone at the scene of the previous fires. *Why is this time different?*

Truman resumed his circular path around the barn, his weapon ready, his focus on the shadows of the terrain beyond the barn. The light cast by the flames extended several yards into the dark, but beyond that the landscape was pitch-black. Anyone could be lurking just out of sight. He widened his circle to use the shadows for cover.

His shirt soaked with sweat and his senses on high alert, he rounded the back side of the barn and spotted two figures on the ground. Motionless.

In the flickering light, he recognized the Deschutes County uniforms.

Please, dear Lord, no.

He sank deeper into the dark and strained his vision, searching everywhere for the shooter. The flames created moving shadows in every direction, and his gaze shot from false movement to false shadow. He pushed his anxiety away, knowing he needed to check the officers even through it would expose him.

"Fuck it." He dashed across the cleared area, feeling the heat singe his shirt, and landed on his knees next to the closest body. He shook Ralph's shoulder, shouted, and then felt for a pulse in his neck. The officer had been shot in the head, and Truman averted his gaze after one horrified glance at the gaping exit wound in his cheek.

I shouldn't see teeth.

He couldn't find a pulse.

Staying low, he scrambled to the next officer. Blood flowed freely from the young deputy's neck, and his frantic gaze met Truman's. His eyes were wide, his mouth silently opening and closing in frantic motions, but his arms and legs held still. Only the deputy's eyes could communicate, and he was clearly terrified.

Spinal injury?

He knows it's bad.

Truman ripped off his coat and pressed it against the wound in the deputy's neck. The fire trucks with their big tanks made their way down the long, rutted road to the barn, and Truman checked his surroundings again for the shooter.

I'm a sitting duck.

He wouldn't leave the deputy alone. He looked the man directly in the eyes. "You're going to be fine. Help just got here."

The man blinked at him, holding his gaze and gasping for breath. Truman spotted his name badge on his coat. "Hold on, Deputy Sanderson. You've got this."

The man's lips moved, and Truman leaned closer, but no sound came from Sanderson's mouth. Truman forced a reassuring smile, ignoring the growing heat on his back. "You'll be okay." He looked up, thankful to see two firemen approach with caution, giving the fire a wide berth and carefully scanning the area.

They got word about the shooter.

A huge burst of air punched him in the back, lifting and hurling him past Deputy Sanderson. He hit the ground face-first, the force knocking away his breath and grinding gravel into his cheek and lips. The sound of the explosion reached him and blew away his hearing for five seconds. He lay in the dirt, his ears ringing as he fought to get his bearings, and an old terror rocketed up from the depths of his subconscious. He battled it down and took mental inventory of his body, spitting the grit out of his mouth.

I'm alive.

Sanderson.

He pushed up to his hands and shaking knees and spun around to look at the injured man he'd flown over.

Vacant eyes stared past him. The mouth had stilled.

"Noooo!" Truman lunged and shook the deputy, but the life he'd seen moments before was gone.

The fire continued to roar.

The morning after the fire, Special Agent Mercy Kilpatrick stared at the smoking pile of burned boards. The old barn hadn't had a chance. It'd been ancient, brittle, and dry when she was a child, so no doubt now, two decades later, it'd gone up in flames as if it'd been soaked in gasoline.

A childhood girlfriend had once lived on the farm, and Mercy had spent several hours rooting around in the barn and surrounding grounds, searching for small animals and pretending the barn was their castle. After her friend had moved, Mercy hadn't seen it again until today.

Now she was an FBI agent assigned to investigate the murder of law enforcement officers. A very angry FBI agent. Cold-blooded murder of her fellow officers in blue did that to her. And to every other person in law enforcement.

She wished she could return to playing princess.

Was the fire set to draw the deputies out here on purpose?

She didn't like to think such a thing could happen in *her* community.

Truman was nearly killed.

She shuddered and put the image out of her thoughts.

Our relationship could have abruptly ended after only two months.

She still hadn't seen Truman. She'd talked briefly with him on the phone, relieved to hear his voice, but he'd been pulled in a dozen directions since he arrived at the fire at midnight. Thankfully he'd suffered only some minor burns. Last night she'd flown into the Portland airport at ten o'clock after two weeks of special training at Quantico. Not wanting to drive home to Bend in the middle of the night after flying all day, she'd slept in her Portland condo, which had been on the market for nearly a month without a single offer.

Seller's market, my ass.

The 3:00 a.m. phone call from Truman had immediately gotten her up and on the road for the three-hour trip home to Central Oregon, the news of the fire, shootings, and explosions driving all sleep from her brain. By the time she'd arrived at her apartment, her boss from the small FBI office in Bend had called.

The two murdered county deputies were now her priority.

As she surveyed the scorched disaster, a frosty breeze shot down the neck of her heavy coat. Thanksgiving was rapidly approaching, and hints of winter had been in the Central Oregon air for several weeks. She'd spent the first eighteen years of her life in the tiny community of Eagle's Nest, but had never returned until she'd been assigned temporary duty in the Bend office for a domestic terrorism case and discovered she'd missed living on the east side of the Cascade mountain range. Less than two months ago, she'd decided to move from wet Portland to the high desert of Bend.

Life in Central Oregon was different from life in Portland. The air smelled cleaner, the snowy mountain peaks were more plentiful, and traffic was a hundred times lighter, although the locals might disagree. Everything moved slower over here. The people were an eclectic mix of families, retirees, ranchers, farmers, cowboys, millennials, and business professionals. Farther out from the main city of Bend, the population drastically thinned and trended toward ranchers and farmers.

Some people moved to Central Oregon to leave all society behind. If you weren't picky about the location, a parcel of remote land could be purchased for a very reasonable price. Some wanted to live on their own terms without relying on the government for their safety or food supply. Sometimes they were called preppers; other times they were called unpleasant names. Mercy had grown up in such a family. Her parents had built a self-sufficient home and lifestyle and embraced the prepper label. It'd been a good, down-to-earth life until she turned eighteen.

After Mercy left Eagle's Nest, she discovered she couldn't fully cut herself off from the prepper lifestyle, so she'd created a balance to ease her mind. While she'd lived and worked in Portland, she'd maintained a remote secret getaway, spending weekends stocking and preparing her Central Oregon cabin. If disaster struck, she was prepared.

She was always prepared.

But no one needed to know that. Only Truman and some of her family knew she slaved like a madwoman in her spare time to ease her worry about a possible future disaster. Her new coworkers and even her closest workmate, Eddie, had no idea that she hid what she thought of as her "secret obsession."

It was her business. People were judgmental. She'd seen it all her life and didn't want that judgment aimed at her.

Plus she couldn't help her entire office if disaster struck and they turned to her because they knew of her resources. She believed in keeping her "wealth" hidden from onlookers. Her hard work was for herself and her family.

She dug the toe of her boot into the wet ground, the area soaked with the thousands of gallons of water trucked in by the fire department. This rural area didn't have fire hydrants every hundred yards, and thankfully, the fire hadn't spread beyond the barn. Pines still stood proudly beyond the smoking pile of rubble. The usually brown ground was black and gray, from the burning of low brush and a thick coating of soot and ash.

She watched the county evidence recovery team crawl through the barn's remains and carefully search a large perimeter under the watchful eye of the fire marshal. Earlier they'd recovered four rifle casings that Mercy's FBI supervisor, Jeff Garrison, had immediately sent to the FBI laboratory instead of the backed-up local labs.

Mercy had never worked a case involving a fire investigation, and she felt out of her element. Truman had been working several arsons around Eagle's Nest, the first of which had occurred just before she went back east for training. Someone had set fire to an ancient abandoned Oldsmobile at the end of Robinson Street. Before the fire, nearby residents hadn't called to have it towed away because they'd assumed someone would eventually come back for it.

Truman had laughed as he repeated the words of an older witness to Mercy. "Hate to mess with someone's car. That's their transportation . . . maybe their livelihood . . . don't want someone getting inconvenienced because I made a phone call to a tow company."

The car had been sitting there for six months.

People had more patience on this side of the mountain range.

Truman had chalked up the car fire to bored teenagers. But then it'd happened two more times while Mercy was training back east. The tension in Truman's voice had increased during their nightly phone calls. The second fire had been in a dumpster, and then the arsonist had burned a shed stocked with prepping supplies.

Mercy's heart had grieved when she'd heard about the supplies. The shed had belonged to a young family who'd worked hard to set aside food and supplies for their future. Mercy understood how much work and sacrifice went into being prepared. The thought of a fire destroying her years of storage work had made her stomach churn uncomfortably. Now the family was struggling to feel safe in their home and wondered if they'd been purposefully targeted.

"The first two fires were set to things people had abandoned," Truman had told her. "But this third fire targeted the hard work of a family. I hope this isn't the start of a new trend." All his spare time during the last two weeks had been focused on the arson cases.

No one had expected the arsonist to suddenly commit murder along with his fourth fire. Now everything had changed.

Mercy stared at the dirt where the deputies' bodies had lain, dark stains still soaking the ground. *Had the arsonist planned to shoot whoever arrived? Or was he simply watching the flames and decided to shoot on a whim?*

One shot is a whim. Four focused shots are planned.

Each of his bullets had found its mark.

She swallowed hard and fought back another wave of boiling anger. Both deputies had families. Deputy Sanderson's baby was three months old.

His poor wife. A baby who'll never know its father.

She watched the fire marshal bend over the shoulder of one of the evidence techs, pointing at something in the pile of wooden debris. The wood all looked the same to Mercy. Wet and burned.

"I wish I understood exactly what he sees," said Special Agent Eddie Peterson. She hadn't noticed him stop beside her, and the presence of her favorite agent immediately boosted her mood. Eddie had applied for the other open position with the Bend FBI office, surprising everyone but the office's intelligence analyst, Darby Cowen.

"I knew Eddie liked it here," Darby had told Mercy confidently. "I saw his eyes light up the first time he went fly-fishing out on the river and heard it in his voice when he talked about the skiing at Mount Bachelor. This area casts a spell over nature lovers. Even when they don't realize they're nature lovers."

Eddie was the last person Mercy would have identified as a nature lover. He was a city boy who paid a little too much attention to how he dressed and fixed his hair. But since he'd moved to Bend, she'd seen a side of him that appreciated the beauty of the area, and she was delighted he'd moved. To her he was a piece of Portland in Central

Oregon. A small link to the good memories from the bigger city. He'd jokingly suggested they rent an apartment together, but Mercy needed her own place. She had a teenage niece to take care of.

Kaylie was seventeen and in her senior year of high school. She'd been abandoned by her mother when she was one, and her father had died recently. His dying wish had been for Mercy to finish raising his daughter. Mercy had reluctantly accepted, feeling as if she'd been thrust into a foreign world. Teenage angst, girlfriend drama, Internet predators, energy drinks, and celebrity crushes. Mercy's teenage years had involved ranch work and hand-me-downs.

"Do we know where the shooter was standing when he shot the officers?" Eddie asked her. His eyes were hard, his usual cheery persona buried under the rage directed at their murderer.

"They found the rifle casings over there." Mercy pointed at a group of pines far to the left of the barn.

"Holy crap. Someone was a good shot." Eddie ran a hand through his hair. "I don't like the thought of that at all," he muttered.

"No one does," said Mercy. "I could never make a shot like that. And I'm pretty good."

"You're much better than me," Eddie admitted.

"I was raised around guns." Mercy had heard the same compliment from several agents she worked with. Firing their weapons wasn't their favorite thing. Most agents spent a lot of time sitting at a desk.

"Everyone out here was raised around guns," stated Eddie with a dour look, and Mercy wondered if he was second-guessing his decision to transfer to the area. The agent was her close friend, but he often made snap decisions. His grumpiness made her want to pat him on the head and hand him a cappuccino with extra foam.

"But why shoot people who are coming to help with the fire?" Mercy said softly.

"That's what I don't understand," agreed Eddie, turning his focus back to the hot pile of burned wood. "Some of the wood looks like alligator skin," he observed. "I think I read that if those marks are large and shiny, it means an ignitable liquid was used."

"Untrue," said the fire marshal as he joined the two agents. "That's often repeated as a fact, but there's no significance to the appearance of the alligatoring." He shook hands with both agents as they introduced themselves. Bill Trek was a short man, maybe five foot six, but he was broad in the chest and spoke with a voice that sounded as if he'd smoked a thousand cigarettes. Or had been exposed to a thousand fires. His eyes were a clear blue, and he had a dusting of gray hair above his ears. Truman had told Mercy that Bill had been working fires for over forty years.

She liked him immediately. "What are your first impressions?" she asked.

"It was a hot one," he said with a half smile. "And I could smell the gasoline the minute I opened my truck door."

She and Eddie both sniffed the air. Mercy couldn't smell it.

"So definitely arson," said Eddie.

"Absolutely. Someone used a heck of a lot of gasoline. I can tell they soaked several areas of the barn, and I've barely started investigating."

"Did you find what caused the explosion?" Eddie asked.

"I can see some remains of a propane tank. It's buried under the debris, but that matches up with the description of the explosion." The investigator looked regretfully at the pile of wood. "I was told the owner doesn't have previous pictures. I guess I'll never know what the barn looked like before."

Mercy looked past the smoking heap, focusing on the image in her brain. "It was two stories. The second level was a loft with a low ceiling. A man wouldn't be able to stand up straight except in the center at the peak of the roof. It had a huge opening on the second level directly over the front double doors. And double doors in the back."

Bill narrowed his eyes at her. "Been here, have ya?"

"I played in it as a kid when someone else owned it." She paused. "Truman—the police chief—said the entire structure was on fire when he arrived." She ignored Eddie's raised eyebrow as she fumbled her words. "Do you know how long it would take to get to that point from when the fire was started?"

Bill stroked his chin, considering her question. "A lot of factors would affect that. Right now I can't even guess. Why do you want to know?"

"I'm wondering about the anonymous phone call that reported the fire," Mercy explained. "It was called in from a gas station pay phone five miles away. Did a passerby report it or did the arsonist set the fire and wait to see that it'd caught sufficiently before he called it in? Then did he come back and wait for the officers to arrive? I'm just thinking out loud here, but he could have just watched it burn, never caring whether anyone showed up or not."

"Firebugs like to watch the reaction of the responders," Bill stated. "I've met enough of them over the years. They can seem like perfectly ordinary folks, but start them talking about fires and they get a weird look in their eye . . . like they just popped a happy pill."

"Did you go to the other arsons that happened in Eagle's Nest recently?" Mercy asked.

"I briefly visited the burned-up shed." Bill shook his head and clucked his tongue in sympathy. "I felt bad for that couple, but they're young and they'll soon rebuild what they lost. Wish they had some insurance, though. I saw the pictures of the burned Oldsmobile and the dumpster fire. My first thought was kids, but you never know." He turned and looked back at the smoking pile. "This was different," he said softly. "I suspect we'll find that setting the fire was only part of his intention."

TWO

Truman found Tilda Brass fascinating. He and Special Agent Jeff Garrison sat in the woman's living room, waiting to ask her about the fire, since it'd occurred on her property. The eighty-year-old woman had answered the door dressed in men's faded jeans and a denim shirt pinned closed with a half dozen safety pins. Her rubber boots looked far too big to be a woman's size, but she wore them gracefully. She had long gray hair, and her manner was that of a society belle—quite at odds with her clothing and boots.

Operating on two hours of sleep, Truman had felt his early-morning adrenaline rush fade away hours ago. The EMTs had applied something that numbed the burns on the back of his neck and then bandaged them, warning him of infection and ordering him to see his doctor as soon as possible. Truman didn't have time. He took some Advil and pushed on. A doctor's visit could wait.

Now he was simply putting one foot in front of the other, running on sheer determination to get to the bottom of his arson mystery.

Murder.

What'd started as pesky arsons had suddenly blown up into the murder of two law enforcement officers.

Deschutes County Deputy Damon Sanderson had been twenty-six and married for two years. His wife had collapsed at the news of his death. His three-month-old daughter would know her father only through pictures.

Deschutes County Deputy Ralph Long had been fifty-one and divorced, with three grown children and four grandchildren. Truman had once bought him a beer at the bowling alley after his team lost to Ralph's.

When the call went out last night that officers had been shot at the location of the fire, every on-duty officer in a thirty-mile radius headed toward the scene. Granted, this was a rural community, so two Oregon State Police troopers, three other county deputies, and two of Truman's officers who got out of bed composed "every on-duty officer." They established a perimeter as the fire department soaked the crumbling building and surrounding brush with the water from its trucks, and then they attended to the murdered men.

There was no sign of the shooter.

By the time the sun came up, Truman had been interviewed by the county sheriff and by Jeff Garrison, the supervisory senior resident agent for the Bend FBI office. Frustration had boiled under his skin all night. He'd been a hundred feet from the murders and hadn't seen a thing to help the investigators find the shooter.

Truman numbly accepted a cup of hot coffee that Tilda had insisted on brewing. He took a sip and it burned its way down his esophagus in a satisfying way, momentarily distracting him from the burn on his neck. His pain relief was running out.

He'd heard about Tilda from the police station's previous manager, Ina Smythe, but he'd never met or seen the woman. Ina said Tilda didn't come into town as much as she used to but made good use of her phone to keep up with the local goings-on. Truman inferred that Ina and Tilda were part of the same gossip tree.

"You didn't know about the fire until one of the county deputies stopped by?" Jeff asked the woman.

"That's correct," Tilda said as she took a sip of coffee from her elegant tiny cup. Each of their cups had a different image of a flower, and the rims appeared to have once been painted with gold . . . or gold-colored paint. Truman could have finished the contents of his tiny cup in three swallows, but he took another minuscule sip, mindful of the temperature.

"I heard the sirens," she added. "But I ignored them. That barn isn't anywhere near the house. I had no idea that's where they were headed."

"Did you use the barn for anything?" Jeff asked.

"Nope. It hasn't been used in years. We bought the property nearly twenty years ago. My departed husband"—she silently crossed herself—"used to store some things in there, but it never held livestock. It wasn't convenient, since it was such a far trek from the house. Now I just pay to have the brush cleared away from all my outbuildings in case of wildfires." She solemnly shook her head. "I never dreamed someone would deliberately set one of them on fire."

"Do you know if there was a propane tank stored in the barn?" asked Jeff.

Tilda thought for a moment. "It wouldn't surprise me if there was, but I can't say for certain."

"Did you recently see any strangers on any of your property who shouldn't have been there?"

"Of course not. Charlie keeps away any intruders. One footstep on the property and if his bark doesn't send them running, then one look at his teeth will."

Truman glanced around for a dog. "Dogs are excellent alert systems. Has anyone come to the door in the past week? Perhaps tried to sell you something?"

"No, I haven't had anyone try to sell me something in ages. I used to have a regular Avon lady stop by, but she died several years ago. Oh! There was a man who stopped by to ask if I'd seen his dog not too long ago. He said it'd run away when his son left the door open."

"Your dog didn't scare him off?" Jeff asked.

Tilda gave him an odd look. "I haven't owned a dog in years. My last dog was Charlie. That's him right there." She dipped her head at her fireplace.

Truman spotted a photo of a German shepherd on the mantel, and a sinking sensation started in his stomach. *A minute ago she told us the dog was alive.* He stood and stepped closer to take a good look. The photo was quite faded, and Truman recognized the car in the background as a Ford Mustang from the eighties. "That's a good-looking dog," he said. He exchanged a brief glance with Jeff. The FBI agent looked grim. Their witness had lost some of her reliability.

"Do you have any other sources of protection in the house?" Truman asked. He took a long look at the woman, wondering if she had a touch of dementia. *Have we wasted our time?* Exhaustion crept up his spine, threatening to make him close his eyes while listening to Tilda's voice.

"I've got my husband's old guns. I practice target shooting every now and then, but I haven't needed to use them recently." She tilted her head. "When those loud teenage boys would ride their four-wheelers on my property, I'd get out a rifle. I never shot at them," she added quickly. "One look at me with the rifle and they'd head back the way they came." She sniffed. "They left tire tracks everywhere."

"How long ago was that?" Truman asked, wondering if any of her answers were reliable.

Tilda sighed and took a sip. "Let's see. It was definitely hot, so it was during the summer."

"This past summer?" he asked faintly, wondering if the woman's memory of time was accurate.

"Yes." She nodded with assurance.

"I'd like to take a look at your rifles," Jeff stated, rising to his feet, a pleasant smile on his face.

Tilda immediately rose and led them down a narrow hall to a bedroom. She moved spryly, making Truman doubt his earlier thoughts about her memory. The bedroom smelled like lavender and he spotted a dried bouquet of the purple flowers next to the bed. The room was clean and airy, but a thin layer of dust covered the nightstands and bed frame. She opened a closet to show a rack with five weapons. Dust covered each one.

Truman sniffed, searching for the odor of a recently fired gun. All he smelled was lavender. If one of Tilda's guns had been used, it wasn't in this closet. "Do you have others?" he asked.

"I keep a pistol in the drawer by my bed," she said. "You never know who might decide to visit an old lady in the middle of the night. I don't have anything worth stealing, but people do stupid things. Especially the ones on *drugs*." She whispered the last word as she leaned close to him and Jeff, her faded blue eyes deadly serious.

Truman fought to keep from smiling and silently wished for more pain relievers. And his bed.

◆ ◆ ◆

Mercy glanced at the clock on her vehicle's dashboard and pressed harder on the gas pedal.

She'd told her boss she wanted an hour to handle a personal errand. She needed to pick up her niece. Kaylie had spent two weeks with her aunt Pearl and a cousin while Mercy was training back east. Mercy knew from frequent phone calls that Kaylie was at her wits' end. Kaylie was used to being the only child and living with her father, so being with the lively male cousin and an overly attentive aunt had turned her world inside out. "I can't get any peace," she'd grumbled to Mercy. "Each time I tell Aunt Pearl I need to be left alone, she spends the next hour asking me if I'm okay."

Mercy had sympathized. She liked her alone time too. But Kaylie's father had just been murdered, and Mercy wasn't comfortable leaving the seventeen-year-old by herself. Pearl had reported that there'd been some crying sessions, but she felt the teenager's overall mental health was solid. Mercy had taken her niece to a therapist after Levi's death and was pleased that Kaylie was still going every other week.

She parked in front of her sister's rural home and stepped out of her Tahoe. The odor from the pig barns wasn't nearly as strong as it'd been earlier in the fall. Kaylie emerged from the house, a backpack slung over one shoulder. She hugged her aunt and dashed down the porch stairs in one leap. "Let's go," she said as she gave Mercy a brief hug, and then hopped in the passenger seat, clearly eager for them to be on their way. Mercy looked back at Pearl, who watched them from the porch. Her sister held up a hand in acknowledgment.

Mercy's legs froze in place. She'd been about to walk up to her sister and at least have a short chat, but Pearl's hand gesture indicated it wasn't necessary. *I guess I'm done here.*

Getting to know her siblings after a fifteen-year absence hadn't been easy. Mercy's fight with her father when she was eighteen had led her family to cut all ties with her. Mercy had never regretted her stance in the argument, but she'd regretted missing out on the lives of her siblings. When she'd been temporarily assigned to a case in Eagle's Nest two months ago, she'd been sick with worry about bumping into people from her past. Now she viewed that case as fate intervening and giving her a second chance with her family.

Not all of her family had accepted her return, but Mercy believed things were moving in the right direction.

Pearl had embraced her on the first day but kept her distance after that. Phone calls were the best way to communicate with Pearl. She was almost chatty on the phone. The oldest sibling, Owen, still refused to talk with Mercy and kept his wife and kids from doing so.

Her other sister was the Rose she'd always known. Wide open, loving, and accepting. Her love kept Mercy sane and optimistic for some sort of relationship with her other siblings. Mercy had been in town less than a week when Rose was kidnapped and tortured by a serial killer, and the slashes on her face were now a constant reminder of his abuse. The killer had been the target of the FBI's hunt after a string of prepper murders in Central Oregon. Her blind sister was also two months pregnant with the dead man's baby.

Levi. Her heart lurched as it always did at the thought of her murdered sibling. Rose had survived, but Levi had not. Mercy would always feel slightly responsible for Levi's murder. The death of his killer at her and Truman's hands hadn't given her much peace, but raising his daughter did. She'd learned to be grateful for every day she had with this living piece of Levi. To her surprise, Mercy had deeply missed the teenager while she'd been gone.

She turned her back on Pearl and climbed in the Tahoe. Kaylie immediately switched on the radio as Mercy started the vehicle. The girl punched buttons until she found a song she liked. Mercy grimaced and turned down the music. They had an agreement: Kaylie picked the station, but Mercy was in charge of the volume. It was one of many small issues they'd had to figure out in their first month of living together.

"Ready to go home?" Mercy asked.

"More than ready." The teen pulled back her long hair, using a band from her wrist to fasten it in a knot on top of her head. The red stud in her nose twinkled in the sunlight. "I think the coffee shop is going to be okay. Aunt Pearl seems to enjoy it."

Mercy blew out a breath of relief. The fate of her brother's Coffee Café in Eagle's Nest had been the subject of many long conversations among her, Kaylie, Pearl, and Truman. Mercy had assumed they would sell the cute store, but Kaylie's emotional attachment to her father's store, where she'd helped since she was ten, had halted those plans. Then had come the discussion of who would run it. Kaylie had insisted she could do it alone, but no one agreed with that plan. Pearl had stepped forward, pointing out that she had spare time.

"She's finally mastered most of the drinks," added Kaylie. "And she lets me handle the baking, *like she should*. She really wanted to do that part, but it's mine," Kaylie said emphatically. "I created most of the recipes and designed the bakery menu. I wasn't about to let her fool with that. I think she enjoys the social part of the café too. She already knew most of the customers, and they like talking with her. That's important."

Mercy glanced at her niece, happy to hear the satisfied tone in the girl's voice. Kaylie had been pessimistic about her aunt's involvement in her father's legacy, but it appeared the two of them had worked out a system that gave both what they needed. "Is Samuel much help in the shop?"

Kaylie sighed loudly at the mention of her cousin. "He's okay. You have to tell him to do everything. He can't see for himself what needs to be done."

Is that a boy thing or a teenage thing?

Judging by Mercy's struggles to get Kaylie to clean up her things around their apartment, it was a teenage thing. Thank goodness Kaylie was a girl. At least Mercy had been one and had an idea of how girls' brains worked. She would have been clueless about a teenage boy, other than knowing to constantly shove food at him. That much she remembered from having two brothers.

Please don't let me mess up with Kaylie.

She wanted to get it right for her brother's sake and for Kaylie. It was a tough world for a teenager without a family. Mercy was determined that Kaylie would never feel the abandonment she'd felt at eighteen when she'd parted ways with her family. At the very least, Kaylie would always know Mercy would be there for her.

Am I exaggerating the benefit of a slightly paranoid, workaholic aunt?

It was better than the complete absence of family she'd experienced.

"I'll drop you off at the apartment, and then I have to go back to work," she told the girl. "I haven't even unpacked my suitcase yet."

"I heard about the fire and dead officers. That's horrible. Aunt Pearl said Truman was there too. Is he okay?"

"I talked to him on the phone. He got some small burns from the fire and banged his head, but he's fine."

Is he?

Mercy knew his history with fire and burns. Just over a year ago, he'd been too late to get a fellow officer and a civilian away from a burning car before it exploded. He'd been severely burned in the blast, and the stress of the deaths had nearly made him give up law enforcement. He still had bad dreams. Her heart ached with the need to see him in person. The quick phone calls during the morning had assured her only that he was still upright and functioning. *He's going to crash tonight.* Possibly in more than one way.

She'd been away from him for the last two weeks. Their relationship was still in an early stage. She firmly believed in taking things slow . . . tortoise slow. If Truman had had his way, she'd be living with him. Kaylie too. He liked the girl and teased her as if he were a good-natured uncle. But Mercy wasn't ready for living together. Hell, they'd only known each other two months.

"What?" Kaylie hollered.

Mercy nearly drove off the road as she frantically looked from side to side for what had made her niece shout. "What happened?" she gasped.

"Did you hear that?" Kaylie stared at the Tahoe's radio. "What the announcer just said?"

"No." Mercy took a deep breath and focused on slowing her heartbeat. "Please don't yell when I'm driving."

"Sorry. But he just said some local idiots are claiming the shooting last night was justified. That the deputies *deserved* it."

Mercy's heart sank. *No. Not here. Not in my state.*

"That's asinine." Kaylie leaned back in her seat, crossing her arms. "People are stupid. Who thinks like that?"

"Sadly, quite a few people." Mercy knew all too well that there were some residents who would prefer the government stay out of their lives. But usually they didn't act so violently on their beliefs.

"Do you think they're the ones who shot the deputies?" Questioning eyes turned toward Mercy. "This is your case, isn't it? Are you going to find the guys who said that shit?"

"Don't swear."

"Sorry. It makes me angry."

"It makes me angry too. And yes, someone will look into it."

THREE

Truman could barely keep his eyes open as he rang Mercy's doorbell.

He'd been up for nearly twenty-four hours. He'd been burned, hit his head, and nearly died in an explosion, and he hadn't seen Mercy in two weeks. He didn't give a shit if Kaylie was here. He needed to feel Mercy against him. His heart and mind were stripped bare, and he felt raw and vulnerable. She would be a balm for his broken parts, and tonight he had a hell of a lot of them.

He swayed as he waited at the door, aching to see the light of her at the end of this very long tunnel of a day.

The door opened and he was in her arms.

He loved her but had never told her. The occasional fear in her eyes made him keep those words to himself. Her anxiety reminded him of a nervous deer. Quivering in front of him, ready to dash away at the slightest wrong move. He kept his movements gentle and slow; he knew he'd win her with time.

He sank against her, loving that she was nearly his height.

"You still smell of smoke," she whispered against his ear.

"Sorry, I haven't had time to shower."

"I don't care." She pulled back and studied his face, her green gaze probing and measuring. "You look like shit."

"I feel like it."

She pulled him into her living room and pushed him down on the couch. The cushions touched the back of his neck and he hissed at the pain.

"Let me see that."

He bent forward and dipped his head to expose his neck. "I need a new hat. The blast pretty much ripped it up."

She gently peeked under one of the bandages. "We'll get you a hat. Do these hurt?"

"Like Satan is sitting on my neck."

"I think I've got something for that. They've barely blistered, so that's good. You won't have to deal with a bunch of oozing sores. Hang on." She vanished down the hall.

Truman sighed, letting go of a dump-truck load of stress, and felt his strength slowly fade away. If she didn't come back soon, he'd be asleep in less than a minute. She reappeared and sprayed something cool on his neck. It felt as though ice were dissolving his pain, and he wanted to kiss the can.

He settled for kissing her.

A minute later she pulled back and spoke. "That spray is only temporary. Take these." She shoved two white pills and a glass of water in his hand. He didn't ask any questions and popped the pills. He was beyond caring. She fluffed a white pillow at the end of the couch and ordered him to lie down.

"Don't want to sleep here," he muttered.

"It's just for a minute. Let me get your boots off."

He lay down and closed his eyes against the pillowcase. More soothing coolness. He swore he'd never slept on a pillow so comfortable. He felt her lift each of his legs and tug off his boots.

Lips pressed against his forehead, and he felt himself fade into sleep.

Mercy watched Truman sleep. There'd been no way she could have gotten him into her bedroom. He'd nearly fallen over the minute he'd stepped inside her place. *How on earth did he drive here?*

Pure stubbornness and determination had guided him.

She understood those elements. It was part of what drew them to each other. They recognized parts of themselves in the other person. He was everything she strove to be. Strong, loyal, honorable. And she admired him for carrying those qualities without any ego. He was unlike any man she'd ever met.

He'd silently hooked her when she wasn't looking. One minute she had been searching for a killer and the next minute wondering how she'd lost her heart along the way.

Truman Daly wasn't the most handsome man she'd ever seen, but she loved everything about his face. The small scar in his chin and the thick five o'clock shadow that'd left burns on her cheeks and breasts in the past. It was if he'd been made for her. Everything about him formed a harmony with her needs. Her heart still jumped at the sight of his stunning smile, and his natural energy boosted hers when she started to lag. Simply put, she felt better when she was around him. So much better that she'd put in for a transfer and moved. An impulse decision. She didn't make impulse decisions; she preferred to analyze and ponder before making up her mind.

So far it'd been the best decision of her life.

She ran her fingers through his hair. He needed it cut. No doubt he'd been too busy to take ten minutes out of his day to sit in the barber's chair.

He's had a hell of a day.

Tomorrow they'd jump back into the investigation with both feet. But tonight he needed to rest. *Stubborn man. He would have pushed himself until he fell asleep at his desk.*

A feeling she knew all too well.

She stood and stretched. Kaylie had gone to bed an hour ago, and now it was her turn. She looked down at the sleeping man on her couch. He was too tall; his feet were propped up on one arm of the couch, but he didn't seem to mind. Her heart overflowed and she wiped her eyes.

"What the hell?" she muttered, grabbing a Kleenex. *Where did those tears come from?* She preferred her emotions firmly under her control. She was pretty good at keeping them in check, but the knowledge that Truman might have been killed last night was making her crumble and shake inside. "I'm tired," she stated out loud, but she couldn't pull her gaze away from his black eyelashes lying against his cheeks. She reached out and touched his face, feeling his stubble grab at her fingertips. More tears flowed and she sniffed, rubbing a hand under her nose.

What would I have done if he died at that fire?

She refused to answer. It hadn't happened. It wasn't relevant.

Or was it?

Instantly awake, Truman flew off the couch and stumbled against a coffee table as his heart tried to pound its way out of his chest. He leaned one hand against a wall and tried to find his balance in the dark. The back of his neck burned in pain and he gently touched the gauze bandages as he peered around, searching for something familiar.

Mercy's apartment.

Understanding flowed through him. He'd driven to her place, desperate to see her, and then he'd fallen asleep. He stood in the dark, taking deep breaths for a few seconds before he strode to the windows and pulled open the curtains. A soft light from the parking lot spilled into the room. It was pitch-black outside. *How long did I sleep?*

The soft click-click of the clock above the fireplace mantel caught his attention. It was nearly 4:00 a.m.

Not long enough.

He couldn't remember what had happened after he'd hugged her at the door. His boots were off, but he was still dressed, and he could smell the smoke that had permeated his clothing and skin.

The events of his day flooded over him. Fire. Explosion. The hole in Ralph's face. His heart started to speed up again. He strode into Mercy's kitchen and got a glass of water, drinking it at the sink, his swallows sounding unnaturally loud in the dark.

Sweat started on his temples, and he bent over the sink, splashing water on his face.

I'm fine. I made it through the fire.

But others had not. He scrubbed at his face and neck with the dish towel hanging from the oven handle. The rough towel brushed one of his covered burns and he hissed but welcomed the distracting pain. He wasn't going back to sleep. That much was apparent to him.

Should I go home?

Thoughts of Mercy in her bed guided him down the hall to the small master bedroom he'd come to know quite well. An outdoor light from the open window spilled over the bed, and he could make out her face. Her mouth was slightly open in sleep, and one of her hands was propped under her chin. The room was freezing as usual. She loved it cold.

He touched her arm. "Mercy?" Guilt racked him for waking her, but it was suddenly important that he hear her voice.

She woke instantly and sat up. "Truman? Are you okay? Do you need more pain medication?" She pushed off her covers and started to swing her legs out of bed.

"No, I'm fine," he lied, putting a hand on her shoulder to stop her. "I just needed to talk to you."

"About what?"

The exterior light caught her profile as she looked at him. He couldn't see her eyes, but he could *feel* her gaze on him. His heartbeat finally slowed. "Nothing. Everything. It's been a trying two weeks . . . and yesterday . . ."

She was silent, and he felt her gaze probing him in the dark. "What is it?"

He lowered himself to sit next to her on the bed. "I should have been there sooner."

"Last night? At the fire? What would have been different if you'd gotten there earlier?"

"I might have stopped him."

She caught her breath. "You think you could have stopped the shooter."

"Maybe. And then those two men wouldn't be dead." His words were thick and heavy as he finally said out loud what he'd been thinking all day. *If I'd been where I was supposed to be . . .*

"If you had been first, you might be dead," she said firmly. "And I'm *not* okay with that."

"But . . ."

"No buts. You can't play this what-if game with yourself, Truman. You'll make yourself sick. What's done is done. You can't bring those officers back."

He faced her in the dim light. "I should have arrived a good ten minutes earlier. It might have made all the difference."

"Are you saying there's a reason you didn't? You can't tell me there was heavy traffic at that time of night."

"I wasn't at home."

There was a long moment of silence. "Where were you?" Dread filled her voice.

"I slept at your cabin."

She exhaled and her spine relaxed. "How come?"

"I slept there the last few nights. The fire at the prepper shed made me worry that maybe more prepper properties might be targeted."

She wrapped an arm around him and rested her head on his shoulder. "You were protecting my work. Is it weird that I think that's the nicest thing anyone has ever done for me?" she asked softly with a catch in her voice.

He didn't answer. He hadn't done it to be nice; he'd done it because he cared. Besides representing years of hard work, he knew the rural cabin and its contents were part of Mercy's core. They kept her sane and balanced. He didn't think sleeping there for a few nights was any big deal. Before her trip they'd been working to transfer some of the stores from his uncle's old home. Upon his death, Truman's uncle Jefferson had left him a wealth of supplies, but he and Mercy had agreed her location was better. Remote and off the grid.

The average home had enough food for a week. Mercy's cabin could keep them fed and warm for months.

Beans, bullets, and Band-Aids.

The three *B*s of prepping.

But there was more to Mercy. She also believed in charity, helping those who were less fortunate. Many of his uncle's supplies had gone to families in town. Mercy could mend a fence, build a shed, and even do some engine repair. Her cabin was stuffed with books that taught medical skills, electronics, tactical skills . . . subjects he assumed could always be looked up on the web. But what if the web was gone?

He even kept a GOOD bag in his truck now. Get Out of Dodge. Small changes.

"You couldn't have stopped the shooter, Truman. Don't drive yourself crazy imagining what you would have done differently. I know you totally exposed yourself to check on those two men. You went above and beyond what is expected of anyone."

Then why don't I feel any better?

"Am I too cautious? Does it affect my work?" he asked.

"Too cautious? *You?*"

"I ran back to get the fire extinguisher the night Officer Madero died instead of getting her away—"

"Stop it!" she ordered, and he slammed the door on the horrific memory of responding to a car fire nearly two years ago. The guilt had nearly ended his career in law enforcement.

She put both hands on his cheeks and pulled his face close to hers. Her pupils were huge, and anger hovered around her. "You know you're exhausted and not thinking straight. You need sleep. Your perspective will be better tomorrow."

His mind had started to slide down a pessimistic narrow tunnel. One where he second-guessed every decision he'd ever made. He recognized the dreaded slippery path but still struggled to break out. She'd seen his spiraling mind-set and knew he needed to snap out of it.

"Sleep," she ordered. "No more discussions. We'll talk about it all you want tomorrow. Now come to bed."

She didn't need to ask twice. He shed his jeans and shirt as she lay down and then slid in beside her. At the touch of her cool skin, every cell in his body relaxed. She snuggled up to him and rested her hand against his cheek. More stress evaporated.

He closed his eyes and felt himself drifting away. "I needed to be next to you."

"Then you got your wish," she said against his neck. Her lips pressed into his skin.

"I missed you, Mercy."

"I missed you too."

"Don't leave town for a while, okay?" he muttered, struggling to form words as he felt himself sucked deeper into sleep.

"I've got no vacation plans." Humor filled her words. "Are you sure you don't need something for the pain?"

"Absolutely. Everything's perfect now."

FOUR

Officer Ben Cooley was covering the night shift.

To be fair, it wasn't a night shift in the true sense. Usually that meant actually driving to a job with a crappy shift from 11:00 p.m. to 7:00 a.m. Eagle's Nest simply had one officer on call from midnight to 8:00 a.m. He didn't mind taking the shift—they all had to cover it at least once a week—but usually he got to sleep in peace. Not much happened in the middle of the night in his quiet town, and getting paid for sleeping in his bed wasn't a bad deal, but lately fires had been on everyone's mind.

Sure enough, at 4:00 a.m., a little more than twenty-four hours after the fire and shooting on Tilda Brass's property, he got a call that suspicious persons were snooping around Jackson Hill's outbuildings. Hill was out of town, but a neighbor had seen someone where there shouldn't be any people. Nothing was on fire, but knowing a young prepper family had already lost supplies and that Jackson was a known prepper, Ben pulled his old bones out of bed.

His wife of fifty years was still sound asleep. As was his custom when leaving to work, Ben kissed her tenderly on the cheek and told her he loved her. Then he got dressed and wished there were a coffee drive-through between him and the call. Instead he heated up the leftover coffee in the pot, poured it into a travel mug, and got into his patrol vehicle. He blinked hard as he headed out of town, trying to get the sleep out of his eyes. He called the dispatch center and flirted with Denise for a few seconds as he let her know he was en route to the call. He knew all the dispatchers at the Deschutes County 911 center. Over the years they'd come and gone, but Denise had been around for a good five years and always laughed at his jokes.

"Busy night?" he asked.

"We've taken just over five hundred calls in the last twenty-four hours, so technically that's a slow day for us."

Ben couldn't imagine. Feeling guilty, he quickly got off the call so she could help someone else and turned his concentration to the dark road. He'd been a cop in Eagle's Nest for over thirty years. In that time a lot of things had changed, and a lot were still exactly the same.

Fights between spouses? Exactly the same. Couples still got drunk and tried to beat the hell out of each other.

Drug abuse? Not much change. The only change was in which drug was popular at the moment.

Drunk driving? Not much change. Even with the big push for awareness over the last several decades, he still pulled over too many drunks each week. Although he'd noticed they were older than they used to be. Perhaps the younger generations were getting the message not to drink and drive.

He still loved his job. He didn't want to do anything else. He liked talking to people and he liked helping his neighbors. Most folks in the area respected his badge. There'd always been a few who didn't, and in the past he could knock respect into their heads, but that was frowned upon these days.

Besides, he didn't have the strength he used to. Didn't have a lot of what he used to. His joints hurt most of the day, and his back had given him grief for the last ten years. His doctor bitched at him to eat better and get more exercise, but Ben didn't see the point in eating boring food and visiting a gym for what he had left of this life. One of the perks of being a human being was eating delicious food. And if it was delicious, that meant his doctor was against it. Ben would rather enjoy his meals than try to please his doctor. His wife was an incredible cook. He patted his bigger-than-it-should-be belly. *A badge of honor.*

He turned off the two-lane highway onto the narrow road that eventually led to the Hill home. A person lurched out of the darkness and into his headlights, waving their hands for him to stop.

"Franklin Delano Roosevelt!" Ben swore. His car skidded as he braked hard.

A moment later he recognized Jim Hotchkiss. The neighbor who'd called in the prowler.

Ben lowered his window. "You waiting for me, Jim?"

"Yep. Took you long enough." Jim was wearing his usual overalls and a heavy canvas coat. The thin man had lost most of his teeth a few decades back and rarely wore his dentures.

Ben put on a patient face. "Came as fast as I could. What'd you see?"

"Two men poking around Hill's three outbuildings. With the fires of the last few weeks, I thought I'd let you confront them first instead of me just scaring them off."

"See any weapons?" Ben asked.

"Too far off. Too dark. And there might have been more than two people, but I saw two for certain."

"Head back home, okay?"

Jim looked out at the highway. "You got some backup coming?"

"They know I'm here. I'll radio if I think it's something I can't handle."

The skepticism on Jim's face stung Ben's ego. He waved off the man and rolled up his window. The chill from the night air had frosted the dried grass along the road, and his headlights gave it a silver cast. In just the short moment he'd had his window down, the interior of his car had completely cooled. He cranked up the heat and cautiously drove on, turning on his brights and watching both sides of the road for anyone else who decided to leap out of the darkness.

"Jim's older than I am," he mumbled. "Jerk doesn't think I can handle myself."

The ruts in the dirt road made his vehicle bounce and jerk, and he heard packed dirt scrape his undercarriage. *One of these days, everyone in the department will have four-wheel drives.* Right now, the department could afford only two.

He turned off the road into the Hills' driveway. Someone had nailed two hubcaps to a pine, marking the driveway. Tacky, but effective, even in the dark.

Keeping his heat blasting, he lowered his window and listened as he drove. Ahead the Hill home was dark. Beyond it Ben could see the outline of a wide, low outbuilding and two small sheds beyond it. Ben stopped the car next to the house, but in a position where he could see all three buildings. He turned off the engine, but kept his lights on and listened again.

Quiet.

Too quiet?

Any moonlight was hidden behind a thick layer of clouds. Ben's headlights were the sole source of illumination, and he didn't see anything out of the ordinary.

They could have driven away in the other direction and not been seen by Jim.

Ben grabbed his big flashlight from his console and stepped out of the car. This wasn't a job for the tiny LED flashlight on his belt. The big one felt good in his hand. Secure and powerful. It was a good friend. It'd been used to bust car windows, pound on doors, and even knock a guy in the temple. A dozen years ago a meth-head had rushed him, and since Ben had the flashlight in hand, he'd used it. The druggie had sunk to the dirt as if his bones had dissolved. Ben transferred the flashlight to his left hand, rested his other on the weapon at his hip, and walked toward the house.

"Hello? Anyone out here? Eagle's Nest Police Department."

He checked the security of the front door and shone his light on all the windows as he circled the home. Everything was intact. Heading to the largest shed, he shone his light as far left and right as he could. The powerful beam was penetrating, but all he saw were fences and bushes. He reached the barn, hollered his identity again, and then slid the giant door open, surprised it wasn't locked. His flashlight revealed several empty stalls, and the strong scent of hay and livestock reached his nose. He strolled in, senses fully engaged, watching for prowlers.

A faint whoosh sounded outdoors. Ben spun around and darted back to the front of the shed, peering quickly around the corner before stepping out into the open. A faint flickering light reflected off the back of the house.

One of the other sheds has been set on fire.

"Eagle's Nest Police Department!" he shouted.

The noise of a dirt bike engine reached his ears. Its sound grew fainter, heading away. Ben took that as a sign the firebug was taking off and stepped out of the low barn to assess the fire. One of the small sheds had just started to burn, and Ben smelled gasoline. He called dispatch for backup and fire support. He spotted a watering trough close to the small burning shed and went to disconnect the hose to play firefighter, suspecting he could have the fire out before backup arrived.

Something whirred by his face, and its wind brushed his cheek. Then he heard the shot.

He dropped to the ground and turned off his flashlight.

He shot at me!

Images of the dead deputies from the other night's fire flashed in his memory. *Thank the heavens above he missed.* His wife's face popped into his head, and he nearly wept with relief that he'd told her he loved her before leaving.

You never know when you won't return.

He called dispatch again, adding that there was an active shooter on the property. He recognized Denise's voice but didn't bother to flirt. Her efficiency calmed him.

"You okay, Ben?" she asked after relaying his information.

"Just need a clean pair of pants."

"Stay low." They ended the call.

He rolled closer to the watering trough and started to crawl around to the other side to put some metal between him and the shooter and get out of the light from the fire. His breath came in short pants, and his knees ached from the cold of the ground. Far off, the dirt bike engine started up again. He hadn't noticed it'd stopped before the shot.

Did someone that far away take a shot at me?

Are they gone now?

He didn't feel like sticking his head up to find out. He cursed, glad his wife wasn't in earshot, as he realized his trusty flashlight had been a beacon to guide the shot. He was crawling into the pitch blackness on the other side of the trough when his hand touched something warm and solid.

He jerked back his hand and strained to see in the black. The dark was too dense.

It's alive.

And human.

His heart tried to pound its way up his throat. He pushed the lens of his flashlight into the ground and turned it on, casting a faint glow behind the trough.

Sightless eyes stared back at him. *No, he's dead.* The corpse was heavyset and thickly bearded, and Ben didn't recognize him.

But the blood that slowly oozed from the long gash in his neck told him the man had been recently murdered.

FIVE

Mercy slept like the dead, opening her eyes only as Truman kissed her forehead.

He was fully dressed and had deep circles under his eyes. She blinked. *How did I not hear him get up?*

"What time is it?" she asked, squinting at her clock.

"Almost five in the morning. Someone took a shot at Ben this morning." His grim tone sped up her waking process.

"Is he all right? What happened?" She sat up and shook the sleep out of her head.

"He's fine. Pissed but fine. He was responding to a prowler call and found a small fire. Then someone shot at him."

"Did he catch the shooter?"

Truman sighed. "No. But they left behind a body. We don't know who he is yet, but someone cut his throat."

Now she was fully awake. "Do you know anything about the body?"

"I know he was murdered at the site moments before Ben found him, and Ben estimated the victim to be in his sixties. A big guy with a lot of graying facial hair."

"Ben didn't know him? Ben knows everyone around here."

"Exactly," Truman said. "Now I'm wondering if our arsonist is from out of town."

"This incident has to be related to my case."

"Our case," Truman corrected her.

She looked sideways at him. "Technically the murdered officers are my case. And now another officer has been shot at? I suspect Jeff will see that as belonging to me too."

"I was already investigating the fires. This is another fire. Sounds like it's a small one . . . more like the first two."

She didn't see the point in arguing details with him; they were both working toward the same goal. She slid out of bed and started rooting in a drawer for clean clothes. "What was set on fire this time?"

"The shed of another prepper."

Mercy froze. And then turned to look at him, dread growing in her stomach.

"Jackson Hill. Know him?"

"I don't think so. How much did he lose?"

"He didn't lose anything. Ben was right there when the fire was started and managed to put it out with Jackson's own hose before the fire department arrived."

"That's good. Ben Cooley is an efficient cop," Mercy observed. She'd liked the older officer from the moment she'd met him. He had a fatherly vibe about him, and she wondered when he would retire. Truman would lose an important asset the day he did.

"He sounded exhausted. I don't blame him. Someone tried to shoot him, he had to put out a fire, and he found the body. Not your average day around here." He took her shoulder and turned her to him. "I'm headed out. I'll catch up with you later."

She kissed him and noticed he smelled of fresh soap and stale smoke. He'd showered but put on his smoky clothes from the day before.

Two days before. He'd never made it home yesterday after the shooting.

"You need clean clothes."

"I have some at the station. I'll change there after I check out the scene."

"The crime is over. The scene can wait fifteen minutes. Go change," she ordered.

He smiled, kissed her good-bye, and left. She grumbled to herself, knowing he was driving straight to check on his officer.

How can I complain about a man who does that?

She went to the kitchen to start her coffeemaker and noticed dirty footprints near the fridge. *Did Truman do that last night?* She frowned as she spotted the distinctive tread of Kaylie's tennis shoes in the dirt. *I don't recall that mess when I was making dinner last night.*

Mercy slid her coffeepot into place in the brewer and headed down the hall to Kaylie's bedroom. The girl's door was open a few inches. She pushed it open the rest of the way and tiptoed in to check on the teen. Kaylie slept on her back. Her mouth was wide open and her arms were flung above her head. Mercy had learned this was her normal sleeping position. At first she'd frequently checked on the teen in the middle of the night, unaccustomed to being responsible for another human being. After a week she'd realized she didn't need to make sure that the girl was still breathing each night.

The sight of the sleeping girl touched something hidden deep in her chest. She'd done it. She'd made a home for the girl, who seemed to be functioning just fine. Kaylie's limbs were still all intact, she hadn't pierced anything, and she seemed happy.

Maybe Mercy didn't suck as an aunt-slash-mom.

The scent of perfume made Mercy's nose twitch, and her moment of basking in pseudomotherhood evaporated. She leaned closer to the girl and the perfume grew stronger. Mercy turned on her phone's flashlight, pointing it away from Kaylie's face, but adding enough light that she could see the girl's heavy eyeliner and eye shadow.

She wasn't wearing makeup when she told me good night last night.

Disappointment filled her. *Here I was patting myself on the back for my excellent adulting skills and she's been sneaking out at night.*

The joke was on her.

She quietly left the room and numbly padded into the kitchen. Her mind spinning, she watched the coffee drip into the pot. *Do I confront her? Do I try to catch her? Do I ignore it?* Maybe she should call Pearl for advice.

But she does still have all her fingers and toes. I call that a win.

It must be a boy.

Visions of Kaylie and some farm boy stealing kisses made her smile. *What if it's an older man? A predator?*

Panic flared and faded. *I'll talk to her.* Her niece wasn't dumb. She had excellent grades and a lot of common sense. The right thing to do would be to sit her down and ask what was going on. And then make her clean up the dirt in the kitchen.

Impatient, Mercy pulled out the pot and poured the small amount of potent brew into her cup. She added some heavy cream and stirred, turning the black coffee a lovely mocha shade.

She'd formulate her questions for Kaylie in the shower.

Truman was pleased to see that one of his other officers, Royce Gibson, had beaten him to Ben's scene. His men were like a small family. They cared about one another, and when one of them struggled, the others pitched in to ease the way. Royce was in his midtwenties, with a young baby at home. He was earnest, direct, and easygoing. He was also one of the most gullible men Truman had ever met, which made him a popular target for pranks and practical jokes by his coworkers. As Truman walked up, he could still make out the faint black Sharpie streak on Royce's face that Lucas, the office manager, had somehow tricked him into putting on himself three days ago.

Truman hadn't asked for the details.

Ben looked pretty good. For someone who'd been shot at and had discovered a murder victim, his chin was up and his posture was relaxed.

Truman slapped him on the back and handed him a protein bar from the stash in his Tahoe. The older cop gratefully took it, immediately ripping off the wrapper and taking a big bite. "Always eat when it's available," he said between chews. "There might not be time later."

Royce nodded as if it was the best advice he'd heard in years.

The Deschutes County evidence team had arrived, and Truman watched them carefully photograph and mark evidence. They'd brought portable diesel light towers to the scene, which Truman eyed with envy. His budget didn't have room for such luxuries. He snorted, realizing he'd just referred to light as a luxury. But it was true. Eagle's Nest didn't have crime scene techs either. It had him and his tackle box from the back of his Tahoe. Gloves, tape, envelopes, containers, tweezers. A little bit of everything. He was thankful the Deschutes County Sheriff's Office or the Oregon State Police were more than willing to give him a hand when things got too technical.

"Nice job getting the fire under control," Truman told Ben.

"Hadn't really taken off," said the humble older officer. "Anyone would have done the same. I was in the right place at the right time. Don't know why they even had the fire department come. They could have just sent the fire marshal."

Truman scanned the people at the scene, not seeing Bill Trek. "He here?"

"Not yet."

"Has the medical examiner arrived yet?" Truman asked.

Ben shook his head. "Nope. The body is over there behind the trough." He jerked his head toward the rusting metal tub.

"What are your thoughts?" Truman asked the older cop. Ben had given him a quick rundown on the phone, but now that the events had had time to percolate, he hoped the cop had more insight.

Ben squinted and carefully chewed the protein bar as he thought. "Whoever shot at me was damn good. They found a single casing way the hell out there." Ben pointed at a portable light far in the distance. "He nearly got me . . . I hope they can find him."

"It's still early," Truman said. "But it's dark."

The older cop grimaced. "Damned dark. I couldn't do anything, the light was so bad. And I walked around with my flashlight on like an idiot, advertising exactly where I was."

"You're lucky he missed his shot."

"I'm certain that the bike motor came from the direction where we found the casing. I assume he's the one who shot at me. I guess someone else could have been on foot and taken a shot, but they haven't found evidence of another person besides our dead guy. County's trying to follow the dirt bike tracks, but the ground's awfully hard. And of course the lack of light isn't helping."

"They'll have better luck when the sun comes up," Royce added.

"Has anyone recognized the body yet?" Truman asked.

"No," answered Ben. "I took another gander at him a while ago. He looks slightly familiar, but I can't place him." He took another bite of the bar. "I can't remember everyone I met over the years."

"I don't expect you to." Truman looked to Royce. "Did you look?"

"Don't know him. We checked for ID and there's nothing in his pockets. Hopefully his fingerprints will tell us who he is."

"Guess I'll give it a shot." Truman doubted he could recognize the man. He had been in Eagle's Nest for only eight months. He'd worked hard to know the people, but if Ben and Royce didn't recognize the guy, there was little chance Truman would.

He strode over to the corpse.

A female evidence tech smiled at him and politely but firmly pointed at a spot of ground. "Please stand over there." Truman stepped carefully and watched for a few moments as she continued to photograph the corpse. He squatted and made his own visual assessment. He agreed with Ben's estimate of the man's being in his sixties. He had to be nearly 350 pounds. His graying beard was at least three inches past his chin, and his hair was plastered across his forehead and looked as if it had needed a cut and wash several weeks ago. His eyes were open and growing opaque. Truman took a long look at the deep cut in his neck and tucked away any thoughts about the terror that must have run through the man's head as he realized what was happening to him.

Who'd you piss off?

The victim wore heavy work boots and jeans with dirt stains on the knees. His coat had seen better days, but it was thick and heavy to combat the cold. Truman spotted his faded John Deere cap a few feet away.

He didn't know the man.

"Good morning, Chief." Dr. Natasha Lockhart had arrived. Her tiny form was overwhelmed by her thick red coat and scarf. He noticed she wore beige scrubs tucked into her fleece-lined snow boots.

"Not the greatest morning, Dr. Lockhart." He'd met the ME a few times. She was smart, quick, and competent.

"I'm pretty certain I've asked you to call me Natasha," she said as she pulled on her gloves.

"Natasha." She had. Every time.

He watched her do a rapid physical exam of the victim and talk in low tones to the evidence tech with the camera. Her hands moved quickly over the body. The evidence tech helped her roll the man to his side, and she scanned his back. "Your man found him just after four this morning?" she asked Truman.

"Yes. He said he was still bleeding at the time."

"Nothing he could have done."

"He knows." Truman eyed the neck wound. No one could survive that.

"I saw Mercy a few weeks ago," Natasha said conversationally. "I wasn't surprised to hear she'd moved to the area permanently."

"You weren't?" Most people were shocked Mercy had left the big city.

Natasha gave him an appraising look, and he felt like a cut of beef in the butcher's case. "Nope. Didn't surprise me one bit."

She winked at him and his face heated.

He and Mercy had tried to keep their relationship quiet. Sort of. His men knew they were together, and most of her coworkers knew she was involved with him, but since her initial case in Central Oregon, their jobs hadn't crossed again until now.

It felt odd. As if he had a poorly kept secret.

Natasha stood and stretched her back. "Not much I can do here. I'll try to get to him today."

"I have a pretty good idea of how he died," said Truman. "What I want to know is who he is."

"I'll print him immediately and send them to you so you can get that ball rolling."

Truman knew running fingerprints wasn't the magic people saw on TV. Sometimes law enforcement got lucky with the first huge database they searched, but with no idea of where the victim had come from, they might have to search a few others. Assuming the man had been printed in the past.

But Truman believed violence beget violence, and judging by this man's manner of death, he'd associated with violence before.

SIX

"Hey, Mercy! Welcome back!"

Mercy's attitude improved at the sound of Lucas's heartfelt welcome as she stepped inside the Eagle's Nest police station. She'd grown fond of Truman's police department manager. The giant young man had a gift for organization and telling people what to do. "Thanks, Lucas. Is your boss here?"

His grin widened. "He's in the back. He's moving a bit slow this morning. I did make him change his clothes once I got a whiff of him. He's been wearing the same thing since that big fire."

So much for Truman following her advice.

She'd checked in at her own office first thing and then driven to the scene where Ben Cooley had been shot at. The body had been taken to the morgue by the time she arrived, but a small crime scene crew and the fire marshal were still present. She'd asked Bill Trek if this fire had any similarities to the fire at which the deputies had been shot. His answer hadn't been helpful. According to his nose, they'd used the same accelerant as in that fire, but that's where the similarities ended. This one was simply too small and had been put out too early to be compared with the other.

But someone had shot a weapon at both fires.

Mercy was relieved that Cooley hadn't been hurt and was determined to find the shooters. A resident had called Truman to say a fire had been started on his property last week and he'd gotten a look at the culprits before chasing them off and putting out the fire himself. She and Truman had agreed to meet him at the Eagle's Nest station.

Lucas scowled at the clock. "Your witness hasn't shown up yet. Clyde Jenkins said he'd be in by now. I'll give him another ten minutes and then call him. He's not known for being prompt."

"What do you know about him?" She didn't recognize the name from when she'd lived in Eagle's Nest years before.

Lucas brushed his hair out of his eyes and tapped the keyboard on his desk. "He was charged once for disturbing the peace. I remember when that happened. He'd fired his gun in the air to get rid of some religious people who knocked on his door. Said he'd told them to leave and they were too slow to get off his property. They filed charges and somehow he ended up only pleading guilty to the disturbing-the-peace charge. I imagine the original charge was something worse. He's sixty-five and lives alone on three acres east of town. Comes to town and hangs around with the old-timers at the feed store or the John Deere dealership. Seems pleasant enough."

Lucas stood up from his desk and walked over to the printer. He moved awkwardly, and Mercy gaped at the giant boot over a cast on his foot. "Is that broken? What did you do?"

"It's nothing, but yes, it's broken."

"How did it happen?" Mercy asked again. The young man seemed flustered and wouldn't meet her gaze as he handed her a sheet of paper from the printer.

"Fooling around. It was stupid."

Truman chose that moment to step in the office and greet her. An overwhelming need to touch him and greet him with a kiss filled her, but she stayed still. They'd agreed to keep it professional around both their coworkers. She tried to transmit her affection through her gaze. The smile in his eyes told her it'd been received.

"Jeez. Get a room or something," Lucas ordered. "I swear the temperature just rose ten degrees in here."

"Send Clyde back when he gets here," Truman said as he led her to his office.

"What happened to Lucas's foot?" Mercy asked as she took one of the wooden chairs across from his desk.

Truman relaxed into his big office chair and leaned so far back she expected it to tip over. "He didn't tell you?"

"He seemed too embarrassed to tell me."

"I had to get the story out of Royce. I guess Lucas and some buddies built a bike ramp and were trying to launch themselves over someone's shed. Lucas didn't make it."

"How's the shed?" asked Mercy, thinking of the muscular bulk of the former high school football player.

"Not a total loss."

"Isn't that the sort of stunt kids do in middle school?"

"Yep. No wonder he didn't want to tell anyone. I often forget he's only nineteen."

Someone paused in the doorway, drawing their attention.

"Morning, Chief."

Mercy assumed the older man clutching a cowboy hat was Clyde Jenkins. Truman made introductions, and Clyde shook her hand as if it were made of glass. He had the eye bags and lined face of Tommy Lee Jones, but that was where the similarities ended. He was taller than Truman and incredibly skinny, with a yellow cast to his skin that made her wonder about his health. His smile was warm, and he flashed perfect movie star teeth.

"Pleased to meet you. I didn't realize the FBI would be here." Caution filled Clyde's tone.

"We're taking an interest in all the recent arson cases in light of the deputies' murders," Mercy told him.

His face fell and the impossibly deep lines around his mouth grew deeper. "I knew Ralph Long well enough to say howdy. I can't believe he's dead."

"It's a horrible situation that's shaken everyone." Mercy gestured at the chair adjacent to hers, and they all took their seats. "Tell me what happened at your place."

"When I heard about Ralph, I knew I needed to come forward." Clyde stared at the hat in his hands. "I heard there'd been some problems with small fires around town, but . . . I didn't think mine was worth mentioning. My neighbor told me two men were killed the other day, so I figured I should at least let someone know what I saw."

He shifted in his seat and crossed and uncrossed an ankle over his knee. Mercy frowned. "Wouldn't most people report an arson started on their property?"

Clyde fingered the brim of his hat. "I didn't want any trouble."

Mercy exchanged a glance with Truman. "How can reporting a fire cause you trouble?" she asked.

The witness set his hat on his knee and gave Truman a pleading look.

Truman twisted his lips. "Did you scare them off with a little gunfire?"

"Am I going to be arrested again?"

Mercy understood, remembering Lucas's story about how Clyde had scared religious folks off his property. "No, Clyde. I don't think that's going to be a concern. Obviously the people you fired at last week never filed a report. We're simply interested in what you saw."

He exhaled and slumped back in his chair. "That's a relief. It took me two years to pay off that fine last time." His demeanor perked up. "This was Wednesday of last week. I spotted two people—possibly three—dashing through my orchard. I stepped out of the house and I could hear them laughing as they ran. I didn't think much of it . . . I'm not far from the highway, and people have been known to park along it and cut through my orchard to the creek. Doesn't matter how many No Trespassing signs I put up. But then a few minutes later I saw a light coming from the area of my burn pile. I'd been waiting for some wet weather before lighting it myself. It was just plain stupid to light anything last week."

"I agree," said Truman.

Clyde nodded vehemently. "It's been dry for weeks. Anyway, I was all pissed as hell and maybe my temper got the best of me, so I let off one warning shot. Since the fire was where I usually burn, everything I needed to put it out was handy, and it was doused in a few minutes."

"Where were the men when you fired?" Mercy asked.

"Heading back through the orchard toward the highway."

"You didn't try to get a look at their vehicle?" Truman leaned forward and rested his forearms on his desk, his entire focus on Clyde.

"I had a fire to take care of," Clyde pointed out. "This might be November, but with our dry spell it could have spread like crazy."

"Not doubting your judgment," Truman told him. "Just hoping you had a vehicle description for us. Did you hear it leave?"

Clyde thought for a moment. "No, all my attention was on the fire."

"What did they do after you fired your gun?" Mercy asked.

"Ran faster."

"Could you make out anything they said? Or see what they wore?" she continued.

The older man closed his eyes. "All I saw was silhouettes. No features. I'm not even certain about how many people. I think there were two or three of them. Could be others I didn't see."

Mercy thought of the large man from the early-morning fire. "Any of them heavyset? Super thin?"

"Average size. I feel like they were younger because they could move so fast, you know?" He opened his eyes and tipped his head in thought.

"They ran as fast as they could once I fired. It's been several decades since I was able to run like that."

"If someone fired at you, you might surprise yourself," Truman suggested.

"Good point." He frowned and opened his mouth to speak but closed it. His thick brows came together, and he picked at a button on his coat.

"What is it?" asked Mercy.

"I could be wrong," he started.

"We're interested in anything you can suggest," Mercy said.

"Well, I think one of them was a woman. I swear I heard a woman's laugh that night."

◆　◆　◆

Mercy couldn't get Clyde's words out of her mind. *A woman? A woman might have done these fires and shootings?*

She and Truman had puzzled over it for a good ten minutes after Clyde left, getting nowhere in their theories except in realizing they needed to be more open-minded. They couldn't assume the shooters and fire setters were all male.

"I feel like I haven't seen you since I got back," Mercy said to Truman as he drove them out to the site of the deputies' murders. They'd grabbed a quick lunch after Clyde left and made plans to meet the fire marshal at the remains of Tilda Brass's barn.

"I'm pretty sure we slept in the same bed last night."

"Briefly. And you passed out within minutes."

"Are you complaining?"

"Maybe a tiny bit." She took a closer look at him, noting the bandages on his neck looked clean and fresh. "You still look exhausted, which doesn't surprise me, since I think you've had five hours of sleep in the last two days. How do the burns feel?"

"Fine."

"Uh-huh." She dug some ibuprofen out of her bag and handed it to him. The fact that he accepted them without protest gave her an idea of how the burns really felt. He swallowed them with a swig from the travel coffee mug in his cup holder. Mercy tried not to think about how old the cold coffee might be.

"What are your thoughts on one of the arsonists being a woman?" she asked him.

"You mean one of the murderers?"

"That too."

"I don't see why not. I'm more hung up on the fact that Clyde saw them sprinting through his orchard. The body I saw this morning hadn't done any sprinting in decades. And he was definitely not of average size."

"Maybe we're looking at more than two or three people." Mercy let that idea simmer in her thoughts. *A group of people starting fires?* She'd been under the impression that arson was generally a single-person crime, unless it was a case of a radical group like the Animal Liberation Front or the Earth Liberation Front. "I can't see the motive yet," Mercy said slowly. "In a case like this, I have to ask, 'Who benefits?' And so far I haven't seen benefits for anyone. No one's getting rich. No one seems to be the focus of revenge."

She'd read Truman's reports on the three small fires. None of the victims had any ideas about why they'd been targeted. There'd been no associations found among them; the arsons had seemed extremely random.

According to what she'd read about arsonists, they loved to see the flames and feel the power of destruction. They could target their fires to hurt someone, but more often it was about self-gratification. And they typically didn't shoot the first responders. They liked to watch the responders in action.

Their arsonists—murderers—were still a mystery to her.

"I can't see the benefit either," Truman said. "The fire at the Brass farm changed it up. You know as well as I do that there's been a backlash against law enforcement in several cities in our country. We can't ignore that."

She couldn't ignore it; it was in her thoughts every day.

His focus was on the road, his profile to her, so she took a long moment to savor the sight of him. Was it wrong that she was thankful he rarely wore a uniform? His badge was on his belt along with his weapon, but at first glance Truman Daly did not look like law enforcement. To her he seemed safer not wearing a uniform that announced his profession. The same went for her. Unless she was wearing an FBI jacket with the letters emblazoned across her back, no one could guess what she did for a living.

Am I a chicken?

Appreciating the anonymity of their jobs when many good men and women in uniform put their lives on the line every day made her feel sick to her stomach.

Who am I fooling? Truman Daly has COP *written on his forehead.*

"I really hate the theory that the fire might have been set for that purpose," Mercy said.

"You and me both."

"That doesn't happen out here."

He lifted a brow at her unlikely claim. "It can happen anywhere," he stated.

I know. It doesn't mean I like it.

A long silence filled the vehicle. Pines and rocks and sagebrush flashed by as they sped down the highway. Mercy waited until they rounded a bend in the road and then leaned forward to look out Truman's side of the vehicle. The Cascade mountains were glorious. The sky was a hazy gray instead of the intense blue of summer, but the peaks were loaded with snow, looking much more white and full than when she had arrived in September. She never tired of looking at them.

She'd considered buying a home, but hadn't rushed into it. The reasonable person inside her wanted to see how things played out with Kaylie, her job, and Truman. Neither she nor Truman talked about the future; it was way too early in their relationship. But she had a good feeling about him. He hadn't raised any red flags for her. Yet.

Sometimes he seemed too good to be true.

He had demons. But he worked to keep them at bay. *Who doesn't have a demon or two under their bed?*

Even she had a few. Ones that made her chop wood half the night and obsessively watch the international stock markets.

She hid nothing from him. He knew it all. Every worry and burden. *But do I know all of his?*

For the most part the man was an open book. With Truman, what you saw was what you got.

But she still watched him, waiting for the bottom to fall out. She couldn't help it; it was part of who she was.

"Have you made Thanksgiving plans?" he asked in the silence.

"When is it?"

He gave her a side-eye. "Next Thursday. Tell me you knew that."

"I can't remember the last time I had Thanksgiving plans."

"Are you kidding me?" The Tahoe swerved slightly as his gaze left the road and he gave her a wide-eyed stare. "Are you anti-American?"

That stung. "No, I haven't been around family in fifteen years," she snapped.

"Thanksgiving isn't only about family. I've celebrated Turkey Day with all sorts of people during the last decade. It's been pretty rare that they're related to me. Usually I don't have the time to fly to see my parents for the actual day."

She kept her gaze straight ahead. Holidays were awkward. And a bit of a sore spot that she preferred not to poke.

"My department in San Jose had a sign-up sheet for people who were looking for something to do on Thanksgiving. It was a different crowd every year and it was always a blast."

"My Portland office had something like that," Mercy admitted. She'd never signed up. Thanksgiving had always been a rare four-day weekend for her, and she'd spent it working at her cabin. Alone.

"I assume you haven't heard from any of your family about the holiday?"

"No."

"Then let's make our own plans. I don't suck as a cook, and we can do it at my house." Enthusiasm filled his voice and the vehicle. "Kaylie might have a friend or two that she'd like to have join us. I can smell roasting turkey already. That's the best part of Thanksgiving . . . the way the house smells all day."

She remembered that smell, triggering memories of the holiday with her four siblings and their parents around a crowded table. *Would they celebrate together this year? Would they even think to invite me?*

They hadn't for the last fifteen years. Why start now?

"That sounds good," she told him, feeling a tiny degree of his excitement for the day. "Kaylie would love to bake the pies." Dirty footprints in her kitchen popped into her head. "Crap." She'd forgotten her plans to confront the teen.

"What is it?" Truman asked as he turned off the highway and down the road to the Brass farm.

She told him about the footprints in the kitchen, the makeup, and the perfume.

"You think she snuck out last night?" He sounded skeptical.

"Of course I do. And I assume it has something to do with a boy, since she wore perfume and a ton of eye makeup. I didn't even know she *owned* perfume."

"Hmmm." He scratched his jaw.

"What? Am I overreacting? I'm sorta new to this parenting thing, you know."

"Didn't you ever sneak out as a teen?"

"No!"

He shot her a look that said he didn't believe her.

"I didn't! Are you saying all . . . or most teens do?"

"You might have been a very good girl while growing up, Mercy Kilpatrick, but I guarantee those two brothers of yours probably snuck out of the house a dozen times or so."

"So it's a male thing."

"Well, when I did it, it was to meet a girl. So, I'd say it's a fifty-fifty split."

She sank into her seat. "I *was* a good girl. So were both of my sisters. That doesn't mean I should overlook what Kaylie is doing now."

"No, you shouldn't. You need to make certain she's not doing anything stupid." He coughed. "Is she on birth control?" he asked weakly.

Mercy covered her eyes. "Oh sweet Jesus." Her hands slid to her ears. "Stop talking."

"I'll take it that means you don't know. Might be a discussion the two of you need to have, considering her age."

I have to talk about sneaking out at night AND birth control?

"But my point about her sneaking out was to suggest that you don't confront her in anger. A lot of kids do it, and I'm not saying it's right, but you need to understand that it's not unusual behavior for her age."

"Next you'll tell me the exact same thing about teens and sex."

"Don't put your head in the sand," he advised. "Kaylie's a smart girl and has a lot going for her. A little guidance from her aunt for her teen years could go a long way."

"Noted." She was relieved as they pulled into the drive that led to the burned barn. She spotted Bill Trek's red pickup.

Truman parked and sat motionless in his seat, staring out the windshield at the destruction. He swallowed, and she noticed his hand shook slightly as he turned off the truck.

"Does it feel different in the daylight?" she asked.

"Very. It's like looking at a sketch of a scene from a movie that I already experienced in 3-D. Still raises all the same feelings, though."

She squeezed his hand and met his gaze. "It's done and over. Nothing will change."

He nodded, and she saw protective walls rise in his gaze as he prepared himself to face the remains of the hell he'd been in thirty-six hours before.

She didn't blame him one bit.

They got out of the vehicle and headed to where Bill Trek dug through the debris. He used a snow shovel to move the piles of ash and wood chunks and was dressed in protective coveralls and a mask to keep the clouds of soot from getting into his lungs. As they approached he pulled off the mask and worked his way out of the pile. It was a contrast to the extreme care and precision Mercy had usually seen in evidence collection. Maybe arson was handled differently.

Fire investigation was a dirty job. Ash covered him from head to toe, but he grinned as they walked up and gestured that he didn't want to shake hands. "Don't touch me," he warned, showing them his soot-stained gloves.

"Not a problem," agreed Truman. "What's with the shovel?"

"I need to see the floor," Bill said, using his forearm to wipe away the sweat that ran through the ash on his forehead. "Can't tell what happened without getting a look at it. It's an important part of my map."

"What have you found so far?" asked Truman.

"Basically I've found support for my original hypothesis. Someone soaked the outside walls with gasoline and did the same with everything inside. They were determined to make it burn big." He gave them a serious look. "I spoke with the owner, asking her what was stored in the barn, and she claims that there wasn't really anything that she was aware of, but I'd like to hear that from some of her friends or relatives too."

"Why?" Truman asked. "I honestly don't think she's been to the barn in years."

"If I get a relative that tells me there was a boat or expensive farm equipment stored inside, then we have a problem." Bill looked pointedly at the burned remains. "Clearly there wasn't anything like that left here."

Mercy suddenly understood. "Someone would have moved things they wanted to protect if they'd set the fire themselves . . . if they were hoping to get the insurance payment for the structure they set on fire."

"You'd be amazed at how many 'accidental' home fires are missing the big-screen TV the neighbor says was in the living room. Or the antique gun collection that just happened to be moved to storage the week before. They want the insurance payout for an accident, but they can't help but first move their favorite belongings. A dead giveaway when a relative tells me the antique gun collection has had a place of honor in the den for twenty years."

"I don't think Tilda Brass set the fire," Truman said.

"I agree. But I need to make certain all my *t*'s are crossed."

"What else do you do outside of examining the actual scene?" Mercy asked with curiosity.

"Well." Bill paused. "A lot. I'll talk to the insurance company and the friends and neighbors. I'll check with the hospital and clinics, looking for someone with burns or inhalation injuries. You'd be surprised how many get burns on their hands or their ankles. The fires always catch faster than they expect. Especially with the gasoline they used here."

Mercy looked at the section of concrete pad Bill had cleared. The patterns meant nothing to her. "The gasoline was also dumped inside the barn? Not just around the outside?" she asked.

"Yep."

"So they must have seen that there was a propane tank inside."

"I assume so," agreed Bill. "Either they didn't care or saw it as a bonus. It wasn't a big one."

"Big enough to knock me a few feet and shoot burning debris onto me," Truman pointed out.

"It was positioned against the wall you were closest to," Bill agreed. "If it had been on the other side of the barn, you wouldn't have felt the same strength of the blast."

Truman turned away and walked over to the far side of the debris pile, staring at the ground. He stopped a few feet from where the two men had breathed their last breaths and shoved his hands in his pockets.

"How's he doing?" Bill asked her in a low voice. "What he went through would send most men to their doctors begging for drugs to make their memories go away."

"I suspect that's crossed his mind," Mercy admitted. "He's been through a similar type of hell before. It nearly drove him out of law enforcement, but he seems well prepared to deal with the emotional aftermath this time. Sadly, it's because he had to learn how the first time."

"No one would blame him for stepping back."

"That's not who he is."

"I can see that." Bill met her gaze. "But he can still crash. He's not Captain America."

Truman often wore a Captain America T-shirt, and Mercy thought it suited him. "Actually, that's a perfect description of him. Captain America has a mushy sentimental core; he's very human. And yes, he can fall apart." She glanced over at Truman. He stood motionless, and she knew he battled invisible demons. Her instincts told her to go to him, but she stood still. Truman would ask when he needed help.

She simply had to be available.

SEVEN

Mercy wrapped her hands around her hot coffee cup at the Bend FBI office but didn't drink. She was coffeed out. Darby noticed and asked if she wanted some juice. Mercy turned down the intelligence analyst's offer. She was tired of eating and drinking on the run. It was all she'd done at Quantico for the previous two weeks, and she hadn't found time to grocery shop since she'd been back. Her body was rebelling against the unusual diet.

I need a week of eating nothing but organic veggies and beef from happy, grass-fed cows.

She'd never dreamed she'd be *that* consumer, the one who questioned the source of the chicken breast on her plate, but after she left home at eighteen, she'd noticed that food tasted different. She'd grown up on meat slaughtered by her father and vegetables grown by her family or by friends. After a few months of processed food, her body had revolted, and she'd learned to seek out local sources.

She'd embarrassed Truman a time or two in restaurants with her questions, and he'd quickly figured out the best places for her to eat, where he didn't have to cower behind his menu as she grilled the staff about sourcing.

She thought of the cinnamon roll she'd grabbed at the gas station that morning. *So sometimes I'm a hypocrite.*

Eddie plopped into the seat next to her. His hair didn't look as perfect as usual, and it appeared he'd run his hands through it a few dozen times in the last hour. Dark circles hung below his eyes.

"How's it going?" she asked.

"Crappy. I've spent the last two days talking with the families of Ralph Long and Damon Sanderson."

"Ahhh." Sympathy washed over her. She'd seen the pictures of Damon's darling baby, and her heartstrings had nearly snapped in half. "Do they have support?"

"Tons of family are hovering around," said Eddie. "I don't know if that's always a good thing. I think Damon's wife needs some alone time."

"Any leads?"

"Not really. I'm looking into a bar fight that Long broke up two nights before he was shot. One of the guys threatened him at that time. Long included it in his report, but I haven't been able to locate the person. No arrests were made."

"That's a stretch," said Mercy. "Any drunk asshole is going to mouth off at whoever is ruining their fun."

"That's what I'm expecting to find. I'm meeting with the bartender and bar owner this evening to see what they remember, and I'm hoping for some camera views."

"Anything jump out about Sanderson?"

"Nope. According to the half dozen people I've talked to, he was a complete angel and impossible to despise."

"Of course that's what they say. Makes me suspicious. No one's that perfect."

"That's my reaction too. I'm still digging."

Their supervisor strode into the meeting and shrugged out of his sport coat, hanging it on his seat back before he sat down. "Where are we?" he asked in greeting. "Mercy, have you heard from the medical examiner? Any news on the autopsies?"

"She found nothing unusual. Both men died within moments from their gunshot wounds."

"When are the funerals?" asked Darby.

"Tomorrow," replied Eddie. "The families have decided to hold a joint service."

"That's unusual," observed Jeff.

"It is, but all members of both families are firmly on board with it."

"I like it," said Mercy. She truly did. It spoke of a unity that resonated within the Central Oregon community, in contrast to the horror of the shootings.

"It's come up several times that the shooter must have some serious skills to make the shots he did," continued Jeff. "Eddie, I want you to contact the ranges in the area. Find out who can shoot like that."

Eddie nodded and made a note on the pad in front of him.

"Keep in mind plenty of people practice on their own property," added Mercy. "Some never step foot in a shooting range."

"What about wanting to show off their skills to their buddies?" asked Darby. "Should we publicly ask if anyone knows someone with those skills? Or are we looking at a level of military training? We have to consider that he may have learned these skills on our tax dollars."

Mercy sighed. She'd wondered the same thing. *Please don't let it be a former soldier.*

Eddie made more notes. "I don't think we should advertise that we're looking for someone with a *particular set of skills*," he said in his best Liam Neeson imitation.

"Agreed," said Jeff. "Later, possibly. For now, let's keep our inquiries quiet."

Darby shuffled through the stack of papers before her and focused on one. "Reports and complaints about militia activity seem to be on a bit of an uptick," she said quietly. "I don't know if it's relevant here."

The room was quiet as everyone weighed her words.

"There's always chatter about militia activity," Jeff finally said. "I don't think a week goes by that something doesn't cross my desk in that regard. Is arson a method they use?"

"Not typically," said Darby. "Most of what I've seen are complaints about open carry and some target practice." She pulled out a piece of paper and stared at it.

"Sounds like business as usual," Mercy said. She'd grown up seeing weapons everywhere. Gun racks in pickup rear windows. Rifles slung across backs or propped behind neighbors' doors. Pistols on hips. But it was much rarer now.

"The most unusual thing I've come across is a rumor of a plan to blow up a bridge," added Darby.

"Holy crap," said Eddie. "That made my skin crawl. How reliable is that rumor?"

"I don't know. I've been trying to trace back the source, but it seems to be a lot of . . . 'so-and-so said.'"

"Assign it to Lefebvre," Jeff instructed. "Give him what you've found so far and that I want a report sometime tomorrow. That deserves a closer look whether it's related to this case or not."

Mercy fully agreed. Public safety was their first priority.

"We know a rifle was used in the deputies' shooting," continued Jeff. "We have the casings and the bullets. It appears the weapon hasn't been used in a crime before, but if we can find the weapon, then our lab can see if the striations match."

"Did they find the bullet that was fired at Ben Cooley?" Mercy asked.

"Not yet. County found the casing, but the actual bullet hasn't turned up. The sheriff theorizes it ricocheted off rock and headed in a different direction. They're combing the area with metal detectors, but it's packed with rock and dense shrubbery."

"And the casing was for a nine millimeter, correct?" asked Eddie. Jeff agreed.

Two different weapons . . . two different shooters? "One shooter missed Ben Cooley, and at the previous fire one shooter hit his targets four times," Mercy said, thinking out loud. "Two different marksmen? Or possibly markswomen?" She updated the group about Clyde Jenkins's observation.

"Your opinion on the quality of the witness?" Jeff asked.

"Solid," said Mercy. "He wasn't positive about what he'd seen, but he felt strongly enough to let us know."

"The descriptions of suspects we're looking for keeps expanding," complained Darby.

"We need to consider that we could be looking at a group," added Mercy.

"I hope it's a group," said Darby. "They'll start to rat each other out at some point. Or they'll become disenchanted with their leader and start talking. I'll take that over one secretive introvert any day."

"Ted Kaczynski," added Eddie. "He was a loner. It took nearly twenty years to find him."

Darby nodded, scowling at the mention of the domestic terrorist.

"Any word on the identity of the victim with the cut throat?" their boss asked.

"Not yet," said Mercy. "I know the ME sent over his prints, and we've forwarded them to our lab."

"He could be an innocent victim *or* one of the arsonists," Eddie pointed out.

"I suspect he'll turn out to be one of the arsonists," said Mercy. "Even if he didn't fit the description from Clyde Jenkins. I'm keeping an open mind, but the fact that no one can place him indicates he's not from around here . . . therefore, he was at that location for a purpose."

"And someone turned on him?" asked Darby. "In their opinion, he did something that he deserved to die for?"

"Possibly," said Mercy. "Maybe he wasn't happy with the murders or who they targeted with the fires. Maybe he wanted out of the group. Assuming there is a group."

"Assume nothing," Jeff stated. "Let's back up a bit and take a fresh look at the beginning. I want new interviews with the victims of the first three small arsons, and I want it done tomorrow. I'll let you decide who talks to whom." He stood and pulled his papers together. "Anything we missed?" he asked without looking up.

Eddie and Mercy exchanged a look. "No," they said in unison.

"Good. See you tomorrow."

"I'd like to talk to the prepper family," she told Eddie.

"You got it, and if you buy coffee all next week, I'll interview the other two victims."

"Deal."

◆ ◆ ◆

Mercy pulled into the driveway of the double-wide mobile home and parked. Julia and Steve Parker had agreed to see her that evening. They'd been pleased to hear the FBI had an interest in their fire. When Steve told her the location of their home, Mercy had realized they lived less than a mile from her parents' home. As she'd driven past the familiar farmhouse, it occurred to her that she hadn't seen Rose in three weeks and promised herself to correct that.

As soon as her case lightened up.

Since she'd been back in Eagle's Nest, she and her sister had developed a routine of meeting for coffee once a week after one of Rose's preschool classes. They'd meet at the Coffee Café and chat for a solid hour, and then Mercy would drive her home.

Rose's facial scarring had faded. She still had some pink lines, but most had disappeared completely. Mercy hoped the remaining lines would completely fade . . . Rose might have some thin silver scars, not that her blind sister would ever be able to see them.

Rose would have another permanent reminder. One she was excited to love and raise.

Mercy's love for Rose's unborn baby was rapidly growing. What she'd once believed would be a burden she now saw as a blessing. Any child would be lucky to have Rose as their mother.

When she dropped off Rose after their chats, Mercy's mother occasionally came to the door and waved. It was awkward, but less awkward than meeting Mercy's father face-to-face. Her mother had shown some spine when it came to their third daughter. She'd even met with Mercy a time or two for an infusion of caffeine. Her mother was careful in their conversations . . . never discussing Mercy's father or anything from the past.

It was better than nothing.

A single light bulb shone over the door of the Parkers' home, casting a small cone of light that barely lit their stairs. Mercy sat in her vehicle for a long moment, straining her vision to see the rest of their property in the dark. It was difficult. She could make out the faintest outline of what appeared to be a small stable and paddock beyond the house, but she had no idea where the shed that had caught fire had stood.

She slid out of her SUV and made her way to the house, thinking about the location in relation to the other fires. She'd already stared at a map, searching for a pattern among all five of the incidents, but she'd come up with nothing. She knocked. The front door opened, and a very pregnant young woman greeted her.

"Agent Kilpatrick?" Julia Parker had impossibly straight blonde hair that hung nearly to her waist. She looked too young to be pregnant, although Mercy already knew she was twenty-two.

Still too young.

A toddler appeared and hugged her mother's leg, frowning at the approaching stranger. Her hair matched her mother's, and her blue eyes were as round as marbles.

Mercy held out her hand. "Call me Mercy." She grinned at the tiny girl, who ducked her face into her mother's pants.

"This is Winslet." Julia patted the top of the toddler's head and ran a supporting hand below her own huge belly as she grimaced. "This elephant will soon be Lola."

"Two girls," Mercy commented. "How lovely." *I never know what to say to pregnant women. Or toddlers.*

Julia led her into the cramped home. She pushed aside a high chair and gestured for Mercy to take a seat at the kitchenette table. Three ceramic Thanksgiving turkeys stood in the center of the table in the middle of a wreath woven from dried leaves. The house had little room to maneuver in, but Julia's personal touches gave it a homey air. Winslet demanded to be on her mother's lap, and Mercy held her breath as Julia lifted her up. *Please don't go into labor.* Julia deftly balanced the girl on the minuscule amount of lap she had beyond her belly. Winslet turned suspicious eyes on Mercy.

She's darling. But the intense stare unnerved her.

"Steve will be in soon. He's finishing up some things in the barn. Oh!" She started to move Winslet off her lap. "I didn't offer you anything to drink."

Mercy held up a hand to stop her. "Don't get up. I'm fine. I just came from a long meeting where I held a cup of coffee and didn't drink a sip of it."

Julia settled back in her chair, looking relieved, and Winslet leaned against her mother's tummy and stroked it with a tiny hand as if it were a kitten. A door at the back of the home opened and Steve Parker came in, removing his boots just inside the door and greeting Mercy in stocking feet. He looked nearly as young as Julia and had a baby face with full pink cheeks. He took Winslet off Julia's lap and sat with the toddler in another chair, giving Winslet a plastic book to play with. "I'm glad to hear that the police aren't done with our fire," he said. "We had a lot of work stored up in that shed. Not that finding the arsonist can replace it, but it'd make me feel a heck of a lot better."

"I completely understand," said Mercy. "I know you haven't lived here that long, but have you met the Kilpatricks down the highway? They're my parents."

Understanding crossed his face and his eyes lit up.

Bingo. We have something in common.

"We lost a year's worth of canning," Steve said. "Along with bins of medical supplies and garden seeds." He placed a kiss on the top of

Winslet's head. "It hurts when you sink hard work and money into preparing for your children and someone destroys it."

"I'm so sorry." The tender way he looked at his daughter and pregnant wife ripped at her heart. *Is that how my father felt about his preparations? That they were primarily about his family?*

Guilt was bitter on her tongue. She'd never thought about it that way. Her father's obsession had always felt a bit self-centered to her.

She turned to Julia. "I read in the police report that you spotted the fire around one a.m. from a window?"

"Yes. I saw the flames out the window above the kitchen sink." A sheepish look crossed her face. "I was getting something for heartburn. Either heartburn or my bladder interrupts my sleep nearly every night now."

"When are you due?" Mercy asked.

"Four weeks."

"A Christmas baby?"

"We hope. That would be really special." Julia and Steve exchanged a look that made Mercy feel like an intruder.

"You told the police you didn't hear or see anything before the fire, correct?" Mercy asked.

Steve looked to his wife as Julia frowned. She said, "I didn't say anything at the time, but I swear I heard children laughing."

Mercy stared at the pregnant woman. *Children?*

"But it was before the heartburn woke me . . . I think I was dreaming. I swear I've had the weirdest dreams while I've been pregnant with this one. But it felt so real at the time."

"So there's a possibility you heard laughter outside," Mercy said as her brain tried to digest this new bit of news. Clyde Jenkins had heard laughter, so Julia's story wasn't that odd.

"Maybe. I know that's not very helpful, but I wanted to tell everything. I should have mentioned it to the police chief when he was here, but it felt ridiculous talking about a dream."

"Not ridiculous," said Mercy. "Please share everything."

"Well, that's the only new thing that's occurred to me." Julia rested her arms on her belly.

"Would you show me where the fire was?"

"I've cleaned up most of the debris," Steve said. "There's just a concrete pad and some boards left."

"I'd still like to look around."

He stood, handed off Winslet to Julia, and gestured for Mercy to follow. He stopped at a cabinet in the kitchen and grabbed two flashlights, handing her a black one and keeping the Minnie Mouse one for himself.

Outside, Mercy could see her breath. The temperature had dropped rapidly, and she zipped up her coat to her chin. The shed was about a hundred feet from the home, closer to the main road. Steve was right. There was just a concrete pad and a neat pile of singed lumber. A faint scent of smoke still hovered.

"I salvaged what I could from the shed itself," he said, kicking the edge of one board. "I can rebuild it after I get some more lumber. And the supplies will eventually be replaced." He shot Mercy a rueful glance. "It just stings, you know? I didn't want to mention it in front of Julia, but it makes me feel unsafe. Julia has enough problems sleeping at night, and this has added to them. Especially after the murders the other night."

"That's completely understandable."

"I've added heavier locks on our house and barn and wired up motion-detector lights that we turn on at bedtime." He gave a short laugh. "It wasn't the best idea. Now we're woken up by lights every few hours as a rabbit or deer runs through the yard. I need to rethink that one." He paused, staring at the concrete pad. "At first I assumed it was stupid kids who didn't care if they caused damage to other people's belongings."

"And now?"

"I don't know what to think since those two deputies were killed. That doesn't sound like kids fooling around to me."

She circled the rectangle of cement, searching the packed dirt with her flashlight, not knowing what she hoped to see. "Have you had any run-ins with people who didn't like the fact that you're preppers?" she asked quietly.

"Not here." Steve pressed his lips together. "My father was a bit of an ass about it, but he's in Arizona. It's one of the reasons we moved to Oregon. To get away from him and the heat."

"Have you found . . . a supportive community here?"

He met her gaze. "We have. Your father has been instrumental in introducing us to people. I like that your mother is a trained midwife."

So they've joined my father's circle.

"What do you do, Steve?"

"I'm a journeyman plumber. Pretty good at construction too. I have a knack for it."

Preparedness wasn't just about accumulating a pile of stuff. People needed practical skills that took training, study, and practice. Anyone could buy up a pile of guns and canned goods, but without the skills, they wouldn't last long. Steve and his family were committed.

That would be reason enough for my father to add him to his small circle of people who have agreed to band together if disaster strikes. Steve's specialized skills would be useful in TEOTWAWKI.

The end of the world as we know it.

Her parents were considered wealthy by prepping standards. They had four vehicles: one powered by gas, one by diesel, one by propane, and one by electricity. Folks just starting out, like the Parkers, probably had one diesel-fueled vehicle, the versatile choice to start with. Mercy suspected the young family was dedicated for life, and had been happy to join the tight-knit prepper community that her father had organized.

"I've met your siblings," Steve said. "Winslet adores Rose. But I don't recall your father mentioning an FBI agent in the family."

"He wouldn't bring it up." Mercy turned and shone her flashlight on a copse of trees a few yards away, wanting to look anywhere but at Steve's questioning gaze.

It's a small town. Time to get used to people asking about my father and me.

"So since you moved here in April, have the people you met have been good to you?" *Talk about anything but my father.* "No arguments with neighbors? No problems with people on your acreage?"

"No problems at all. It's very quiet out here. If we don't go into town, we might not see another person for days."

"That's why my father originally built in this area," Mercy said.

"It's a good location," Steve agreed. "A bit cold and dry in the winter, but the rest of the year's weather is good for growing and getting work done. We considered the west side of the Cascades in the Willamette Valley, where the weather is milder, but the cost was too high. And there were too many people."

She wanted to tell him that there was more to life than judging an area by how ideal it was in case of a natural disaster or government meltdown. *Try to enjoy life now. Don't focus entirely on what hasn't happened yet. Don't ignore your children for the sake of an obsession.*

She remembered how he'd looked at his daughter and wife. There'd been genuine love and affection. Had her father ever pressed his lips against the top of her head when she was a child? *Surely he had.*

Hadn't he?

She couldn't remember any outward signs of affection from the man. Ever.

Steve Parker wasn't her father. Yet.

"You have a beautiful family," she told him. "Lola will be very lucky to join it."

Even in the poor light of their flashlights, she could make out his happy reaction. "We can't wait. I don't care that it's another girl. Girls are awesome."

"I agree."

EIGHT

Kaylie silently closed the door and tiptoed down the apartment stairs, excitement rushing through her veins. Freedom gave her a heady rush as anticipation about seeing Cade made her feet move faster. She hit the sidewalk and jogged through the dark night to their usual rendezvous spot, her breath creating big clouds in the cold air.

Am I in love?

No matter what this sensation was called, she felt fantastic. The energy bubbling through her was oblivious to the fact that it was one in the morning. She and Cade had been dating for over a month. He was three years older than she, and she'd known who he was for a long time, but they hadn't spoken until she waited on him at the Coffee Café early one morning on his way to work. He came back three mornings in a row and finally asked her out.

He'd been the best thing to happen to her since her father died. Aunt Mercy was great, but with Cade she felt beautiful and special. He'd bought her a gold necklace for her seventeenth birthday, lessening the pain of her first birthday without her father. He was tall and gorgeous and kind. When his brown eyes looked into hers, she felt like the only woman in the world.

She jogged faster, the icy air invigorating her.

Aunt Mercy will kill me.

But she didn't care. She was happy and energetic around Cade, and she'd do whatever it took to spend more time with him. He worked twelve-hour days on a ranch far out of town. At first they'd simply texted and FaceTimed in the evening, but soon it wasn't enough. Nights were his primary free time.

She spotted his old Toyota pickup parked up ahead, and elation raced through her.

She'd kept the relationship quiet, unsure what her aunt would think of her having her first boyfriend. Especially one who was three years older. Her father had told Kaylie that his sisters hadn't been allowed to have boyfriends in high school. Would Mercy continue that legacy? She didn't seem like the type to look down on young love, but she did preach self-sufficiency. And Kaylie felt as if she couldn't breathe without Cade.

There was nothing independent about that.

It was enough to make her keep her mouth shut. Mercy had her own romance going on. Kaylie knew Chief Daly had spent the night a few times in their apartment. He was always gone before Kaylie got up in the mornings, but *she knew*. Her aunt always seemed more introspective those mornings. Quiet and content. A small smile on her lips.

Kaylie dashed up to the driver's window and knocked, laughing as she made Cade jump. She ran around to the passenger side and climbed into the warm truck. They leaned toward each other and kissed, his hand running through her hair. She'd worn it down because he liked it that way.

"Hey, babe," he said in his low, sexy voice, stroking her cheek, pressing his forehead against hers. The smell of his cologne made her heart race. Simply put: he made her feel alive. When she wasn't near him, it felt as if she were moving through a fog, simply biding time until they could be together again. She was addicted.

"What do you want to do tonight?" she asked. "I shouldn't stay out more than two hours. It's too hard to get up for work in the morning."

"Your aunt didn't hear you, right?"

"I don't think so. She seemed exhausted when she got in this evening and went straight to bed."

"Good." He kissed her again. "I missed you."

"I missed you too," she said between kisses.

"Landon and Jason want to hang out. They said they'd be at the gravel pit off Lincoln. Finn will probably be there too."

Her heart fell at the news that they wouldn't be alone. At first she'd been excited to meet Cade's friends, but once she'd spent time with them, she'd found them to be full of themselves and immature for twenty-year-olds. Cade wasn't like that. He was mature and thoughtful while his friends tended to be loud and obnoxious. Especially when they'd been drinking. Someone always brought a case of Coors or Budweiser to every gathering. Kaylie would accept one and nurse it. She didn't care for the taste, while the guys liked to see how fast and how many they could drink at one time.

"Sounds great," she said with a smile. "You won't drink, right? I need to be back on time."

"I promise. I have to get up for work too."

"Text me in the morning and I'll have your coffee ready when you stop by."

"Deal." They drove toward Eagle's Nest with her sitting in the center of the bench seat and his arm around her shoulder. He cranked up the heater, although the cool of the night didn't bother her. Nothing bothered her when he was near. Every cell in her body worked overtime when she was with him; she was never cold.

Cade steered with one hand on top of the wheel, smiling as he frequently glanced down at her. He turned off the main highway and weaved down a few back roads. Kaylie had a general idea of the location of the gravel pit but was mildly lost by the third dark turn. Cade drove with confidence.

"I haven't actually been here," Kaylie admitted. "I think I drove by a time or two with . . . my dad." The words stuck on her tongue. She'd learned her days passed easier if she didn't spend time thinking about her father. Every evening she spent a few minutes looking at pictures of the two of them and telling him about her day. It sounded weird, but it worked for her. After his death, at first she'd felt guilty if she didn't think about him every minute of the day. Mercy had taken her to a therapist, and together they'd worked out a system whereby Kaylie could move on with her day because she knew she'd spend time with her father's memory in the evening.

"It's a cool place." He took a sharp left, and the truck lurched as he guided it down a steep gravel road. Kaylie spotted three other pickups at the bottom. They were parked side by side with their headlights on. Three guys stood in the headlights, and she spotted a rifle in the hands of one of them. Another tipped his head back as he took a long drink out of a silver can. The headlights reflected off the can, sending a flash of light at her and Cade. The figure smashed the can in his hand and threw it to the side.

She straightened and Cade's arm slipped off her shoulders as he parked, adding his truck to the line. "What are they doing?"

"If they're at the gravel pit, it means target practice," Cade said. "It's a good place to shoot because it's deep."

"In the middle of the night?"

He shrugged. "Why not?"

"Isn't this private property?"

"No one comes out here at night." Cade opened his door and she slid out his side, wishing they'd gone somewhere else. Alone. Cade's friends ambled over and greeted them, thrusting beers in their hands. Jason was the tallest, but he wasn't fit like Cade, and even though he was only twenty, Jason had a beer belly.

Landon gave her the creeps. He always stared a little too long and sat a little too near. He was whipcord lean with hawklike eyes that were set close to his long narrow nose. She'd heard he'd flunked out of high school.

Finn was the follower and people pleaser, always anxious to do what everyone else wanted. Kaylie figured Landon kept Finn close at hand to stroke his ego and so he'd have someone to order around.

Kaylie handed back her beer. "I have to work in a few hours."

"Same here," said Cade. He tossed his to Finn. "Some of us have jobs."

"I prefer to sleep in," said Landon. "Especially on the weekend. Why in the hell would you work at a job that made you work weekends?" He took a long swallow of beer and studied Kaylie over the top of the can as he drank. "That's right," he said directly to Kaylie after wiping his mouth. "You're still in high school. I don't miss that hell."

She looked away, discomfort curling in her stomach.

Cade claimed his friends thought she was cool even if she was young. But every time they hung out together, one of them said something about her school, as if to remind Cade that he was dating someone beneath him.

"You're up." Landon handed a rifle to Cade. "Five bucks says you can't land them all in the head."

Kaylie spotted several paper targets on the tall, sheer rock wall. Her dad had taught her to shoot, and she was the best out of all her cousins, but she didn't want to show off to this group. Landon was excellent. She'd learned that weeks ago when she and Cade had stopped by his farm. Landon had taken them out back to a shooting range he'd built. Hay bales had dotted the field, labeled with their distance and targets. When Kaylie's father taught her to shoot, she'd aimed at bull's-eyes. These guys used huge images with real faces—not the standard faceless human form. It was creepy.

"I haven't shot in weeks," Cade said. "Not since the last time we were at your place."

"Forget the bet then, loser. Just shoot." Landon stuck a cigarette between his lips and lit it with the flick of a lighter. He caught Kaylie watching him. He blew out a giant breath of smoke, holding her gaze as he toyed with the lighter, making it flame over and over.

A chill shot through her limbs. *Does he act creepy on purpose?*

Cade stepped aside and fired the rifle. Three-quarters of his shots found the head.

I could have hit all of them from this distance. Easy.

Kaylie smiled when he was done. "Nice job!"

"Want a turn?" He held the weapon toward her.

"No, thanks. Not my thing."

"Come on, Kaylie," Finn said. "You won't get hurt."

"Scared, Kaylie?" Landon asked. He pulled a weed out of the gravel and lit it, watching it wilt and burn.

She didn't like the glint in his eye. "I'll pass."

"My turn." Finn grabbed the rifle from Cade, and he tripped as he went to line up his shot.

He's drunk.

Kaylie looked back at Cade's truck and desperately tried to think of an excuse to leave. *I'm tired? I don't feel good?*

Cade slung an arm around her shoulders as he watched Finn shoot. "Hey, Jason," Cade said. "I changed my mind about that beer."

Oh shit.

The headlights of Truman's Tahoe caught the battered sign for the gravel pit. He yawned and took the turn, proceeding slowly through the dark, not bothering to turn on his light bar. He'd received a call about a gunfire complaint. Usually locals would roll over and ignore the sounds of gunfire in the middle of the night, but since the shooting, people had been overly cautious. Truman knew what a call about gunfire near the gravel pit meant: a couple of guys blowing off steam. He'd tell them to go to the shooting range. During daylight hours.

His vehicle reached the bottom, and he spotted four vehicles lined up with their lights on. Five figures stood in the headlights, a rifle in the hands of one man and silver cans in the hands of a few others. There was a rapid shuffle as they spotted the silhouette of his Tahoe with the light bar on top and tried to set aside the cans. The man with the rifle leaned it against the tire of a truck and took a few steps away from it.

Crap. *Alcohol and shooting.*

He scanned the vehicles and recognized one as Jason Eckham's old pickup. *At least one minor is here, and judging by how they ditched their cans, there's more.* He stopped behind the other vehicles and called in support from Deschutes County. If he had a few minors with alcohol, he couldn't let them drive. He eyed the rifle, wondering if there were other weapons. The group appeared nonthreatening in their stances, and he appreciated the guy who'd set the rifle aside, but he trusted no one.

If there's one weapon, assume there's more.

He'd caught Jason drag racing a few weeks ago. He sighed. The kid had a mouth and no respect for law enforcement. Truman studied the other figures in the lights of the vehicles. They held up their hands in front of their eyes to block his headlights, but were trying to get a look at who had arrived. They all looked about Jason's age—

Is that a girl?

He wasn't too surprised.

His backup was three minutes away.

Truman got out of his vehicle and walked toward the group, resting his hand on his weapon at his hip. "Evening guys. And gal—*Kaylie?*" His heart dropped. Mercy's suspicions about Kaylie's nighttime activities were correct.

Kaylie leaned into a tall guy who had his arm wrapped protectively around her shoulders. "Hi, Chief," she said quietly. Jason and one of the other guys shot her an irritated look for acknowledging the enemy.

Determined to not single her out—any more than he just had—he refrained from asking if Mercy knew what her niece was up to. He gave a pointed glance to the silver beer cans on the ground. "Jason, I know how old you are. Let's see IDs from everyone else."

"You can't charge us unless the beers are in our hands," said the skinniest of the bunch.

Great. A teenage lawyer. "I don't know where you got your information, but that's not true for minors in possession in Oregon." He met the gazes of the other three guys. "You know this is private property, right?"

"No one cares if we come here," Jason said quickly. "Everyone does it."

The ultimate defense.

"I assume you're all underage?"

"I'm twenty-one," said skinny. "But I don't have my driver's license with me." He smirked at Truman.

"What's your name?" asked Truman.

"Landon."

"Landon, I count four vehicles behind us, and I happen to know that none of them belong to Kaylie Kilpatrick. That means you drove one here . . . Are you stating that you drove here without a license?"

While the young man struggled with his answer, Truman stared at the other men. "Let's see them."

All reached for their wallets in their back pockets. He collected the IDs and watched Landon reluctantly dig in his pocket. All four men were under twenty-one. Landon had the decency to keep his eyes lowered as Truman handed back his license without saying a word about the fact that he'd lied about being twenty-one. Kaylie hadn't moved. The expression on her face said she wished the gravel pit would open and swallow her. He knew it wasn't him she was nervous about; it was her aunt. Mercy was going to flip.

He took a long look at the ID of the young man with Kaylie. Cade Pruitt. Truman hadn't met any other Pruitts, but he knew there were a few on the far east side of town. At least the young man looked him in the eye and seemed respectful. Jason and Landon were surly and full of attitude. Finn had pulled out his license first, and Truman had seen his hand shake as he held it out for inspection.

"Did Cade drive you here?" he asked Kaylie.

"Yes." She kept her gaze on the ground.

Your aunt is going to explode.

Truman met Cade's gaze, taking his measure. He wasn't mouthy and didn't look away. "You have anything to drink this evening, Cade?"

"That's my first." Cade pointed at a silver can a few feet away. "I didn't even get through a third of it."

"It really is his first," Kaylie interjected. "We just got here."

"And you?" Truman asked Kaylie.

"I didn't drink anything. I have to work in a few hours." Her shoulders slumped.

"She didn't," Cade added. He glared at the other three men, and they gave a weak chorus of agreement.

Truman had already figured that out. Alcohol wafted from the men as from a brew house, but not from Kaylie. He'd purposefully stepped closer to her and inhaled as he took Cade's license.

Truman stepped over to where the men had rigged up a small table with sawhorses to shoot from. Cans littered the ground around the stand. Truman counted the cans out loud. Thirteen.

"If Cade's only had one beer, that means the three of you have split twelve."

Lights flashed from the gravel pit entrance. Two Deschutes County sheriff's cruisers entered, their light bars flashing, but their sirens silent.

"I called you some rides. I'm going to let them process the four of you while I take Kaylie home."

Landon stepped forward. "But we didn't—"

"Shut up." Cade cut him off and put out a hand to stop him from advancing toward Truman.

Two deputies joined Truman, big grins on their faces. "You catch some young ones tonight, Truman?"

"Yep, I'm going to drive the juvenile home." He gestured at Kaylie, who seemed to shrink two inches. "The other four are minors and reek of alcohol."

"We're happy to help. Turn around," the first deputy ordered Landon.

Truman took Kaylie's arm and tugged her away. "We're leaving." She resisted, digging in her heels.

"I need to say—"

"Call him later," Truman ordered. "If Mercy lets you keep your phone." He gave her a don't-mess-with-me glare and she followed meekly after giving a quick wave to Cade.

They were both silent as he drove out of the gravel pit. Kaylie crossed her arms on her chest and stared out her window into the dark nothingness, her nose piercing glittering in the lights from his dashboard. She was a pretty girl—she looked a *lot* like Mercy, and he felt a need to protect her. For her own sake and her aunt's.

"You need to watch who you hang out with." Truman finally broke the tension. "Cade seems like a decent-enough guy, but those others are trouble."

"I know. I didn't want to go to the pit. I didn't realize what was going on until we arrived."

"Then you need to speak up and say you want to leave. If Cade has any decency in him, he'll not make you do something you don't want to."

"I know."

"But you didn't want to rock the boat."

Her silence was his answer.

"How long have you been seeing him?" Truman asked in a gentler voice. For a girl who'd lost her father two months ago, she seemed mentally and emotionally healthy. But appearances could be deceiving. He'd told Mercy it was normal for teens to sneak out at night, but now that he'd caught her niece, he realized his view had changed a bit. Looking at it from a parent's or guardian's point of view was completely different: what if she'd gotten hurt?

He'd found her around alcohol and guns. Every cop's and parent's nightmare.

"A few weeks."

"If you do . . . anything . . . with him, he could get in trouble. You're under eighteen and he's twenty." His face grew warm in the dark.

Kaylie covered her face with her hands. *"Oh my God."*

"It's not something to take lightly."

"We haven't done anything!"

Relief flooded him. "Good. Then I don't have to arrest him."

"You wouldn't!" She turned in her seat to face him. "What if I love him? That's a stupid law."

"Not my place to judge the laws," Truman answered. "I just enforce and follow them." He glanced over at her, and her eyes were wide and pleading. The sting he felt at the sight surprised him. "Stay on the right side of the law. No more sneaking out. You know there's a curfew between midnight and four a.m. for juveniles, don't you? I don't want to catch you out again."

She slumped back in her seat. "You hate me."

Truman snorted. She sounded like his sister when she was in high school.

"I don't hate you, Kaylie. Not at all. In fact, I like you quite a bit. Your aunt adores you, and I can see why. But by the good Lord above, I don't want to be in your shoes when she finds out about this. You know she suspects you've been sneaking out, right?"

"She does?"

"Yep, she mentioned it to me yesterday."

"I'm so dead."

"Talk to her. Tell her how you feel. No one's out to stop you from having fun, but she needs reassurance that you're safe while you live under her roof. Hanging around with drunk idiots and guns isn't safe."

"Are you going to tell her that part?"

"You better believe it."

NINE

Mercy steamed as she drove to Eagle's Nest hours later.

Truman had called that morning before arriving at her apartment with Kaylie in tow, shocking her out of a dead sleep and gently breaking the news that he'd caught her wayward niece running wild in the middle of the night. When the two of them arrived, he'd given her a kiss, and Kaylie a thumbs-up, and then had nearly run down the stairs, leaving the girl in Mercy's confused hands.

Chicken.

Her brain still spun with the story Truman had told.

Alcohol? Guns?

Mercy couldn't get the image out of her head. *And Kaylie was the only girl in a group with four guys?*

She shuddered. Kaylie had claimed the guys were her friends, but it didn't calm Mercy's nerves.

"What if they'd decided to attack you?" she'd nearly shouted at the defensive teen. She'd amazed herself that she'd kept her voice even.

"They wouldn't do that. I *know* them."

"Well, *I* don't know them. From now on I want to meet whoever you're going out with. *And* I want to know when you're going out. No more sneaking out at night. You can go out in the daylight like the rest of the human race."

"I don't want to go out at night anymore," Kaylie had muttered. "I'm done with that."

Mercy hoped she was telling the truth. Figuring out a punishment had been the hardest part. She could rescind the girl's driving privileges, but then Kaylie wouldn't have a way to get to school and work. She could take away her phone, but she needed it in case of emergencies, and Mercy liked being able to immediately reach her.

So that left extra projects.

Kaylie was now in charge of *both* bathrooms *and* the rest of the apartment for the next month. The teen had already proved she cleaned up after herself most of the time, so it didn't feel like much of a punishment to Mercy, but she'd been at a loss about how to punish a kid who was usually very responsible.

Now she had to figure out a way deal with Kaylie's relationship. According to Pearl, Mercy would make it worse if she forbade Kaylie to see him. "Keep him close," Pearl suggested. "Invite him over and suggest they do things at the apartment when you're there. Or take the two of them out to dinner."

Mercy couldn't imagine anything more uncomfortable. When she suggested it to Kaylie, the girl's stunned look had said she felt the same.

Either way, there was a new understanding between Mercy and Kaylie: more communication.

Restless energy radiated through her. She hadn't been to her cabin in over two weeks. Truman had assured her everything was in fine shape, but she liked having her weekends to get away and futz around in her own space. Kaylie had been to the cabin, and together they'd moved a lot of items from Levi's house to the storage space in Mercy's barn. Levi had laid in good supplies and had a wealth of equipment that thrilled Mercy. Everyone had agreed that his belongings should go to Kaylie, along with the proceeds from the sale of his home. Kaylie now had a nice college fund.

Kaylie had embraced Mercy's cabin as if it were her own, and Mercy had started to think of it as belonging to the two of them. It'd been a rough mental transition at first. For several years she'd always pictured herself alone in the cabin if disaster struck, but now there was comfort in knowing her niece would be there. Kaylie was her family.

And there was Truman.

A smile turned up the corners of her lips. She liked having him around, but it was too soon to know if he would stick around permanently. Mercy wouldn't allow her brain to travel down that path just yet. Caution and habit stopped her from relying on his presence. Maybe later. She needed more time.

She parked in front of the Coffee Café and went in, putting Kaylie and her punishment out of her thoughts. Rose smiled at her from a table as Mercy approached, her sweet face beaming.

"You knew it was me, didn't you?" Mercy hugged her sister.

"I heard your steps outside. I know what you sound like."

Mercy slid into a lime-green-painted chair. "Do my steps sound the same as when I was a teenager?"

Rose's forehead wrinkled in thought as she wrapped her hands around her mug of coffee. "No. But after spending one evening with you, I learned your sound and it replaced the old file in my brain."

"Old file?"

Her laugh was like sunshine. "That's how I think of it. The sounds I hear open the correct file and tell me who's coming." She turned her face toward Kaylie as their niece came to their table, a white apron wrapped around her waist. She had dark smudges under her eyes, but Mercy didn't feel the slightest bit sorry for her.

"Do you want your usual, Aunt Mercy?"

"Please. And one of your cacao oat bars too."

"I'll take one of those too," said Rose.

"Yes, Aunt Rose," Kaylie said as she walked away, and Rose immediately whispered to Mercy, "What's wrong with Kaylie?"

Rose's perceptiveness didn't surprise Mercy. "She didn't get much sleep last night. That's what happens when you sneak out and are brought home by the police at two in the morning."

Her face lit up. "Ohhh. Tell me!"

Mercy shared the story. Rose's wide grins and questions helped her see a degree of humor in the situation. A very small degree.

"Too bad you don't have a farm," Rose mused. "Mom and Dad would have come up with all sorts of grueling work punishments."

"They sure would have." Mercy was done thinking about Kaylie for the moment. "How are you feeling these days?"

"Good. Less puking this week." Rose's skin glowed and her happiness radiated. Her usual calm seemed more pronounced to Mercy. In fact, Rose had been calm about the pregnancy from day one. At least as far as she shared with her sister. Mercy had been the one with anxiety, but Rose's attitude had brought it into check.

Kaylie dropped off Mercy's Americano with heavy cream and two plates with cacao bars. Mercy took an immediate bite of the bar, relishing the bitter taste of the chocolate and the crunch of the almonds. It was her favorite of Kaylie's recipes—dark, dense, and not too sweet.

Rose took a bite of hers along with a sip of coffee. "The girl has talent." Bliss filled her face as she chewed.

"She does. And she can pursue it all she wants *after* she gets a college degree."

"I think Pearl can handle the café if Kaylie leaves for college," added Rose. "I hear an excitement in Pearl's voice when she talks about the café. She hasn't been excited about anything in a long time."

"I've noticed it too," Mercy agreed. "Has she not had a job in recent years?"

"No. Rick liked her staying at home with the kids and managing the house. I think Pearl liked it too, but after Charity left home, I think she felt a bit useless. Samuel doesn't need a lot of parenting. Working here has given her something to look forward to."

"How's Rick feel about that?" Mercy had spoken only briefly with Pearl's husband and son. She saw Pearl's need to currently keep a wall between Mercy and her immediate family and tried to respect it. But one day she'd get to know her other niece and nephew.

She'd know Owen's kids too.

Rose held up a palm and tipped it from side to side. "There've been some complaints from Rick. I don't think he likes having to make his own breakfast." Her lips tightened in mirth.

"It's good for him," Mercy said. "And definitely good for Pearl." She watched her sister behind the café bar. Pearl moved with confidence and threw back her head as she laughed at a comment from a customer. She was definitely happy, and her laughter gave Mercy warm fuzzies.

"I agree. It's not good to be stuck in a rut."

Mercy changed the subject. "Do you know the Parker family very well? The young family that lives pretty close to you guys? I met Julia and Steve last night when I went to interview them about the arson at their place."

"I do know them. Their little Winslet is a doll." Rose's nose twitched. "I smelled the smoke from their fire the morning after it happened."

"Have you heard about anything unusual going on?" Mercy asked, abruptly realizing her sister was an excellent source for gossip and rumor in town. "I mean—"

"I know what you mean. If I've listened to talk about the shootings and fires. Who do people think might be responsible, or who has a beef they want to take out on a neighbor? Or who is angry with the police?"

"Exactly."

"I haven't heard anything very useful."

"Then you've heard *something*."

"Well, of course. It's all anyone can talk about."

"What are they saying?" Mercy knew leads could be buried in casual conversations. She hadn't been in town long enough for the residents to talk openly around her, but everyone talked to Rose.

"Well, until those two deputies were shot, people were up in arms about kids or teenagers starting the fires. They were convinced that someone's kid had an issue with fire and that the parents needed to pay more attention to what their kids were doing before someone caused a lot of damage."

"I'd call the Parkers' situation quite a bit of damage. It could take them a few years to rebuild what they lost."

"I agree." Rose nodded. "I heard Mom and Dad say they'd do what they could to help them catch up."

Pride and sadness warred inside Mercy. Pride that her parents watched out for and helped their own; sadness that she no longer fell beneath their umbrella of concern.

I can't fix what they've torn down.

"But after the deputies were shot, people became nervous. What had first been perceived as kids being stupid suddenly became a threat embedded in the community. When they believed it was kids, their voices were filled with anger and disgust. After the shooting, their voices were quieter and infused with worry. People felt vulnerable."

"Understandable." Mercy knew exactly what Rose meant. "What kids did people speculate about to start with?"

"The only names I heard tossed around were the two Eckham boys. But it was just talk based on their previous behaviors, you know?"

"Have they had trouble with fires before?"

"Not that I know of. The two women I heard talking about it seemed to be basing their assumptions on a history of behaviors like smoking and drinking and riding dirt bikes through the middle of town."

Jason Eckham was one of the young men with Kaylie last night. Mercy took a sip of her drink, remembering how her brothers had been at that age. Stupid behaviors were often par for the course with males of a certain age.

"Do you know Tilda Brass? The owner of the property where the deputies were shot?"

"I've met her once or twice. She seemed like a quiet woman. Moved softly and spoke as if she was only partially present."

"Truman said she has memory issues. Maybe the start of some dementia."

Understanding crossed Rose's face. "That would explain my impression. I assume she didn't have much helpful information?"

"None."

"Those poor deputies and their families," Rose whispered. "Are you going to the funerals this evening?"

"Yes. Do you need a ride?"

"No, Pearl already offered."

She and Rose sat silently as memories of a recent funeral swept over them.

"How is Kaylie holding up?" Rose asked.

"As good as can be expected. I encourage her to keep busy. Keeps her from thinking about Levi too much."

"Sometimes I simply sit and remember him," Rose said, her fingers playing with her coffee mug. "It's important to think about the good times."

But then you remember that last day.

A pink scar terrifyingly close to Rose's right eye held Mercy's gaze, and she let the anger and hatred toward her sister's attacker out of a locked closet in her mind. He'd murdered her brother and brutalized her sister. She'd wanted to castrate the man for what he'd done to her family. Instead Truman had tried to save his life. To no avail. She didn't feel guilty for hating the dead man; she fed on the hate, using it to fuel her current search for the cop killer.

"I need to get back to work." Regret filled her. She'd rather sit and gossip mindlessly with her sister. Talk about baby names and drink too much caffeine.

Rose stood and kissed her good-bye. "Be careful."

Mercy left the coffee shop after a wave to Pearl and Kaylie, who were filling drink orders for a family of five.

Kaylie was a good kid, and again Mercy hoped that she could continue to guide her, not create a divide between the teen and her other relatives.

Losing all family support was a level of hell Mercy didn't wish on anyone.

Mercy opened the door to her Tahoe and spotted two men in conversation across the street. Her heart had felt happy after her conversation with Rose, but her carefree attitude vanished at the sight of her brother Owen.

He hates me.

Owen was talking to an overweight man with a thick beard. Mercy didn't recognize the man but immediately noticed the bulge at his hip under his heavy coat. Their conversation seemed calm, but Owen glanced around several times, as if making certain no one was listening in.

Mercy froze with her boot on the running board. *Should I approach him?* She'd made some inroads with her mother and Pearl. Maybe it was time to start working on Owen too. *I only have one brother left.*

She slammed the door and crossed the street before she could talk herself out of it. Both men glanced in her direction, and Owen did a double take, his shoulders straightening as he recognized her. His face hardened and he plunged his hands into the pockets of his coat as he looked away. He pivoted, turning his back to her.

Keep going.

Mercy stepped up onto the curb and stopped before the two men. The bearded man gave her a curious look and touched the brim of his cowboy hat. His eyes were a dark brown, and two red spots burned high on his cheeks. He was even bigger up close, his girth rivaling that of a giant pine near her cabin. The lines around his eyes told her he was older than she'd first assumed from a distance. Now she estimated him to be in his late fifties.

"Hey, Owen," she said. "I just had coffee with Rose." Owen glanced at her and looked away. She held out her hand to the other man. "I'm Mercy Kilpatrick. Owen's sister."

Comprehension washed over the other man's face and he blinked several times. He took her hand, giving it a weak shake. The type a man gives when he's afraid to crush a woman's hand. "Tom McDonald. I've heard of you." His beard and mustache needed a trim. Hairs curled under his lip and covered half of his teeth as he spoke.

Owen looked miserable. "All good, I hope," she said with a wink at the bearded man. She didn't recognize his name, but he felt familiar even though she couldn't recall any men of his size from her youth.

Tom smirked at Owen, and Mercy kept her gaze locked on his eyes, startling Tom when he turned his focus back to her.

Great. Owen's friend is a jerk.

Tom excused himself and headed toward a big Chevy king cab with three rifles in the rear window gun rack. Two other men in jeans and heavy coats leaned against the fender, clearly waiting for Tom to join them. The three of them got in the truck and left.

"Pleasant guy," Mercy said, mentally filing away the license plate number of the Chevy.

Owen glared at her and started to walk away.

"Owen, wait!" She sped after him, speaking to his back. "I want us to be able to talk to each other. You don't have to like me, but let's at least get to the point where we can be in the same room. We've got a new niece or nephew coming in seven months. I'd like to welcome the baby without feeling like I'm hated at family gatherings."

He whirled around, making her halt, anger shining in his eyes. *He looks like Dad when he's mad.*

"*You* killed Levi. It's your fault he's dead. Don't talk to me about family."

Mercy couldn't move. Her lungs crashed to the sidewalk and her vision narrowed on his face. Whatever she'd been expecting, it hadn't been that.

"What?" she finally croaked.

"You cops stuck your nose in everything. Levi would still be alive if you hadn't come to town."

"Craig Rafferty shot Levi! You can't blame me for that. Craig was *your* friend. Didn't you ever see how unhinged he was? *He killed Pearl's best friend.*" A high-pitched buzz started in her ears.

"You shot Craig before he could prove his innocence." Owen spit the words. "It's impossible for a dead man to defend himself. That's the cops' solution for everything."

"You're making excuses for the man who murdered your brother," she whispered. *Does Owen truly believe what he's saying?*

"The real problem is at the core of our society," Owen continued, his eyes fierce. "Law and order need to be back in the hands of the people . . . They should govern themselves."

"Who do you think makes our laws?" she snapped at him. "Cats? Aliens?"

"Laws are made by bureaucrats who sit on velvet chairs in mansions somewhere. They're totally out of touch with the common man. We need to have a say."

"You do have a say. Everyone does. It's called voting."

"Our process has gone haywire. It's time to return the power back to the average guy. He's the one who understands what life is truly like." Passion burned in his voice. "People sitting in Washington . . . hell, the people sitting in *Salem* don't understand what life over here is like. Why are they the ones telling us what to do?"

Are we really arguing about politics?

"You cops are a by-product of the problem."

A red haze started at the edges of her vision. "Excuse me?"

"Levi and Craig shouldn't be dead," he hissed at her. "You and your cop boyfriend are just tools. Tools of the assholes running this country. We don't need you. We can take care of ourselves."

Mercy opened her mouth to argue and then shut it, studying the anger in his expression. *He's not in the mood to listen.* "What's happened to you, Owen?"

"I've wised up. I'm tired of bending over and taking it up the ass. Levi was the last straw."

"I miss him too."

"You don't miss him. You don't even know who he was." The hatred in his tone tore at her heart.

"He was my brother," she whispered.

"Well, you didn't act like much of a sister."

"I'm here now. I want—"

"Leave it, Mercy." He cut her words off with a jerk of his hand. "Do whatever you think you need to do. Just keep it away from me. You slunk into town and won over Kaylie and Rose, but don't you dare come near my kids."

She couldn't speak.

He spun on his heel and strode away.

Mercy watched him walk, seeing echoes of their father in his stance and stride.

I tried. She firmly set aside the anger and sorrow he'd ripped out of her heart and replayed his words in her brain. *Tools. Bureaucrats. Take care of ourselves.*

She didn't like where his mind was spending its time.

TEN

Truman's dress uniform felt unnatural on his body, as if he'd borrowed someone else's clothes. He'd worn it three times since he'd taken the job as chief of police. Once for his swearing-in and the other two times for special events. Today was an event, but it wasn't a good one. It was a necessity that he passionately wished didn't exist.

Two law enforcement officers would be put in the ground today. He'd spent half the day trying to get his stomach under control. Waves of nausea struck him at random times, bringing memories of the night the men had died.

It could have been me.

Twice he'd escaped death where other officers had died.

In their entire career, most officers would never have to fire their weapon, let alone nearly die twice. Why did he feel as if his luck was about to run out? By the odds, he should be safe for the rest of his life. Instead he was antsy and anxious, as if death were waiting for him just around the corner, angry that it'd missed him twice.

Beside him in the Tahoe, Mercy was silent, looking authoritative in her elegant navy suit and heavy coat. Kaylie sat silently in the back seat. Earlier in the day, Mercy had questioned the teen, uncertain she'd want to attend a funeral so soon after her father's, but Kaylie had been firm. She wanted to honor the officers who'd died in the line of duty.

Glancing in the rearview mirror, Truman noticed Kaylie's face was pale, but determination shone in her eyes and her posture. She looked like a younger version of Mercy. Lighter hair and a few inches shorter, but just as stubborn and tough.

He was proud of her.

He parked, and the three of them walked across the lot toward the small crowd as it moved into the county civic center. Satellite news trucks filled the far end of the parking lot. Cameras and reporters stood behind a rope, their lenses silently pointed in the direction of the mourners. A few county deputies stood in a sparse line, facing the cameras, enforcing the distance between the watchers and the attendees. Truman spotted two national cable news network trucks and heard Mercy quietly swear under her breath. He squeezed her hand. He had taken hold of it as she got out of the truck and wasn't about to let go. Kaylie paused as her gaze found the cameras, and he wrapped his arm around her shoulders.

"Ignore them," he told her.

"It's CNN," she muttered. "Why are they here?"

"Police shooting." It was all he needed to say.

"This shouldn't be a *thing*," Kaylie muttered as she wiped her cheek.

"Damn right," Truman agreed.

The parking lot was packed with a variety of patrol cars. He saw logos from Washington, Idaho, and Nevada. The majority were from Oregon's east side of the Cascades, and his heart swelled as he spotted logos from tiny rural towns whose officers must have driven for hours and left their communities shorthanded to pay their respects.

When officers died, you did your damnedest to show up.

Kaylie's attention wandered, and he noticed as she zeroed in on a tall young man, her steps slowing and her shoulders straightening. Cade Pruitt was up ahead with what appeared to be his parents. He hadn't seen Kaylie yet, and he stopped to greet a cluster of people. Truman recognized Cade's three buddies from the other night among the several older men in the group.

Truman tried to place the older members. *More family?* Some of them wore heavy camouflage jackets and carried their hats in their hands, appearing to be typical hardworking rural men. One or two of them looked slightly familiar, but not enough for Truman to remember names.

Cade stood out among the men of his age. He didn't slouch, and he was wearing slacks where the others wore jeans.

Maybe Kaylie picked a decent one.

He saw Mercy's gaze dart between her niece and the young man, two lines deepening between her brows.

Mother bear.

They filed in and took their seats, Mercy sitting between him and Kaylie, his hand still tightly gripping hers.

The next forty-five minutes ripped out his heart.

The slide show of Damon Sanderson's life. Images of him and his pregnant wife. And then pictures of his new baby girl. Ralph Long's brother valiantly spoke without shedding a tear about Ralph's love of his job, but left the entire audience holding wet Kleenex. A police solo-ist had been flown in from Seattle and made grown men weep with his version of "Amazing Grace."

As they exited the building, Truman nearly asked Mercy to drive. He'd left his strength and heart on the floor in the auditorium. Even Kaylie appeared to struggle to hold up her head, her energy sapped.

"I feel like I just ran a marathon. Jenna and I probably won't do much tonight," Kaylie told the two of them as Truman drove toward her friend's house. She'd made plans to spend the night with Jenna to work on a school project. Mercy had questioned letting Kaylie stay with a friend while she was still in deep water, but then she'd seen how much work was left on the presentation that was due soon.

They dropped her off, and Mercy gave the teen a hug along with a few stern words about staying put that night. "I have no desire to go anywhere tonight," Kaylie told her. "We have to get an early start in the morning, so I need sleep."

Truman couldn't complain that the teen was gone for the evening. He was emotionally spent and selfishly wanted Mercy all to himself.

Mercy watched Truman check the doors of his house again. He hadn't stopped moving since they walked into his home. So far he'd fed the cat, poured drinks for the two of them, straightened up the family room, and unloaded the dishwasher. She expected him to start vacuuming next.

She took a sip of the orange juice and vodka he'd mixed for her. It was extremely strong. Another out-of-character action of his. Or else he figured she needed it after the emotional freight trains of the memorial service.

She sat as still as possible at the dining nook table. As if her lack of movement could calm him and slow him down. His restlessness filled the house, and she had to fight to keep it from taking over her own energy level.

Simon hopped up onto the chair next to her and silently requested attention, her golden gaze fixed on Mercy's. She stroked the cat's silky black fur and wished Truman would sit down so Simon could settle on his lap and infuse him with some of her calm.

Truman strode back into the kitchen, spotted the cat, and stopped to scratch her under the chin.

"What's wrong?" Mercy didn't beat around the bush.

He kept his gaze on Simon. "It was a pretty crappy day."

"I completely agree, but I feel like there's something else eating at you." She set the cat on her chair and moved to him, putting both of her hands on his upper arm. "Tell me."

His throat moved and she saw a vein pulsate in his neck.

"I'm sure the memorial service was hard for you. You were there," Mercy continued. "You were with both of them at their last moments."

"It wasn't just that," he said, still petting Simon. "Something happened this morning."

Mercy waited, fighting the need to stroke his arm as he stroked the cat.

"It was a simple traffic stop."

"No traffic stop is simple. They are completely unpredictable." She pulled him over to the couch and made him sit, positioning herself beside him, her leg pressed against his from hip to knee as she clasped his hands.

"I really don't want to talk about this now." His gaze wouldn't meet hers.

"Tell me, Truman," she whispered. He needed to unburden himself, and she wanted to be the one he sought for solace. The desire was foreign to her. Before, she'd wanted people to keep their problems to themselves and not disturb her life with their issues. But something inside her ached to know his pain. It was an intimacy she craved from him.

She touched the rough stubble on the side of his jaw. He flinched and took her hand, turning to face her. The shutters had vanished from his eyes and his agony slammed into her like a rock.

"The truck had two taillights out. *Two of them.*"

"So they definitely needed to be stopped," she agreed. "They were a hazard on the road."

"I pulled them over on the highway just east of town. You know where it's two lanes wide and twists near the Polk farm?"

"Yes, there's a nice wide shoulder for them to pull over. Plenty of room."

"There is." He looked straight ahead, his gaze distant as he remembered. "Everything was fine. I'd run their plates, called in my location, and had just approached the driver's window."

He stopped speaking, and she waited a long moment before prodding him again. "What happened?"

"It's stupid. I look back now, and you can't understand how pissed I am that I reacted the way I did." His hand tightened on hers.

"Traffic stops can be anxiety producing."

"Another car sped by as I reached the window, and its tires threw up a rock." He looked down at their clenched hands. "I thought it was a gunshot when it hit the truck's fender."

"Ohhhh." *Now I understand.* Her heart cracked for him.

"Exactly. I darted behind the bed of the truck and had drawn my weapon before I could think."

"What did the driver of the truck do?"

"I don't think he even noticed that I'd abruptly vanished. It wasn't until I heard him swearing at his passenger about the rock hitting his fender that I realized what actually happened.

"I was terrified, Mercy. My fucking heart was trying to beat its way through my rib cage and I was sweating as if it was a humid day in Houston. *Instantly. It all hit instantly.* And it took me twenty seconds before I could even leave my position at the back of the truck."

"Did you talk to the driver?"

"I could barely speak. All I wanted to do was get in my vehicle and leave. He must have thought I was an idiot. I had to ask him for his license twice because the first time I handed it back without even reading what was on it. My brain was short-circuiting. I finally gave him a warning and then sat in my vehicle for another ten minutes, trying to figure out what'd happened."

"It's totally under—"

"Don't patronize me!" he snapped. "I fell apart over a rock. *A damned rock!* And then I could barely go back to work. An hour later I saw someone blow through a stop sign, and I couldn't bring myself to do a damn thing about it. I just watched them speed off. I fucking froze."

Her heart split in two, the ripping sensation as painful as the time she accidentally tore a huge hunk of skin off her thigh on a bolt. *He doesn't need me to tell him it's normal after what he's been through. He doesn't need me to logically explain away his reactions.*

He just needs me to listen.

"I don't know if I'm fit to do this job anymore," he whispered. "I've fallen down this hole before and it was a hell of a lot of work to drag myself out of the pit. I don't know if I can do it again."

"You don't need to decide tonight." She held her breath, terrified to say the wrong thing.

He leaned forward and buried his head in his hands. "I'm so fucking exhausted, I can't think straight."

"That memorial today completely drained me," Mercy admitted. "I can't imagine attending it after what you went through today."

"But I didn't go through *anything*. It was a traffic stop with a flying rock. Anyone else would have ducked and laughed. Not fallen apart and hid."

"You aren't *anyone else*. You're *you*, and we're all the results of our past experiences. It's what makes us unique. No one else has gone through what you have or what I have. It's nothing to be ashamed of."

"But am I fit to be the chief of police? I came to Eagle's Nest because it sounded like a job I could handle and I needed to get away from a city where I saw horrible things I couldn't fix. Did I run away from my fucking fears only to have them resurface in the quietest town in the United States? Am I fooling myself? If I had to go to that fire from the other night right now, I don't think I'd have the guts to run to Damon as he lay dying on the ground." Terrified eyes met hers. "Am I no longer enough?"

She took his face in her hands and turned it toward her, touching her forehead to his. "You do so much good here. Don't let this stop it."

"But—"

"No buts right now. We aren't going to solve this tonight. It will look different in the morning." She stood and pulled him up to her, tucking her head under his chin and wrapping her arms around his chest. They stood still for several long seconds, and she felt his pulse pound against her hair.

"Take me to bed," she whispered.

His arms tightened around her and she didn't need to ask twice.

ELEVEN

He'd lost himself in Mercy last night. She'd opened herself to him in a way he'd never experienced. She didn't talk; she spoke with her body and he'd found himself caught up in her emotions. After opening his heart to her on the couch, he'd been convinced he was too broken to function, and she'd shown him he still had something inside.

Where had the energy and passion come from?

Despite having been thinking of bed and sleep since noon yesterday, he'd found the energy to stay awake for another hour, satiating himself with her. It'd been hard to get out of bed this morning, and now he drove mindlessly around town, his brain still reliving the previous evening.

His radio crackled and Lucas told him there was a domestic disturbance at Sandy's Bed & Breakfast.

Truman turned right at the next corner. "I'm a minute away. What's going on?"

"Sandy says one of her customers is beating on his wife behind her building."

He sped down a deserted street, leaving a wake of brightly colored fall leaves spinning behind him.

The grand old house sat on the main drag through town. Truman parked along the curb and let Lucas know he'd arrived. Lucas told him Royce was minutes away. Sandy came out the front door and jogged down the steps. The tall redhead had a rolling pin in her hand and looked ready to use it on someone's head. "They're around back in the gazebo. Go that way." Anger flashed in her eyes as she pointed at the side of the house. "I was going to grab my cleaver and address it myself, but I figured you could handle him better than me."

Truman eyed the rolling pin and her grim stare. Sandy could be pretty intimidating. "See any weapons?" he asked as he strode around the house. Sandy kept pace with him as they circled to the rear of the house, fury keeping her jaw tight.

"No. I've seen him carry a few times since he's been here, but there's nothing that I could see today. Doesn't mean he's not carrying."

"How long have they been staying here?"

"Four nights."

"Name?"

"Wayne and Kimberly Davidson. From Coeur d'Alene."

"Stay here," Truman ordered as shouts reached them. He took a quick peek around the corner of the home and spotted the gazebo just as the man standing in the romantic structure hauled back and landed a fist on the woman's cheek. She stumbled backward two steps, her hand covering her injury. She paused, staring at him in shock and stiffening her back. After a split second she flew at him with her nails bared.

Truman stepped forward. "Eagle's Nest Police Department!" He flicked the release on his holster, holding his hand above the weapon, but didn't draw.

The couple fell apart. "You're in deep shit now!" the woman yelled at her husband.

The man touched his hip, making Truman believe he was used to wearing a firearm, and scowled at the intrusion. *Doesn't mean he doesn't have another someplace else.* He stopped a safe distance from the couple. Kimberly had a dripping bloody lip and a red gash on her cheek. Her husband had a few slashes on his forehead, and his hair looked as if she'd tried to rip out several chunks.

"You two done?" Truman asked politely.

"This is none of your business," Wayne snapped. "We're having a private discussion."

"When you start drawing blood and trying to skin each other in my town it becomes my business."

"Don't you have something better to do than harass the public?" Wayne sneered. "What happened to cops that respected their citizens? Go find someone who's actually committed a crime."

Truman nodded at Kimberly. "Her face tells me that person would be you. Now step away from each other, and for my own safety, I'd like both of you to place your hands on your head so I can see them."

Kimberly immediately complied, but Wayne was slow. He held Truman's gaze as he slowly lifted his hands, making a deliberate show of linking his fingers and resting his hands on his hair. Truman took a couple of steps closer and saw the signal in Wayne's eyes as he decided to be stupid.

The man took two steps and lunged at Truman. Having anticipated the move, Truman stepped to the side, neatly grabbed one of Wayne's arms, twisted it, braced it, and applied pressure behind the elbow.

"FUUUUUUUCK!" Wayne froze with his arm in Truman's grasp.

Truman applied a little more pressure and Wayne's knees started to buckle. He let up a fraction and the man shuddered in relief.

"You're a fucking public servant! You've got no right to put your hands on me!"

"But I have to put up with you attacking me? Your level of customer service from this fucking public servant depends on your cooperation. So far it sucks, so I'm returning the favor."

"Let him go!" Kimberly took a step in their direction.

"Come any closer and I'll break his arm." Wayne screeched as Truman pressed on his elbow.

"Don't hurt him," she pleaded.

"Oh please." Sandy strode up and pointed her rolling pin at Kimberly. The woman shuffled back several steps and put her hands back on her head.

Smart woman.

"You defend a man who did that to your face?" Sandy asked in disgust. "Next you'll tell me that you had it coming." Sirens sounded out front as Truman's backup arrived.

Although Sandy is solid backup.

"You have no right to do this," Wayne bitched.

"I thought we already addressed that issue," said Truman. "Simply put: you're wrong."

"You cops are nearly done around here," Wayne continued. "You're going to be out of business."

"If my job is no longer needed, then that means that assholes like you are no longer beating their wives. I'll gladly accept that change."

Glowering, Wayne turned his attention to Sandy. "Your place is a rip-off. Your prices are insane."

Sandy's smile was saccharine sweet. "I'll miss your business. Not!"

"Be nice," Truman ordered, pressing on the elbow. Wayne trembled and Truman eased up.

Hurry up, Royce.

An hour later Truman finished up the paperwork on the arrests of Wayne and Kimberly Davidson. The couple deserved each other, he decided. Their antigovernment rage was more than he could stomach. Apparently they both wanted to live in a utopia where Wayne was free to beat on his wife as much as he wanted. Nothing Truman could say would change Kimberly's belief that it was her husband's right.

Truman was ready to send them to utopia.

What he didn't find out was why they were in Eagle's Nest. Both had said for vacation.

Who vacations here?

It turned out Wayne had a bit of a record from Idaho. Speeding tickets. DUI. Assault (not on his wife). These didn't surprise Truman, but there was a different charge that caught his attention. He'd called the arresting police department for more details and found out Wayne had been part of a group who'd decided they were done paying taxes and had taken their gripes to court. But instead of appearing in court, they'd gone to a judge's home and delivered their protest in person.

Wayne had spent a month in jail for that stunt.

Breaking up the morning's fight had restored a bit of the confidence Truman had been lacking last night. There was also something very satisfying about twisting the arm of a wife-beating asshole. Sandy's gratitude had helped too.

His cell phone rang, and his heart happily sped up as he read Mercy's phone number. He answered, and the sound of her voice washed away his thoughts of the morning.

"How's your day going?" she asked.

"I arrested two people, and Sandy gave me a dozen fresh-baked cookies for dealing with the problem."

"Sounds like it was worth it. Don't eat them all."

"Too late. Lucas, Royce, and Ben smelled them the second I stepped foot in the office. I was smart to eat one on the way back to the department. What's new over there?" The tone of her voice had told him she had news.

"We identified the body Ben found at the fire. Joshua Pence from Nevada."

"Nevada? What was he doing here?"

"Good question. We tried to trace his movements through his credit cards, but he doesn't appear to have any. He owned a small property in Nevada that was foreclosed on a year ago. We can't figure out where he's been living since then. His vehicle registration is four years out of date, and his driver's license was to be renewed two months ago. It didn't happen."

"What kind of vehicle?"

"A ninety-five Ford Ranger. Red."

"I'll keep an eye out for it. What about family?"

"Long divorced. There's a daughter who lives in Oregon—but she lives in the Portland area. Not over here. I guess he could have been staying with her."

"There has to be some recent information on him. It sounds like everything you're finding is ancient history."

"That's exactly how it looks."

"How can you drive a vehicle with plates that expired four years ago?" Truman ran a hand over his eyes. "Never mind. I answered my own question. Sometimes I forget that not everyone is a law-abiding citizen like me."

"I'm not sure how you could ever forget that," Mercy replied, a smile in her tone.

"Call me an optimist."

"That's a good thing. Don't lose it."

"It's hard some days."

"But then someone hands you a dozen cookies."

"And all faith is restored. Did Joshua Pence have any arrests?"

"One charge from nearly ten years ago, which is how we matched the prints. He's been clean since then."

"Huh." That didn't sit right with Truman. He'd expected the dead man to have a hefty record. "That sound odd to you?"

"It did. We're checking to see if we missed any aliases."

"Maybe he was an innocent passerby at that fire," he suggested, grasping at straws.

"In the middle of the night?" Mercy asked. "And he had gasoline splashed on the lower legs of his jeans and on his hands. In my book—and Bill Trek's book—that indicates he was spreading the accelerant. The big question is, who decided they no longer needed Pence's help and the only way to fire him was to cut his neck?"

"I'd hoped his identity would answer that question. Maybe the daughter will have some answers. Do you have a job history for him? Where did he work?"

"He hasn't been employed in six years. He was collecting some Social Security, and the checks were being delivered to one of those private postal places in Nevada where you can rent a box. They don't have a forwarding address for him, and this month's check was still in the box."

"I'm surprised. From the sound of things, he needed that check. Seems unusual he'd not pick it up immediately."

"My thoughts exactly."

"Anything else going on? How is Kaylie?"

"She's still working on the school project at her friend's. She checked in and sounds optimistic they'll finish it today."

"I'm going to take a closer look at Cade Pruitt," Truman admitted. "He's a bit old to date a high school student."

Mercy laughed. "You sound like a protective father."

"I feel like one. I can't tell you how rattled I was to see her with those four guys the other night. My inner Jedi wanted to run a light saber through them and whisk her out of there."

"Do you think they're trouble?"

Truman thought. "I don't know. Frankly, I identify with them quite a bit. I remember what it was like to be that age and live around here. Maybe that's why I want to take a closer look," he admitted sheepishly. "I know how guys that age think and act."

Someone started talking to Mercy in the background, and she wrapped up the phone call with a promise to keep him up-to-date on any Joshua Pence information.

Truman hung up and immediately started to dig for his own facts on Joshua Pence. The man's lifeless face was burned into his brain, and he had an overwhelming need to trace the man's last months.

Who killed you?

TWELVE

Cade sank another nail into the board. The knot-filled wood wouldn't have been his first choice to build the new bunkhouse, but he understood the wood was cheap, and it wasn't his place to offer suggestions. Tom McDonald was the boss, and Cade was there to do as he was told. Tom paid well and had plenty of work for him, so Cade wasn't about to rock the boat with something as unimportant as his opinion of lumber quality.

At least it smelled good. This was much better than tending Tom's cattle or pigs. Cade's familiarity with framing had earned him a recommendation from one of his neighbors and gotten his foot in the door at Tom's ranch. His savings were slowly building, and he'd soon be able to afford a payment on a newer truck. It was a bit embarrassing to pick up Kaylie in his current POS, but she didn't seem to mind.

A new truck should impress her.

He slammed the palm of his hand against the board, pleased at the solid feel, and grabbed the next board to place.

Chip stuck his head in the bunkhouse. "Hey! Go get some more nails out of the storage shed by the barn. We're about out."

Chip was a dick. He was perfectly capable of getting his own nails, but he liked to order Cade around. Especially when there was someone close by to listen. Cade had learned to bite his tongue and just do what the prick wanted. He knew the type of man Chip was: a bully. It was best not to show any emotion around bullies. That was what they fed on: emotions and reactions.

"You bet." Cade set down his hammer and passed by Chip as he stood in the doorway. Chip and a few other guys were working on an adjacent building, where they were expanding an existing small kitchen along with a large mess hall and meeting room. The new construction lifted Cade's spirits. Some people said Eagle's Nest was drying up and dying, but according to Tom McDonald, he had work for lots of men and wanted the facilities to house them.

Cade's current project would sleep ten men. Four bunkhouses were already built, and he'd heard there were plans for ten more. He wondered if he could get construction work for some of his friends. But why did McDonald need to build so many bunkhouses? There wasn't that much to do on the ranch. One guy handled the small herd of cattle and the few pigs. Cade didn't see work that justified housing so many men.

But a lot of men lived on the isolated ranch. As far as Cade could tell, they primarily talked a lot. The construction crew was currently five guys, including him and Chip, and all five of them went back to their own homes at night. But he'd seen a dozen unfamiliar pickups come and go during the weeks he'd been here, men intent on meeting with McDonald in his small old farmhouse.

They were out-of-towners. Idaho, Montana, and Nevada plates. A few Oregon plates. Men who ignored him for the most part. Occasionally McDonald would bring a few men to take a tour of the bunkhouses and mess hall. They'd meet with the men who lived in the bunkhouses and go off on foot tours of the ranch's woods. *Perhaps McDonald plans to start logging?* Sometimes they'd stand around and nod approvingly as McDonald pointed out the sites for the next few bunkhouses. Cade would stand out of the way and watch as the men examined his work. It didn't bother him; he knew his work was solid.

All the men were salt-of-the-earth types. Heavy boots, Wrangler jeans, cowboy hats or caps, and serious faces. They didn't smile. They scratched their beards or scowled, their heavy eyebrows creating a solid line across weathered foreheads.

Were they looking for jobs?

Cade didn't understand their presence. Maybe they were investors in McDonald's plan for his ranch. But judging by the age of the pickups and the stress in their faces, they didn't feel like the type of men with thousands to spare. So Cade nodded respectfully and kept his ears peeled. He'd already made the mistake of asking Chip what plans McDonald had for the new buildings. That question had drawn spit aimed at his boots and a sneer, along with, "None of your business. You're getting paid, right?"

"Yep."

"Then shut up and do your work. Consider yourself lucky to have work."

Cade took his advice. Mouth shut. Ears open.

He slid open the heavy door to the shed and headed toward the shelves where he knew nails were stored. He grabbed a few boxes and turned toward the door but stopped as an odd odor reached his nose. Sort of sweet, but unfamiliar. In the poor light he squinted at the back of the shed, noticing a stack of wooden boxes he'd never seen before. Someone had tossed a weathered canvas blanket over them, but the far ends of the boxes weren't covered, showing dovetailed corners. He lifted a corner of the blanket and read the side of one. DuPont Explosives.

He dropped the blanket and spun around, striding out of the shed.

Dynamite?

When he was a child, he'd seen similar boxes in his grandfather's old barn, and his father had ordered him to stay away from them. So of course, he'd looked inside the first moment he could. Old, fading paper-wrapped sticks. Specks of a drying sticky clear substance that oozed from under the paper.

It'd been disappointing and thrilling at the same time.

As far as he knew, dynamite wasn't around anymore. The boxes in McDonald's shed looked nearly as ancient as the boxes in his grandfather's barn. Decades ago it'd been normal to use on a ranch. In fact, he remembered his grandfather saying he'd been able to buy dynamite at the feed store. Cade was certain those days were long gone. But no doubt it was still found in forgotten corners of old-timers' barns.

He walked across the gravel to the slow-growing mess hall, the boxes of nails in his hands, his brain spinning, wondering where the dynamite had come from. He'd been in the shed last week and was positive nothing had been in that corner. Tires sounded on the gravel, and he watched a newer Chevy stop near the house. It was clean and shiny, unlike most of the visitors' trucks. The man got out, glanced in Cade's direction, and then disappeared into the home without knocking.

Cade blinked, his stride slowing.

Was that Kaylie's uncle Owen?

He took another look at the truck, spotting the local high school bumper sticker, and remembered Kaylie had cousins who attended the school.

Thinking hard, he remembered he'd seen the truck on the property another time or two, but hadn't seen the driver. He'd met Kaylie's uncle a few times in town. His father knew him from way back, although Cade had never mentioned that to Kaylie. It was expected that most people knew one another around Eagle's Nest. It was the norm, not the exception.

Cade silently delivered the nails to Chip, who accepted them with a smirk. "Hey, give Mitch a hand for a minute. He needs someone to hold those boards."

Across the room Mitch glanced back with surprise on his face, clearly balancing a board with no problem. Cade said nothing but went over and braced the far end for the man, giving him an I-just-do-what-I'm-told look. Mitch nodded and said nothing as he hammered the board into place.

Cade handed him the next one and braced the end.

"Thanks, Cade," Mitch muttered. "You can head back to the bunkhouse now."

Ignoring Chip, who was futzing around with some electrical work, Cade walked as quietly as possible out the door, hoping to escape Chip's notice. Cade got more work done when he was out of Chip's sight. Chip had an overwhelming need to order him around, assign him useless tasks, and keep him from finishing the work he was supposed to do.

Outside the mess hall, he nearly bumped into Tom McDonald and Owen Kilpatrick. He nodded at both men, making brief eye contact, and hurried toward the growing bunkhouse.

The flash of recognition in Owen Kilpatrick's gaze stayed with him.

◆ ◆ ◆

Mercy parked in front of the tiny Craftsman home in an old Portland suburb, admiring the perfect landscaping. Joshua Pence's daughter, Debby, had agreed to meet her and Truman. Ava McLane, one of Mercy's colleagues from the Portland FBI office, had already informed the woman in person that her father had died. Mercy had talked to Special Agent McLane after the visit and learned that Debby hadn't spoken to her father in six months. The daughter had been crushed over his death—especially the manner of his death. Mercy had specifically asked Ava to deliver the notification, knowing her friend would handle it with sensitivity and tact.

Mercy and Truman had decided to make a trip over the Cascade mountain range to talk to their victim's daughter in person. She glanced at the time on her dashboard, hoping it wouldn't be too late by the time she and Truman made the long trek home.

"Nice house," Truman commented. "But I don't want to live with this sort of traffic anymore. It's not even a weekday and it's crazy."

"Amen." Mercy had been surprised at her own impatience at the traffic on the interstate. She'd driven in it for years, wasting hours bumper-to-bumper as the vehicles crawled toward their destinations. But tonight she hadn't been able to sit still as the traffic slowly crawled north. "If one more person had pulled in front of me, I would have rammed their bumper."

"I think it's also because Thanksgiving is this coming Thursday. Seems like that always increases the traffic."

She didn't say anything. It was the first time he'd mentioned the holiday since their discussion the other day. She'd agreed to have him cook dinner, but a very tiny part of her held out hope that she'd receive an invitation from her parents.

Probably not if Owen had any say in the matter.

The heavy wooden door had a lovely fall wreath that looked straight from a Pinterest project, or else from one of the most expensive florists in the city. Mercy wanted to snap a picture to show Kaylie. She had no doubt the teen could recreate the wreath in a matter of hours.

The door opened, and a petite female with chic, short hair and heavy black eyeliner greeted them. Mercy was about to ask if her mother was home when she realized this *was* Debby Pence. Mercy knew she was thirty, but she looked as if she should be slinging caffeine in a drive-through coffee hut that blasted rock music. The type where you had to yell to place your order. Ava had told her Debby was a successful lawyer in a big firm downtown.

Now she understood the touch of amusement she'd heard in Ava's tone.

Mercy shook her hand, feeling like a giant next to the small woman. Energy radiated from her, although her eyes were sad and slightly red. Debby gave Truman an admiring glance as he introduced himself, and Mercy was surprised by the possessiveness that flared in her chest. She quickly smothered it.

They stepped into the living room just to the right of the entry. Immaculate period built-ins, dark wooden crown molding, and wainscoting glowed in the soft light.

"This is beautiful," said Mercy, admiring the light fixtures. They looked straight out of the first half of the twentieth century, but she suspected they were recreations from one of the hip lighting stores where your firstborn was a required down payment for a chandelier.

"Thank you. I've restored most of the home myself over the past two years. It's a hobby of mine," Debby said with a touch of pride.

"Don't you work in one of those law offices that require sixty-hour workweeks?" Truman asked.

"I do. But that still leaves a hundred and eight hours in a week. I like to stay busy."

Mercy chuckled, liking the woman immediately. She hated idle time too.

"Some people occasionally sleep," said Truman.

"Yes, they do." Debby didn't claim she was one of them. She gestured for them to sit on the couch. After offering something to drink, which they refused, she sank into a chair with a sigh. "I feel like I haven't sat down since this morning."

"Thank you for meeting with us on a weekend," said Mercy.

"It's not often I get two visits from the FBI in one day. Never, actually."

"We're very sorry for your loss," Truman said in that calming voice of his that made Mercy want to crawl in his lap and take a nap. From the sudden expression on Debby's face, she'd felt the same desire.

"Thank you. Like I told the agent earlier today, I hadn't seen my father in a long time. The last time was five years ago, when I was in Reno for a conference. I drove out to see him then." Curiosity filled her features. "I understand he was murdered, but why is the FBI taking an interest?"

"It's a bit of a long story," Mercy said. She immediately held up her hand at the look of distrust from Debby. "But I promise to tell you all I can. But first can you tell us more about your father? Do you know why he was in Central Oregon?"

"I have no idea. I was shocked that he was so close and hadn't called me. We don't call each other anymore." She looked down at her clenched hands in her lap. "He's so awkward to talk with on the phone. He never has anything to say and I have to come up with question after question to keep the conversation going. He did start emailing quite a while ago, and that replaced phone calls. Texting replaced email about two years ago, and that was a relief. It's so much easier. But one way or another, I'm shocked he didn't tell me he was so close."

"We haven't found out where he was staying or how long he's been here. Do you know if he's always avoided credit cards?"

Debby threw back her head as she laughed. "Lord, yes. He hates the plastic 'devil cards.' I honestly don't know how he's managed to get by all these years without one. It seems like you can't do anything without securing it with a card these days."

"It is hard," Mercy agreed. "What about his work? He appears to not have any work history for six years."

"That sounds about right. He hurt his back at the lumber mill back then. When I saw him five years ago, he was happy about not having to do the physical labor anymore. He said he was getting disability." She sat up straighter, looking them firmly in the eye. "As he should. He really was messed up. He gained nearly fifty pounds after the accident because he could barely get around. He wasn't looking for a handout."

"Of course not," Mercy said. "Was he able to get by living on his own if he was hurt?"

"That was my concern too. But everything looked good when I was there. He had helpful neighbors."

"Your parents divorced when you were young, correct?" Truman asked.

"Yes. And my mother died two years ago." She pressed her lips together. "I was an only child. Now both my parents are gone," she whispered. Her chin was still up and her gaze solid, but Mercy saw faint cracks in her facade.

"Did you know his home in Nevada had been foreclosed on?" she asked gently.

Debby's jaw dropped open. "He told me he sold it."

"Where would he have been living?" Truman asked.

"I don't know." Shock sharpened her voice. "He never said he needed a place to live. I guess he could have rented a small place." She looked from Mercy to Truman. "I take it you couldn't find any rental records?"

"No. But it could have been off the books or a casual situation."

"But was he living in Oregon?" Debby asked. "How long ago did he leave Nevada?"

"We were hoping you could shine some light on that." Mercy paused, looking for a delicate way to phrase her next question. "Would you say your father preferred to be . . . independent? Maybe complain a bit that laws interfered in people's lives too much?"

Understanding crossed Debby's face. "You're asking if he was part of some weird group who thinks the government needs to mind its own business." Amusement twitched in her lips.

"Something like that."

"Let's just say my father was rather shocked when I went to law school."

"Was he angry?" Truman asked.

Debby looked thoughtful as she considered the question. "He's always been angry," she said quietly. "His parents' home was foreclosed on a long time ago. He's been bitter about that for as long as I can remember. He's always preached that people need to be left alone to live their lives instead of being taxed every time they turn around."

"What about his view of law enforcement?" Mercy swallowed hard, not sure she wanted to hear Debby's answer.

"He's always hated cops," Debby replied. "Cops and the military. I remember that from when I was young. I never knew the reason why."

Mercy saw Truman tighten his jaw. *I hope those fires weren't aimed at hurting law enforcement.*

"Now tell me why the FBI is involved." Debby's tone and demeanor shifted into lawyer mode.

"Eagle's Nest had a rash of small fires that I was investigating," Truman said. "But then two deputies were murdered when they responded to a larger fire. Then someone shot at one of my officers at the fire where we discovered your father's murder. The FBI was brought in to investigate the deaths of the deputies. They're including your father's death in their investigation."

"Is your officer okay?" Debby asked.

"Yes. They missed. Thank you." Truman nodded at her.

"You're wondering if my father was involved in starting the fires. And the murders."

Mercy and Truman were silent, watching the young woman. Debby looked away and shuddered slightly. "That's horrible. I'm sorry for the other deaths, but I honestly can't see my father being involved." She met Mercy's gaze. "He was a harmless big teddy bear. He was kind and gentle and couldn't hurt a fly. It just wasn't in him. Sure, he talked hard words about police, but I don't think he would actually act on it."

"I know he had two weapons registered at the time of his death," Mercy said. "Did he own more?"

Debby shrugged. "You're asking the wrong person. I don't know what he had. My dad loved to shoot and even won some awards. He was an amazing shot with a rifle." She turned her gaze to Truman. "But he would never kill anyone."

Silence stretched among the three of them.

"You can't think of any acquaintances he had in the Bend area?" Mercy asked, feeling the need to end the silence.

The woman stared at the floor to her right, pressing her lips together. "I just don't know. I really didn't pay much attention when he talked about people I wasn't familiar with." She blinked hard and turned back to Mercy. "I don't know who his friends have been over the last decade. Does that make me a rotten daughter?" she whispered.

"Not at all." Mercy's stomach simmered as she felt the rotten label on her own forehead.

"Did he ever talk about moving to Oregon?" Truman asked.

"I guess he might have said something." Debby's face cleared and she straightened. "When I came here for my job four years ago, he'd said he'd never leave Nevada. But about a year ago"—she rubbed at her chin as she concentrated—"I think it was around Halloween. He mentioned that someone he knew was moving to Oregon and joked that he was now considering it. At least I assumed at the time he was joking." Her dark-brown gaze flicked between Mercy and Truman. "That was about the time he lost his house, wasn't it?"

Mercy nodded.

The daughter's shoulders slumped. "I should have listened better. Maybe he was trying to ask for help with a place to live." She pressed the heels of her hands against her eyes. "Dammit. I think I laughed it off. Told him I knew he'd never leave Nevada. I wish I could remember who he said was moving here, but I honestly can't remember the names of any of the people he used to talk about. I can't even tell you the name of the nice neighbors who lived next door so long ago."

"Since we haven't figured out where he lived yet, we don't have any of his belongings outside of the clothes he was wearing," Mercy said. "Surely someone will come forward when his identity is publicly released tomorrow, and we'll learn more. We wanted to speak with you before it happened."

"Someone must know where he's spent the last year." Debby's eyes were hopeful. "I'll tell you right now you are welcome to go through any of his things to figure out who killed those deputies." She paused and continued in a thoughtful voice. "My father is dead, and there's nothing in his past I need to protect."

"Thank you." Mercy caught Truman's gaze and lifted a brow. *Anything else?*

He shook his head. He stood and handed Debby his card, stating the usual request that she contact them if she remembered anything else. Mercy did the same, and they said their good-byes.

The air outside was nippy and Mercy pulled her collar up around her neck as they walked down Debby's driveway. "I can feel it's about to rain."

"The air is definitely damper over here," agreed Truman. "What do you think about her description of her father as a teddy bear?"

"I think she's a grieving young woman who lost her father."

"She's sharp," said Truman. "I think she would have known if he had it in himself to kill someone."

"I don't think *anyone* can truly know what another person is capable of. Doesn't matter if you are the daughter, son, or wife. People see only what you want them to see." She looked away as Truman glanced over at her. "She admitted he's a good shot. Whoever shot those deputies had true skills."

"On our side of the mountains, there are plenty of people with those skills."

"True," Mercy admitted. *Our side of the mountains.* She wanted to go back to their side. In a matter of short months, Portland had ceased to be her home. Maybe it never had been. Had she simply been biding her time when she lived here? Nothing in town made her want to stay.

Well, almost nothing.

"Have you ever had olive oil ice cream?" she asked, suddenly swamped by a craving.

He recoiled. "What the hell? That sounds disgusting."

"Do you trust me?" She paused at her side of the vehicle, looking at Truman over the hood.

"Not right this moment." He looked pained.

"It'll change the way you look at ice cream. I promise. We need to make one stop before we head home."

He took a deep breath. "This better be good."

THIRTEEN

Truman tried to focus on his email at his desktop. He yawned several times, even though he'd gotten a good six hours of sleep.

Last night Mercy had been right. The olive oil ice cream was unique. He didn't have an overwhelming urge to rush back to Portland and get some more, but it'd been an eye-opening experience. He wished he'd had the courage to try the flavor made with bone marrow and smoked cherries instead of settling for the sea salt and caramel, which had sounded safe.

He'd watched Mercy indulge in her odd ice cream and had enjoyed the blissful look on her face. She was weird about food. Selective and particular in a way he'd only read about online or seen in movies. But when it came to ice cream, all her rules went out the window. He'd never seen her pass up the dessert.

Someone tapped at his door and pushed it open. Mercy's sister Pearl stepped in. "You got a moment?" she asked.

Surprised, he stood and gestured at the chair in front of his desk. "Absolutely, Pearl. What can I do for you?"

She wore her apron from the Coffee Café and had her hair pulled back in a long ponytail. It was nearly 8:00 a.m., and he was shocked she wasn't behind the counter during what had to be a busy time. She didn't sit and he continued to stand.

"Some of the customers told me the man that was found at that fire had been identified." She tipped her head to one side as she spoke to him, her hands buried in her apron's deep pockets. "I pulled up the article from the paper on my phone this morning. It said the FBI is trying to track his whereabouts for the last few months. Is that right?"

"That's true. We don't have a current address for him. Do you know him?"

"I don't know him, but I recognized his picture. I didn't know his name was Joshua Pence until I read it. He's been in the shop recently. Maybe a half dozen times over the last month or two."

"So he was definitely living around here."

"I don't know that for certain," Pearl clarified. "He could have lived an hour or two away and his route to work brought him through town."

"Good point." Truman watched her. She fussed with her pockets and had a hard time looking him in the eye. "I take it you don't recall discussing where he lived with him."

"I don't remember him as being a talker. But his size stood out to me, which is why I recognized him."

Truman waited. Pearl wouldn't have left her coffee shop to tell him she simply remembered a customer.

"He came in with Tom McDonald a few times."

There it is.

Truman didn't know McDonald except to nod at him in the street. His ranch was far out of town, and the police had never responded out there for any incidents. Truman liked that in a resident, but he also liked getting to know his people. McDonald hadn't made himself available to get to know. He kept to himself.

"McDonald's a big guy too," Truman commented.

"That's why I remembered him. Together they made quite the pair."

"So McDonald is the guy to talk to," Truman said. "Hopefully he can shine a little more light on Pence's history."

"I need to get back to work. That was all I had to tell you. I wasn't certain it'd be helpful."

"It was definitely helpful."

Pearl turned to leave, and Truman came around his desk. "Hang on, Pearl." She stopped and looked at him with a deer-in-headlights gaze. "That newspaper article said the FBI was looking for any information on Joshua Pence, right?"

She nodded.

"How come you didn't contact Mercy?"

Her gaze darted from side to side. "I figured you would know what to do with the information. And it was easy to dash over here."

"You could have called her just as easily," he said gently, knowing he was on fragile ground. Pearl looked ready to dash out the door.

"This was easier," she admitted.

"I understand." Although Pearl's efforts to avoid her sister hurt a mushy spot in his heart.

She tilted her head again. "Do you?"

"I think you try to walk a tightrope between your sister and the rest of your family." He lightly touched her arm. "You feel like you're in the middle. Trying to keep the peace, not piss off either side. But still keep a tenuous contact."

Her lips tightened.

"I think you just want everyone to be happy."

"I do."

"What are you doing for Thanksgiving?" he asked.

He might as well have poked her with a cattle prod.

"Probably going to my oldest's house."

"You don't have plans yet?"

Pearl shifted her weight from foot to foot. "It's a given. It's what we've done the last couple of years. We haven't really talked about it yet."

Truman found that hard to believe. He remembered when his mother would plan Thanksgiving dinners. She had the menu delegated among family and the grocery list written down two weeks before the date. Pearl struck him as the same type of organizer.

"Perhaps you and your family can swing by my place for dessert. I'm cooking for Mercy and Kaylie, but we'd love to have everyone come by."

She relaxed a fraction, as he'd expected. He knew dessert would feel less threatening than the entire meal.

"I'll check with everyone and let you know."

Truman held her gaze. "Please do. Kaylie will be baking, and I'm sure there will be ton of goodies."

Pearl looked thoughtful. "In that case I may skip baking any desserts. Kaylie always outbakes all of us. Even my mother."

Relief flowed through Truman. *She's considering it.* He didn't want to overwhelm Mercy with a crush of family, so Pearl's family was a good choice. He'd heard about Mercy's last conversation with Owen and knew better than to try to contact him. He didn't know what to do about Mercy's parents. Maybe a quick word with Rose would shine some light on the question. "Thank you, Pearl. It means a lot to me."

Contemplative eyes regarded him. "You're a different man, Truman Daly. In a good way. My Rick would never consider stirring any pot but his own." She laughed. "That's a good thing for me most of the time, but sometimes I wish he *saw* beyond his dinner plate."

Truman wondered if Pearl dished up Rick's plate for him. Twenty years ago he'd had dinner at an aunt's home where she'd done that for her husband. His mother had rolled her eyes, but his father had liked it. It'd led to an interesting car ride conversation on the way back home. "What's he think of your hours at the coffee shop?"

"Mmmph." Her lips turned up the littlest bit at the corners.

"That good, huh?"

"He'll get over it. With one kid out of the house and the other nearly independent, I needed this. It feels good that I'm adding financially to the household. I know Rick likes that part too . . . it's just taking him a while to come around."

"Good luck."

"Thanks." She turned again to leave but stopped and glanced back. "Take care, Truman," she said awkwardly, dipping her chin as if slightly embarrassed.

He watched her leave, feeling good about their conversation. He'd do whatever it took to smooth Mercy's transition back to Eagle's Nest. He wanted her to stick around for the long term.

◆ ◆ ◆

Mercy had received a call from Truman to tell her that Joshua Pence had been seen in town with Tom McDonald over the past few months, so she immediately found his address and recruited Eddie for the ride out to the McDonald ranch. Eddie had been supervising the evidence processing from all the fires, which he stated primarily involved a lot of emails and phone calls begging people to speed up their work.

Following her GPS, Mercy turned off a highway, and her Tahoe bounced through deep ruts on a dirt road.

"Are you sure this is right?" Eddie grabbed the "oh shit" handle above his door. "It looks like no one has driven here in a few months."

"I suspect that's exactly how he wants it to appear." Sure enough, after a minute the rough road was replaced by a well-tended gravel road. "Maybe there's a back way in that gets used more often."

"Why does everyone out here spend so much effort trying to avoid people?" Eddie muttered.

Mercy grinned. "I don't have an answer for you."

"They've got too much time on their hands," Eddie mused. "And I think they watch too much conspiracy TV."

"Maybe."

They drove between two buttes as they climbed in elevation. The vegetation around them was dry and scarce, giving the area a dull beige tone amid the rocky landscape, typical of the Deschutes County high desert. The road took a sharp turn and Mercy drove into a large level area of several dozen acres. A small old farmhouse sat far off to one side, looking as if it'd been lonely since the 1950s. Barbed-wire fences surrounded multiple pastures. Fresh lumber framed several outbuildings, and a dozen pickups indicated that humans were around somewhere.

Mercy parked next to the pickups and hopped out, studying the new construction. A few older buildings sat beyond the new ones, looking as old as the farmhouse. Mercy glanced at the farmhouse and then back at the buttes they'd driven past, feeling a sense of déjà vu.

She was positive she'd never driven out to the ranch before, but it had the same aura of another place she'd visited. She continued to scan the buildings, searching her memories for the connection and waiting to see who'd greet her and Eddie.

My uncles' ranch.

That was it. Satisfaction curled through her. Her mother's five brothers had owned a similar ranch in southeast Oregon. Three of the uncles had passed away over the years. Two had died from heart problems, and the youngest had been killed in the eruption of Mount St. Helens back in 1980. The two remaining uncles now lived somewhere in eastern Washington, and Mercy hadn't given them a passing thought since she'd left home fifteen years ago.

She remembered long car trips from her childhood that had ended at her uncles' ranch on the far side of the state. She and her siblings had been let loose to explore the property while the adults talked for hours. Thinking hard, she figured their last trip had occurred before she turned twelve. She wasn't certain why the trips had stopped, but once two of the brothers had died, she knew the others agreed it was time to sell and go their separate ways.

Her memories were of a property dominated by men. With so many uncles and their numerous ranch hands, that was understandable. She couldn't remember much interaction with her aunts outside of helping with cooking and chores. Her remaining uncles' contact with her mother seemed to dissolve once they moved to Washington, and Mercy suddenly wondered if there'd been a falling out on that side of the family that she'd been blissfully unaware of.

A perk of being a child.

"This reminds me a lot of my uncles' ranch," she told Eddie. "I used to visit it when I was a kid. A great place for playing hide-and-seek with my siblings."

"Was it this remote?"

"More so."

The look on Eddie's face said he wasn't surprised.

Someone stepped out of the closest new construction building. The young man was wearing a tool belt and glanced around as if looking for someone more senior to take charge of the visitors. Mercy took pity on him and strode over, deciding to make the first move.

"Good morning," she said. "I'm Special Agent Kilpatrick and this is Special Agent Peterson."

The young man stared at her for a moment and then blanched as he ducked his chin. "I'm really sorry. I didn't mean to get her in trouble." His words tumbled over one another.

"Excuse me?" Mercy was lost. He was a good-looking kid who had clearly misunderstood the reason for their visit. She saw Eddie stifle a grin out of the corner of her eye.

"Can you tell us what happened?" Eddie asked in a serious tone.

Mercy wanted to elbow him for harassing the man.

The young man straightened and turned to Mercy, meeting her gaze directly this time. "I really like Kaylie," he said with a quiver in his voice, and nervously licked his lips. "I'm sorry I talked her into sneaking out at night. That was on me, not her."

Comprehension dawned. "You're Cade?" Mercy exclaimed, as she realized this was the young man she'd seen exchange a brief look with Kaylie at the memorial service. She didn't know whether to give him a piece of her mind or admire his guts for standing up to her.

He blinked rapidly. "Ummm . . . yes. Isn't that why you're here? To talk to me? Kaylie told me you wanted to meet me."

"Well, yes, but I imagined it'd be over dinner somewhere," Mercy managed to say. "I didn't know you worked here."

Cade looked from her to Eddie in confusion. "I don't understand."

"We're here to talk to Tom McDonald," Eddie told him. "Not you." He turned to Mercy. "*This* is the guy who Kaylie snuck out with?" He gave Cade an evil eye. "How old are you?"

"I-I-I'm twenty."

"She's in high school," Eddie pointed out, still using his tough-cop voice.

"Stop it," Mercy interjected. "This isn't the time or place. Is Tom around?"

"What's going on? Everything okay, Cade?" A new voice spoke as two men came around the building. Like Cade, they wore tool belts, but they were at least a decade or two older. One was short and wiry, while the other was a few inches taller and hung back, looking slightly uncomfortable at the sight of visitors.

Mercy immediately disliked the shorter man who'd spoken. His eyes were mean and squinty. "We're looking for Tom," she said pleasantly.

"Who's looking?" said the jerk as he crossed his arms and challenged her with those eyes.

"The FBI." She smiled, showing all her teeth, as she introduced herself and Eddie.

"Tom's not here," answered Squinty Eyes.

"He went to Salem," added the second man in a friendlier voice. "He said he might not come back today." He received a glare from Squinty for sharing the extra information. Or for being helpful.

Eddie held out the photo they'd lifted from Joshua Pence's old DMV records. Mercy estimated he weighed quite a bit less in the photo, but the hair and beard looked about right. "Know this guy?"

Squinty glanced at the photo and looked away. "Nope. Never seen him before."

Liar.

The second man shook his head while keeping his gaze on the picture.

Too chicken to challenge Squinty.

Eddie held the photo so Cade could see it. Cade studied it for a few seconds and frowned. "I'm not sure," he said slowly. "Did something happen to him?"

"He's dead. Murdered. We're trying to find out where he lived and worked for the last six months."

Cade paled. "That's too bad, but I don't pay much attention to the people who come visit. A lot of guys drop in here."

A safe answer.

"Why is that?" Mercy asked. She made a show of looking around the property. "Tom sell cattle or pigs? I don't see a lot of livestock. What causes all the traffic?" She smiled innocently at Cade.

"Not livestock. I dunno, I guess. I just work here and don't ask a lot of questions." His gaze dropped to his feet, and he kicked some gravel in the dusty dirt. "I haven't been here that long. I just do my job."

"What exactly is that?" Eddie asked.

Mercy watched Squinty out of the corner of her eye as Cade answered. The man had shifted his weight to his toes and leaned forward an inch, his intense stare on Cade as he spoke.

"Construction." Cade pointed to the building that smelled of fresh wood behind him.

"And you two?" Eddie asked the other men.

"Same. Construction," answered Squinty. The other nodded silently.

"Tom must have some big plans," Mercy stated, taking an obvious look at all the new buildings.

No one answered her.

Fifty yards away a woman stepped out of another building. Her braids were tucked inside a man's heavy canvas coat, and she wore camouflage pants with heavy boots. She glanced at the visitors and proceeded to empty a large pot of water a few feet away from the door, then disappeared back inside.

"We'd like to show this photo to a few other people," Eddie said.

"I'm not comfortable with you walking around Tom's property when he's not here," said Squinty. "I don't think he'd like you to interrupt his employees while they're working. I'm sure he'd be happy to set up a time to meet with you." Squinty decided it was his time to grin at Mercy.

She held eye contact and ignored his crooked teeth with the black bits of chewing tobacco stuck between them. "We'll leave our cards, and you can pass them on to Tom. Tell him to give us a call when he gets back." She deliberately handed the cards to Cade, who reluctantly accepted them, as if he were getting a traffic ticket. She didn't let go until he raised his gaze to look at her. She met his confused look and then released the cards.

"Nice meeting y'all," said Eddie with a little wave as they turned to leave.

"Where'd the Southern accent come from?" Mercy muttered to him as they headed to her vehicle.

"It felt like the right thing to say at the moment."

"Were you expecting a 'Y'all come back now, ya hear?' in reply?" She yanked on the handle to her Tahoe.

"A man can hope. Think Cade will reach out to you?"

"A woman can hope." She started the vehicle, pulled a tight U-turn, and headed out in the direction from which they'd come. "Actually, I'm certain I'll hear from him soon."

Twenty-five years ago

"Hold steady, honey."

Mercy could smell pipe smoke on Uncle John's breath as he crouched behind her and moved her eight-year-old arms and hands into the correct position on the big rifle. Straw from the bales of hay poked the skin of her stomach and knees as she knelt on one to properly reach the weapon on the gun rest.

Behind her Owen muttered about her turn taking too much time.

"She's faster than you were at this age," Uncle John informed her brother. "Better shot too."

Mercy smiled but kept her eye turned to the sight. Sixteen-year-old Owen could do everything better than she. But if her uncle said she was a better shot than he at her age, then it was true.

"Just let her shoot, Owen," Rose added. "Your turn was a lot longer."

"But it's useful for me to learn. It's stupid for a girl."

"Back off for a minute," her mother's brother said in her ear.

Mercy took her finger off the trigger and looked over her shoulder. Owen wore his pouty face, and Rose was shaking her head. Beside her Levi crouched, ignoring the small squabble and drawing something in the dirt with a stick. It was a rare moment when all the siblings got along. Discord between at least two of them was the norm.

Her uncle John stopped in front of sixteen-year-old Owen. "You don't think your sisters deserve to learn to shoot?"

Owen shrugged. "I don't see the point."

"What if they're out hiking and come across a pissed-off bear? What if someone breaks into their home when they're adults and tries to attack them? What if their husband is hurt and unable to defend them?"

Owen looked away and gave a smaller shrug. "I guess."

"Everyone benefits from learning to shoot. Being able to defend ourselves is our right."

"It seems stupid to teach a child."

Uncle John slowly shook his head, and disgust filled his tone. "How do you think you learned? Your dad and my brothers agree it's best to learn early respect for weapons to eliminate the fascination of the untouchable. A kid who's taught the proper respect is less likely to cause an accident. This is serious business, and I'm proud your daddy let me have a hand in teaching all of you."

"Even me," Rose said. She'd learned right alongside all of them. Studying the weapons with her fingertips, learning the recoil of each gun. She couldn't hit a target, but she knew how to fire, and their uncle had said she just needed to fire in the right direction to scare off any threat.

"That's right," he said to Rose. "You never know when a person will have to take up a weapon to defend themselves," he told Owen. "Maybe even defend yourself from your own government. I hope it never comes to that one day, but if it does, we'll be ready."

"Why would the government attack us?" Owen asked.

Her uncle ran a hand over his beard, his gaze distant. "That's not something you need to worry about now. Just be prepared for every uncertainty and you won't have to worry about anything. Now keep your mouth shut until I'm done with your sister."

Mercy turned her eye back to the sight, deliriously happy that Owen had gotten in trouble.

"Quit your grinnin'," her uncle whispered in amusement next to her ear. "Take a deep breath and let it out and then shoot. Five shots."

Mercy did as he asked and was pleased to see five holes in the third and fourth rings of the bull's-eye fifty yards away.

"Nice job, Mercy."

She beamed and lined up her next series of shots.

That night at the adults' dinner table, her uncle bragged about her precision. It was a packed table. Her parents, her mother's four brothers, and two of their wives had squeezed together while the five kids ate on folding chairs around a card table. Owen had sulked because he'd been made to eat at the kids' table, and her uncle's statement about Mercy's shooting made his shoulders sag even more.

As he sank lower, Mercy sat up straighter. She listened closely to the adults' talk, and ignored Levi and Pearl's argument about who got to ride which horse tomorrow. She enjoyed visiting her uncles' ranch. The four men had lots of horses, which made the long car ride worth it to her. Mercy loved to ride the horses, explore the vast ranch with her siblings, and help her aunts cook big meals for the ranch hands.

Her aunts were always very quiet at dinner, letting the men do most of the talking. Even her mother spoke less here than at home. Probably because there were more people to listen to. Her uncles had a way of talking over one another, each one getting louder than the others to get his words heard. Especially when they talked about the government. That subject was certain to get them fired up. They didn't trust the government and would argue over the best way to avoid any interaction with it.

She grew bored as the adults changed the topic to cattle, and her gaze strayed to the family photos on the wall. She knew them by heart. They never changed from visit to visit. There were pictures of her mother's parents, who had both died before Mercy was born, and there were pictures of her mother as a little girl, younger than Mercy was now. Everyone said Mercy looked just like her mother as a child, but Mercy didn't see the resemblance. Her mother had worn impossibly short bangs and had a ton of freckles. Her uncle Aaron had a place of honor on the wall. He'd been camping near Mount St. Helens when it erupted and been one of the nearly sixty deaths. Multiple pictures of him were hung in a circle around his high school senior picture.

She had no memories of this uncle who'd died in his early twenties before she was born, but his picture showed a strong resemblance to her other uncles. Uncle John was her favorite; he was always a lot of fun.

"Eat your peas," Pearl ordered her.

Mercy glared at her older sister. "You're not the boss of me." She hated peas.

"Pearl's the boss when Mom's not here," Levi stated, shoveling peas in his mouth. He chewed and then showed her a tongue covered with green mush.

"Mom's here." Mercy shot a nervous look at the adult table to see if her mother was paying attention to their argument. Any other day she would have told on Levi for being gross, but she didn't want to call her mother's attention to the uneaten peas on her plate. "And I ate all my carrots. So there."

She glanced at the big table and caught her uncle John's eye. He'd been listening. He winked at her and made a show of pushing his peas to the edge of his plate. Her heart warmed, and she ducked her head in embarrassed happiness.

Even with the large number of men on her uncles' ranch, she didn't feel outnumbered as she did at home with just Levi and Owen. Her brothers had a way of dictating every moment of her life.

There were three more days left in their visit, and Mercy planned to enjoy every minute.

FOURTEEN

"I heard Tom McDonald is out of town," Jeff, Mercy's supervisor, commented as she stopped in the doorway to his office.

"I take it Eddie told you about our visit already?" Mercy asked. "I was stopping by to bring you up-to-date. What are you doing in the office on a weekend, anyway?"

"When someone has murdered law enforcement officers, every day is Monday for me. Will McDonald call you when he gets back?"

She raised a brow at him.

"Didn't think so. Continue to stop by his place until you talk to him."

"His ranch isn't exactly on my way to work. Today's trip took a big chunk of my day, but I'll keep at it."

"Don't go alone." Jeff tapped at his keyboard, his gaze on his screen.

Mercy's hackles rose. "Would you say that if I was Eddie?"

Jeff sighed and leaned back in his chair, bringing his hands together across his chest in a way that made her feel as if she were about to get a lecture from her father. "I *would* say that to Eddie. A remote location staffed with a bunch of rednecks who don't want law enforcement poking around? You bet I'd tell him to not go alone."

Mercy backed down. "Sorry. You're right. And I wouldn't have thought twice about heading out there on my own, so it's a good thing you brought it up. I grew up around places like that and it feels familiar . . . as if I share roots with them. But I need to look at it from an LEO perspective, not as a local." She frowned, realizing she'd hit the nail on the head. She still saw herself as one of them; therefore they wouldn't hurt her. A potentially reckless train of thought. People saw only her badge.

"Your roots offer you no protection around here. You haven't been a local for a long time."

"I keep being reminded of that, but some days it feels like I never left. Any additional updates on our cases?"

"We haven't had a new fire in a few days."

"Does that mean we're due for flames or that they've backed off?" Mercy asked.

"Perhaps Joshua Pence was our fire starter. He did have the gasoline on his clothing."

True. "But I'm bothered by Clyde Jenkins's report that he saw his fire starters running. And the Parkers thought they heard young voices. Pence doesn't fit either of those descriptions."

"We're still processing evidence from the first two big fires. Hopefully we'll catch a break before the next one."

"I hope so."

Jeff waved her away and went back to his keyboard. Mercy stopped at her desk to grab her bag and headed out the door to her Tahoe, feeling the need to revisit the scene where the deputies had been shot. She could stop and chat with Tilda Brass, even though Truman and Jeff had reported she suffered from some memory loss.

A quick call to Tilda Brass resulted in an invitation to tea at 4:00 p.m. Mercy didn't think she'd "had tea" since she'd held tea parties as a child with Rose. Tilda's home was far out of town, so she got an early start and drove past the Bend city limits and down the two-lane highway toward the Brass property, making a mental note to check in with Bill Trek and see if the fire marshal had any fire investigation updates.

A pickup started to pass her on the highway and she slowed the slightest bit, remembering how the long straight stretch of road had always been a favorite with teenagers for impromptu drag races.

Her Tahoe jerked hard as the passing truck smacked her left rear fender and her vehicle spun in front of the truck across the oncoming lane. Her mind blanked and she clenched the wheel as the landscape blurred outside her windows. She hit the brakes as her vehicle flew off the road and rocketed down the shoulder.

Metal screeched and scraped on rock as she hit the lava rocks at the bottom. Her airbag smacked her in the face and knocked the breath out of her lungs. Her Tahoe rocked to an abrupt stop at a sharp angle, the rear of the vehicle too high and her chest pressing against her seat belt, which suspended her in the cab. She fought to catch her breath and slow her pounding heart.

He pulled a fucking PIT maneuver!

A favorite move of officers everywhere to stop errant vehicles. She'd trained on the maneuver at Quantico, but memories of how to respond when on the receiving end had disintegrated the moment he'd struck her Tahoe. And to be fair, she'd never experienced it at sixty miles an hour.

She braced herself, hit the seat belt button, and slid out of the SUV, dropping two feet more to the ground than usual, and brushed airbag dust off her clothes. Her legs shook as she stepped back to inspect her vehicle, and she leaned weakly against a big rock, welcoming its solid, immovable presence. The rear axle of the Tahoe had come to rest on huge boulders, its back tires nowhere near the ground.

I'm not going anywhere.

She pulled out her phone, trying to recall any description of the pickup that'd hit her. She had impressions, not memories. She thought it had been dark red, and there might have been two men in the cab, but she wasn't certain.

Why? Who'd run me off the road?

Her brain refused to consider the question; its current primary goal was to get help.

She called 911 and reported the incident, advising the operator that the truck might have body damage on its right front end. After reassuring the operator that she wasn't injured, she hung up and scrambled up the incline to the highway. Her truck had ended up in a spot a dozen feet lower than the road.

They picked a good spot. If I'd been injured, no one would have seen me.

She fumed. Pure luck had kept her Tahoe from rolling. The shoulder where she'd gone off the highway was wide and level before gently angling down to the rocks. If it'd been soft dirt or a more abrupt incline, she would have rolled across the big lava rocks. She called Eddie.

"Are you sure you're not hurt?" he asked. "Sometimes you don't realize it until later."

"My back and neck probably won't be happy with me tomorrow," she admitted. "But I'm okay now. Can you pick me up and then take me to get a rental car?"

"I'll pick you up, but then I'm taking you to the hospital. You're not going anywhere until your spine is x-rayed. And Jeff will agree with me."

"Crap." She didn't have time for this.

"Did you call Truman?"

"Not yet."

"Do it."

"I don't want to interrupt him while he's working. I'm fine and you're my ride. I'll tell him later tonight."

Eddie sighed in the phone. "You don't know anything about men, do you?"

"I don't need Truman to come pick me up. I'm on the job, so I called a coworker. That's what I should do, right?"

"Call and tell him what happened. Don't make me call him."

"Why would you do it?" Exasperation made her want to shake him.

"Call it a man code thing. When your friend's woman has been in an accident, you let the dude know."

"That's the most caveman thing I've ever heard you say." She didn't know whether to be shocked, flattered, or amused. "I didn't realize there was a *thing* between you and Truman."

"Just do it, okay?" he pleaded. "Tell him I'm on my way and that I'm taking you to the hospital."

"Call me a tow too," she said before they ended the call.

She looked down at her vehicle and wondered when it'd be drivable again. She liked the Tahoe. It'd become her buddy, and she felt safe and secure while driving it. *What if the damage underneath is too much to repair?* The thought depressed her.

She went to clear her things out of the vehicle, starting with her always-ready backpack stashed in the back. Her truck was also well supplied with equipment for her job. She'd have to transfer it to Eddie's car before the tow truck arrived.

She sat on a rock by the Tahoe and called Tilda, canceling their tea date, promising to do it tomorrow.

Then she called Truman.

"So I wrecked my Tahoe," she blurted when he answered.

"Are you okay?" he nearly shouted.

"I'm fine. There's no fuss needed. I'm just pissed because I screwed up and now I'll have to miss an appointment."

"What happened?" he asked in a calmer voice.

She relayed the whole story, feeling slightly unnerved as he grew very, very quiet while she spoke.

"That's all you remember of the vehicle that ran you off the road?" he finally asked.

"Sadly yes. Some investigator I am."

"Did you go anywhere for work today?"

She told him about her and Eddie's trip to Tom McDonald's ranch.

"Any chance the vehicle could have been from there?"

"I can't rule it out." She rubbed at her forehead, feeling a dull ache start in her brain. *Why didn't I look closer at the truck before it passed?* Could that little squinty-eyed ass from the ranch have run her off the road?

The thought made her headache worsen.

"When's Eddie going to get there?"

"Soon. And I'm supposed to tell you he's taking me to get my back x-rayed."

"Good."

"Then I'll need a rental."

"You won't get one tonight. By the time you're out of the ER, it'll be too late."

He's right. Dammit.

"I'll meet you at the ER."

"That's not necessary. I don't want you to have to—"

"I'll meet you at the ER." Anger infused his tone.

Eddie's earlier words about Truman ran through her head. "Okay."

They ended the call, and she went back up the slope to keep an eye out for Eddie. A Good Samaritan stopped to see if she needed help. The driver had to be in her seventies and insisted on waiting until Mercy's ride showed up. "I can't leave another woman alone on the side of the road out here. If you don't want a ride, I'll just wait here until yours shows up." She offered Mercy the warmth of her car, but Mercy turned it down, preferring to stand outside where Eddie could easily see her.

The cold cleared her head, and the more she thought about the wreck, the more convinced she became that someone at the ranch had followed her. She could understand that she'd ruffled some feathers, but not enough to make them hurt her.

Hell, I could have died.

The decision to stand outside resulted in two more Good Samaritans stopping. Mercy finally decided to accept the offer of the warm car, and she called Eddie to tell him to keep an eye out for a two-decades-old white Cadillac on the side of the road.

The woman chatted pleasantly as they waited, and Mercy learned she was a retired nurse.

"Weren't you worried about stopping for a stranger?" Mercy asked.

"Oh no, honey. I could tell by your face that you were a good girl."

Mercy thought on that for a while, uncertain whether to take it as a compliment or not.

Eddie showed up and charmed her companion as Mercy transferred the things into his vehicle. The tow truck showed up a minute later, and the driver scratched his head as he eyed the Tahoe stuck on the rocks below the road. Mercy didn't have any advice to share. He was the expert, and it was now his problem to figure out.

Minutes later they were en route to the ER. Mercy leaned her head against the back of her seat and sighed. "I don't have time for this."

"Get over it," said Eddie. "Let's make sure you aren't going to wake up tomorrow with some devastating injury from shards of bone working their way through your spinal cord or internal organs."

She glared at him. "Thank you for that visual."

"Truman said he'd be there in about an hour."

"You called him? I told you I would do it."

"He called me to see if I'd picked you up yet."

She didn't say anything. Knowing that people had talked about her when she wasn't present made her want to pout like a cranky toddler. Even if their intentions were good. When that was combined with the growing certainty that someone had tried to hurt her, her mood grew darker by the minute.

◆ ◆ ◆

Tension ratcheting through his veins, Truman followed the nurse's direction to the curtained-off bed at the end of the small emergency room. He spotted a man's shoes below the curtain hem.

"Eddie?" he asked.

The FBI agent pushed back the curtain as relief and exhaustion showed in his eyes behind the thick frames of his glasses. "Glad you're here. I'm taking off." He tipped his head at Mercy, who perched on the side of the hospital bed in a gown, looking ready to run out the front door. "She's all yours."

"I don't need to be handed off," Mercy snapped. "I'm not six."

Eddied rolled his eyes at Truman. "Enjoy," he silently mouthed.

Truman sat next to Mercy and pulled her into him, kissing her soundly. She leaned into the kiss after a moment of sitting stiffly and then sighed as she rested her head on his shoulder. He swore stress evaporated from her like rain on hot pavement. His own stress lessened as he held her against him and felt her skin touch his. The entire drive to the hospital, he'd worried about hidden injuries, terrified he'd arrive and find her unconscious.

He hugged her tighter.

"Did the X-ray confirm that you're in one piece?" She smelled like the hospital—bandages and disinfectant. He noticed a Band-Aid on the crook of her arm and wondered if they'd tested her blood for alcohol. If the police had brought her in, he could understand the need for a draw.

"I haven't been told if I'm in one piece. They took the X-ray thirty minutes ago and I'm waiting for someone to review it. I haven't busted in half yet, so I assume I'm okay." She followed his gaze to her arm. "I requested the blood draw. I don't need some overseeing agency asking if I was drunk when I wrecked government property. Better safe than sorry."

Irritation dripped from her tone, and he knew it was hard for her to wait. Mercy was a doer. No doubt she would have rustled up her own radiologist and been checked out by now if she'd been allowed. The irritation encouraged him; she sounded like her usual self.

She asked, "Any leads on the vehicle that hit me?"

"None," said Truman. "Both Deschutes County and my guys are keeping an eye out for a red pickup with some front-end damage."

"If he's smart, the driver would have immediately hidden the vehicle."

"If he was smart, he wouldn't have run an FBI agent off the road."

"True," she agreed.

"Why did they do it?" he asked bluntly. "You must have some ideas." On the way to the hospital, he'd talked with her boss, who'd also theorized that she and Eddie had stirred up some anger out at the McDonald ranch.

Mercy looked at the floor, clearly mulling over her options. "Most likely it was someone from the McDonald ranch. The move was clearly deliberate, for God's sake. I spun in front of their vehicle. If it had been accidental, they would have stopped."

"Unless they were uninsured or scared."

"True again."

"Joshua Pence had a red truck that we haven't located yet."

Mercy's gaze flew back to him. "That crossed my mind too. You think it's been commandeered by someone at the McDonald place?"

"Pearl said Pence came into the coffee shop with McDonald a few times, so it's possible he worked out there, even though that's not the story you got when you visited the ranch. The vehicle hasn't turned up yet, so I wouldn't be surprised if someone who knew he was dead simply decided to start driving it around."

"Idiots," muttered Mercy. "We need to go back there and look at the vehicles out—"

A tired-looking young doctor stepped inside the curtain. "Ms. Kilpatrick. Your films look fine." He wore light-blue scrubs and running shoes Truman had considered buying until he saw the price was nearly $200. He glanced at Truman and kept talking. "A radiologist will also review the films. You'll get a separate bill from their office and—"

"I know," Mercy said, cutting him off. "But *you* don't see any issues?"

"No."

"Can I leave?"

"I'm printing out your discharge papers. You might have some pain and stiffness tomorrow morning. Take some OTC pain relievers and use ice as needed. If you have any severe headaches, I want you back here, or go to your doctor right away."

"I don't have a doctor yet," she said. "I've only been here a few months."

"A good time to find one then," he said with a polite smile that indicated this wasn't his problem. He vanished.

"Get dressed." Truman stepped outside the curtains and stood guard as she changed. A weight lifted off his shoulders in his relief that she hadn't been hurt.

But who would purposefully run an FBI agent off the road?

He had hard questions for the men at the McDonald ranch.

Truman drove toward her apartment, wishing she would come home with him. She'd said she wanted to be home for Kaylie, to make sure she got up in time for school in the morning. He'd known it would be tough dating a woman with a teenager. Even though Kaylie was pretty self-sufficient, Mercy had a need to be available for her. He had to get over it; the girl had just lost her father.

But sometimes he wanted Mercy to himself.

"Thanks for the ride. You didn't have to come to the hospital."

This is enough!

Fury shot through him, and he took a deep breath as he pulled over to the side of the road and turned off the ignition. They were a few blocks from her home. He turned toward her in the SUV's driver's seat, his heart pumping and frustration rushing through his limbs. "Why shouldn't I give you a ride?"

Wide eyes blinked at him. He had her attention.

"Eddie could have driven me. He was already there."

"Maybe I *wanted* to drive you. I *wanted* to be at the hospital."

"But—"

"No *buts*. Don't tell me what I feel."

"I didn't want you feeling obligated."

"I know Eddie had to convince you to let me know about the accident."

She glared. "That little—"

"He didn't tell me. Jeff did. Eddie mentioned it to him and Jeff told me when I called him."

She threw up her hands. "*Why is everyone talking about me behind my back?*"

"Because we care!" He shoved the words through his clenched teeth to keep from shouting at her.

She opened her mouth to reply, but slammed it shut as she stared at him in the dim light of the cab.

"Why is it so hard for you to let people take care of you?" he asked in a normal voice.

"I don't need to be taken care of," she snapped. "I'm an adult."

"*Taken care of* isn't the way I should have phrased it . . . Why is it hard to let people do nice things for you? Why didn't you want me to know about the accident?"

"Because I knew you'd leave work, and it's important that you do your job. People rely on you. Cases need your attention. Important cases."

"You're important too."

"But I had Eddie. Why did I need two people to respond? How many people was I supposed to notify that I'd screwed up and gotten run off the road?"

"It wasn't your fault, and I want you to always call me when shit happens to you."

A passing car's headlights illuminated the inside of the SUV, making her green eyes shine. *Are those tears?*

"Why is this so hard for you?" he asked, gently taking her hand. It was like holding ice.

"I don't rely on other people. I rely on myself." She paused for a long moment. "If I wasn't able to rely on my family—people who are supposed to love me unconditionally—how can I rely on someone I barely know?" Her words ended in a whisper.

It was a fragile moment. She had pulled aside her emotional curtain, exposed her vulnerability. He was scared to move, let alone speak, for fear of her shutting him out. *How do I reassure her that she is safe?*

"Tell me this," he said carefully. "Do you want Kaylie to rely and depend on you?"

"Yes! Her world was yanked out from under her, and she needs stability. I want her to know I'll always be available . . . something I didn't have after I turned eighteen."

"Because it's important that she knows she has people in her life who love her," he added.

"Absolutely. I wish I'd had that during those hard years."

"I'm trying to be that person for you." He held his breath, watching for signs of flight.

She blinked rapidly. "You don't know me . . . We've barely—"

"You haven't seen Kaylie since she was one. Does that matter to you? Do you need to spend a year getting to know her before you commit to her?"

"It's not the same!" She tried to jerk her hand out of his, but he tightened his grip, not willing to let her hide so easily.

"Listen." He waited until she made eye contact. "You're scared I'm going to not be here tomorrow. Or two months from now. So you hold back, refusing to put your heart out there. I'm telling you I'm a safe bet."

"You can't promise—"

"Don't try to tell me what I can or can't promise. I know what I'm capable of. I'm not scared of exposing my heart to you, Mercy, but I know you are terrified of doing the same."

She was silent.

"But that's okay. I get it. I know being abandoned by your family ripped a deep hole inside of you and you've got high walls built up around your heart to protect it. But you need to understand that it's not a sign of weakness to allow yourself to be loved."

"I can't do that," she whispered.

"Not yet," he agreed. "Eventually you'll learn it's a sign of strength. You'll learn it's one of the hardest gambles in the world, but damn . . . when it's right, the payoff is out of this world." He touched her cheek, worried he'd pushed too hard, but she hadn't run away. Yet.

She was so stubborn and independent.

But he wouldn't have fallen for her if she were any other way.

FIFTEEN

Mercy liked Tilda Brass on sight.

She felt right at home with the elegant, mannered woman who wore men's overalls and rubber boots and spoke in a kind voice. Tilda poured her a cup of tea and Mercy declined the milk, opting for a wedge of lemon. She'd asked Tilda to reschedule their tea to midmorning and Mercy was glad she'd already had her hit of caffeine for the day. Tea wasn't her poison of choice.

She'd woken with a stiff neck, but a hot shower and some ibuprofen had made short work of it. Eddie had picked her up, stopped at Starbucks, and then dropped her off at a rental agency, where she'd waited impatiently behind two groups of tourists who couldn't decide what type of vehicle to rent. Each time the twentysomething clerk glanced aside and caught Mercy's stare, he seemed to completely lose his concentration and had to ask the customers to repeat themselves. Forty minutes later she was on her way in a Ford SUV, feeling as if she were cheating on her Tahoe.

Truman's words from last night were fresh in her head. In fact, they'd ricocheted in her brain for most of the night. He was willing to risk a broken heart for her.

She wasn't ready to risk one for him. Yet.

There's nothing wrong with needing more time.

She sipped her tea and admired the intricately carved wooden mantel of Tilda's fireplace. Photos and pictures littered every surface in the formal living room. Mercy liked the contrast of the delicate doilies and crocheted afghans with the attire of her hostess, because she firmly believed in dressing to be comfortable. "How long have you lived here?" Mercy asked, knowing Truman had written twenty years in his report. The home no longer resembled the small house her childhood friend had lived in on the property. It appeared to have been expanded several times.

"Over two decades," Tilda answered. "I was nearly sixty at the time, but I still had more energy than most twenty-year-olds. Buying this big farm didn't seem like a big deal, but after a dozen years or so it became a bit much for my husband. He was ten years older than me and had slowed down quite a bit." She eyed Mercy over the rim of her teacup. "I hear you're sleeping with that good-looking police chief who interviewed me the other day."

Mercy nearly spit out her tea. Tilda might have lovely manners, but apparently she said whatever she felt like.

"Don't look so shocked. I've heard it from two different sources in town. People talk, you know."

"I thought you didn't get to town much," Mercy said faintly.

"I don't. But I have a phone. Still like to talk and catch up on some things. Who's sleeping with who is always a topic my girlfriends want to discuss. They seem to approve of the two of you."

"Uh . . . that's good."

"I like being able to put a face to the names I hear about, so I was plumb delighted when you called and wanted to get together." She looked Mercy up and down, assessing and nodding as if she liked what she saw. "I bet you're nearly as tall as him, aren't you?"

"Almost."

"That's good. I was taller than my first husband and it never bothered me that much, but when I remarried, I realized how nice it was to be able to look eye to eye with my second husband."

"I understand." Mercy did. She'd been taller than a majority of the guys she'd gone to high school with. Few were willing to take an interest in a girl they had to look up to.

"Doesn't really matter in bed, though, does it?"

Mercy kept a straight face. "I guess not."

"Your police chief reminds me of my second husband. Tall and dark with kind eyes and a nice smile."

Her own smile spread across her face. "Yes, that's Truman."

"You've got that look about you," Tilda said thoughtfully, scanning Mercy's face. "When you said his name, I could see how important he is to you. You looked like a woman in love. I remember that feeling."

Mercy caught her breath. She and Truman still hadn't said those three little words to each other. Several times she'd felt as if he was waiting for her to say it, and she'd been convinced he was going to say it during their discussion last night.

He hadn't. *Was I disappointed?*

A bit. Part of her wanted to hear it, and the other part screamed that she wasn't ready.

Because if he said it, then she should too. *Right?*

Am I ready?

She recalled the bit of taped cotton she'd ripped from the crook of her arm in the shower a few hours ago. She'd led Truman to believe the blood draw was intended to check her nonexistent alcohol level. But when Mercy couldn't swear she was not pregnant in preparation for the X-rays, the doctor had ordered the quick test. "Better to play it safe," the doctor had said.

Mercy had spent the next few minutes in fear that she was pregnant. She wasn't.

"But then there's times where you want to hit them in the head with a shovel and bury them deep in the back pasture because they pissed you off," Tilda continued with a grin. "That usually leads to makeup sex. And then everything is better until you want to brain them again."

Mercy took a drink of her tea, still at a loss for words.

"But you're not here to talk about your man, you want to know if anything else has occurred to me about that fire."

Relief swamped her. "Yes. Anything new?"

"Nope. Nothing." Tilda took a big swig of tea. "I remember when your parents moved to town, you know. We lived out their way for quite a while. In fact, my man helped your dad dig fence post holes one year."

"I didn't know that." *Tilda needs some gossip time, not an opportunity to talk about the fire.* She wondered how to steer the conversation back to the crime.

"I remember them being young and motivated and out to protect themselves from the world."

"That sounds like my parents."

"They weren't nutty like some preppers are. Never saw them practicing drills with gas masks or digging a bunker to protect against radiation. They seemed to want to get back to a simpler time when people relied on themselves."

"That was exactly what they wanted to do."

"They were good neighbors. We moved to the other side of town right after your mama had her first baby. My husband liked to move a lot. It was always a pain in the ass. Seemed like I always had to do most of the packing and unpacking." She sighed. "I guess it's time to do that again. Maybe I'll hire some strong young arms to do that part for me."

"You're moving?"

"I've had a good offer for this property."

"I didn't realize it was for sale."

"It's not. But when someone knocks on your door and offers money for your home that has been feeling way too big, you take it as a sign from the good Lord above."

"Where will you go?"

The woman tipped her head and looked off in the distance. "I think it's time I find myself one of those old-people homes. The ones where you live on your own, but someone is always available to help you when needed. Sort of like an apartment complex, but specially run for us old biddies. I know how old I am. I've thought about what could happen if I slipped and broke a hip. I think that offer for my property came at a good time, and I intend to follow up on it. I hope he understands it's a woman's prerogative to change her mind."

"You already told him you wouldn't sell?"

"I did. I admit it was an emotional reaction. I didn't care for him marching up to my front door and talking to me like I was some infirm old woman. I sent him packing. He came back a few days later and was politer, but I still wasn't interested. He left his phone number. I'll mull it over a few more days and then give him a call."

"Only if you're ready. And get the property appraised. He might believe he can get it for a steal."

"No problem on that front. I've got a grandnephew who's a Realtor. He'll take care of me."

Tilda's earlier frankness had thrown Mercy for a loop, but talking real estate had helped get her brain back on track. "I read over the notes from your first interview, and you mentioned that the only person who'd come to the door recently was looking for a lost dog. How long ago did the man make the offer for your house?"

Tilda's eyes widened. "Well, aren't you a sharp one. You're absolutely right. I forgot to mention that visitor to your man and that other FBI agent. The buyer first stopped by at the beginning of November. I remember because he commented on my fall wreath on my door. I'd already taken down the Halloween cat that'd been hanging there for a decoration."

"Would you mind sharing the name of who made you the offer?"

"Not at all. I'll find his card." She stood stiffly but strode out of the room with the energy of a younger woman. Mercy glanced at the picture of the German shepherd on the fireplace, remembering how Truman said she'd claimed at the beginning of their interview that the dog was alive. *She seems sharp as a tack today.*

"Well now, I'm not sure where I put that number," Tilda said as she returned. She scanned the room, looking for the offending piece of paper. "I swear I left it right by my phone. I threw it away at first, but I fished it out of the garbage thinking I might change my mind at some point."

"Do you remember his name?"

Tilda tapped a finger on her chin as she thought. "I don't. It was on the card. I hadn't met him or heard of him before."

It probably isn't relevant. But it niggled at her. Arson had occurred on Tilda's property after she'd refused to sell. It warranted a closer look.

"I'll keep looking."

Ready to leave, Mercy pulled out her card and handed it to Tilda. "Don't lose this one. Call me when you find the other. I want to know who your eager buyer is."

"You don't think he set the fire to scare me away, do you?"

"That sounds a little extreme, don't you think?" Mercy asked, hoping she was right.

"If they want me off the property, burning down that old barn isn't the way to do it. I don't miss that barn one bit. But try it on my house and they'll be in for a surprise." Tilda patted something in the baggy pocket of her overalls, and Mercy realized she'd been drinking tea with an armed woman.

Way to be on your toes, Kilpatrick.

Several sets of tires crunched on the gravel outside, and Cade stopped to listen. It was nearly 9:00 p.m. and he'd never worked so late before, but there was no point in rushing home, because Kaylie couldn't meet him later anyway. Twice he'd had to pull apart work he'd completed because he'd made stupid mistakes. Both incidents were a result of him thinking about Kaylie's aunt's visit instead of focusing on his job. He'd decided he wasn't going home until he had the damn thing right.

Multiple voices sounded outside, and he picked out Tom's distinctive low rumble. The other voices sounded concerned and upset. Cade moved against the wall right next to the door of his bunkhouse and listened. Chip was mouthing off. Cade couldn't make out the words, but his tone was higher-pitched than usual. He thought he heard "FBI" mentioned a few times. And Joshua Pence's name. Tom answered in a soothing rumble, and footsteps sounded as the group headed toward the growing mess hall.

Cade exhaled, suddenly aware he'd been holding his breath as he tried to listen. No doubt Chip had conveyed the news of the FBI agents' visit. Cade had nearly fallen over when Kaylie's aunt showed up at his job. Finding his tongue to speak to her had been a hundred times harder than he'd imagined. It'd felt as if she knew all his secrets as she spoke to him, her green eyes penetrating his brain. He'd wanted to tell her that he knew Josh Pence. That the man had been working at the ranch before Cade was hired, and that he'd been kind and jolly but had gotten into arguments with some of the other men.

Then one day he hadn't shown up for work. No one seemed concerned. Cade had asked Mitch, who'd simply shrugged and said, "Guess he found something better." He'd noticed the quick exchange of glances between Mitch and Chip after the reply.

But now Josh had been murdered?

Cade tried to Google Josh's name, wanting the details about his death, but the cellular service out at the ranch was temperamental. Tonight there was none. Nada. Zip. It'd have to wait until he got home. Wondering over and over what had happened to Josh had added to his distraction and faulty work.

Go eavesdrop.

He swallowed, his throat suddenly dry.

Something happened to Josh, and they know about it.

Cade opened the bunkhouse door and spotted the men still walking toward the mess hall. The sun had set hours before, and the light was poor. In the weak light above the mess hall door, they were a group of silhouettes in the dark night. The two guys who had taken to going everywhere with Tom walked right beside him. Cade never saw Tom without them anymore. They seemed like guards.

Is Tom at risk like Josh?

Is that why he never goes anywhere alone?

His feet were moving before his brain acknowledged that he was following the group. Cade scooted to the far edge of the gravel lot, preferring to walk on the silent dirt. His breath hung in the air as his eyes adjusted to the bad light. He broke into a slow jog, keeping his steps as quiet as possible. He reached the mess hall and slunk around to the back, where Mitch and Chip hadn't finished the back door that led directly to the kitchen. If he bumped into one of the kitchen women, he'd say he was looking for something to eat on his way home. The unfinished door easily swung open, and Cade stepped into an empty, dark kitchen. Relief made his knees weak. Voices sounded from the other side of the wall between the kitchen and the larger seating area.

He dug through one of the cupboards and grabbed two pieces of bread and slathered some peanut butter on them, squinting in the dim light.

A sandwich for my alibi.

He bent down and followed the long counter to the pass-through, which let some light into the kitchen from the mess hall. It was a large window at the far end of the kitchen where the cooks could put up food to be easily grabbed from the seating area. Cade crouched below the raised counter of the pass-through and listened.

"The Davidsons can't stay in town anymore. They fucked up and caught the notice of the cops."

I'm not sure who's speaking.

"What were they thinking?" asked Tom McDonald.

"Dunno," said the first voice. "Kimberly did something that set Wayne off."

"Ten straight days' KP for her," ordered McDonald. "All meals."

What's KP?

"Where are they going to sleep? We're currently full."

"They can stay in the bunkhouse that's nearly finished and spread out some sleeping bags in there. The cold will be good for them," declared McDonald.

Murmuring voices agreed.

"Now, Chip. Explain to me how we caught the notice of the FBI," said McDonald.

There were a pause and a few boot steps as, Cade assumed, Chip stepped forward. From the volume of the voices, it sounded as if McDonald was a few feet from the pass-through while the other men stood in a group and faced him.

Except for his two shadows. Cade imagined them standing to the right and left of McDonald.

"I don't know, sir." Cade had never heard such a polite tone from Chip. "Somehow they connected Pence with the ranch. They had his picture and asked if we knew him."

"What'd you say?"

"Mitch and I said we didn't recognize him. Cade said he was unsure and then proceeded to mention that a lot of men come and go from the ranch."

McDonald cursed, and another assenting murmur sounded from the small group. Cade wiped the sweat that had formed on his upper lip.

"The kid did okay."

Cade perked up at Mitch's words.

"For someone with two FBI agents staring at him, Cade played it cool," continued Mitch. "I thought he seemed genuine. He acted how you would expect from someone who knows nothing but is trying to be helpful to the cops."

The room was silent, and Cade hoped Mitch wouldn't regret sticking his neck out in his defense.

"Watch him," McDonald ordered. "I'm holding you responsible for keeping him out of sight and his mouth shut if they show up here again."

"Yes, sir," Mitch replied.

Cade's spine relaxed a fraction.

"What about their questions about Pence?" asked the first voice.

"Answer them. We know nothing about him," said McDonald. "And figure out why they think we do. Someone had to say something that led them here."

"Are you going to call them?" Chip asked.

"What for?"

Silence.

"This is my property and I don't owe them anything. Pretty soon we won't have to put up with them anymore."

The men made pleased sounds along with a few "Damn right" responses.

"You've all chosen to be here," McDonald said in a solemn tone. "You've put your faith in me, and we have a common goal. I'm going to see we achieve that goal. Pence screwed up and he paid the price. It's a lesson that we all need to keep our eyes on the prize. I see a grand existence in our future. The one we were supposed to have as Americans."

More replies of "Damn right!" This time with volume.

"What about Owen?" asked a second voice Cade didn't recognize. "His sister is one of the FBI agents."

"I'll handle Owen," promised McDonald. "Don't worry about him one bit. He can barely stand the sight of his fibbie sister."

"I can stand the sight of her just fine," muttered one man. Laughter shot through the group.

"She won't be a problem. And don't worry about having women to look at. They'll be flocking here soon enough. You'd be surprised how women are strongly drawn to men in power. Deep down they want to be taken care of, and they'll soon see that this is the place for that."

Appreciative noises reached Cade's ears. Along with the sound of the kitchen door suddenly scraping open. On his hands and knees he scrambled behind a stack of produce boxes, hoping the person wouldn't turn on the lights. He leaned his back against the boxes, pulling his long legs as close as possible to his belly. A faint light came on and the boxes cast a shadow over Cade. He slowly slid his right boot out of the light that'd found his toe.

Please God, please God, please God.

The light blinked off and he realized someone had opened and closed the fridge. Boot steps walked behind him and to the door between the kitchen and mess hall. It opened and closed, and Cade buried his head in his knees in relief.

I need to get out of here.

He unfolded his legs and silently crawled back toward the door, his heart pounding in his ears. He was nearly to the door when the word *dynamite* reached him. He halted and listened, trying to hear past his heartbeat.

Laughter filled the mess hall. Whatever McDonald had suggested, it'd been hilarious.

Cade couldn't think of anything hilarious about dynamite.

Fear drove him out of the kitchen and through the door. He hurled the sandwich into the brush, knowing he'd vomit if he ate. He jogged back to the bunkhouse, straightened his tools for the next day, and got in his truck. His limbs shook as he drove off the property, and he felt the weight of Special Agent Kilpatrick's business card in the pocket of his coat.

Did McDonald order Joshua Pence's death?

SIXTEEN

Can you meet me for lunch?

Giddiness swept through Kaylie as she read Cade's text. She immediately replied that she could, and then spent the next thirty minutes of third period staring at the clock, barely able to sit still and listen to Mr. Hausman drone on about the creepiest book she'd ever read, *Lord of the Flies*. How could she focus on child-aged murderers when Cade was coming?

The bell finally rang, and she bypassed her locker and tore out the front door of the school, ready to make the most of her thirty-minute lunch. Her nerves tingled at the sight of Cade's truck idling at the front of the school.

I wish I was out of high school.

It was hard to attend school each day when the man you loved did not.

She opened the passenger door, hopped in, and slid across the bench seat, admiring the sight of him in jeans and leather coat. He pulled her close and kissed her deep.

She melted.

"Why aren't you at work?" she asked once the kiss ended and he put the truck in gear.

"I needed to come to town for some supplies. I don't think they'll notice if it takes me a bit longer than it should."

"Can we go to Dairy Queen?" A burger sounded heavenly.

"Absolutely."

She snuggled into his shoulder as he drove, inhaling the scent of fresh-cut lumber that clung to him.

I can't skip the rest of the day. But boy was she tempted. It was a good thing he needed to get back to the job site.

"Has your aunt said anything about me?" he asked.

"Nope. We still need to figure out a day you can come over for dinner so she can meet you."

"She brought that up again?"

"No. She hasn't mentioned it since our huge discussion the other day, but I told her we'd schedule something."

He nodded and hit his blinker to turn into the Dairy Queen parking lot.

"What kind of cases does she work on at the FBI?" he asked.

"I know she's working on the murder of those two county deputies. That includes the guy who was found murdered a few nights ago. They believe the cases are connected . . . along with some other minor fires. She doesn't talk about it at home very much."

"She's probably not supposed to."

"True. And she needs a break from thinking about them. I try to distract her during dinner because she gets so quiet and I know she's having a hard time getting them out of her head."

"Dedicated."

"She is."

"So she works murder cases," he said, his voice catching on the word *murder.*

"Not always. Since she's transferred to Bend, she gets a little bit of everything. In Portland she was assigned primarily to domestic terrorism. Out here they have a lot fewer agents, so everyone works on everything."

He parked but turned to look at her instead of opening his door. His brown eyes were thoughtful. "Did you know any of the men who were murdered? The deputies . . . or that other guy?"

Kaylie shook her head. "No. I know Truman had worked a bit with the deputies, and they just identified the other guy, but I'd never heard of him. They aren't sure where he's from."

"That must be frustrating."

"Aunt Mercy said he has a daughter in Portland and she's made arrangements to have him buried there."

Relief filled his face. "That's good."

He's so sensitive. "Hungry? We probably should grab our food and go eat in the school parking lot, so I'm not late."

"Let's go."

Inside they placed their order. And waited. *Why is this place always so slow?*

She was calculating how many minutes she had left with Cade when she heard him greet someone. She looked up from her phone to see Landon's snarky grin and Finn standing right behind him.

She forced a smile, hoping their food order would be called that second.

"You skipping?" Landon asked her.

"It's lunch."

"Did you call the cops on us the other night?" Landon asked with a wide smile, but his tone was deadly serious.

"What the hell are you saying?" Cade asked as Kaylie stared, fear swirling in her gut.

"What I'm saying is I don't think it's a coincidence that a cop showed up that night. And who was the only one who got off scot-free?" Behind Landon, Finn attempted to look supportive but withered under Kaylie's glare.

"Did you see her make a phone call?" Cade snapped. "Do you think she's got some telekinetic power to summon the police chief? Because that's the only way she could have done it."

"I didn't call anyone," Kaylie asserted. "If you don't want to get caught by the cops, then don't do anything stupid." Fury tunneled her vision. Landon could go screw himself. And if Cade couldn't see what an ass he was by now, they needed to have a serious talk.

"Did you talk to your boss about that extra work?" Landon asked Cade, changing the subject.

Kaylie bristled. *No way in hell should Cade try to find him work.*

"They're not looking right now," Cade said. "But I'll keep my ears open."

I can tell he's lying. Maybe he is starting to see the type of person Landon is.

"Number twenty-three!"

"That's us." Kaylie lunged forward to grab the bags of food. "I need to get back to school." She headed toward the door, leaving Cade to say good-byes to the guys. She'd had enough.

Outside he took the bags from her and held her hand as they walked to the truck. "You don't want Landon working out there, do you?" she asked.

Cade opened the truck door for her before answering. "I don't think he'd be a good fit." He shut the door and walked around to the driver's side.

"I wouldn't recommend him," Kaylie stated. "I get the feeling he's not very reliable." She watched Cade closely, waiting for his reaction.

"He's not. There's a reason he's been fired so many times."

She took a deep breath. "I know he's a good friend of yours, but I don't like him very much."

Cade didn't say anything and focused on driving.

"Every time I see him, he insults me."

"That's just—"

"I don't think there is any excuse for that sort of rudeness."

He was silent again.

"You lied to him about the job. Did you even ask your boss about it?"

"No. But I can't tell him that."

"That's understandable." She respected that Cade and Landon had been friends for a long time, but she wasn't going to stay silent about his treatment of her. "I can't believe he accused me of calling Truman that night."

"He always looks for someone to blame," Cade said slowly, as if finally seeing the truth.

"Not cool."

"It's not. I'll make certain we stay away from them when we're out together." He pulled into a parking spot at the school. Turning off the truck, he slid an arm around her shoulders and kissed her. "I'm sorry my friends are dicks."

She laughed against his mouth. "They really are. I would like to do things with other couples, though. Are there some guys at work you'd rather hang around with?"

He pulled back slightly, frowning. "No." He opened a bag and handed her a burger.

She waited, expecting a clarification. But she didn't get one. "No one? Really? You don't like the guys you work with?" She unwrapped the sandwich and caught a huge drip of grease with her napkin. She took a bite, savoring the flavor of the salty, juicy meat with the cheese.

"They're older. I don't think we'd have much in common." He studied the other cars arriving in the parking lot as students returned from lunch.

"Well, I'll figure out an evening you can come over for dinner so Aunt Mercy can meet you."

He flinched the slightest bit. "I already met her."

"What? When?" Kaylie nearly choked on the bite of burger in her mouth. "My aunt never told me that!"

"She came out to the ranch yesterday. She was asking about the murdered guy who'd had his throat cut."

"Oh, that makes sense. You introduced yourself?"

"Sorta. I don't think she likes me."

"She doesn't know you. Don't judge her by how she is while working. I've seen it; she's all business. When she's not working, she's much more relaxed."

"I don't know . . ."

"Can you come over in the evening on Thanksgiving? We're doing dinner earlier in the day, but having some people over for dessert. Would that work?"

He looked uncomfortable. "Yeah, that'd probably be okay."

Kaylie inhaled the last of her burger and wiped her mouth. "I need to run. I'm so glad you came, even though we didn't have much time." His kiss made her consider skipping her math test during last period. *He needs to get back to work too.*

She slid out of the truck and waved good-bye. He looked a little upset, and she was secretly pleased that he didn't like parting either.

SEVENTEEN

Cade unloaded three pieces from the stack of lumber in the back of his truck and carried them into the shed where he'd found the dynamite the other day.

It was gone. He stared at the empty spot, wondering if he'd imagined it.

No. I know *it was there.*

In a daze he walked back and forth, unloading more boards as he wondered where the dynamite had disappeared to.

Did they move it so I wouldn't find it?

What are they planning to do with it?

Why do I care?

He repeated the last phrase ten times in his head. Whatever Tom McDonald did on his property was none of Cade's business. He was here to work. He got paid well, and he enjoyed seeing the buildings slowly come together. It was rewarding to see the results of his labors. Chip had mentioned they'd pour the foundation for another bunkhouse next week. To Cade that was confirmation that they had more work for him. It was good money. More than he'd ever made, and he'd be damned if he was going to screw it up.

He dropped a board into place, spun around to grab another from his truck, and nearly ran into Tom McDonald.

McDonald blocked the entrance to the shed, his large girth silhouetted by the bright sky behind him. Cade stepped aside, assuming McDonald needed to get into the shed. McDonald didn't move, and Cade couldn't see his eyes with the sky behind him. He automatically glanced behind the big man, looking for his ever-present duo of . . . bodyguards? Lackeys? Monkeys? McDonald was alone for once. Cade squinted and blocked the daylight with one hand, bringing McDonald's face into focus.

"Excuse me, sir."

McDonald didn't move. "You're a polite kid, Pruitt. I like that. Not enough people have manners these days."

"Thank you, sir." Cade didn't care if McDonald called him a kid. McDonald could call him whatever he wanted as long as he kept paying him.

"I was just looking at your work on the bunkhouse. It's solid and clean. I like that. I'm glad I listened when you were recommended." McDonald continued to stare at him.

Is this some sort of test?

"Thank you again, sir. I like the work."

"You've got a good work ethic." McDonald nodded. "Wish more people around here had that. You finish in one day what it takes both Chip and Mitch to do."

I'd wondered if anyone would notice that.

Cade eyed McDonald with a little more respect. The man had been paying attention. Truthfully, Cade hadn't seen him around the ranch that much and had wondered how he kept his finger on the pulse of everything.

"Sometimes you must do jobs you hate," McDonald went on. "But I've always believed in giving one hundred and ten percent no matter how shitty the job is or how much you don't like the people you work with. What's important is how you feel because you did what needed to be done and you did it well." McDonald's eyes were tiny in his bulging, wide face. He always had pink cheeks, but today they seemed more red. His breathing was heavy. Understandable from the effort it must take to move his bulky weight. But he wasn't a slacker, he was always moving and giving orders.

Cade felt sweat under his armpits. *What is he getting at? Is he angry about something?*

"Did I do something wrong, sir?"

McDonald's face lit up. "Oh no, boy. You've done good. I couldn't be more pleased. I just wanted to hear your impressions of the FBI visit."

"Oh." More sweat. "They had a photo and asked if I knew him."

"Did you?"

Cade held eye contact with the large man. "I thought I'd seen him around, but I wasn't certain. Not enough to say I knew him."

A thoughtful look came into McDonald's eyes, and he evaluated Cade's words for a long five seconds. "He worked around here a bit. It didn't pan out and I let him go. I don't know what he was doing at that farm with the fire . . . Maybe he was sleeping in the barn. I don't think he had another place to go after I fired him." His eyes seemed to darken. "The FBI doesn't need to know he worked here. Sometimes I don't keep the best employment records."

Cade grabbed the excuse in relief. "Understandable, sir."

"Sometimes it's best for an employee if I just pay them under the table. I hate to see the government take more taxes than it deserves."

"That's decent of you."

"Our government takes more of everything than it should. Where does all that money go? They wouldn't give me a handout when I needed it. How much tax do they need to build and maintain our roads? That's all I need from them. Something to drive on."

Cade nodded. He'd heard the refrain all his life. He didn't necessarily agree with it, although he did hate to see that chunk taken out of his paycheck every other week.

Is he offering to pay me under the table?

Discomfort made him shuffle his feet. That wasn't a road he wanted to start down. He wanted to build a good work history and stay on the right side of the law—all of it.

"Don't understand why it takes so many bureaucrats to build something as simple as roads," continued McDonald. "That's where a lot of our taxes go—paying unnecessary people. Same thing with the police around here. They don't work for us; they work for the government and are restricted to enforcing a lot of stupid laws that no one wants. We're capable of policing ourselves; we know what's right and wrong. We don't need a lot of politicians deciding that for us."

His stare seemed to penetrate Cade's skull. *Am I supposed to agree?* Instead he kept his mouth shut. *When in doubt, say nothing.*

McDonald continued to stare at him, and Cade felt sweat trickle down his side. Then a big grin cracked the man's face. "Smart one, aren't you? I like that you keep your mouth shut even though your eyes say you don't quite agree with me. Shows you're capable of listening."

"Everyone is entitled to their opinion. I try to respect that."

"Good." His gaze was thoughtful as he studied Cade. "I'll see what I can do to find you some other tasks around here. Maybe some more responsibility. But if those FBI agents or any other cops show up, you let me know. We don't have to answer any of their questions. They're just being nosy. The government hasn't liked me for a long time because I don't put up with their shit. They take every opportunity to hassle me. Something tells me this is just the beginning. I left Idaho because things were getting too complicated. I'd like to avoid that here."

"Not a problem." *More responsibility? Is he trying to bribe me? Keep me quiet?*

What if he finds out my girlfriend's aunt works for the FBI?

Cade felt a touch of dizziness as the thought struck him. Was he already lying to his boss by not telling him about Kaylie's aunt Mercy?

What if he already knows and this is one big test?

His gut went liquid and his knees buckled slightly. He continued to hold McDonald's eye contact, but inside he was ready to collapse, and he wondered if his sweat was visible through his shirt.

McDonald slapped him on the shoulder. "See you around, Pruitt." He squeezed Cade's shoulder, turned around, and left, the shed suddenly brighter inside because the doorway was no longer blocked. Cade took two steps and leaned his back against the wall, then bent over and rested his hands on his thighs. He fought back the urge to vomit.

Did I just fail his test?

Now what?

I've got to keep Kaylie away from here.

Mercy recognized her brother from the back as he talked to Rose. Rose sat in a booth at the diner, her face turned up to Owen as he stood at her table. Mercy paused, not wanting to intrude, but then she saw *a look* cross Rose's face and she stepped closer, blatantly eavesdropping.

Her last discussion with Owen was fresh in her mind. *Discussion* was a kind word for the way he'd spoken to her, and she didn't care to rehash any of their conversation, but the expression on Rose's face overrode her caution. Since she'd returned to Eagle's Nest, Mercy had discovered she'd walk through fire for any member of her family. Even Owen.

The distaste in Rose's expression kept her feet moving forward.

" . . . both think it's the right thing to do," Owen was saying firmly to Rose.

"You're out of your mind," answered Rose.

"He's a really nice guy. I met him yesterday for the first time, and I think you'd like him."

"You've met a guy once and you're ready to marry me to him? Christ, Owen. Do you know how many things are wrong with what you just said to me?"

"Marry?" Mercy couldn't stay back any longer. Relief filled Rose's face as she heard her sister's voice, and Owen spun around.

"Maybe you can talk some sense into Owen," Rose said. "He and Dad are desperate to find me a husband."

"*A husband?*" Mercy whirled on Owen. "You think she needs a *husband?*"

Owen's chin shot up and he squared his stance. "She's pregnant."

"So what?"

"It's the right thing to do."

"What century are you living in?"

Anger shot from his eyes, and Mercy looked away to Rose. "You're not having any of this, right?"

"Hell no."

"She needs someone—"

"Are you listening to yourself?" Mercy said. "Do you know anyone more capable or stronger than Rose? She can do anything!"

"You don't understand," he started to say.

"I understand just fine," Mercy retorted. "You think a woman needs a man to take care of her. Yes, it's wonderful when two people fall in love and start a life together, but jeez, Owen, you don't *force* it to happen!"

"Mom and Dad are getting older. They aren't going to be able to take care—"

"Stop right there." Mercy held up a hand. "Who takes care of who? From what I've seen, Rose takes care of everyone at that house. The only thing she can't do is drive." She looked closely at her brother. "Have you forgotten we grew up together? Did Rose ever let her lack of sight stop her from *anything?*"

"It's a different world now," he argued. "She needs a male protector in her home. We all need to be able to defend ourselves."

"Then teach her how. Frankly, I don't know what there is to teach her." She looked at Rose, surprised she couldn't see steam coming out of her sister's ears. "You've done every self-defense class you could get your hands on, right?"

"Absolutely."

"It didn't keep her safe two months ago!" Owen snapped.

Silence filled the diner.

"See?" Owen lowered his voice. "You know I'm right. She's vulnerable."

"Did you forget it was your *friend* who attacked her?" Mercy hissed. "I wouldn't trust any man you recommend. Your track record stinks. And you're recommending a guy you just met? How do you know he's not a wife-beating asshole? Your protective instinct is screwing with your judgment." She glared. "Or maybe it's not. Maybe that's what you truly believe . . . that any man is better than none."

"Can I say something?" Sarcasm filled Rose's tone.

Both Owen and Mercy looked at her.

"You're both overreacting and both trying to protect me in your own way. Get over it. I'm perfectly capable of speaking for myself. Owen, give it up. Don't *ever* talk to me about men again. Mercy, settle down. I can fight my own battles."

Mercy took a deep breath and pressed her lips together, determined not to speak. Rose was right. It was as if they were children again and Rose were taking her siblings to task for trying to ease her way. She'd always been capable of getting things done; she didn't need Mercy to defend her.

But sweet Lord above, it's damn hard to keep my mouth shut.

Mercy eyed Owen and saw he was fighting the same battle. Recognition flowed between their gazes. Rose didn't need the two of them for anything.

"Sorry, Rose," Owen mumbled. "I feel like I'm a teenager trying to protect my little sister again."

"No more husband talk," she ordered.

"Agreed," Owen said gruffly, looking as if he'd just agreed to never eat red meat again. "But the baby—"

"*Owen!*"

He wisely said no more.

"I can't wait to meet my new niece or nephew," Mercy said. "You're going to have more help than you know what to do with."

Owen said his good-byes and strode out of the diner. Mercy slid into the booth across from Rose, enjoying the flush of color on Rose's cheeks. *She's going to be an awesome mother.* Fear still struck Mercy when she thought about Rose having the baby of her rapist. But the moments of fear were outnumbered by her moments of pride in her sister. She knew people would talk behind Rose's back, but if Mercy got wind of it, they'd never utter a word again.

If they treated Rose's innocent child any differently because of who its father had been, they would have Aunt Mercy to deal with. If anything was left after Mother Rose handled them.

"Owen is different," Rose said. "He's always been overprotective, but I've never heard him so angry before."

"He was angry with you?"

"No, it's not directed at me, but I hear it in the way he says his words. It's like he needs to vent . . . get a million things off his chest. It's been like that since Levi died. He hasn't been the same."

"I know." *But I don't really know. I didn't have time to get to know Owen again before Levi died.* "I still carry a lot of guilt about that," Mercy whispered, suddenly overwhelmed by images of her murdered brother.

"Don't," ordered Rose. "It had nothing to do with you."

"I know," Mercy repeated, lying for the second time. *But it will always feel that way.*

"Hello, ladies!" Ina Smythe, Barbara Johnson, and Sandy from the bed-and-breakfast greeted the sisters, and Mercy slid over in the huge booth to make room. A few seconds later Pearl showed up and took the last bit of room in the booth. Mercy was silent as she let the conversation flow around her. Rose had invited her to join the small group of women who met every few weeks to chat and gossip. It sounded self-serving, but they also discussed who in the town needed help. The hidden power of the town sat at the table, Mercy suddenly realized. These women knew everyone, knew about their situations, and were driven to help. Since Mercy had joined the group, they'd raised money for school supplies and clothes for a young family. They'd also supplied three weeks of dinners when Sarah Browne's husband died.

Families were their priority.

"How's that baby treating you?" Sandy asked with an envious look in her eyes. Mercy didn't know why the tall redhead wasn't married and didn't have children. She had one of the most nurturing personalities Mercy had ever encountered. It was perfect for running her business.

"I'm feeling great," said Rose with her usual sweet smile. "Lots of energy."

This answer triggered mutters from Ina, Pearl, and Barbara. "I was exhausted from day one," said Pearl. "With both kids. And it didn't go away until they left for school."

Ina and Barbara nodded emphatically.

Mercy glanced at the time, knowing she couldn't spare more than just a few minutes with the group before heading back to her office.

"Celie Eckham says her son, Jason, needs a job," Sandy said. "Anyone have any leads?" She looked around the table hopefully.

"I heard Tom McDonald is hiring," Barbara said. "But it's a bit of a drive out to his place."

Mercy was instantly alert. "I've met Tom," she said casually. "What's he hiring people to do?"

Her old high school English teacher frowned. "I think he's looking for construction workers. I overheard someone say he's planning to house quite a few hands eventually."

"Does he have some herds? What's he raising?" Mercy asked.

Barbara raised a brow at Ina, who shook her head and scowled. "I don't know and I don't like him," said Ina. "Let's not send anyone out his way. Young Jason can find a job somewhere else." She looked at Mercy. "I don't know what he's got going on out there. He's only been in town for a year or so. Him and the guys who moved out there with him."

"Why don't you like him?" Ina Smythe knew everyone, and Mercy trusted her judgment of character. That she didn't like someone was a big black mark in Mercy's book.

The older woman thought for a moment. "I was in line behind him at the grocery store. He berated the poor checkout clerk, who was doing nothing wrong. Rudeness is uncalled for. When I ran into him on the street, my Scout growled at him and tried to hide behind my legs. Scout likes everyone, and I trust that dog's instinct."

Mercy didn't know what to say.

"You can't go by a dog's opinion," Barbara countered. "I'm sure Tom McDonald's money is as green as anyone else's. Sometimes you have to do a job you hate to pay the bills. Celie says Jason barely gets off the couch and eats junk food while watching TV all day long. It's wearing on her, not to mention expensive."

"He needs a swift kick in the tush," Ina stated. "Celie's never been one to discipline her boys. Now look at them."

"What brought McDonald to the area?" Mercy asked, wanting to know more about the man. She knew from research on McDonald that he'd bought the ranch a year ago and had spent most of his squeaky-clean, law-abiding life in northern Idaho. His record was disappointingly dull. As she'd studied his driver's license picture on her computer, she'd thought he looked good for his seventy years of age, but some people are gifted with good genes. He'd also never married or had children; maybe that was the key to looking young. Most of the women at the table would probably agree.

The women exchanged more looks among them. No one seemed to know the answer to Mercy's question.

"I heard he had a falling out with a neighbor in Idaho," Pearl finally said in a quiet voice.

"That must have been some argument if he moved to another state," observed Mercy.

"It was Silas Campbell."

"Oh!" Mercy straightened in her seat. Silas Campbell was one of the FBI's most watched militia leaders in the West. He'd spent some time in prison back in the eighties but had walked the straight and narrow for a long time. The men who'd followed him were another story. *Does that mean McDonald favors or is against his views? Why was that not in his file?* She would have noticed if Silas Campbell had been listed as a known associate.

"Oh, phooey on that!" said Ina. "It's all rumors. I'm more concerned that Scout doesn't like him. And why hasn't he ever been married? That tells me a lot about his character right there."

Nods went around the table.

"I'm not married," blurted Mercy. "What's that say about me? Or about Sandy and Rose?"

Ina reached across the table and patted her hand. "Give it a little more time, honey. You're next." Her faded eyes were kind, and beside her Barbara Johnson beamed.

"Wait a minute. Don't be marrying me off so soon. I *like* being single. It'll take a hell of a lot to make me give up my independence."

"Picking the right man will protect your independence, dear," said Barbara. "And we think the man you've chosen won't change a thing about you."

They've been talking about me?

Of course they have.

Mercy fumed and looked to Sandy, who sat silently with a big grin on her face. Rose had the same expression. *They're just happy the attention isn't on them.*

"Nothing is set," argued Mercy. "We barely know each other. We haven't even—"

She snapped her lips closed. *Said I love you.*

Ina tipped her head and studied Mercy. "It'll come. Truman has the patience of a saint. He knows what he's doing."

"What's he doing?" muttered Mercy, feeling as if a spotlight were shining on her face. The focused attention of the women made her armpits dampen.

"He's waiting for you to see what's right in front of your face, dear. A good, steady man."

More nods.

Mercy studied each woman in turn. *They're serious.*

She swallowed, feeling trapped.

Is that what Truman is doing?

EIGHTEEN

Cade couldn't sleep.

Lying on his back, he tucked his arms under his head and stared at his ceiling in the dark.

He kept reliving his conversation with Tom McDonald, wondering if he'd answered appropriately.

Why do I care what he thinks?

Because he needed the money from the job. Right now he was willing to look the other way and say whatever it took to keep the money coming in. Last week he'd put in ten hours of overtime at time and a half, and McDonald hadn't even blinked. At this rate he'd have enough for a down payment on that new truck before Christmas.

But what about Joshua Pence?

Was it wrong to keep his mouth shut?

Mercy Kilpatrick's determined face at the McDonald ranch popped into his head.

He didn't have any information to help her case. He felt bad that Pence had died, but that didn't mean he could help find who'd killed him.

He sat up and threw off the covers. Standing up, he started to pace his room, nervous energy flowing through every nerve. An overwhelming urge to go for a drive with the windows down hit him. He wanted to feel the cold night air whip across his face.

Maybe Kaylie . . .

No. There was no way she'd meet him.

He paced some more, knowing that if he got in his truck, he'd find himself outside her aunt's place.

Don't do it.

He grabbed his phone and called her. He listened to it ring, wishing he could FaceTime her, but knowing she wouldn't appreciate that in the middle of the night.

"Cade?" her sleepy voice sounded in his ear. "Is everything okay?"

"Just wanted to hear your voice." It was true. Hearing her speak had instantly calmed his nerves and quieted his brain.

"What are you doing?" She sounded more awake now.

"Trying to go to sleep, but I want to take a drive."

She made a small sound. "I can't meet you," she whispered.

"I know. I just have a lot of energy, and I miss our late-night meetings. I think I got used to them."

Her soft laugh made his stomach warm. "I miss them too. Although it's much easier to get up in the morning now. And you saw me during lunch today."

"It's not the same."

"I agree."

They were silent for a long moment as he fumbled for the words to explain how much he missed her without sounding like a lovelorn idiot. "I miss you," he said, knowing it conveyed only a fraction of the emotion he felt.

"I do too. Are you going back to sleep?"

He wasn't. "I don't know. I'm wide awake."

"I might be jealous if I know you're out driving in the night without me. How lame is that?"

"Very. But I understand. It's our thing." He didn't tell her that he liked that she was jealous.

"We'll think of something new. We both knew we couldn't keep that up for very long. It was so hard the next day."

"Are you going to hate me if I tell you I'm going for a drive? I don't think I can go back to sleep."

She was silent for a moment. "Don't come over here."

"I won't. I promise." He ended the call and got dressed, feeling oddly hollow, and knew a drive wouldn't fill the empty pit in his stomach.

◆　◆　◆

"I'll be right there," Truman said in a sleepy voice, and Ben knew he'd woken his boss.

This time Ben had notified Truman before responding to a midnight prowler call.

"I'm covered. I called Deschutes County to back me up," said Ben. "A month ago I would have gone on my own, but after last time—"

"I'm coming," stated Truman. "We need to put a stop to these fires. I don't care if the prowler turns out to be a deer. From here on out I want multiple cars at each late-night call."

Relief swept over Ben. He'd felt like a wuss calling county *and* his boss, but Truman was right. They had a killer to catch, and nights were his prime operating time.

Tonight's call was a report about dirt bike noise behind the Cowler property. Ben knew exactly where he'd find the noise makers. Next to the creek bed that created the north property line of the Cowler farm stood an abandoned tractor shed. At one point it'd housed various pieces of the Cowlers' equipment, but since the Cowler patriarch had died in the early nineties, the shed had stood empty and slowly fallen apart, board by board. All that stood now was a framework of old timbers, waiting to collapse on some teenage head. Ben had responded to a half dozen calls about teens drinking in the location over the last two decades. He'd asked the Cowler family to tear down the structure, but their last response had been that someone would deserve a beam to the head for trespassing.

The shed was isolated, hidden in a small copse of trees next to a dry creek that came alive during the fall and spring months. Adjacent to the old shed was a field with naturally formed jumps and ramps that dirt bike riders couldn't stay away from. The noise of the dirt bikes couldn't be heard at the Cowler house, but if the wind was blowing from the east, their neighbors could hear the bike engines. They were the ones who had called the police tonight.

Ben turned off his headlights and took the dirt road that wound its way to the back of the Cowler property. It was a cold and clear night with stars that looked unnaturally close and a partial moon that aided the officers with its faint light. When the road widened a few hundred yards in, he pulled over and waited for Truman. He lowered his window and smiled as he heard the faint whine of a dirt bike. Whoever it was, he was still there.

Checking the clock, Ben saw it was just after midnight. His breath showed in the cold air flowing in through his window, but he didn't want to raise the glass. As long as he could hear the bike, he knew they would catch their trespassers. He radioed for the county cars to set up camp at the bridge that crossed the creek north of the shed, effectively cutting off an escape route. The bikers' only choices would be to ride either straight toward Ben or up the creek toward the county units.

A louder engine sounded behind him, and he spotted the outline of Truman's Tahoe in his rearview mirror. He'd also turned off his headlights. Ben stepped out of his vehicle and walked up as Truman lowered his driver's window.

"I hear 'em," said Truman. "See anything?"

"I spotted the headlight of one for a few brief seconds. Sounds like there are two bikes. Probably racing."

"County says they've got the north end covered if they decide to make a run for it."

"No place else for them to go. Unless they plan to plow through fences."

"That might work in our favor," Truman joked. "Ready?"

"Waiting on you." Ben headed back to his vehicle. He pulled back into the road, pleased that Truman waited for him to lead. Any other boss would have taken the point, but Truman had no problem letting Ben go first. It made sense; Ben knew the area best. But for some men, ego would have demanded they go first. Not Truman.

It was one of the reasons Ben liked him so much.

His tires made nearly no sound on the packed dirt. He pulled up to the edge of the trees and parked. Here the engine noises were louder, and he could hear laughter. Female laughter. *Could it simply be teens fooling around?*

Disappointment filled the back of his throat. He'd wanted to catch their killer.

Truman was suddenly right beside Ben's door, and Ben realized with a start he'd been sitting in his seat, letting his mind wander.

"I hear women," Ben said as he quietly shut his door.

"I hear them too," Truman said grimly. He gestured for Ben to lead the way, and followed.

Ben stepped carefully. The ground was a mix of packed dirt, ruts, and tall grass tufts that could easily trip a person.

"What's that?" Truman asked in a hushed voice.

Ben looked up from the ground at the light that'd suddenly filled the copse of trees. "Fire. They just lit something."

"Shit." Truman started to jog, and Ben took off after him.

Music filled the night. A Southern rock anthem that Ben had heard for the last thirty years but whose title he'd never bothered to learn. Happy whoops and female laughter sounded over the music. It'd become a party.

As they reached the clearing, Ben spotted the silhouettes of two women dancing in front of the burning remains of the Cowler shed. They both had beers in hand, and ten feet away two guys sat on the ground by the dirt bikes, watching the women dance. A rifle leaned against a tree stump a good twenty feet from the men. Ben automatically scanned the foursome for more weapons and rested his hand on the butt of his gun.

"Eagle's Nest Police Department," Truman yelled as they approached, his hand near his weapon.

One woman gave a small screech and dropped her beer, but they both froze with their hands raised. The guys instantly stood and raised their hands, their feet planted. Ben didn't see how it happened, but the music went silent.

Good.

The flickering light from the burning frame of the shed cast odd shadows across the faces of the foursome. Ben wrinkled his nose, smelling gasoline. He spotted a plastic gas can tossed to one side.

Bingo.

"A little cold for a party, isn't it?" Truman asked. "But I see you decided to provide some heat. You know it's a crime to light someone else's property on fire, right?"

"It's falling down," said one of the women. "We're doing them a favor."

"Did you ask first?" questioned Truman.

Silence.

"We aren't doing anything illegal," said one of the guys. "We're just having a little fun."

"To start with, you're trespassing," said Ben. "And burning private property."

"And I happen to know that you two aren't twenty-one," said Truman, nodding at both men. "How about the rest of you? Is anyone here of drinking age?"

Silence again as the flames crackled in the background.

"Know them?" Ben asked in an aside to Truman.

"Yep. Caught both of these guys drinking and shooting earlier in the week. Jason Eckham and Landon Hecht. Don't know the girls."

"Is that a knife on the second guy's belt?" Ben murmured. "We've got dirt bikes, a gas can, the fire, and a knife."

"Radio Deschutes County to get in here," ordered Truman. "And the fire department."

Ben scanned the young faces. *Was their killer standing in front of them?*

NINETEEN

Could I see him shooting a cop?

Hell yes.

Mercy had been in the room with Landon Hecht for sixty seconds.

The young man slouching in a chair across the table from Mercy gave off enough disdain to fill a football stadium. He was all sharp angles. Pointy elbows and chin and shoulders. Even his eyes seemed sharp—not in an intelligent way, but in an angry way. As if the world were out to get him and he was constantly on the edge of striking back. The contempt he directed at her and Truman told her he wasn't the sharpest tool in the shed; most people at least pretended to give officers respect. Especially in an interview room. If he'd shot the deputies, he did it on a whim, she decided, not because he'd planned some elaborate scheme. He didn't seem to be the type who thought further ahead than two hours. Or one.

Truman had called her an hour ago and said he was delivering four subjects to the Deschutes County Sheriff's Office for questioning. When she'd found out he'd caught them at the scene of a fire with dirt bikes and weapons, she'd leaped out of bed. Now Eddie was questioning the other male subject in a different interview room, and the two female subjects were talking separately with county detectives. Truman leaned casually against the wall in the interview room with her and Landon, keeping quiet as she decided how to get Landon to open up.

The county deputies had taken his rifle, a lighter, and a knife big enough to slaughter a horse.

Not unusual items to carry in Central Oregon.

Mercy knew her father and brothers had carried the same sort of gear. In fact, she carried the same in her emergency pack. Except for the rifle. She kept hers in a safe in her apartment.

"I understand you already got in trouble this week for alcohol possession," she stated.

Landon threw a glare at Truman. "Yeah."

"Seems to me like a rational person would wait until they were twenty-one."

This time the glare was aimed at her. "It's a stupid law."

"A lot of people would agree with you, but the fines alone keep most of them in line. They can hurt the wallet."

Landon shrugged.

"You were trespassing for the second time too."

"Are you here to remind me about what I've done this week? Because my memory's pretty good," Landon said. "Did you hear I ate at Burger King three times?"

"How do you eat out so much when you don't have a job?"

"I get money."

Mercy waited, but Landon didn't take the bait. He leaned back in his chair, tucked his hands behind his head, and held her gaze.

Creep.

He injected a sexual predator vibe into his stare that made Mercy want to shower. Behind her she heard Truman shift his stance. No doubt Landon's creeper aura was affecting him too.

"What's an FBI agent doing here in the middle of the night?" Landon asked. When she'd first introduced herself, he hadn't blinked at her title, but it seemed to have finally sunk into his skull that being interviewed by the FBI wasn't the norm.

"The county sheriff is a little shorthanded," Mercy replied.

"Huh," was his response.

"Are the two girls good friends of yours?" she asked.

"Just met them tonight. They were at the 7-Eleven when we stopped to buy—" His lips slapped shut.

"That wasn't very smart of them to leave with guys they'd just met," Mercy observed, purposefully passing up the chance to ask him if he had a fake ID to buy alcohol.

Landon grinned. "They wanted to party."

Mercy sent up a silent prayer that Kaylie used better decision-making skills.

"How often do you ride dirt bikes?" Mercy asked, changing the subject.

Landon rubbed his hands on his thighs as he thought, pointy elbows poking the fabric of his plaid shirt. "More during the summer. We took them out tonight because Jason wanted to test the new brakes on his. Usually we have our trucks, but since the weather was clear it seemed like a good time."

"I assume you take them off road usually?"

"Yep."

"Where do you like to go?"

He thought. "There's good riding back of the old gravel pit place. And around the Smalls's farm. They don't care if we ride back there," he added quickly.

"Do you always ride with friends?"

"Usually. Kinda boring by myself."

"I understand you were target shooting when you were arrested the other night." She jumped to another subject.

"Yeah." The gaze darted to Truman again.

"You a good shot?"

"Not bad."

"Better than your friends?"

"Lots better." He grinned.

"You have contests with them?"

"All the time. I usually kick their butts."

"Rifle or pistol?"

"Both," he said with pride. "I'm better with the rifle. I have three-hundred-yard targets set up at my place, and I practice all the time."

Mercy made a mental note to add the shells from Landon's home-made firing range to the warrant that was currently being written up to search his home for his weapons. She slid a piece of paper across the table. "These are the weapons that are registered to you. Does this list everything you have?" The FBI was especially interested in one of the rifles.

He leaned forward and studied it, his head hanging over the document. It took forever for him to read it, and she wondered about his reading skills. It listed three rifles and two pistols. He should have been able to verify that with one glance.

"That's everything." He shoved the paper back at her.

"Nothing else? Maybe a gun a friend gave you or a relative passed on?"

"Nope. That first rifle on the list was a gift from my uncle. We did it by the book." His smug look made her skin crawl.

Mercy nodded and changed the topic again. "Do you always carry gasoline with you?"

"The tank on my bike doesn't hold much. Better to be safe than sorry."

"So it was simply convenient to set the Cowler shed on fire."

"I didn't plan it, if that's what you're asking."

"Why did you light it?"

He shrugged again and looked away.

"Your friend says you have a thing for fire," she lied. She hadn't heard anything from the other interviews. But he'd sat alone in this room for nearly an hour before she'd entered. He'd had plenty of time to wonder what was being said in the other rooms.

Landon sat up straight. "He's a liar."

"Know anything about a fire on Clyde Jenkins's property? Someone lit his burn pile in the middle of the night two weeks ago." Mercy mentioned a fire that hadn't been a source of gossip. Since Clyde had waited several days to report it, the only people who knew about it were the police, as far as she knew.

Landon ducked his head to the side, a sly grin on his face. "It was a burn pile. Nothing illegal about that. They're supposed to be burned."

One fire admitted. Two including tonight's.

"Who was with you that night?"

The ceiling suddenly became very interesting to the young man. "Jason was there," he said as he stared at the tiles in the ceiling. "The usual group. Finn. Cade." He glanced behind her at Truman. "Same people as the other night."

Mercy held her breath. *The night Kaylie was with them?*

"The night at the gravel pit?" Truman asked.

"Yeah."

"The girl too? The one I took home?"

"Yeah, she was into it," he sneered. "Don't let her age fool you. She leads Cade around by the nose."

All speech left Mercy's brain. *Kaylie?* She couldn't think of another question.

"Who was with you the night you lit up the dumpster?" Truman asked.

"Nothing happened with that," Landon pointed out. "The fire was contained by the dumpster. It was perfectly safe to light."

"Who?" repeated Truman.

"Just Finn."

Mercy's brain came back online. "I don't have Finn's last name." *Three fires admitted.*

"Gaylin," said Truman.

Does he believe these fires are no big deal? She studied the young man. He seemed to thrive on the attention from her and Truman, and every time he admitted to having set a fire, his ego seemed to get a boost. He sat straighter, smiled more, exuded more confidence.

Reel him in slowly. Don't think about Kaylie right now.

It was a giant effort to put the teen out of her mind. Mercy kept picturing Kaylie as one of the people described by Clyde Jenkins, a teen dashing through his orchard and laughing. Then she remembered the dirty footprints on her kitchen floor. Evidence the girl had been outside. If it'd happened once, it'd probably happened a few times.

She focused on the man in front of her. The cocky creeper. She smiled at him, and his returning smile made acid rise in the back of her throat. She shuffled through the small stack of papers in front of her until she found a police report. "What about the old car on Robinson Street?"

The smile broadened. "I did its owner a service. They shoulda got insurance money for that. The stupid thing hadn't moved in months."

"It wasn't insured," Truman said. Mercy heard the barely leashed anger in his tone. "The owner had to pay to have it hauled away after that. It *cost* them money."

Landon's face fell ever so slightly. "That's a bummer."

Does he think he's some sort of Robin Hood?

"You know the Parkers lost a lot of supplies in their fire," Mercy said. "They'd worked hard to prep and save. It might take them a few years to catch back up."

"Stupid preppers," Landon said. "They think they're better than everyone else. All self-righteous like they're the only ones living the correct way. Nothing wrong with shopping at Walmart."

Mercy cocked her head. It wasn't an admission, but Landon definitely held a grudge. "You know Steve Parker?" Her heart still hurt for the young family.

"No." Landon looked away.

"Sounded like you did."

"I know the type. They can squeeze blood out of a turnip."

"And? Is there something wrong with being thrifty?"

"They're not going to help anyone if it all goes to shit. It's all about protecting themselves. Fucking elitists."

I've never been called an elitist before.

"So you think they should share their supplies with others if we get decimated by a natural disaster."

"Everyone should help each other," Landon said piously.

"How are you prepared to help?"

"I can work. I can do whatever is needed. I'll help out wherever someone needs me."

I'd like to see you when you're cold, wet, tired, and hungry. Take away your TV, beer, and fast food, and we'd see the real person underneath. Desperate, savage, and cruel.

Mercy leaned forward, resting her folded arms on the table. "How about you start preparing now and—"

"I think we're going off topic," Truman stated. "What *do* you know about the fire at the Parkers', Landon?"

She sat back in her chair, biting her tongue, which wanted to lecture.

"I don't know nothin' about that one."

Liar.

"Do you know where you were the Wednesday before last?" Mercy threw out the question, ready to hear his excuses about the fire that Ben Cooley had put out. And the murder of Joshua Pence.

Landon thought. "On Wednesdays we usually go bowling."

"But did you last week?"

"Yeah, I remember now. I slaughtered everyone." The confidence was back.

"How late do you bowl? Do you do anything after?"

"We're done by eleven. Then I went home." He looked expectantly from Mercy to Truman.

"Anyone at home with you?"

"My mom," he admitted. A frown crossed his face. "Why are you asking about that night? Nothing happened that—" His face cleared and his eyes widened. "That was the night they found that guy with his neck slashed!" He sat up straight in his seat. "I didn't have nothing to do with that! Just because someone started a fire doesn't mean it was me!"

Truman's hands were sweating.

Mercy had neatly questioned Landon Hecht, jumping from topic to topic, feeding his ego, and keeping him talking.

But everything about the young man had changed once he realized they were looking at him for the fire where Joshua Pence had been murdered.

Truman discreetly wiped his palms on his jeans. *That wasn't the reaction I'd hoped for.*

He was a pretty good judge of character and was certain that Landon Hecht was lazy, full of himself, a liar, and an idiot. But he wasn't lying about the Pence fire.

"You just told me you started the fire in the dumpster, the vehicle, and tonight's fire," Mercy stated calmly. "But you weren't at the fire last Wednesday? That seems odd."

"*I wasn't there!*" Landon half stood, his hands on the table, terror in his voice. "Sure, I might have had something to do with some other fires, but I didn't kill *no one!*"

Mercy was silent.

"*I didn't!*"

"Sit down," Truman ordered. "We heard you."

"Did you know Joshua Pence?" Mercy asked.

Truman heard the subtle change in her tone; she believed Landon's claim.

Are we following the wrong lead?

"No. Never heard of him until they said on the news he was the one murdered that night." Landon wiped the moisture on his upper lip. He'd gone from being a cool customer to squirming and sweating in less than fifteen seconds. His gaze shot from Mercy to Truman and back again.

"And I didn't set the fire the night the two deputies were shot! I didn't kill no one!"

"But you're now our local fire starter," Mercy said. "You've just admitted setting several of them. And you're a crack shot with the rifle. I assume you heard the deputies were shot from quite a distance?"

"It wasn't me!" Landon looked ready to vomit.

Truman grabbed the trash can in the corner and set it next to Landon's chair. The young man glanced gratefully at it, and his Adam's apple bobbed as he swallowed hard. Truman could smell his body odor.

"Then where were you when the two deputies were murdered?" Mercy asked, emphasizing the last word.

"I don't know." Landon's gaze bounced around the room. "But I wasn't *there.* Give me a minute to remember." His breathing had sped up, and he continually wiped his temples and upper lip.

A small twinge of sympathy touched Truman's chest. A *very* small twinge. *He's still a menace.* He didn't believe Landon was a murderer, but he was guilty of breaking a number of laws and needing a kick in the ass. He wished he could see the expression on Mercy's face, because it was making Landon squirm like a restless toddler.

"Do you want to tell us again who was with you the night you lit Clyde Jenkins's burn pile?" Truman asked. He'd seen Mercy's shoulders tense and Landon's gaze turn conniving as he claimed Kaylie was there.

Landon looked away. "Jason and me. And some girl Jason was trying to impress. I don't remember her name. Jason can tell you."

"Why'd you claim other people were there?" Truman asked.

A childish and sour look crossed his face, but Landon was silent.

"You think Cade and Kaylie called me that night at the gravel pit, don't you? You're trying to get some innocent people in trouble." Truman fumed.

Landon looked anywhere but at Truman.

"Neighbors reported shooting at the pit," Truman said. "No one else. Let's try to keep your answers to the truth, okay? Especially tonight."

He nodded.

Mercy stood up. "I'm going to have a word with Eddie." She shoved in her chair, and Truman followed her out of the room.

"Let him stew for a little while," she said, arching her back. "I needed some fresh air. He was starting to stink."

"I noticed that," said Truman. "I couldn't believe he tried to get Kaylie in trouble."

"He had me going for a few minutes," Mercy admitted. "Thank you for clearing that up. I assume he doesn't know she's my niece?"

"I don't think so. He just knows that I was shocked to find her at the gravel pit that night."

"Jerk."

"Yeah, he's got some problems, but I don't think he pulled the trigger that night the deputies died," Truman admitted.

Mercy slumped against the wall. "I think you're right. He was willing to admit to setting a few fires, but he panicked once he figured out where my line of questioning was going. Could he be involved somehow? I have a hard time believing we suddenly have two people setting fires. Maybe he didn't kill anyone, but was involved in the fire part?"

"I think he would have given up any names he knew. He was quick to throw Kaylie and Cade under the bus for nothing. I can see him instantly ratting out anyone he suspected was involved in the murders."

"True. Maybe some time alone will help him come up with a name."

One of the county detectives came down the hall, a cup of vending machine coffee in his hand. "Those girls aren't going to be of much help," he told Mercy and Truman. "They never met the two men until a few hours ago. They claim they went with the guys because they had beer and bikes. I guess that's the adult equivalent of offering candy to little kids."

"Only for some people," Mercy countered.

"Well, it was enough for these two," said the detective as he took a sip of the coffee. "They thought it was funny when Landon lit the crumbling building on fire, and said they didn't talk to them about any other fires the two men might have started. Do you want to talk to them?"

"That's the same story they told me earlier," said Truman, looking to Mercy. "They were pretty embarrassed to be picked up. I don't need to talk to them again, do you?"

"Not tonight," agreed Mercy.

The detective nodded, muttered something about paperwork and lack of sleep, and then continued down the hall.

Eddie stepped out of the next interview room, annoyance on his face.

"How'd it go?" Mercy asked him.

"According to Jason, Landon likes his lighter a little too much."

"We gathered the same," said Truman. "Did Jason say which fires Landon had set?"

Eddie glanced at his notes. "The car on Robinson Street. A dumpster. The Parker family shed. Clyde Jenkins's burn pile, and he claims tonight was all on Landon too."

"Nice going," Mercy said. "Landon wouldn't outright admit to the Parkers', but he seemed to enjoy telling us about the rest."

"Jason claims he wasn't present the night of the deputies' deaths or the Pence murder."

"He thinks Landon was there?" Truman asked.

"He does."

Mercy straightened. "Did he ask Landon about it?"

"No. He said when he heard about both fires, he instantly knew it had to be Landon but didn't dare talk to him about it."

"Seriously? But he still hung around with the guy?" Truman was disgusted.

"That's what I asked him," said Eddie. "He said he was waiting for Landon to bring it up so Jason could tell the police he'd confessed."

"Bullshit," stated Mercy. Truman agreed.

"He's a coward," said Mercy. "Kaylie told me the guys follow Landon around, and she thinks it's because they're afraid to stand up to him."

"They're afraid of him?" Truman asked. "What do they think he's capable of?"

"I pressed Jason on that," said Eddie. "I asked if Landon had ever threatened him, and he wouldn't give me a clear answer. What I gathered is that Landon is a mean drunk and says threatening crap that keeps people on their toes around him."

"Half the people I know are like that when drunk," said Truman.

"I hear you, but Jason seemed really uncomfortable when I tried to get a clear answer out of him. What was Landon like?"

Mercy said, "Terrified and vehemently vocal that he didn't kill anyone or set those two fires." She paused. "I believed him."

"I did too," added Truman. "But I'm having second thoughts on hearing what Jason had to say."

Frustration filled Mercy's face. "Me too. It could have been fear of being found out that we saw, not fear of being accused of murder."

"We got the warrant signed for the weapons where Landon lives, at his mom's house," Eddie said. "We'll serve it in the morning. Hopefully that will give us some concrete answers."

"It needs to include a search of the target range Landon uses at the house," Mercy added. "If we don't find the weapon we're looking for, we might find evidence that it's been fired at his range."

"Beat you to it. I had it written up to include anything weapon-related." She high-fived him. "First thing in the morning?"

"Yes," said Eddie, who looked to Truman. "You'll be there?"

"You couldn't keep me away."

TWENTY

Early the next morning Mercy watched the evidence techs remove the weapons from Landon's house. Every registered weapon had been accounted for, and Mercy had half expected they'd find a few illegal weapons, but they did not. Landon's mother leaned against a wall and smoked as her steely eyes watched every move. She'd known the officers were coming but had still given them a mouthful of grief when they arrived.

Mercy saw her resemblance to Landon. His mom was incredibly skinny and looked as if she subsisted on cigarettes and dry toast. She worked at the grocery store in Bend, and it took Mercy a moment before she realized she'd rung up Mercy's groceries several times. His mother wasn't a service-with-a-smile checker, but she was fast and efficient and never had to look up the produce codes, which was more important to Mercy than a fake smile.

No recognition had shone in her eyes as she met Mercy that morning.

She'll remember me after this morning. I'll have to go through someone else's checkout line.

"Come look at this," Eddie said to Mercy. After ignoring an angry stare from Landon's mother, she followed him out the back of the house. They walked for several minutes, heading to the far end of the property. Mercy looked up at the gentle hills that bordered the Hecht property. The sun was just peeking over the rise, and she watched her breath float away. The sky was clear, but it was going to stay cold all day.

"How many acres do they have?" Mercy asked.

"About ten."

"Have you found any other outbuildings?"

"Just the big one beside the house. It's got a couple of dirt bikes, quads, and an old truck that hasn't run in over a decade."

"Get copies of the tread patterns from the bikes?"

"All of them."

"Ms. Hecht didn't protest?"

"I know how to turn on the charm. She would have handed over her brand-new iPhone if I'd asked."

Glancing sideways at Eddie and taking in the handsome profile and nice build, Mercy agreed. He was excellent at schmoozing.

"Maybe you could freelance as a gigolo," she said dryly.

"We prefer to be called escorts."

Mercy spotted Truman far ahead, bending over next to a tech and a few Deschutes County deputies. They wore gloves and were picking up shells and tossing them in a bucket. As Mercy drew closer she saw the bucket was nearly full and the ground was still littered with shells. "Jeez. If he'd spent sixty seconds after each practice to clean up after himself, it wouldn't look like this."

"Did you see his bedroom? I doubt the phrase *cleaning up* is in his vocabulary," said Eddie.

She had seen it and was thankful that the techs were responsible for finding the weapons. She would have needed to shower before returning to work.

They reached the others, and Truman handed her a pair of gloves. "Hope your back feels strong this morning."

Mercy eyed the group as they bent and squatted to get the shells. "If I say no, can I just watch?"

"No."

"I'm going to show her the targets," said Eddie. "Then we'll help." He pulled Mercy past the working group and toward another tech who was far downfield, meticulously digging bullets out of wooden targets.

"What about the targets?" she asked.

"Whoever has been shooting here is damn good, and there aren't any shells closer to the targets. They're all back there." He gestured back at Truman and the group.

Mercy looked ahead and then back. Landon's three-hundred-yard claim looked accurate to her. "So Landon wasn't exaggerating about his skills last night."

"Assuming he's the shooter."

"With this many shells, it has to be him or his mother. No one else lives here, right?"

"Nope. And I already asked Mom if anyone else uses their range. She said Landon occasionally has friends over, but it's usually just him."

"He needs a different hobby."

"Or a job," added Eddie.

Mercy's phone rang and she answered as they continued their trek. "Kilpatrick."

"Agent Mercy?" said a female voice.

"Yes."

"This is Tilda Brass."

"Good morning, Tilda. I hope everything is all right?" Mercy stopped walking and gestured for Eddie to continue ahead. He raised a brow at her but kept walking.

"I found that phone number I told you about. I don't know how the piece of paper ended up in this drawer, but if I hadn't been looking for my candy thermometer, I wouldn't have found it for another month. I need to make some divinity for Thanksgiving. I'll make a few more batches when Christmas gets closer."

"What's the number, Tilda?" Mercy wasn't a fan of divinity. Too sweet. But she respected the skill it took to get the candy to set just right.

The woman read off the number, and Mercy punched it into the notes on her phone. "Is there a name?"

"Jack Howell. Is it okay if I call him to let him know I'm reconsidering his offer?"

"Can you wait twenty-four hours? I'll mention you're still interested."

"I hope hearing that the FBI is poking around doesn't make him change his mind," she fretted. "I'm ready to move on."

"Has anything else happened?" Mercy asked sharply.

"No. Nothing has. It just feels like this house is telling me to leave." She cleared her throat. "I hear voices sometimes . . . not as if someone is actually in the house—they're more like echoes of old conversations. And I swear one of my old dogs still wanders around. Last night I could feel him sleeping on my bed like he used to, but when I looked nothing was there."

Mercy didn't know what to say.

"I know. You're thinking that I'm an old woman who shouldn't be living alone."

"No—"

"Well, I am old. And I should set myself up in a safe place while I'm still able to make my own decisions." Her voice fell. "Although I do like thinking that my good Charlie is sticking close. He was always a protective dog."

"I suspect he is," agreed Mercy. "He's watching over you. He'll probably be happy if you're living where there are more people around." She believed the spirit of a beloved pet would hang around a vulnerable owner. Tilda ended the call, and Mercy did a quick Google search on Jack Howell as she jogged to catch up with Eddie.

"He's a real estate agent," she said in surprise as she reached Eddie.

"Who?"

She brought him up-to-date.

"Sounds like you need to find out who his client is," said Eddie. "Unless he's one of those agents who personally buy property as an investment."

"She really should sell," Mercy said. "I don't think she should be living alone."

"Does she need to sell to afford to move?"

"I didn't ask. From our conversations, she implied it."

"Do you want to call and ask who his client is or set up an appointment to talk to him?"

"I'm always about asking first," said Mercy. "Why jump through hoops if people will tell you what you want to know over the phone?"

"I'm always shocked by the personal stuff people tell me," Eddie said. "I'll call to ask a question about a purchase they made and get their life history."

"Every time," Mercy agreed. She dialed the number and the agent answered the phone.

"Jack Howell here!" he said with gusto. "What can I do for you today?"

Mercy identified herself. "Tilda Brass said you were interested in buying her property."

"Brass . . . Brass . . . ," he muttered. "Oh! The spread out east. Oh yes. That's a great piece of land. Way too much for her to handle."

"You know Tilda?" Mercy asked, slightly irked that this stranger had voiced a judgment about the woman.

"I met her twice," he said. "Lovely woman, but she seemed overwhelmed by the amount of land she had to manage."

Such a salesman.

"How big is the property?" Mercy asked. She faintly remembered that her parents had talked in awed tones about how big the property was when her childhood friend lived there, but she'd assumed it'd been sold in parcels and winnowed down over the decades.

"Six hundred acres."

Mercy had to agree with the agent that it was a bit much for one woman to handle. "Who are you representing?"

Jack was silent for a moment. "Are you interested in buying the property?"

"No, I'm interested in who you're representing."

More silence. "Well, my buyer has asked to remain anonymous," he finally said. "I'm sure you can respect that."

Mercy's interest level quadrupled. "Actually, Mr. Howell, I can't. We're investigating the two murders of police officers on the property, so I'm sure you can *respect* that I'd like to know the name of the person who was interested in buying this property before its barn was set on fire."

Listening, Eddie grinned and gestured with his hands for her to keep it up.

"Can I call you back?"

"Have you forgotten the name of your buyer?"

"No . . . I need him to tell me it's all right to tell you his name. He'd been very emphatic about his confidentiality." His earlier gusto had evaporated.

"You do realize I can get a warrant for the information, right? But I'd much rather spend the time working on the deaths of these officers instead of filling out paperwork."

"I understand." Judging by the amount of discomfort in his voice, he was squirming in his seat and reluctant to let his buyer know the FBI was demanding his name. "You're creating an ethical issue for me. When a client asks me to keep—"

"Mr. Howell." Fury filled her. "I don't give a damn about your code of ethics at the moment. I care about finding a killer. I'll give you five minutes to call your client and get back to me." She rattled off her number and ended the call.

"Nice," said Eddie with an admiring grin. "I suspect he's dialing as fast as he can."

"Jerk. Who do you think his client is?"

"I suspect we'll know in five minutes."

They continued to the end of the target range, and Mercy had to agree with Eddie that whoever had used the range was an excellent shot. Five minutes came and went. And then ten.

Mercy called Jack Howell, and the call went to his voice mail. She dialed again with the same results.

She fumed as they traced their steps back to where Truman and the others had just finished picking up the shells.

"Nice timing," he told her as he deliberately stretched his back.

"Sorry." She told him about her phone call with the real estate agent.

"Sounds like you need to pop into his office and have a chat with him," said Truman.

"It'll be my next stop."

Truman shook the door handle of Jack Howell's real estate office. It was a one-man shop, and it appeared the agent had stepped out for a midmorning coffee. He glanced at Mercy; she was ready to strangle someone.

"I left two more messages," Mercy stated. "Clearly he's avoiding me."

"Not for long," Truman said.

"Damn right." She stared at the name on the glass door as she chewed on her lip. Inside they could see two desks, but only one had a computer set up. Flyers advertising homes for sale papered part of the building's windows. The office was a tiny storefront in a small strip mall that also housed a vape shop, a pawn shop, and a Hispanic bakery.

"Hungry?" Truman asked as the smell of fresh pastries reached his nose. He knew the bakery was a good one. He tried to stop by whenever he was on this side of Bend.

"No." Mercy scanned the parking lot, looking frustrated. "I'll get his home address and pay him a visit."

"Why do you think his buyer would want to stay private?" asked Truman.

Clear green eyes met his. "They have something to hide."

"Or maybe they had a bad history with Tilda or her husband and were afraid she wouldn't sell to them," he suggested.

"Could be. But she's been adamant that she doesn't know of anyone who'd burn her barn, so I don't know if there is someone she'd refuse to sell to."

"Are there any financial issues with the property?"

"I don't think so. I know Bill Trek investigated any possible liens and title issues on his end. He said there were no problems." She checked the time and made a sour face. "I need to get back to the office."

"You're not the only one," said Truman. He hesitated, enjoying their time together though they were hunting for a Realtor who clearly didn't want to be found. They'd had too little time together lately and he didn't like it. He took a quick look around the parking lot. Seeing they were alone, he kissed her, a lingering kiss with his hands on her face. She leaned into the embrace and sighed.

"When this is over . . . ," he started.

"We'll find a place to relax. Together," she finished.

He reluctantly let her go, promising to meet up later.

TWENTY-ONE

Tom McDonald watched the woman carry the coffee across the yard as if it were liquid gold, knowing he could easily meet her halfway, but not wanting to. Laurie handed him the mug, and Tom thanked her as if she'd handed him a hundred-dollar bill. Her eyes lit up and she whispered, "You're welcome." She dipped her head and dashed off the front porch of the farmhouse, headed back to the mess hall, where the scent of bacon still hovered outside.

He took a sip of the coffee, watching as she hustled away. Laurie must have noticed that he'd missed breakfast. The drink was hot and dark and bitter. He smiled. He liked that the women on the ranch respected him and tried to anticipate his needs. They kept the mess hall clean and always had hot food ready when needed. The kitchen in his farmhouse had a small refrigerator and microwave, but no working stove or oven. He'd decided funds were best spent building one large, central kitchen. One day when he had more money, he'd get the house's small kitchen up and running, but right now it wasn't a priority. His priority was to create a place where men wanted to live and work.

Food, shelter, and community. These were men's core needs. Provide those three items along with a desirable goal and he'd have plenty of happy followers. He was working hard on getting their shelters built. The bunkhouses were bare bones, but over time he planned to add small houses and more luxuries. The men who stuck with him from the early days would be rewarded first. Newcomers would start in the bunkhouses and see the rewards they could earn if they worked hard.

It would be perfect.

He'd be surrounded by men who would defend him and their way of life against anyone who threatened it. Anyone. No government was going to stick its nose in his business. If it did, soon he would have his men well drilled to fight for the property and their God-given rights.

But he needed more men to form his regiment.

Slowly. Take it slowly. Build up my force with the best.

This wasn't a project to be rushed. He'd do it right.

He took another burning sip and started down the steps to get a late breakfast, hoping that the bacon wasn't gone. Food was expensive. Especially bacon. But soon they'd be producing everything they needed. *Maybe I should start rationing some of the meat.* He'd noticed yesterday that Chip had taken as much bacon as his plate could hold.

This is no place for greed.

A small dust cloud billowed behind a low hill far off to his right, and he stopped to watch. The dust meant a vehicle was coming. A moment later a truck came around the bend, and Tom squinted, not recognizing the heavily built vehicle.

Shit.

The truck had a light bar on top of its cab, and even though it was completely blurred, he recognized the Oregon State Police logo on the side of the vehicle. Tom glanced around, feeling exposed. *Where are Al and Deke?* Usually the two men weren't far from his side, but his morning hadn't officially started, and he insisted they leave him alone until the beginning of his workday.

No doubt they're eating all my bacon.

The truck came closer, and Tom strode over to meet it. By the time he reached the flat parking area, he was panting heavily, and he knew sweat beaded his forehead. The truck was a utility vehicle with a bulky covered back end to store equipment. After the truck parked, a stocky man in his thirties wearing the navy clothes of an OSP officer hopped out. A second officer stayed in the cab, talking on a phone. "Tom McDonald?" asked the first man.

"You found him." Tom held out his hand, and the other man gave it a firm shake. "What can I do for you?"

"Nathan Landau. OSP Arson and Explosives. I understand you've got some dynamite you want us to take off your hands?"

Tom nearly dropped his coffee. "What?"

Nathan frowned. "Dynamite. We got a call that you found some old dynamite and want it off your property."

Sweat ran through his eyebrow and stung his eye. "I didn't call you." He rubbed at the stinging eye. "Who said I called you?"

"You did according to the report, but we don't care where the dynamite came from, you know," the man said carefully. "All we care about is that it's disposed of properly. Old dynamite isn't something to play around with. It's common that people discover boxes of dynamite in Grandpa's barn. They used to sell the stuff in feed stores all the time, but we like to get the call so we can take care of it."

Tom struggled to speak, his mind spinning away from him. "I don't have any dynamite, and I didn't call you. I don't know who told you I had some."

"None?" Nathan was skeptical, lines forming across his forehead. "Maybe someone didn't tell you they found it and called us first."

"There's no dynamite on this property," Tom said from between clenched teeth. *Who called the police?* "I don't need to ask my men. If one of them had found dynamite, they would have let me know. I'm afraid you received a prank call."

"You're shitting me," Nathan pulled out a pen and made notes on his clipboard, shaking his head. "Why in the hell would someone do that?"

"Either they thought it'd be funny to see you waste your time, or they thought it'd be funny to see me get harassed," Tom stated, fury replacing his earlier confusion. "I suspect it's the latter."

Nathan looked up from his clipboard, his eyes narrowing. "Someone getting back at you for something?"

"Something like that."

"You know who? We take false calls like this pretty seriously."

"I wish I knew." His brain spun with possibilities. *Who would do this to me? And how did he know about the dynamite?*

Because he works here.

"Crap."

"What?" Nathan asked.

"Nothing. Just pissed. Now I have to figure out who thought it'd be funny to see me squirm." He forced a laugh. "I'm sorry you wasted your morning driving all the way out here."

Nathan sighed and held out a business card. Tom glanced at it and saw Nathan was some sort of certified hazardous device technician. They made some more polite talk, and Tom spoke on autopilot, not registering any of it. His brain was preoccupied. As the truck drove away, anger filled him again as his brain focused on one question.

Who?

Silas? Would he cause trouble for me?

Tom had believed he'd left his arguments with Silas Campbell in Idaho. He'd left the state to put more room between the two of him. At one time Silas had been his closest confidant and he'd thought he was Silas's. But it hadn't taken much to shatter the fragile trust between the two men. Especially given how paranoid Silas was.

He'd learned a lot from Silas in their decades together. He'd been drawn to the man's philosophies before he'd ever met him. He'd known most of his life that the government had brainwashed the general public into believing that it cared about them. During his time with Silas, he'd watched and listened, learning to be a leader of men.

It'd been a big deal for Tom to leave, but he'd seen the writing on the wall. Either you were with Silas or you were against him; there was no other option in Silas's book. When the two men no longer saw eye to eye on some key issues, their relationship was over. Tom had stood at a crossroads, carefully deciding which road to take. He'd thought through all the options, deliberated all the possibilities, and committed to his decision a year ago.

Echoes of another huge crossroad had briefly clouded his mind at the time, but he'd made the right decision back then, and it had given him confidence to move forward last year. He'd gathered the men who supported him and believed in his philosophies and moved to the ranch in Oregon.

He'd been hesitant to return to Central Oregon, but he'd spent time here decades ago and believed enough time had passed that residents wouldn't be startled when they saw his face. He'd known he'd find the right men in this part of the state. Men who thought and believed as he did. He'd been right.

It hadn't been easy. He'd started from scratch and been careful to toe every legal line.

Until recently.

That wasn't my fault.

To create a strong base, he'd had to surround himself with the right people. When one of those people had turned poisonous, he'd had to sever the infected limb. If he allowed active dissent, he'd lose all respect. Enforcing discipline and creating examples of naysayers were the ways to maintain control. If everyone respected everyone else, then they would live in harmony. When the dissenters caused problems, they needed to leave. And if they wouldn't leave, they needed to be forced.

Joshua Pence had created a problem.

Tom had addressed the problem.

Simple.

A twinge of regret touched him. Joshua had been an enthusiastic supporter. He'd firmly believed in Tom's mission, speaking to the other men with fervor and encouraging them to stay strong to support Tom's cause. But Joshua's enthusiasm had become his undoing.

Tom's phone vibrated in his pocket, and he answered without looking at the screen.

"It's Jack Howell."

"Hey, Jack. Got good news for me yet?"

"Not exactly."

Caution crept up Tom's spine. Jack was unusually calm. Typically the real estate agent enthusiastically talked a mile a minute, but today he sounded subdued.

"Spill it."

"I had a call from the FBI. They want to know who is interested in buying the Brass ranch."

"Shit." For the second time that morning, Tom was punched in the gut.

"I didn't tell them anything," Jack said. "I told them my client insisted on confidentiality, but I'd check with him. Does it matter to you if I tell them your name?"

"Fuck yes, it matters!" His brain spun out of control again.

"She gave me five minutes to call you and get back to her."

"Who?"

"The FBI agent."

"I know she's an FBI agent. *What's her name?*" He held his breath, knowing what Jack would say.

"Uh . . . Kilpatrick. Mercy Kilpatrick."

Tom pulled the phone away from his ear as he cursed. *Owen's sister again. Was I wrong to bring him in?* "Don't call her back."

"What am I supposed to do? She said she could get a warrant for the information." Jack sounded miserable.

"Let her. If she wants to waste her time, that's fine with me."

"She'll find out eventually."

"Your job is to avoid her until then."

"I don't understand why you insist on remaining anonymous. Eventually your name will be the one on the property deed."

"You haven't written my name down anywhere, right? You agreed no one would be able to find my name in your paperwork."

"All our dealings have been oral. I haven't even sent you anything by email, because I respect what you want."

"Thank you. I appreciate that. Of course, I don't have an email address. You know the government reads all that stuff, right?"

"I've got nothing to hide," said Jack. "The government is welcome to read all my boring contracts if they want."

"I think we need another meeting," Tom said. "I got a look at a property nearby that I'd like to get your opinion on."

"What's the address? I'll pull up all the info before we meet."

"Nah, just come out. I'll tell you about it when you get here."

Jack agreed, but Tom heard the reluctance in his voice. With commissions dangling in front of him, Tom knew Jack would jump through any hoop Tom asked him to.

Tom ended the call and tossed the coffee out of his cup. It'd cooled to an undrinkable temperature. He looked up at the hills surrounding his property, feeling as if a net were slowly tightening around him. The morning had been so promising, and now it had turned to garbage.

Kilpatrick. When he'd heard that Al and Deke had run her off the road, he'd laughed his head off and slapped them on the back. He'd hoped she'd scale back some of her nosy questions. It hadn't worked. Was it time for bigger measures?

Who reported the dynamite?

How did the FBI find out about the offer for the Brass property?

The old woman had told them, of course.

If only Joshua hadn't interfered. *How am I going to handle this new twist?* Could he admit he was the buyer? It wasn't illegal to offer to buy land, but it was instinctive for him to stay under the radar. So what if he was interested in buying her land? Would they think he'd set the fire to scare her off?

He wasn't that stupid.

Some people were, but not he. He knew how to stay out of the limelight. Hell, he knew how to completely stay off everyone's radar. He'd been doing it all his life. No one was better at staying in the shadows than he was.

He'd known when he cut ties with Silas Campbell that he'd have to step forward more, but he hadn't expected this. Maybe he needed to tone things down until the FBI stopped asking questions. What it was interested in had nothing to do with him.

Not really.

Could Owen Kilpatrick be the source of his problems? The thought made his heart hurt a bit. When he'd first encountered Owen, Tom's initial instinct had been to hide. But instead he'd looked Owen in the eye and shaken his hand. Owen's eyes had reflected Tom's own, and Tom had known instantly he could trust the type of man Owen was. Owen's father, Karl, was a straight shooter, and Owen had the same blood.

So did the FBI agent. But she was a woman. It wasn't the same as looking a man in the eye and knowing him.

There were men on his property with less character than Owen Kilpatrick. Character meant a lot to him, but sometimes it took time to be exposed. What seemed perfect and shiny on the outside could house a rotting center . . . or a weak center. Sometimes it was that weakness that kept a man from fulfilling his potential.

But who would call about the dynamite?

And why?

To stop Tom from using it. Someone didn't like his plans and was too chickenshit to tell him to his face.

Maybe someone was afraid of becoming the next Joshua Pence.

Do I need to make another example?

Jack Howell would come in handy.

TWENTY-TWO

Truman had nearly arrived back at his department when his phone rang. It was the Deschutes County Sheriff's Office reporting that it had found an abandoned red pickup with some minor front-end damage.

"Who's the owner?" asked Truman.

"The tags are long expired," said the deputy. "But it's registered to a Joshua Pence in Nevada."

"Crap." The theory about Joshua's truck having been used to run Mercy off the road appeared to be accurate.

"Have you towed it yet?"

"Nope. We're waiting for the tow truck."

"Give me your location."

Truman took the next turn and floored his accelerator, wanting to get to the scene before the truck was moved.

Nearly twenty minutes later he pulled up behind a county cruiser on a little-used side road and spotted the tail end of a truck in the brush off the side of the road. No tow truck in sight.

"Did you touch anything?" he asked the deputy.

"I opened the door and looked through the contents of the glove box. Once I radioed it in and heard about the BOLO for the vehicle, I backed off."

Little effort had been made to hide the vehicle. They'd picked a quiet road, but the vehicle was still visible from the street. Truman wondered if an empty gas tank had led to the poor hiding spot. "See any keys?"

"Nope. It was unlocked and one of the windows left down."

Truman walked around the vehicle. It'd had a hard life. The bed of the truck was well dented and had a few holes. The tires should have been replaced ten thousand miles ago, and a headlight was missing. He crouched down to look at the missing headlight. The truck had minor damage around the missing headlight, and he could see scrapes of black paint in the dents.

Mercy's Tahoe.

Slipping on gloves, he opened the driver's door and did a quick visual inspection. There were holes worn in the fabric bench seat on the driver's side, and the floor was littered with fast-food wrappers, Big Gulp cups, and soda cans. Truman opened the ashtray; it was full.

DNA.

Probably DNA on the straws in the cups too.

Not that we'd use DNA to figure out who abandoned a truck.

The mess could be from Pence, but if Truman had a suspect for who had run Mercy off the road and he wanted to handle the expense, he could test to see if it matched.

I'd rather get someone to confess.

No doubt he could intimidate a suspect with the fact that they'd left their DNA all over the inside of the truck. Cheaper too.

He backed away from the vehicle and looked at the towering pines in the area, trying to get a mental picture of where he was. "Do you know how far we are from Tom McDonald's place?" he asked the deputy.

"Who?"

"Never mind." Truman strode back to his vehicle and pulled up his location on a map on his phone. He zoomed out, getting a bigger picture of the area. McDonald's ranch was less than ten miles away. He stared at the screen for a few seconds and knew he needed to pay a visit.

Once Mercy had admitted the McDonald crew might have run her off the road, Truman had done as much digging on Tom McDonald as he could. She'd said what she'd uncovered on McDonald was clean. Truman had found the same.

It was too clean. Given that he was associated with the Idaho militia leader Silas Campbell, Truman felt there should have been a few skirmishes on McDonald's record. Truman had never had a real conversation with Tom, but he'd seen the man around Eagle's Nest a few times. He'd pulled up what information the state had on Tom McDonald before heading to the ranch, and let the information percolate in his brain on the drive. Something about McDonald niggled at his brain, but Truman couldn't see any issues.

McDonald was boring.

Too boring?

He pulled into the remote property and parked next to a few trucks. Four men stepped out of a large building fifty feet away, and Truman immediately identified the girth of Tom McDonald. Two others were the men who always accompanied McDonald. To his surprise the fourth man was Mercy's brother, Owen.

As they got closer and he recognized Truman, Owen missed a beat in his stride. His jaw tightened.

"Morning, Chief." McDonald held out his hand to Truman. "What brings you all the way out here?" He didn't bother to introduce the other two men, who hung back a few feet behind him. Big guys who wore bulky outerwear that could hide a multitude of weapons.

Truman nodded at the silent trio, his gaze lingering on Owen, who looked away.

Fine. I'll play it your way.

Truman shook McDonald's hand, ignoring his obvious hint that Truman was stepping outside the Eagle's Nest city limits. "We recovered a red Ford pickup a couple miles down the road from here," he said, stretching the truth a bit. "Was wondering if any of your men know anything about it?"

McDonald didn't look at his men. "Who's the owner?"

"Joshua Pence."

"Don't know the name. Why'd you come here instead of going to his house?"

Truman didn't flinch at the obvious lie. "The home address is in Nevada, and the registration is out of date. I'd heard he was working for you."

"I don't have any employees by that name. I don't know where you got your information, but it's not right." McDonald held his gaze, his face expressionless.

"Joshua Pence was the man whose body was found at the Jackson Hill fire last week." Truman watched McDonald carefully.

"Is that the guy the FBI harassed my employees about the other day? They were poking around, asking if anyone knew him. Why's everyone think I know something about him?"

"I don't know anything about the FBI's visit. You'll have to ask them." Truman felt Owen's stare on him. "I'm here about the truck."

McDonald finally glanced at his men. "Anyone know about an abandoned truck?"

Three heads shook in unison.

McDonald turned back to Truman. "I think you're barking up the wrong tree."

"Sounds like it. I appreciate the help." Truman let his gaze wander across the ranch buildings. "Looks like things are coming along. I heard you've got some good employment opportunities going on. Planning on lots of building?"

"Some."

"I can put the word out around town if you're looking for workers."

"I've got plenty at the moment."

Behind McDonald, the man wearing a camouflage parka shifted his stance and intensified his glare at Truman. Truman met his gaze and gave him a friendly smile. "I think the red truck was involved in an accident the other day. Someone nearly killed an FBI agent when they ran her off the road. They got real lucky she wasn't hurt."

The guard's glare turned into a subtle smirk.

"Don't know anything about that," said McDonald. "Not our truck."

Truman eyed the camo-wearing guard and decided to see if his fast-food theory was right. "Well, it's been driven since Pence died. Whoever took it for a joyride left all sorts of garbage inside. Soda cans. Straws. Cigarette butts." Camo's smirk evaporated as he realized the items Truman mentioned could harbor DNA, and Truman contained his grin. *Gotcha.* "It's got some front-end damage too. With residual paint from the federal vehicle it hit."

Tom McDonald kept his cool. "Sounds like you'll have plenty of evidence when you catch whoever stole it. Probably teenagers."

"Probably," agreed Truman. He took a last quick glance at Owen. Mercy's brother looked slightly nauseated.

That's right. You're hanging around with guys who nearly killed your sister.

Truman touched the brim of his hat and made polite good-byes. He felt their stares burn hot on his back as he walked back to his SUV. He sat in the cab for a while, pretending to work on his computer, letting them sweat about what he was doing. As he fiddled with his console, he realized he hadn't experienced an ounce of anxiety about confronting the men. None. Zip. Nada. Pleased, he tried to identify what had changed since he'd fallen apart the other day.

I care. I care about justice for Joshua Pence. I'm not thinking about myself.

Mercy too. He was determined to find out who'd tried to kill her in that car accident, because he didn't want it happening again.

215

He started the vehicle and pulled a tight circle to head back the way he'd come. He noticed that one of McDonald's two guards was still in the spot where they'd spoken, waiting for him to leave.

Go tell Daddy I left.

He fumed as he drove off. He suspected all four of the men knew where the truck had been for the last week. Possibly Owen did not, but without him opening his mouth to defend himself, Truman would group him with McDonald's crew.

No matter that he was Mercy's brother.

◆ ◆ ◆

Tom McDonald watched the police chief drive off his property. The asshole had sat in his truck for five minutes before leaving and completely screwed with Tom's peace of mind. The chief didn't have any authority here, and both of them knew it. He'd come out only to stir up trouble and try to intimidate him and his men again.

He'd heard good things about the police chief of Eagle's Nest, but now Tom had his own opinion. The chief wasn't afraid to overstep his bounds to harass innocent men. Just like every other cop. He might have his townspeople snowed about the type of man he was, but Tom knew he had the inflated ego that always came with the badge.

Unnecessary. Cops were government tools to enforce its extraneous laws. Tools to protect itself from the very people who'd given it power.

Soon.

Owen Kilpatrick paced in the small living room of the farmhouse as Tom watched him out of the corner of his eye. He wanted to believe Owen was with him 100 percent, but in the last few minutes Tom had started having doubts. The police chief had rattled Owen. Even Deke watched Owen, distrust settling into his features.

Did I bring him into the fold too fast?

"What's going through your head, Owen?"

"A lot of officials have shown up here," said Owen as he continued his pacing. "First the FBI, then the state police looking for dynamite, and now the local police chief. It's getting hot."

Tom wished he hadn't told Deke, Al, and Owen about the state cop looking for dynamite. All three men had started to sweat and then had grown angry at the thought that there might be a traitor in their midst. Their reactions had felt genuine to Tom, and he was nearly certain none of them had reported the dynamite. But that left forty other men and women who might have made the call.

"Are you worried?" Tom asked. "None of the cops had any facts. They were all just following rumors."

"Who's spreading these rumors?" asked Owen.

Al came through the farmhouse door, his face full of annoyance. "Don't know why the chief waited so long to leave."

"He was trying to intimidate us more," said Tom. "More proof that he's got nothing on us. He was just blowing hot air."

"We should have cleaned out the garbage," muttered Al.

Owen froze midstep. "What garbage?"

"Nothing."

Owen stared at Al for a long second, and disappointment flashed across his face. Tom knew he'd suspected that his two men had run his FBI-agent sister off the road, but now he was positive.

What will he do about that?

"Do you have a problem with my plans for the dynamite?" Tom asked Owen.

The tension in the room tripled. Al and Deke slowly turned toward Owen, waiting for his response.

His hands clasped behind his back, Owen looked at Tom and then the other two men. "I don't. You can do whatever you want on your own property."

"But it's not my property yet."

"It will be soon," said Deke. "She'll come around." He nodded emphatically, as if he could will it to happen.

Tom studied the large man. Deke was a few peas short of a casserole, but he had heart and was one of the best shots Tom had ever seen. That was the primary reason Tom had picked him to watch his back. Another reason was that he was usually silent.

"I didn't ask your opinion," Tom told Deke.

Deke clamped his mouth shut and straightened his spine, focusing his gaze on a spot past Tom's shoulder. "No, sir."

Tom turned his attention back to Owen. "Your sister could have been hurt the other day. That was the fault of these two boneheads. It wasn't my intention." He held Owen's gaze. "But I won't stand for federal agents trying to walk all over me. I'll strike back when warranted. Do you have a problem with that?"

Owen hesitated a split second too long. "No, sir."

Disappointment washed over Tom. *I had such high hopes for him.*

Owen was different from the other men who'd come to him. He was successful, smart, and motivated. Anger had driven Owen to Tom. His brother's death as a result of shoddy police work had opened Owen's eyes. He wanted what all the other men wanted: change. They wanted change that returned their dignity and pride.

Not this constant stealing of their taxes to support greedy politicians, or to have to look over their shoulder every time they stepped outside their own front door. They wanted to simply live their lives. Instead they were being nickel-and-dimed while the government created new laws to give itself power to sweep in and take whatever it wanted.

A forest your family has owned for fifty years? Hand it over. We need to protect an owl.

Pastures your cattle have grazed for the last decade? Keep off. We need to protect the river your cows drink from.

Then the federal officials would show up with their guns and all the power.

Unfair.

"Maybe this isn't the place for you," Tom said to Owen.

Owen took two steps toward him, passion flaring in his eyes. "You know we want the same things. You've got the strength to sway men to support you. I *believe* in what you're doing." He held Tom's gaze, sincerity ringing in his tone.

I believe him.

Tom had strong faith in his gut instincts. His temporary doubts about Owen vanished. Owen might have a soft spot for his sister, but he wouldn't let it get in his way. Tom held out his hand to Owen, who grabbed it and shook it firmly.

"I'm with you," Owen stated.

"Good," said Tom. "Now how are we going to figure out who the leak is around here?"

Owen blew out a breath. "I have my suspicions about that young kid working on the bunkhouses."

"Cade?" Tom was shocked. The kid was polite and worked hard.

"Maybe he didn't do anything intentionally, but it's possible he mentioned the dynamite to his girlfriend."

"And she reported it? Why would some teenage girl care about dynamite out here?"

"She's my niece . . . Her dad died, and she lives with Mercy."

Understanding struck Tom. "You think she told her aunt? And that's why things have heated up around here? Why didn't you mention this sooner?" He was horrified. One of his workers was dating the live-in niece of an FBI agent?

Owen pressed his mouth into a hard line before answering. "I only put it together recently. I didn't realize he was the guy I'd seen with my niece until I bumped into him here the other day. Even then I wasn't sure."

"So you could be wrong."

"Could be. But I'm thinking it's the same one."

"I think I need to have a talk with Cade." Tom turned to Deke and Al. "Go find the kid."

"He's off today."

"Dammit." Frustration heated his face. "I want to see him first thing tomorrow."

TWENTY-THREE

Truman's desk phone rang and he snatched it up, crossing his fingers that it was the call he'd been waiting for.

It was. Bonner County Deputy Chad Wheeler's voice came booming through the line. "Truman? Chad here, returning your call. Did you want to beg for another fishing trip?"

"You've got the best fishing in the Pacific Northwest."

"We do. But it's too damn cold now. Where were you three months ago? I told you the guys were getting together."

Chad had attended high school with Truman. Truman had always assumed Chad would end up behind bars instead of on the law-abiding side. No one had been more surprised than Truman when he joined the police force. It'd been good for Chad, calming his wild ways and focusing his energy for good. Every few years they pulled together a few old classmates and fished in Chad's backyard of northern Idaho.

The same area Tom McDonald had left a year ago.

"I wish I'd reached out to you about fishing, but I've got business I need to discuss."

"What do you need?" Chad's tone shifted to full-on cop mode.

"Information on a Tom McDonald. He moved here from your area a year ago. As far as I can tell, he lived in northern Idaho all his life." He gave Chad the Idaho driver's license number he'd found for Tom.

He heard Chad's keyboard clatter in the background. "Yep, I see him. I've got previous addresses for him in Sandpoint, Coeur d'Alene, and Bonners Ferry. I don't see any record. The guy never even got a traffic ticket."

"I've heard he was an associate of Silas Campbell."

"Ohhh." The interest in Chad's tone shot up. "Let me nose around in some other files. Is he causing problems for you?"

"Not yet," admitted Truman. It was true. So far all McDonald had done was ignore the FBI's request for a phone call and act like a pompous jerk to Truman that morning. "But I suspect he's involved in something. His name keeps coming up in regard to a case I'm working on, but there's nothing concrete yet."

"Where there's smoke, there's fire," said Chad. Keys continued to clack in the background as he searched for information on McDonald. "I wish his name wasn't so common. I'm searching some of the files we have on Silas Campbell to see if your subject's name is mentioned. Why couldn't he be named something easy to find, like Keziah Moreau?"

Truman agreed.

"I've got a Tom McDonald mentioned several times in relation to Campbell, but I don't see any illegal behavior. It looks like he was always in the background, not stirring up any fuss, but simply being present."

"He's careful."

"Looks that way. I've got all sorts of long lists of people who've been arrested in conjunction with Campbell's organization, but your guy's name isn't on any of them."

"What sort of things has Campbell done?"

Chad sighed through the phone. "Depends who you ask. Either he's a saint and speaks for the oppressed or he's a right-wing nut job who's never met a law he likes. His record has been clean for the past decade; he knows how to stay out of trouble now, but plenty of his fervent followers screw up."

"I remember there was a problem with a lake."

"Yes, Campbell spoke out when the federal government put up a fence to keep cattle out of a newly protected marsh area. Families had been using that area to water their cattle for a hundred years. But you know what happens when a species becomes endangered."

"I do." Truman knew all too well. Emotions would run high, and the little man always felt powerless in the face of a federal government that believed it was doing the right thing. Truman usually could see both sides of the issue, but he knew it felt different when a family's livelihood was threatened. He didn't always agree with either side. Usually he fell somewhere in the middle.

"What's the date of birth you have for him?" Truman asked as he looked at a photocopy of McDonald's relatively new Oregon driver's license. Chad rattled off the same date that Truman had. "Does this guy look nearly seventy to you?"

Chad was silent for a moment. "Hell no."

"I met with him face-to-face this morning," Truman said. "I'd put him in his mid to late fifties. He's really heavy, so he doesn't have the facial wrinkles, and sometimes that can make someone look younger, but seriously . . . I can't even see him as being in his sixties. He's a rural guy; he runs a ranch and I get the impression he's worked a ranch most of his life. He should look *older* than his age."

"You think he's taken on someone else's identity," Chad said. "Hang on. I'm going to email you the driver's license photo we have on file from twenty-five years ago. I think it's the same guy in every license photo we have, but maybe you'll disagree."

"How far back do you have photos?" Truman asked.

"I'm sending you the oldest one."

Truman opened his email and spotted Chad's address at the top of his in-box. He clicked. "Yes, that's him." McDonald was younger in the photo, but still had the heavy beard he wore today. "He's supposed to be forty-five in this one. I don't see that. He looks younger than you or I right now."

"I agree. But the beard makes it hard to estimate his age. He's worn it in every photo we have."

The men were silent for a long moment.

"If this isn't his identity, he's been using it for a long time," said Truman. "I don't even know where to start to figure this one out." *How am I going to dig around in another state?*

"I have some ideas," said Chad. "One of our reserve officers would get off on solving this puzzle. He's semiretired and there's nothing he likes better than to research this sort of thing. He's damned good at it. Let me talk to him for you."

"I'd appreciate it."

Truman ended the call after a few more minutes. Frustrated, he sat silently at his desk, hating to wait on someone else to do his work for him. *How long will it take to get results? What if he can't find anything?*

Was it relevant if Tom McDonald wasn't who he said he was? If he had used an assumed identity, it didn't change what he'd been up to. Clearly the man had been living as McDonald for a very long time.

Maybe he's wanted for an old murder.

Truman let his mind wander for a long moment, listing reasons for someone to assume a new identity. None of the reasons suggested a moral purpose.

He pulled up the McDonald property on a map on his computer, studying the surrounding landscape. McDonald had picked a very rural location. His large piece of land was surrounded by either a dense forest, steep hills, or a river. If Tom had wanted isolation, he'd found it. The best route in was the horrible road that fed in from the south that Truman had driven earlier that day. The only other way into the property followed winding roads that added ten miles and crossed a river. Truman shifted the map so he could follow the winding roads and land to the west of the property. He traced the long way in with his finger, starting at Tom's property and working his way out.

Only someone with too much time on their hands would try to use this road.

His finger finally reached a country highway. He paused with his finger on the screen, staring at the number that labeled the highway, knowing he'd recently visited a home with that highway address.

Tilda Brass lived on that highway. He searched for her property lines. Her acreage turned out to be one of the oddest-shaped properties Truman had ever seen. It was long and narrow and curving.

But it shared a property line with the McDonald ranch.

TWENTY-FOUR

Mercy was in her vehicle when Truman called. She pulled into a fast-food restaurant parking lot to give the call her full attention, and ignored the heavenly smell of frying beef.

"I just had an interesting call with a buddy of mine in north-ern Idaho," he started. He proceeded to lay out his theory that Tom McDonald wasn't who he claimed to be.

Mercy listened in shock, letting the concept sink into her brain.

I'm glad I parked before I heard that bit of information.

"I can see how you came to that conclusion," Mercy admitted. "McDonald doesn't look as old as he should. And the fact that he has absolutely no record? That tells me he's been trying extra hard to stay clean over the years. Do you think his real past is hiding something horrible?"

"I don't want to jump to conclusions," said Truman. "Let's wait and hear what this officer in Idaho finds. We could be way off course."

"And does it really change what's happened here?" she asked. "The deputies are still dead, and we don't know who set two of the fires. Past or no past, something is up. Although I think it's an excellent theory, and I'll mention it to Darby. Maybe she can help your Idaho guy."

"I went out there today."

Mercy tensed. "Went where?"

"The McDonald ranch."

"Why?" Her boss's warning about not going out to the ranch alone echoed in her head. Male or female, he hadn't believed it was safe, and Mercy agreed.

"The truck that ran you off the road was found today."

"I heard they found *a truck*. I wasn't going to pay much attention until the evidence proved it was the right vehicle."

"Well, I went to check out the truck. There's black paint on the front right corner. That was good enough for me."

"Who does it belong to?" She took a deep breath, suspecting she knew the answer to her question.

"Joshua Pence. And it was found less than ten miles from the McDonald place, so I decided to go see if they knew anything about it."

"Did they still deny that he worked there?"

"Yep. I had a short chat with Tom that went absolutely nowhere. And Mercy . . . Owen was there."

She froze.

"He was standing behind Tom like one of his lackeys and pretended he didn't know me."

Mercy closed her eyes. *Why, Owen?* "I can't control what he does."

"Of course you can't, but you should be aware that if we find dirt on Tom McDonald, it could affect or incriminate a lot of his followers."

In other words, Owen will have more reasons to hate me.

"He's chosen his path. I've done what I can."

"I'm sorry, Mercy," Truman said gently, and his soft tone nearly broke her heart.

"I'm doing the best I can with my family. Owen has been the hardest to get to talk to me, let alone accept that I've returned. I think I have to stand back and just let him have his anger. He knows I'm here when he's ready to talk."

A long silence dragged out between them.

"Anything new in the cases?" Truman asked.

"The dirt bike treads from Landon's home don't match the ones at the fire scene where Joshua Pence was found."

"That was fast work."

"According to one of our lab techs, it was a no-brainer. He took one look and knew it didn't match."

"What about the weapons and shells?"

"That takes longer. This isn't TV, you know."

"No one knows that better than me," said Truman. "But I'm still waiting for my hot FBI girlfriend to show up in heels and low-cut blouses."

Mercy laughed. "Are you making fun of my boots?" She glanced at the heavy-treaded boots she'd slipped on that morning to wear while searching Landon Hecht's home. There was nothing glamorous about them; *glamorous* was a word never used to describe her. She preferred being comfortable and practical.

"Of course not. I find you particularly attractive in jeans and boots. Especially when you're swinging an ax. That whole look works for me." He gave a low chuckle that curled her toes. "Have you heard from Jack Howell yet?"

"I haven't. I should stop by his office again."

"Something tells me he's going to be out for the rest of the day."

"You're probably right. I suspect it would be a waste of my time, but I'm going to continue with my phone messages every few hours. That should get under his skin a bit."

A beep sounded in the vehicle, and she saw she had an incoming call from Rose.

"Truman, Rose is calling."

"I'll let you go."

She ended his call and picked up the second. "Hi, Rose."

"Mercy? Is that you?" asked a high-pitched voice that didn't belong to Rose.

"Mom?" Mercy caught her breath at the stress in her mother's tone.

"I'm on Rose's phone."

"What's happened?" Every cell in her body tensed, and her finger hovered over the start button to the rental vehicle.

"Someone threw rocks and mud at Rose today. And they called her a whore."

Mercy couldn't breathe. She hit the button and fired up her vehicle. "Where are you?"

"We're home now, but we were in Eagle's Nest. I was in the post office while Rose went to Hackett's store."

"I'm on my way. Is she hurt?" *I will make someone wish they were dead if she is injured.*

"Not really. Just some small cuts from the rocks, but she's very shaken."

"Assholes. I'll be there as soon as I can."

Mercy parked at her parents' house and slammed the door to the Ford rental, fury racing through her veins. She took the stairs two at a time and pounded on the front door. "Mom?" she hollered, wanting to throw open the door and walk right in. Instead she forced herself to stand and wait.

I will find out who did this.

Footsteps sounded behind the door, and her mother opened it. Her face was lined and drawn, and Mercy didn't like the fear in her eyes. She stepped back. "Rose is in the kitchen."

Mercy started to pass by, but she stopped and placed a hand on her mother's shoulder. "It's going to be okay. I called Truman and told him Rose needed to file a police report."

"We don't want to—"

"It's assault. There needs to be a record."

Dismay wrinkled her mother's forehead. "I don't think—"

"Do it for me . . . Hell, it's not for me. *Do it for Rose.* Don't look the other way and let this happen unnoticed, Mom."

"I'm not looking the other way! I just don't want to make a fuss."

"*Make a fuss!* People need to learn that his sort of behavior is *not* okay."

"Mercy?" Rose's voice sounded from the kitchen, and Mercy locked eyes with her mother.

"It's the right thing to do."

Her mother broke eye contact and disappointment stung. *At least she didn't refuse.*

"I'm coming, Rose." Mercy left her mother at the door and passed through the living room area to where Rose sat at the kitchen table with a plastic bag of ice against her cheekbone. Her hair was damp.

She showered to wash off the mud.

Tears burned in Mercy's eyes, and she forced the worry out of her voice. "Hey. Let me take a look at that." She sat in the chair next to Rose and placed a hand over Rose's fingers holding the pack in place.

"It's not so bad," Rose said, but Mercy noticed she was slow to pull the ice away.

Rose's perfect cheekbone now sported a gouge surrounded by fresh bruising. Two tiny cuts graced her forehead.

Mercy wanted to hurt someone. Most of Rose's facial slashes had healed, and now this had happened.

"Truman is sending someone to take a police report," Mercy said as she took stock of her sister, visually inspecting her for any other problems.

"That's not—"

"Humor me," Mercy ordered. *What is with the women in my family?* A knock sounded at the door and her mother opened it. The sound of Truman's greeting made Mercy relax a few degrees, pleased that he'd come instead of sending someone else. A moment later his hand squeezed her shoulder as he greeted Rose. He pulled out another chair.

"You don't know how angry this makes me," Truman started.

"Get in line," snapped Mercy, glancing at him, looking for understanding of her temper. She found it in his calm brown eyes.

"Tell me what happened," said Truman as he clicked the button on top of his pen and opened his notebook.

Mercy clenched her hands in her lap as she listened to Rose's story.

"There were two men," began Rose. "One had tailed me for about twenty feet. I heard him walking behind me as I walked down the sidewalk to Hackett's store. His steps sped up, and as he got closer he started saying horrible things in a low voice behind me."

"Like what?" asked Truman.

"He said I was having the baby of Satan and that I was a whore. Basically these were repeated several different ways with some of the nastiest language I'd ever heard."

Mercy sat very still, feeling as if she would shatter if she breathed too deep.

"Then I heard a truck pull up at the curb. His steps changed and I heard him open the door. There was an exchange between him and the person I assume was the driver that I couldn't quite hear." She sucked in a deep breath and raised her chin. "Then he called my name and I stopped and turned around . . . I shouldn't have stopped! I should have kept going!"

Mercy's mother stopped behind Rose and bent over to wrap her arms around her shoulders, burying her face in her daughter's hair.

"That's when I felt the rock." Rose indicated the gash. "And then softer blows hit me. It was mud." Rage filled her voice. "He continued to call me a whore. I heard a second voice echoing his words. Probably the driver. Then the truck door slammed and his tires squealed as he took off."

Mercy held her breath. Her fingers felt like ice, and she didn't know if she could speak without bursting into tears.

"Did you recognize either voice?" Truman asked. He struck the perfect tone of caring and calm.

Be like Truman.

"No."

"You know everyone around here," Truman pointed out.

"I do. I don't think they were from around here."

"But they knew your name," said Truman. "Have there been other incidents about the baby I haven't heard about?" He looked at Mercy's mother.

Baby. Mercy stared at Rose's still-flat stomach as her sister shook her head. She'd forgotten, even though the assailant's words had referred to Rose's pregnancy. *Rose isn't the only innocent victim here.* "They knew she was pregnant, and it sounds like they know how she got pregnant," Mercy pointed out.

"Word travels," said Truman.

"Who would do such a thing?" Mercy's mother asked in a distraught whisper. She continued to cry into Rose's hair. Rose raised her hand and patted her mother on the arm, her face wearing an expression of a measured calm.

Rose is handling it better than Mom.

Rose had always been the stoic sibling, and Mercy wondered if it was truly her nature or if she'd adopted it for self-preservation. She could remember incidents that had gotten her brothers up in arms over someone's treatment of Rose, but Rose had always been the one to defuse the situation. Rose's serene face made her wonder if her sister simply buried her emotions to help other people stay calm. Or did she truly feel that peace?

Mercy buried her own fury. *If Rose can do it, so can I.*

The back door opened and her father walked in. He slammed to a stop and stared at the group at the kitchen table. The tension in the room tripled.

"What happened?" he asked sharply. His gaze rested briefly on Mercy before he nodded at Truman.

Nice to see you too.

"Rose—" Truman started.

"It's nothing," Rose interjected. Her hand tightened on her mother's arm.

"What happened to your face, Rose?" He moved his gaze back to Mercy, and she felt the heat of his penetrating stare.

Rose gave a brief account.

Pain flashed on her father's face, and his stare continued to move between Rose and Mercy. But when it landed on Rose, it was soft and gentle. On Mercy it burned.

"We'll handle it from here," Karl Kilpatrick stated to Truman. He hadn't moved from his original stance in the kitchen. Boots, jeans, heavy jacket, hat in his hands. Nothing about her father had changed in decades. Just the color of his hair and the lines on his face.

And the way he looks at me.

"And leave the Parker family alone," her father told her.

She froze.

"Why?" asked Truman. "They were the target of serial arsonists. It bears investigating."

Her father's gaze shifted to Truman, and Mercy managed to take a breath. "It's done and over. Let them get on with their lives. We'll keep watch over them. We don't need outsiders sticking their noses in things. Seems to always end bad."

Truman stood and glanced at Mercy. "We'll be headed out then. Rose, I'll start asking some questions around town."

Mercy glanced at her mother and Rose. Both women were silent, her mother avoiding eye contact. She caught a movement of Rose's hand below the table, out of sight of her father's gaze. Rose shifted her fingers into a thumbs-up. Something she'd done as a child when any of them were in trouble with their father; her silent gesture of support, meant to show she'd comfort them later.

Their father had never caught on.

Rose has been attacked, but she reaches out to make me feel better.

Fierce love for her sister threatened to make Mercy cry. "Thank you, Rose." She let her gaze linger on her father before she led Truman out of the house.

When will he forgive me?

Even though I did nothing.

She grabbed handfuls of her hair and pretended to pull it out.

"I hear you," Truman said. "I really don't know what goes through your dad's head."

"I suspect it sounds a lot like 'Levi is dead because of Mercy.'"

Truman stopped her. "Don't talk like that." He moved in front of her, his countenance deadly serious.

"I don't believe it," Mercy pointed out. "I'm stating what I think is on repeat in his brain."

"He'll come around." Truman pulled her to him, wrapping his arms tightly around her. "I'm sorry you had to go through that. It was hard enough hearing Rose's story."

"Enough about my dad." Mercy pressed her nose against his shoulder, inhaling the icy scent of fall from his coat. "All I care about is protecting Rose. I can't believe someone would attack her. This town has always loved Rose."

"They still do. Like she said, I don't think they're from around here."

"But how would they know those things about her?"

He didn't answer. Neither of them knew.

"You should have seen the look on your face when I first got there," Truman said. "You looked like a mother bear whose cub was in danger."

"Rose does that to me."

"Anyone in your family does it to you. I saw the same look with Levi and Kaylie."

"Hurt my family and I'll make you pay."

He pulled back and smiled at her. "I like that about you. Your world is very black and white, isn't it?"

Mercy thought. "About some things. My family is the same way. It's the inability to see the shades of gray that keeps my father from accepting me. He's always insisted that there is no middle ground in most issues."

"Everyone needs to bend a little," said Truman.

"I'd like to buy my dad a bumper sticker with that quote." She quickly kissed him. "Thank you for taking Rose's report. That meant a lot to me."

He gave a sheepish grin. "I was the only person available."

"Hmmmph. I'll let you keep the kiss anyway."

He grinned and she gave him another.

TWENTY-FIVE

Tom weighed his choices.

Al and Deke would do whatever he said. No questions asked. And he trusted them to keep their mouths shut. They'd already proved themselves several times, so they were scheduled to handle the second part of today's task.

He eyed Owen Kilpatrick out of the corner of his eye. He wanted more from the man. He needed to know where Owen stood once and for all. No doubts.

Pounding sounded on the front door. Tom waved off Deke as he got up and opened the door himself. Jack Howell stood on the front stoop, looking annoyed that he'd been summoned to the ranch. *His timing is perfect.* Usually the real estate agent acted as everyone's best friend, but the FBI's hounding had taken his level of enthusiasm for Tom's friendship down a notch. But he was here; Jack was still hungry for the sale.

"Let's take a walk, Jack," Tom suggested. "I need to get out of the house for a bit." He glanced back at Owen. "Why don't you come with us? I think this might interest you."

Owen glanced at Al and Deke as he slowly stood, a questioning expression on his face. Tom's usual companions sat motionless. Tom had already told them he'd use Owen as an escort for his conversation with Jack Howell. Neither man had questioned his decision.

He liked that.

They had a different assignment while he was out with Jack and Owen.

Tom, Owen, and Jack headed toward the east side of the property, following a path that led through a dense copse of pines. All three of them wore heavy coats to combat the chill in the air. Tom glanced at the sky and saw no sign of rain, just high, thin clouds against the pale blue. The men were silent as they walked, and Tom enjoyed the tension he'd created. He could feel their questioning glances on his back, but neither man asked where they were going.

Respect.

The path went up a gradual slope, and Tom's lungs burned as he pushed himself. He wasn't ignorant of the extra energy it took him to walk the path while the other two men seemed not to exert themselves at all. Both were younger, with lean builds. He'd tried for years to lose weight and had finally given up. He was what he was. He'd rather eat the food he enjoyed than spend years restricting himself. But there were times, like right now, when he despised the extra weight that made him sweat and strain.

"How far are we going?" Jack finally asked. "I need to get back to the office. It takes quite a while to drive out here, you know."

Subtext: I'm spending a lot of time on you, and you haven't put money in my pocket yet.

"You know the FBI might be waiting in the parking lot at your office to ask questions." Tom glanced back at Jack and spotted a hitch in Owen's stride at his words.

"I won't say anything," Jack said. "If that's how you want to carry out this deal, I'm good with that. I don't have to reveal your identity to anyone. You'll be glad to know that Tilda Brass left me a voice mail about an hour ago," he added in a more chipper voice. "She wants to know if I'm still interested in the property."

"I told you she'd come around," said Tom.

"So you definitely want to move forward with the offer we made? Or do you want me to lower it a bit? Now, since she came back to us, we have a bit of an upper hand."

"I'm a man of my word," answered Tom, puffing heavily. "I'll honor the first offer."

"When I leave, I'll call to let her know."

"You're sure my name isn't floating around on documentation in your office anywhere? And Tilda doesn't know that I'm behind the offer, right?"

"Absolutely. I already told you this," Jack said.

Anger shot through Tom at the exasperation in Jack's tone. He didn't tolerate his orders being questioned, and he didn't like the signs that Jack's respect for him had taken a hit.

Tom stopped to study their forested surroundings. Beside him Jack also stopped, annoyance still on his face.

I'm done tolerating that.

Tom took a long look at Owen. *Time to find out exactly what Owen thinks.*

Clearing his mind, Tom drew the pistol out of his deep pocket and shot Jack in the forehead.

The man's body slumped to the ground. His eyes still open in surprise.

I'll never get that image out of my brain.

"*Holy shit, Tom! What the fuck?*" Owen shouted as he jumped back from the body. He stumbled over his own feet and fell backward on his ass, his legs moving in crablike motions as he scrambled to put more distance between him and Jack. "What did you do?" Owen's face went pale as he stared at the body and then at Tom. "What did you do?" he repeated, his eyes wide.

The sound of the shot continued to echo in Tom's ears, and a wave of cool relief surged through him.

"He could lead the police to me."

"I think they're already watching you, Tom. You've been visited by every agency in the area." Owen panted in deep gasps from the ground. He scooted another foot away from the body.

"I needed to eliminate any links between me and the fire at the Brass property."

"The one where the deputies died?"

Tom didn't answer, keeping his gaze on Jack. The agent's body was impossibly still as blood slowly oozed from the red circle in his face. *I thought dead men don't bleed.* As if it read his thoughts, the bleeding stopped.

"Are you responsible for those deputies' deaths?" Owen hissed in a low voice.

Tom stayed silent as he turned his attention to Owen. Sweat covered the man's forehead. "Get up," he ordered.

Owen stared at him for a moment but obeyed. He slowly moved to his feet, his gaze alternating between Tom's face and the weapon in his hand.

"There's a ravine about a hundred feet in that direction." Tom pointed, keeping his gun neutrally at his side with his other hand. "Drag him up there and throw him over. The wildlife will make short work of him."

"No."

Don't disappoint me. "What will you do? Go to the police?"

Owen didn't say anything. Tom saw the indecision in his eyes.

This is his make-or-break moment.

Tom moved his finger back to the trigger. "You don't know this, but I spent time in this area several decades ago. I knew your dad, Owen. And I knew all your uncles on your mother's side too."

He had Owen's attention.

"I know what you're made of. I know the thoughts in your head. I *know* how you were bred. It's why I was willing to bring you into my circle so rapidly. Most men spend years getting to the level of trust that I have in you."

"Why me?" he breathed.

Tom knew Owen balanced on a tightrope, ready to leap off. But he paused, wanting Tom to convince him that everything would be okay. Tom was an expert at that sort of thing. He had the skills to show men like Owen what they really wanted.

"I just told you. I know your blood," he said earnestly. "This country was built on the backs of men like your relatives. You can be one of them too."

"Murder makes us no better than the ones trying to change us."

"Sometimes you have no choice." He kept his tone soft, regretful, knowing occasionally sacrifices had to be made for the greater good.

Owen weighed his words. "You had no other option?"

"None."

Owen broke eye contact and stared at the body, his face expressionless. "I'll help you this once. But then I'm done. This isn't what I signed up for."

Tom released the magazine from his pistol and popped the round out of the chamber before handing the weapon to Owen, who refused to take it. "Look closely at it," Tom suggested.

Owen looked and turned a pale shade of green. "Is that my gun?"

"It is." Tom thrust it at him again and watched Owen's gaze go to the thin leather gloves on Tom's hands. He saw the moment Owen realized that the only prints on his gun would be his own. His gaze shot to the body.

Yes, your bullet is in his brain.

"I assume there are plenty of bullets from this gun in that homemade firing range at the back of your property."

Owen stared at him, and Tom could see the gears spinning in his brain, searching for a way out.

But Tom had already covered all the exits.

"Al and Deke will swear they saw you shoot him."

"But I didn't—"

Tom held up his hands. "It doesn't need to come to that. No one can trace Jack Howell to me."

"They can pull his phone records." Owen still wasn't sold on Tom's plan.

He needs another small push.

"Nothing illegal about talking to someone on the phone."

Owen opened his mouth to argue and then shut it. Again he looked at the body on the ground. "How many men have you killed, Tom?" he asked quietly. "How many men have died because of what you're trying to do?"

Tom didn't reply. His answer wasn't relevant. Right now it was important to bind Owen to him.

"I have faith in you, Owen. I know you're the type of man I need at my side. We both want to do away with the police running wild all over our civil rights. Together we provide a united front. Once the government realizes we're capable of policing ourselves, they'll back off. Hell, we'll be saving them money."

He wasn't seeing the confidence he needed from Owen, so he pulled out the last weapon in his arsenal.

"I *know* your wife and kids will support you."

The fear in Owen's eyes pleased Tom.

Tom pointed at the body. "I'll wait right here while you dispose of that."

Mercy decided to swing by Jack Howell's office after her gut-wrenching encounter with Rose and her parents.

She was still seething over her father's comments, but knowing Rose saw right through his blustering gave Mercy some calm. One day she and Rose would stand up to her father. Rose was quite good at calming him, but Mercy knew her sister couldn't change his beliefs, and Pearl and her mother would never be any help.

Or would Pearl?

Working at the coffee shop had given her a confidence Mercy hadn't seen in the two months she'd been in Central Oregon. But Mercy didn't know if Pearl could ever supplant her need to be the peacemaker. It was odd how all the women in her family were adept at calming the people around them. Her brothers had never acquired that skill.

Maybe it's not that odd.

Mercy stopped in heavy traffic a block from Jack's office. She leaned to the left, trying to see around the truck in front of her. As far as she could tell, drivers were rubbernecking at something. Her vehicle slowly crept forward, and she spotted the fire trucks in the parking lot of Jack Howell's real estate office. Thick gray smoke oozed from the collapsed building.

No. It can't be.

Mercy ignored the police officer gesturing that she couldn't enter and pulled into the lot.

The real estate office was gone. Her stomach churning, Mercy got out of her vehicle and stared at the destruction. Next door the vape shop was nearly decimated, but the pawn shop and the bakery had escaped unscathed.

Did I pressure the Realtor to do this?

"Hey! You can't park—"

She held up her FBI ID to silence the approaching officer. "Who's in charge?"

He pointed. "Sergeant Herscher."

Mercy strode in the sergeant's direction, wondering what his reaction would be when she informed him the fire was now part of an FBI investigation.

What did I stir up?

TWENTY-SIX

Hours later and smelling of smoke, Mercy joined Eddie in her boss's office. She glanced at the time, feeling her exhaustion down to the marrow in her bones, and considered calling Kaylie to cancel the late dinner for Mercy to officially meet Cade. Mercy knew it was important to all three of them that they get their relationships back on the right track. She needed to see how Cade acted around her niece instead of standing on a remote ranch with a couple of belligerent construction workers. And it would be a good time to question him about activities at that ranch.

Mercy wished she'd grabbed a cup of the horrible office coffee before sitting in front of Jeff's desk. Their primary concern was that no one could locate Jack Howell.

"How many times did you call the Realtor?" Jeff asked her.

"I don't know. A half dozen? I was annoyed that he hadn't called back when he said he would. But I left only two messages," she pointed out.

"So the rest of the calls were just harassment?" Jeff tapped his pen on his desk, his mouth in a grim line, avoiding her gaze.

"I thought of them as polite reminders to return my call. Maybe he has short-term memory problems."

Jeff finally looked at her, and she raised her eyebrows in an innocent expression.

"I requested his phone records. Hopefully we can trace who he called or his location before the fire." Eddie broke the tension. "When I went to his home to notify him of the fire, no one was there and his car was missing. I've requested an APB on the vehicle. A dog barked like crazy when I knocked, and when I peeked in the window by the door, I saw the dog had wet on the floor. I have to think that Jack planned to come back and let the dog out. I left a patrol car in front of his house to wait to see if he returns."

"Married?" asked Jeff.

"Divorced. I contacted the ex-wife. She hadn't heard from him in a few weeks."

"Are we sure he wasn't killed in the burning building?" Jeff frowned.

"We aren't sure," said Mercy. "But Jack's car wasn't at the office, and the owner of the vape shop said Jack always parks in a particular spot. The fire marshal says he won't know if there's a body inside until the building cools down enough for him to go through the debris."

"Does he believe it's arson?" asked Jeff.

"Bill Trek wouldn't give me a definitive answer on that because he hadn't done the inspection yet, but he pointed out the gasoline odor. It was overwhelming even with the smell of the smoke."

"Do you think Jack burned down his own office and left town?" Jeff asked.

"Who'd leave their dog locked in the house?" Eddie pointed out.

"A person who is scared," said Mercy. "Someone who's not thinking straight."

"Just what did you say to him?" Jeff leaned forward. "Did he burn it because we asked him some questions?"

"All I asked about was his purchase offer for Tilda Brass's property. I didn't threaten him at all."

"Then what did he hide by burning the office?" Eddie shrugged his shoulders. "Did we open a can of worms that we simply aren't aware of yet? Was Jack running something illegal through his office and was paranoid that we knew about it?"

"Keep digging into him," ordered Jeff. "Something made him cut and run. I want to know what it was."

"I called Tilda a little bit ago and asked if she had any idea who the mystery buyer could be. I wanted to know if there was someone she'd refuse to sell to for whatever reason," said Mercy. "She couldn't come up with any person who would stay anonymous to buy her land. She stated again she doesn't have any enemies and would sell to anyone who offered her a decent price." Mercy paused. "Unless they were followers of Bhagwan Shree Rajneesh. She was very adamant that she wouldn't sell to anyone associated with him."

The office was silent.

"Who?" asked Eddie.

"Didn't he die thirty years ago?" asked Jeff in a stunned voice.

"Something like that," said Mercy. She smiled at Eddie's confusion. "He was an Indian guru whose followers took over a small town not far from here in the nineteen-eighties. It got ugly. I think Tilda feels it happened a lot more recently than that."

"I think I read about it," admitted Eddie. "Rolls-Royces and red pajamas?"

"That was him," said Mercy.

"I think we're pretty safe that the buyer isn't associated with them," suggested Jeff.

"I agree," Mercy said. "While I was talking to Tilda, I wondered if the anonymous buyer burned down the real estate office. Maybe he didn't like that Jack told him the FBI wanted to know his identity."

Eddie stared at her as the theory sank in. "That would be one very nervous buyer," he said slowly. "That sounds a bit extreme, don't you think?"

"Maybe Jack knows more about the buyer than he should. Or maybe the buyer panicked when Jack said the FBI was asking questions."

The theory was growing on Mercy. The more she thought about it, the more she liked it. "Someone set Tilda's barn on fire. It seems logical they'd revert to fire again to take care of another problem." She paused, her brain rapidly processing. "It's all connected somehow . . . I can't see it yet. But the fires are a common denominator."

"I agree," said Jeff. "But whether Jack set this latest fire or not, we still need to locate him."

"Is there any connection between Jack Howell and Landon Hecht?" Mercy wondered out loud. "Could our presence at the Hecht home this morning have set something in motion?"

"Ask Hecht and his mother if they know Howell," ordered Jeff. "You're right. We're missing some pieces here. Anything else I need to know?"

Mercy and Eddie looked at each other and then shook their heads.

"Get back to work." Jeff waved them out of his office.

"I thought you were coming over this evening," Kaylie said into her cell phone as she lay on her bed, staring at her ceiling. Frustration shot through her. Cade didn't sound like himself.

"I am. I need to run out to the ranch for a bit first," Cade answered in a consoling voice.

Kaylie wasn't consoled and wondered if he was avoiding dinner at her house. Uncertainty shot through her nerves. "It's your day off. Why would you go out there on a day you don't work?"

"I won't do any work." Cade hesitated, and she felt his discomfort through the phone.

"What's going on?" *Is there someone else? What isn't he telling me?*

"It's nothing. Just something I need to check out."

"Then do it tomorrow when they're paying you to be there," she argued. "I don't understand why you're cutting into our time like this."

Cade was silent.

"Cade?" Her voice caught. "Is there someone else?"

"Oh God. No! Don't think like that, Kaylie!"

"Then why won't you tell me what you're doing?" She cringed at the nagging-girlfriend tone in her voice.

He sighed into the phone. "It's not another girl. It's work stuff. I need to go look for something . . . I saw something the other day and then it was gone. I need to know what happened to it."

"Like you lost some tools?" She tried hard to sound patient, but he was being deliberately vague.

"Something like that."

"Are you nervous you'll get in trouble if they find out you lost something?"

He paused again. "Not quite." He lowered his voice. "I think something illegal might be going on at the ranch."

Kaylie swung her legs over the edge of her bed and sat up, her anxiety skyrocketing. "Illegal? Should you be going back out there? Is it dangerous?"

"I think I'm okay. I don't think it's dangerous. The owner likes me; he says I have a good work ethic."

"Then what are you nervous about?"

"I came across a whole bunch of dynamite."

A large chunk of her anxiety vanished. "That's not a bad thing. My grandpa keeps dynamite in his barn. Says he'll never know when he might need it. He always made us grandkids stay away from it, although one of my cousins got into it one time. Grandpa was furious."

"I know. But this was a lot. And then when I looked for it again, it was gone."

Kaylie still didn't see the problem. "So they moved it. Or they got rid of it."

He exhaled impatiently.

He's still not telling me everything. "Why are you worried?"

"I heard some stuff."

She waited.

"I heard the guys talking about your aunt showing up at the ranch and asking questions. They didn't like it."

"That's her job. She can't help it if her questions make people uncomfortable. She's trying to find out who set those fires and killed three people."

Cade was silent.

"Oh my gosh! You think some guys at your ranch had something to do with those deaths?" Kaylie pressed her phone against her ear, tension making her heart race.

"Isn't that why your aunt went out there? Looking for answers about one of the victims?"

"I don't know. I don't keep track of what she's doing. But what did you overhear?" *Something is making him very nervous.*

"I'm not sure. Could just be a bunch of guy talk. Trying to sound tough. But someone said Josh Pence paid the price for screwing up."

"His death was the price?" she squeaked.

"Or he just got fired," Cade assured her. "I could be reading too much into it."

"Uh-huh." Kaylie knew he was trying to convince himself. The whole situation made her uncomfortable, and she didn't want to talk about the ranch anymore. "You're supposed to be here for dinner at seven. Are you going to make it?"

"I swear I'll be on time," Cade told her. "I don't want to miss it."

"Does meeting my aunt here scare you? She's very nice once you get to know her."

"She doesn't scare me. Sure, I'm a little intimidated, but I like that she's insisting on this dinner. It shows me she cares about who you hang around with."

"She's the best."

"I'll see you in a couple of hours," Cade promised. "I love you, Kaylie."

She caught her breath. "I love you too."

Cade ended the call, and Kaylie fell backward on her bed, arms outstretched and adrenaline pumping through every muscle. Glee made her brain spin in a heavenly, intoxicating manner.

He told me he loved me!

She couldn't wait for dinner.

TWENTY-SEVEN

At 7:05 p.m., Kaylie texted Cade. WILL YOU BE LATE?

At 7:10 p.m., she tried to call him and got his voice mail. As Mercy watched, she left a message asking what time he thought he'd arrive at dinner.

At 7:30 p.m., she hid briefly in her room and shed a few tears. *He didn't mean to tell me he loved me, and now he's staying away.* Mercy knocked on her door and suggested they eat.

By 7:45 p.m., dinner was over. More than two-thirds of the pizza that Kaylie had made from scratch and baked on her new pizza stone still sat on the table. Mercy stood and started to wrap up the pizza. To her credit she didn't ask why Cade had stood them up. She didn't seem too concerned about his absence. In fact, her aunt appeared extremely distracted.

Kaylie wallowed in self-pity in her chair, tracing the pattern in the tablecloth as her aunt cleared the dishes, unable to bring herself to jump up and help.

We're over. I pushed too hard.

She knew some guys were unable to break up with girls, so they simply went silent. Stopped texting, stopped calling, stopped showing up. End of relationship. *Is this the first phase?*

But why did he say he loved me?

She checked her phone again, and her finger hovered over the app to locate Cade's phone. They'd exchanged passwords a month ago to be able to trace each other's location. Cade had suggested it for emergencies, and she'd immediately agreed, flattered that he cared about her safety. Looking back now, she saw the creepiness factor. No doubt some guys used it to track their girlfriends, but it sent a notification to the missing phone if a search was activated. No one could secretly search with this app.

Would he think I'm a stalker if I check his location?

He could be hurt in a roadside ditch somewhere.

She tapped the screen and ran a search.

The app told her it couldn't locate his phone.

She stared at the screen. *What does that mean? Is he avoiding me? Did his battery die?* A million thoughts raced through her head. Some good, but mostly bad. Most circled around him trying to dump her.

Who is he seeing?

Mercy turned on the kitchen faucet and rinsed out her wineglass. Kaylie watched, torn between wanting to beg her aunt for advice and wanting to hide under her covers for the next month. At least Cade didn't attend her school, where she'd see him with some other girl, but her friends would ask how the relationship was going. What would she tell them?

Placing her wineglass in the dishwasher, Mercy glanced her way and did a double take. "Kaylie? Are you okay?"

She couldn't speak. She bit her lips together as tears ran down her face.

"Oh, honey." Mercy closed the dishwasher and sat in the chair next to Kaylie, taking her freezing hands in her warm ones. "I'm sure there's a good reason he's not here."

"But he's not answering my texts! And I checked the location of his phone." She swallowed hard, humiliated she'd admitted her stalking behavior to her aunt.

"Where is he?" Mercy didn't blink at her confession.

"It can't find him. His phone must be off," she whispered. "I think he turned it off on purpose."

"Oh, honey." Mercy leaned forward and pulled her into a hug.

Kaylie buried her face in her aunt's long curls. "He told me he loved me a few hours ago. Why would he do that if he planned to break up with me?"

Her aunt stiffened in the middle of the hug. "He told you that? You've only been together a little while. Even I haven't—" She abruptly cut off her words. "I'm so sorry, Kaylie. That's horrible."

Kaylie took a few deep breaths, getting her voice under control. "I believed him," she said softly. "Part of me still believes him. Maybe he was in a car accident and he's out of cellular range. Maybe the app can't connect with his location."

Mercy patted her on the back and didn't say anything.

She knows I'm grasping at straws.

"He was driving out to the ranch before coming here for dinner. There are a lot of isolated roads out there."

Mercy pulled back and met Kaylie's gaze, her eyes sharp with questions. "Why did he go out there? You told me today was his day off."

Kaylie wiped her nose with the back of her hand, unable to meet her aunt's intense stare. "He's nervous about something. He said he found a big stash of dynamite and then it disappeared. He also heard some of the men talking about your visit. He wouldn't tell me what they said, but I think he's scared they're involved with those murders."

"Shit."

Kaylie blinked.

Her aunt pulled away and grabbed her phone off the kitchen counter. "You haven't heard from him since he said he was headed out to the ranch, correct?" She tapped a few buttons on her screen, not looking at Kaylie.

Mercy's tone unnerved her. Her aunt had suddenly shifted into FBI-agent mode. "That's right."

Holding her phone to her ear, Mercy met Kaylie's gaze. "You need to tell me everything he's told you about working out there. Everything. No matter how inconsequential it seems to you."

◆ ◆ ◆

Nearly an hour after Mercy called him, Truman took the final turn onto the long road that led to the McDonald ranch. He'd nearly missed it in the dark, but beside him in the vehicle, Mercy had been watching, her gaze glued to the side of the road. He'd called Deschutes County to request backup at the ranch and to request the county's patrols keep an eye out for Cade's pickup. The state police had also been notified and warned that the truck might have gone off the road between the ranch and Bend. The entire trip to the ranch, Mercy had studied the side of the road, watching for skid marks or signs that a truck had disrupted the brush.

The pitch dark made for difficult searching. Twice he'd pulled over because she'd seen something, only to discover no truck. Each time Truman had recalled the image of Pence's abandoned truck. Would they find Cade's truck in a similar situation? And what did that mean for Cade?

"I don't think he would have stood her up. I think he's in trouble," Mercy repeated for the third time. Her gaze was laser sharp, searching for the truck, but he felt her distraction, her brain considering every situation they might encounter when they arrived at the ranch.

"Sounds like their relationship is serious," Truman said.

"As serious as you can be at seventeen," replied Mercy. "I think it's mostly hormones and heartbreak at that age, but if he's purposefully avoiding her, he's going to get an earful from me."

A sideways glance showed she was deadly serious. Her baby had been hurt, and Truman enjoyed seeing her mama bear instincts. Kaylie had exposed a whole new side of Mercy that he deeply appreciated. When Mercy had first come to town, she'd hid behind a professional unemotional wall, and immediately Truman had felt challenged to chip away at it. He'd succeeded, but her relationship with Kaylie had ripped away bricks only a daughter could reach, exposing a tender side of Mercy that made his heart warm.

"How far out is our backup?" she asked.

"I think they're about twenty minutes out."

"I also let Jeff know what's going on," Mercy said. "He's sending a team in our direction. Anytime I mention McDonald's ranch to him, he gets antsy."

"I think he has good reason."

Mercy shifted in her seat. "Kaylie told me Cade was scared of some of the men he works with. He also told her he heard that Pence paid the price for screwing up. That statement has to refer to his murder."

"That's a steep price for messing up. What could he have done to deserve that?"

"Who knows? But he's dead, and I think someone out here knows what happened."

"What do you think McDonald is doing on this ranch?"

"According to some of what Cade shared with Kaylie, it sounds like he's forming his own militia. Our office has heard chatter of a new militia in the area. They also heard about plans to blow up a bridge. When Kaylie told me about the dynamite, it raised an alarm in my head."

Truman's gut told him she was right about McDonald's plans for a militia. He'd seen the signs. The growing group of men. McDonald's constant guards. His attitude toward law enforcement. The rumors surrounding his ranch. He had the ego and the personality to drive men to do what he desired. *Could he inspire men to kill for him?*

Possibly.

Mercy scanned an email on her phone. "They didn't find a body in the ruins of Jack Howell's real estate office."

"Now he's another missing person."

"I think he torched it and left town."

Truman suddenly remembered what he'd discovered about a piece of real estate earlier that day. "Did you know Tilda Brass's property shares a border with the McDonald ranch?"

"*What?*" Mercy's entire body swung toward him. "Where did you hear that? That can't be possible. They're miles apart."

"I looked it up. Her property is a weird shape that follows the creek. The far east end butts up against a remote part of the McDonald ranch."

He could nearly hear the gears spinning in her brain. "Why didn't you tell me this?"

"I just did. I found out today."

"Could he be the anonymous buyer for her property? Wanting to expand his own?"

"Seems a logical guess. Although I think his ranch is big enough. Why does he need more?"

Mercy slowly slid back into her seat, her fingers beating a rhythm on her thighs. "That's a question I'd like to ask McDonald. I can see him remaining anonymous during real estate negotiations. He seems to appreciate his privacy."

"Based on my phone call with my deputy buddy in Idaho this morning, McDonald is a very private person. Too private. I suspect the reserve officer is going to dig up some interesting dirt on Tom McDonald."

"If McDonald is the buyer, would he torch the real estate office?" Mercy suddenly asked. "We're already considering that he had Joshua Pence killed at that other fire. Is he our fire starter?"

"I think Landon Hecht is our firebug," said Truman.

"Me too, but even he said he didn't start the fires on Tilda's property or where we found Pence's body."

"If you're suggesting Tom McDonald started those fires, then he might have shot the deputies." Truman's stomach seethed with acid as his anger built.

"If he's forming a militia, he may not have any regard for law enforcement," Mercy stated. "He ignored my FBI visit and didn't feel a need to be respectful during your visit."

"I don't know." Truman's mind tried to catch up with Mercy's theories. "We're making a lot of assumptions."

"I'm thinking out loud."

Truman slowly drove around the last bend to the McDonald property and spotted a few building lights. "We need to wait for our backup. I was ready to knock on doors and ask about Cade, but now I don't think that's the best course of action."

"Absolutely not. Park at the edge and we'll sit tight until they get here. I have no desire to confront some wannabe militia members in the dark."

TWENTY-EIGHT

Mercy sat in the dark next to Truman, her eyes straining to see through the night. Truman had stopped near the vehicles parked farthest from the buildings, not wanting to stick out by parking alone. The ranch was silent. They'd cracked their windows, and the lack of noise made her want to crawl up the inside walls of the vehicle. Truman sat quietly, his focus and calm keeping her nerves from leaping out of her limbs.

No anxiety in him this evening.

She could see a half dozen lights on different buildings. The brightest was on the farmhouse in the distance. It was after 9:00 p.m., and no silhouettes moved in the shadows. *Is everyone in bed already?* Her gaze traveled over the small bunkhouses. Cade had told Kaylie that McDonald planned to house more than a hundred men.

The thought made her insides shudder.

"What's that?" Truman whispered. "Over there. By the king cab truck."

Mercy stared into the dark. Sure enough, she spotted the outline of a figure darting between the vehicles, working toward their end of the parking area. "It's moving this way."

Truman touched the handle of his door.

"Wait," Mercy said almost silently. The figure passed between two trucks, a brief silhouette in the night. "It's a woman!" she exclaimed under her breath. Disappointment filled her chest. She'd hoped it was Cade.

"You're right."

Hunched over, the woman dashed through the dark, using the vehicles as cover. As she drew closer, Mercy saw she carried a duffel bag and glanced over her shoulder several times. *She's scared.*

"I'm going," she said. "Don't let the inside lights turn on when I open the door."

"They're off, and I'm going with you."

"I'll talk."

"I've got you covered."

Mercy opened her door as quietly as she could and breathed a sigh of relief as the Tahoe's cab lights stayed off. The woman reached a nearby car, and Mercy heard the grate of a key sliding into the lock of the door. She took several steps toward the woman, stopping with twenty feet between them.

"Excuse me," Mercy said as calmly as she could.

The woman whirled around, her hand pressed to her chest, her terror apparent in the dark.

Mercy raised her hands. "I didn't mean to scare you," she said kindly, as every piece of her focused on the position of the woman's hands. *She hasn't reached for a weapon.*

Yet.

"You scared the crap out of me," the woman said. The dim light lit her blonde braid, and she was nearly as tall as Mercy. She squinted in the dark. "Who are you?" Her voice shook, and she reminded Mercy of a doe ready to bolt at the slightest hint of danger.

"I'm looking for a friend." *Don't scare her away.*

"This isn't a place to find friends," the blonde stated. "I definitely wouldn't come here alone. Especially as a woman at night. You're just looking for trouble."

"I'm not alone." Mercy tipped her head in Truman's direction. "He's helping me."

The woman took a half step back as she spotted Truman's tall shadow for the first time. She glanced at Mercy. "He's safe?"

"Yes. Are you worried for your safety?"

"Not anymore. I'm out of here."

"Why are you leaving?" Truman asked.

"I'm done working for this guy." She opened the passenger door, quickly tossed her bag inside, and shut it, keeping the noise to a minimum. She moved like a bird, rapid and fluttery.

"McDonald?" Mercy asked. "What did you do for him?"

"Cook. Clean. Whatever was needed. I thought McDonald was okay at first . . . but now I have my doubts. He's good at presenting an honest front, but behind the scenes he's ruthless. He'll do whatever it takes to get what he wants." Her voice lowered and she glanced behind her. "People have died. People who crossed him. But he claims he had nothing to do with it."

Joshua Pence?

"And the guys he attracts are also a problem. They think I'm here for more than labor." Her voice was steady but full of anger, her pale profile proud. "I'm not putting up with it anymore."

"Do you have somewhere to go?" Mercy asked.

"Yep. I'll go crawling back to my sister's house. She told me not to accept this position, and she was right." She strode around the front of her car to the driver's side.

"Do you know Cade Pruitt?" Mercy took several steps closer, unwilling to let her leave just yet.

The woman froze and turned around. "Why?"

"He's the friend we're looking for."

In the dark, Mercy saw the blonde's gaze go from her to Truman and back. "He screwed up." Her voice wavered, and Mercy worried she'd bolt.

"What does that mean?" Fear bloomed in Mercy as she remembered how Cade had told Kaylie that Joshua Pence screwed up.

"I was going to call the police once I left." She stood still, a motionless bird in the split second before it rocketed into the sky.

Truman stepped next to Mercy. "Why? What happened to him?"

The woman took a half step in their direction, her eyes black holes in her pale face, and whispered, "They've got him locked up. They said he ratted them out to the FBI."

Mercy caught her breath.

"All the men are furious. I don't want to know what they'll do to him, but I've heard how Tom McDonald takes care of people who go against him." Her head dipped in Mercy's direction. "I'm really sorry about your friend, but it's too late to help him. The only thing you can do is call the police and hope they'll respond all the way out here."

"Has he been hurt?" Truman asked.

"He's still breathing. For now."

"The police are on their way," Mercy said. She showed the woman her ID. "I'm with the FBI. We're waiting for our backup."

"I don't know whether to be relieved or scared for you," the woman said, backing away again. Her hands shook.

"Why would you be scared for us?" asked Truman.

"Because that crowd sees the police as the enemy . . . and that kid isn't going to survive the night."

Cade could see out of only one eye. Not that it mattered in the pitch dark.

The rough wooden floor was gritty under his cheek, and both hands were numb from his having his arms tied behind his back. He was tired of lying on his stomach, but he was also grateful that they'd stopped kicking him. The darkness was his closest friend, hiding his tears and allowing him to take inventory of his injuries.

His ribs hurt every time he breathed, and he'd puked up the soda he'd drunk on the way to the ranch. He breathed through his mouth, his nose smashed and clogged with drying blood.

Kaylie will think I stood her up.

He had bigger things to worry about, but his thoughts kept straying to Kaylie, concerned with her feelings.

I need to focus on getting out of here.

He knew they wouldn't let him leave alive.

Earlier, Chip had been the first one to spot him on the ranch. Cade had parked in the dark and casually walked in the shadows to the shed, determined to prove to himself that the dynamite hadn't disappeared. It had to be somewhere in that shed. What he hadn't expected to find was Chip and one of his buddies, Rob, going through the supplies in the shed. They'd looked up in surprise as Cade came around a corner. Playing it cool, he'd greeted the men, planning to come up with some story about searching for his backup tool belt. Instead Chip drew a gun.

Cade's words had dried up in his mouth as he stared at the end of the barrel.

"Scared, smart boy?" Chip had sneered. "The boss man told everyone to keep an eye out for you. He's pissed as all hell that you ratted us out to the police and feds."

"I—I don't know what you're talking about," Cade had stuttered as icy fear threaded through his limbs. He slowly raised his hands, praying Chip wouldn't shoot.

"We know about your girlfriend," Chip stated. "We know she's the niece of that FBI agent who harassed us the other day."

"I haven't told her anything! I don't have anything to tell her!" Cade said earnestly, using his gaze to plead with the two men. Chip's finger was on the trigger of the pistol, and the look in his eyes was just left of crazy.

He wants to shoot me. Just to enjoy it.

"Tell it to the boss," said Chip. He directed Rob to tie Cade's hands behind his back, and then Chip poked him in the ribs with the gun as they walked through the dark to the mess hall. Cade couldn't see the ground and stumbled several times, hoping Chip didn't accidentally trip and shoot him through the heart.

They made it to the mess hall, where some sort of meeting had just taken place. About forty men milled around, looking ready to wrap up their night until Cade had been pushed through the front door. Every face turned in his direction. After a moment of surprise, a small cheer went up from the crowd. Cries of "You got him!" and "Fuck that bastard!" met his ears.

His knees turned to water at the frenzied looks on their faces. Angry, bitter eyes glittered at him. Cade blinked. These were his fellow workers and acquaintances. Men who made a living with their hands and embraced an honest day's labor. They dressed like him in boots and Wranglers. Men he'd never dreamed would turn on him.

Seeing their hate and anger rocked him to his core. It was a mob.

Is this what happened to Joshua Pence?

Tom McDonald emerged from behind the group, and Cade's gaze latched on to his face in hope. His boss had told him how much he admired his work; Cade had seen the respect in his eyes. *He'll straighten this out.* But McDonald's current expression was of a subdued rage. Cade couldn't look away as the man stepped closer through the crowd, his huge bulk driving men to step aside to make room.

He stopped in front of Cade.

The room had gone quiet. Eager faces looked from Tom to him and back again, repressed energy bubbling under their surfaces, thirsting for blood.

Cade tried to swallow, but his dry throat wouldn't follow directions. On either side of him, Chip and Rob each gripped one of his arms, presenting him to their leader. Chip's fingers dug into the underside of his upper arm, and Cade wondered if he could feel his sweat.

"What brings you here so late on your day off, Cade?"

Cade couldn't speak.

"Snooping for the FBI?"

He vehemently shook his head. "No," he croaked. "I've never talked to the FBI."

Mutters of "Bullshit" filled the room. Boots shuffled, men adjusted their stances. Eyes continued to stare at him, their heat boring into his skull.

McDonald tilted his head the slightest bit. "You told the FBI about us. You pretended not to know that agent who was here the other day when you're *dating her niece!*"

Louder mutters.

"You managed to fool Chip and Mitch. Mitch even stuck up for you."

Cade met Mitch's gaze over Tom's shoulder. Mitch looked at him with dead eyes. "I'd never met her before that day. Seriously." He spoke directly to Mitch. The one man he wanted to convince. It was suddenly important to him that Mitch know he hadn't stuck his neck out in vain.

McDonald shook his head. "Too late. I'm disappointed in you, Cade. I had high hopes that you could join us one day. You showed a lot of promise, but you let a woman lead you around by the dick."

Cade spotted Owen Kilpatrick standing next to Mitch. His face was blank, his arms crossed over his chest, his stance stating he was as angry as the rest of the men.

"Who knows you're here?" Tom asked.

"I told Kaylie I was coming here. I'm supposed to be at her house by seven." At least his voice sounded normal.

"You're not going to make your date," Chip taunted.

McDonald held up a hand to silence Chip. "I don't believe you," he said to Cade. "You're just saying that."

"Check my phone," Cade stated. *They need to think someone will come looking for me.* "You'll see I called her in the last hour."

Rob pulled the phone out of his pocket and pressed it against Cade's right thumb to unlock the screen. He poked around for a few seconds. "He's right. There's a call to her."

McDonald pressed his lips together as he regarded Cade. "We'll settle his fate later. Put him in the pantry. Tie his feet too."

Rob knocked Cade's feet out from under him, and he fell to the floor, catching his weight on his left shoulder and knocking the breath out of his lungs. The group of men pressed closer, and scuffed boots moved threateningly close to his face. His feet were lifted; someone produced a rope and bound his ankles together.

That's when the kicking started. Boot tips to his face, chest, and back. Cade rolled to his side and tried to bring his head to his knees, protecting his chest and belly. He vomited the soda, and the blows continued until McDonald ordered them to stop.

They'd dragged him into a small room off the kitchen and slammed the door. He heard McDonald order someone to clean up the mess.

Cade slowed his breaths, inhaling as gently as possible to stop his ribs from sending lightning jolts of pain to his brain. He searched for something optimistic about his situation.

I'm not dead.

Kaylie knows where I am. But would she tell anyone? Or would she go to bed upset that he'd blown off their dinner?

If it had been one of his buddies he'd told, he'd probably wait a week before mentioning he hadn't heard from Cade lately. And didn't a person need to be missing for two days before the police took any action?

I'm not dead.

Voices sounded from the mess hall. The men were protesting something McDonald had said. Cade awkwardly scooted closer to the entry and placed his ear against the wide crack under the door.

"I don't care that it upsets you. I can't shoot him," said McDonald. "His girlfriend knows he was coming here, and if they find his body with a bullet hole, where do you think they'll focus their attention?"

Cade shuddered at the casual tone. McDonald spoke about killing him as if he were debating whether to throw out an old head of lettuce.

"I know he betrayed us," McDonald said. "I wish I hadn't hired him, but we needed to get the bunkhouses done as quickly as possible. From here on out, all labor will come from our circle. No more outside help. We will trust and rely on ourselves. The way I wanted it to be in the first place. Our need to expand the facilities will no longer affect my decisions."

"We'll get it done!" "We don't need anyone else!" "No more outsiders!"

Cade's neck ached from the uncomfortable position, but it was a small pain compared with his others. And small in relation to the utter burning fear in his stomach.

"Stage an accident," suggested a voice from the crowd. Other voices seconded his idea.

"I like the idea," said McDonald.

Proposals for car accidents, fires, and hunting accidents were put forward. Cade couldn't make out all the words of the discussion on the best way to kill him, but he heard enough. He rolled onto his stomach, resting his neck.

"Are you guys crazy?" said one clear voice. "He's just a kid."

That was Mitch.

Relief at the knowledge that he had one friend in the group made tears burn in both his eyes. Snot ran from his injured nose, and he wiped it carefully against the floor.

The muttered tones and angry voices that followed told Cade that Mitch was in the minority.

"We handle our own problems," announced McDonald. "We don't wait for the narrow-minded police and backed-up courts to spend our taxes as they dawdle over making decisions. The kid broke my trust and has put a lot of people in danger. That needs to be punished." He paused. *"Do you have a problem with my decision, Mitch?"*

Silence.

Cade held his breath.

"All I'm asking for is mercy," said Mitch. "A little leniency. You said he's shown a lot of potential, Tom. I agree you should go ahead and punish him . . . he's got that coming, but I don't think he deserves death."

Thank you, Mitch.

"This is why I'm the leader, Mitch. I don't let emotions mess with the need to take action. I've decided on the best way to handle the kid, but your input has been noted, and we'll debate his sentence a little later."

Murmurs of agreement reached Cade.

He's humoring Mitch and trying to show the other men they have a voice in his decisions.

They don't.

"Whether he lives or dies will be decided tonight."

TWENTY-NINE

Truman couldn't stand still.

"We need to wait for our backup," Mercy argued as they watched the woman's taillights disappear down the road from the ranch.

"I vote we go in. We can't wait. Waiting could mean Cade's death. You saw how scared she was." Truman's muscles buzzed as if he'd had three hits of espresso.

"But—"

"If there was an active shooter, we'd already be in there."

"That's different."

"Cade needs us to take action now. For all we know, we're too late. You know I'm right." He watched Mercy look back at the road, where they expected their backup to appear. "We've got good cause to go in. Now."

"Dammit. Get me a vest."

Truman opened the rear of his Tahoe and grabbed another vest as she updated her boss on their actions. "You should've already had one on," Truman muttered as he handed it to her. His own vest suddenly felt heavy and too tight around his chest. *Breathe slowly.* He took a couple of deep breaths and fought off the claustrophobic feeling. *How can I wear it all day with no problem and suddenly feel like it's drowning me?*

Fucking nerves.

I'm not waiting to find Cade.

He'd promised himself he'd never hesitate again. He knew better than to rush every situation, but he'd heard enough from the woman to know Cade's situation was deadly serious. As Mercy strapped on the vest, he called the dispatcher and asked her to inform the Deschutes County sheriff that they were going inside.

"Jeff said Eddie and another agent are headed out here," reported Mercy as she tightened the Velcro straps. "They're in touch with the Deschutes County deputies that are en route."

"Let's go." Truman wove through the parked vehicles toward the light above the door on the mess hall, and wondered what they'd find inside. The entire ranch was eerily quiet. There was no indication that a mob stood ready to tear apart a young man.

Did she exaggerate?

"Truman," Mercy whispered urgently. "Get down!"

He immediately spotted the figure and ducked behind the bed of a truck next to Mercy. Moving silently, he stretched to peer around the truck. Tom McDonald's recognizable bulk moved across the compound. His steps were stiff, and he walked with a noticeable waddle. He was alone. Truman watched for a long moment, searching the darkness for McDonald's ever-present guards.

Truman pulled back into the protection of the truck's shadow. "I didn't see his entourage."

"I didn't either. He's headed toward the farmhouse."

Their gazes met in the dim light. "Follow him," Truman stated as Mercy nodded. They changed direction and moved after the man. They kept to the shadows, constantly checking over their shoulders for McDonald's guards. Truman doubted Cade was in the farmhouse, but surely McDonald wouldn't authorize any punishment of Cade without his direct supervision. McDonald struck him as the type to keep a firm thumb on top of every command.

If we can stop McDonald, we can stop him from telling his men what to do.

What if we're too late?

Truman refused to consider that possibility, positive that their best course of action was to cut off any communication between the leader and his men. According to what they'd learned from the escaping woman, McDonald had to be stopped. Period.

No hesitating.

He and Mercy watched McDonald lumber up the steps to the farmhouse and disappear inside.

"Think his guards are already in there?" she whispered.

"No, I suspect they're watching over Cade." *I hope.* "We'll move in assuming that there are other people in there." Standard operating procedure.

Weapons ready, they did a quick circle around the tiny house, peeking in windows and noting exits. The brightest light in the house was in a rear room Truman figured was the kitchen. Ancient half curtains blocked them from seeing in, their red rickrack trim reminding him of the curtains in his grandmother's old home. Reconnaissance finished, they silently worked their way up the stairs to the front door. Truman opened it, thankful for the bare light bulb that lit the interior, and together he and Mercy covered the hidden corners of the room before moving in.

Walking in tandem with their shoulders touching to keep in sync, he and Mercy rapidly cleared the lower level of the house, leaving the well-lit room at the back for last. Truman nodded at Mercy and held his breath as they entered the kitchen simultaneously. Tom McDonald sat at the table eating a bowl of stew, and he froze with his spoon halfway to his mouth. Mercy trained her weapon on McDonald while Truman checked the corners. McDonald had stew in his beard. He slowly lowered the spoon to the table and lay his hands flat on either side of his bowl, his gaze darting between Truman and Mercy.

"Well, look who it is," said McDonald, drawing out his words. "I don't suppose you're here to share my stew."

Truman stepped behind him and checked him for weapons, removing a revolver from his belt and then handcuffing him. It took two sets of handcuffs linked together to bring McDonald's arms in place behind his back. Truman rattled off a statement about temporarily securing McDonald for the safety of the officers, and McDonald shot him a black look over his shoulder.

He silently watched McDonald while Mercy took the stairs to the upper level of the house. He traced her movements by the sound of her footsteps overhead. Each hushed shout of "Clear!" as she moved from room to room steadied his breathing. She was back within less than a minute.

"Where's Cade Pruitt?" asked Mercy.

McDonald took a long moment to size her up. "Not sure who you're talking about. I have a lot of men working for me."

Truman resisted an urge to whack him in the head to jolt his memory.

Mercy gave a smile that made Truman's skin crawl. "Is he still alive?" she asked sweetly. "Or has he met the same fate as Joshua Pence?"

McDonald stared calmly at her. "Again . . . not sure what you're getting at."

"In five minutes this ranch will be crawling with FBI agents and Deschutes County deputies," she said with the same smile. "How about you do some work on restoring your memory before they arrive?"

He leaned back in his chair and gave a lazy smile, a man in no hurry.

Truman sighed.

"I believe you're trespassing," offered McDonald. "Neither of you have jurisdiction to be here. I've declared this property to no longer be part of the United States. Therefore you're subject to our laws, and both of you are breaking them."

Mercy rolled her eyes.

"I warned you," McDonald said. "I'm not liable for what might happen to the two of you. You've trespassed on my land, taken away my weapon, and handcuffed me against my will. The two of you are the reason why this country is taking a stand against the police."

"We've been informed that Cade Pruitt's life is in danger on this property," stated Truman.

"That's no business of mine," said McDonald. "Or yours."

A soft noise sounded from outside the kitchen's back door, and Mercy's head jerked at the sound. She nodded at Truman, her weapon still trained on McDonald. Truman visualized the space they'd reconnoitered moments before. A few concrete steps led to the door. No debris or fencing for someone to hide behind. It was a wide-open area at the back of the house. The only cover for an assailant would be the corner of the house. Truman moved to the side of the door and shouted, "Eagle's Nest Police Department! Who is outside?"

Silence.

No sounds of footsteps leaving.

He shouted again.

"I'm going to check," he told Mercy. She nodded and moved to back him up.

Weapon leading, he opened the door and did a rapid two-step and swing of his arms to check the entire area. *No one is out here.* He jumped off the steps to the left and placed his back against the house as Mercy covered him and the right side from the top of the stair. He took a few steps to the left, welcoming the calm that'd taken over his limbs. Even his heartbeat felt steady. *No fear.*

"Oooof!"

He whirled around in time to see Mercy collapse and be dragged back into the home, her feet trailing. The door slammed behind her. *"Mercy!"*

His vision tunneling, Truman rushed for the steps but was grabbed from behind around the waist, his weapon arm pinned, and thrown to the ground. *Noooo!* The man's bulk landed on top of him, knocking the air from his lungs. A burst of energy lit up his brain and instinct took over. *Fight back!*

Truman brought his elbow back into his assailant's chest and kicked with every ounce of his being, determined to keep the man from grabbing his weapon, which was stuck between his stomach and the dirt. *I won't let them take her!*

"Hold still!" hissed in his ear, and Truman flung back another elbow, connecting with something hard. *"Fuck!"* The grip around his stomach and weapon arm tightened.

"It's me, Owen! You've got to get out of here!"

Truman stopped kicking. *Owen?* "They've got Mercy!"

"There's a half dozen of them in the house now. *You can't take on all of them!*"

Truman lay still, his mind racing and his heart pounding against the ground. *How do I get to her?*

◆ ◆ ◆

I'm an idiot.

She hadn't watched her back.

At least Truman got away.

She sat on the floor in the kitchen, her back to a wall, wearing a pair of Truman's handcuffs, as McDonald's men searched the property for Truman. She'd been focused on clearing the yard when she'd been rushed from behind. She'd heard the boot steps a split second too late. A half dozen men had taken her to the floor, knocked the breath out of her lungs, and disarmed her before she could breathe again. Now she had a growing bruise on the back of her skull and a sore breast from the joker who'd thought he had the right to maul her as the others bound her hands. He sported a new falsetto.

Mercy glared at another man, who hovered over her. He had a lascivious smile on his face that made her stomach crawl. He deliberately adjusted his jeans at his crotch. "Give me a break," she muttered.

"I'll give you something." More leers.

"Grow up."

"Oh, I'm old enough for you, darlin'." Two of his bottom front teeth were missing.

For all his sexy advances, the man hadn't touched her. He'd kept a pistol aimed at her head, but he stayed a good distance from her feet. She'd already proved she could kick.

Four men had been left to guard her.

I think that number is a compliment.

Three of them kept a healthy distance, but the fourth had slowly worked his way closer as he tried to seduce her with his charming banter. She uncrossed and recrossed her boots, holding his gaze, amused when he scooted back six inches. She wasn't scared; she was on edge, her senses on high alert, watching and analyzing every word and action around her. Whatever was going to happen would happen, and she'd do her damnedest to get out without getting hurt. For all their blustering, they were now keeping their hands off her. There weren't a lot of IQ points in the room, and her mind was preparing arguments for her release.

Heavy treads in the hallway told her McDonald had returned.

He entered the room and the four men stood at attention, snapping to with nonmilitary precision. McDonald waved a hand at them and they relaxed.

At least they didn't salute the man.

McDonald stopped at her feet and stared down at her. Mercy looked back, moving only her eyes, not her head, and raised a brow at him.

"How fast the cards change," stated McDonald. "Are you a betting woman?"

"No. I don't gamble."

He nodded in approval. "I didn't think so. Waste of money."

"I'd like to take a gamble on her," muttered her dentally challenged guard.

"Show some respect," barked McDonald, surprising Mercy and the guard.

"She's a lying fed," argued her admirer. "You said the women were here for us. I'd think this one should make the full rounds."

Just try me. Keeping her lips closed, Mercy ran her tongue over her teeth and paused on a particularly sharp canine. *I'll use whatever I can as a weapon.*

"Not now," huffed McDonald. His face was redder than when Truman had cuffed him earlier. "We've got other problems. Go help find that police chief," he told the frustrated man. "But first tell Owen Kilpatrick I want to see him." He jammed his hands in the pockets of his coat and focused on Mercy again.

Mercy briefly closed her eyes. *What will Owen do?*

"Where's the chief?" he asked her.

"Like I would know. You saw how your men yanked me back into the room."

"Who else is here?"

She smiled. "I expect the FBI and Deschutes County to be here any minute."

McDonald held her gaze, assessing her. "I want a dozen men covering the road," he said over his shoulder. "Tell them to move some vehicles to block the entrance. No one gets in."

One of the men darted down the hallway to carry out his command. He returned five seconds later. "They found the police chief's truck!"

"Where?"

"Right with all the others. They want to know if they can break in."

"Of course not!" McDonald shook his head in exasperation. "No one touches the truck until I say so." The messenger dashed away again.

McDonald pulled on his beard as he looked from Mercy to the two waiting men. Frustration emanated from him, and he paced in a small circle, continuing to stroke his beard and take quick glances at Mercy.

The two men left in the room exchanged confused looks, and Mercy wondered if they'd never seen their leader struggle with a decision.

She considered his options. Believe her story that more police were on their way and get ready for a standoff. Kill her and prepare for a standoff.

Or give up.

She wasn't sure if he'd kill her first in the giving-up scenario. Probably not.

"Get her up. Take her to the mess hall."

The men each grabbed an arm and hauled her to her feet. She deliberately met the stare of one of them; he looked away after a few seconds and shot a glance at McDonald, who ignored him.

That's right. Your leader is losing ground. You can feel it.

She walked slowly, making the men try to drag her. As they took the gravel path toward the mess hall, McDonald shouted into the dark, "Hey, Chief Daly! Your woman is about to provide entertainment for my men this evening!"

Mercy stumbled, tripped up by the memory of a man who'd once tried to force her. He'd died as a result.

But the terror he'd created had never died. It'd simply gone underground in her psyche, waiting to pop out in moments like this.

No one responded to McDonald's taunt from the shadows.

Breathe. She worked to control her breaths, which deepened and slowed. Searching for calm.

"Did Joshua Pence have a final walk like this?" she asked her escorts. "Did two men lead him to his murder?"

Hands tightened on her arms. "Shut up," muttered the man on her right. He smelled of cigarettes.

"Is that a sore topic for you?" she hissed at him. "Maybe you'll be next if you don't toe McDonald's line. He seems the type to simply eliminate anyone who disagrees with him."

"I suggest you keep your mouth shut," Tom McDonald said from behind her. He shouted his taunt again.

"I know how your type operates," said Mercy over her shoulder. "You're the big cheese. Everyone around you is terrified you'll hurt them if they don't jump when you say jump. But you know what? That gets old after a while. Pretty soon people get tired of jumping for no reason."

Cigarette Breath dug his fingers under her bicep. Pain shot to her brain.

"Joshua Pence went rogue," announced McDonald. The men escorting her solemnly nodded.

"How is that possible? Don't you run a tight ship?" she prodded.

"My men have free will," McDonald stated. "They make their own decisions."

"And what happens when one makes a decision that goes against what you've decreed?"

"They're asked to leave."

Out of the corner of her eye, she watched Cigarette Breath exchange a look with her other handler.

"What did Joshua Pence do?" she asked.

"He shot those deputies."

"And how did he end up with his throat slit?"

"I don't know the answer to that," McDonald said. "I ordered him to leave my ranch when I heard about it."

"If he murdered the deputies, why didn't you turn him in to the police?"

"It wasn't any of my business."

"Was he killed by someone wanting revenge for the deputies?"

"Probably," agreed McDonald. "To me that would indicate another cop caused his death. I've noticed you aren't investigating his death as heavily as the two deputies'. No doubt you've already realized it was an inside job."

Her escorts gave fierce nods in agreement.

"We have no leads that Joshua Pence was killed by a cop in revenge for the two deputies."

"Maybe you need to take a closer look at your own kind."

"Was the Brass fire started because you were trying to intimidate Tilda to sell to you?"

McDonald laughed. "I don't know what you're talking about."

Again, Cigarette Breath exchanged a glance with his coworker.

You guys need to take a class in reading body language.

They arrived at the mess hall, and Cigarette Breath yanked open the door, pushing her inside. Mercy was immediately hit with the odor of sweaty men. The room was large, but there were enough bodies inside to make it smell like a men's locker room. Every one of them turned to stare as she stumbled through the entrance. The attention brought her to a halt, her mouth going dry.

There are so many of them.

And each one is angry.

She searched for her brother's face, wanting to see his eyes in the crowd. Surely he wouldn't be looking at her with the anger and disgust of the dozens of other men right now. She fought to keep her knees from shaking. She met several stony gazes and was overwhelmed by a thought: she *knew* these men. They were the type of men she'd grown up with, been raised by, and encountered every day of her youth. She'd always felt safe around them . . . these men with their canvas coats, boots, and callused hands. They were the salt of the earth, people who loved to work the land and respected their neighbors.

But she'd never felt threatened until now.

There was no comfort in their familiarity.

Unshed tears burned.

How can they turn on me?

I'm one of them.

Or had it been too long? Her clothes had changed, and some of her beliefs had changed. When they looked at her, did they see only these changes? Someone who didn't belong? Someone who threatened their way of life?

The irony nearly made her laugh.

She gave a coughing hiccup, and the hands on her arms tightened again.

The staring men took a collective step closer, and terror settled in her heart.

THIRTY

Truman tried to catch his breath. The aftereffects of Owen's body slam made it feel as if his ribs were poking into his lungs. The two men had darted away from the farmhouse and into the woods, circling back to a forested area far from the vehicles. Truman leaned against a tree, wrapped an arm around his rib cage, and tried to ignore the painful stabbing.

Owen huddled behind a second tree, watching the flashlights hover around Truman's truck and keeping a sharp eye out for followers.

"When's your backup getting here?" he hissed at Truman.

"Any minute." *I hope.* He pulled out his phone. No service. "I don't have service."

"It's nearly impossible to get a signal here." Owen said, checking his own phone and shaking his head.

Truman heard Tom McDonald shout his name and say something about Mercy. As McDonald's threat penetrated the fog of pain around his brain, Truman numbly stepped out from behind his tree.

"Get back!" Owen ordered. "He won't hurt her."

Truman couldn't meet Owen's gaze in the dark. "Are you sure?" The thought of Mercy being handed off to a crowd of men made his intestines turn to water.

"Yes."

Owen hesitated a split second before answering, adding flames to Truman's already hot anxiety.

"He's not into that sort of thing," Owen whispered. "He'll use her to keep them in line, hinting that they might get some time between her legs if they obey. But I don't think he'll just hand her over."

"You don't *think*," Truman repeated as he tried to calm his nerves. "That's not good enough for me."

"She's *my* sister!"

"Don't give me that line! You've ignored her or verbally attacked her since she came back to town! If there's any family loyalty there, I haven't seen it!" Pain shot through his side, and he fought for breath. "As far as I can tell, you think following through on McDonald's threat would be good riddance to her!"

Owen went silent, but Truman could feel the weight of his stare in the dark. Tension weighed heavy in the air between them.

"I was wrong," Owen finally whispered. "I'll get her out of there."

"The two of us can't take on forty men." Truman wouldn't place a bet on Owen's honesty, but he heard a sliver of truth in the man's voice that gave him hope.

"Not everyone is happy with the recent developments around here."

"Some of McDonald's men won't back him up?" asked Truman.

"If they know they're not alone, I think they would take a stand."

Truman weighed Owen's words. "What about Cade Pruitt?"

Owen shook his head. "I think it's too late for him. McDonald needs to set an example, and he sees Cade as expendable." Owen wiped the back of a shaky hand across his mouth.

"He's just a kid!" said Truman.

"Not in McDonald's eyes."

"What else do I need to know about McDonald? Did he set fire to Tilda Brass's barn?"

Owen blew out a breath and hesitated.

"Fucking spill it!" Truman ordered.

"He did. Joshua Pence and another guy set the fire under his orders."

"Why? To get her to sell the property?"

"Yes. There's a bridge on her property that crosses the river and is the only other way into the McDonald property. He wants to blow up the bridge, isolating his piece of land except for the one defensible road in."

Truman pictured the road to the ranch, surrounded on both sides by hills. Easy to defend it and keep people out. He remembered the map with the curving river that formed a border between the Brass and McDonald properties. Destroying the bridge would nearly isolate McDonald's land. The mountains were too steep on the other sides to access the land. No doubt a team of Navy SEALs could infiltrate the property, but not the local police. "Is that what the dynamite was for?"

Owen nodded in the dark. "He was waiting to buy the property before blowing up the bridge, but when she kept refusing, he was weighing whether or not to blow it anyway." Owen paused. "He's a little paranoid."

"A little?"

"I kept telling him to wait. He knew the explosion would call attention to what he was doing out here, but his paranoia increasingly pressured him to cut off the outside world. Some of the other guys wanted to use the dynamite to send a message. They'd talked about blowing up the FBI office in town, or even your department."

Truman's blood chilled at the thought of his murdered staff.

"I called in a report about the dynamite, hoping the state police would take it off his land, but Tom was here the day they came and stopped them."

"What is McDonald doing here?" Truman whispered. "He's forming a militia, right?"

Owen's shoulders slumped. "In a way. That's just one element."

"Explain," Truman snapped. Part of his hearing focused on the mess hall where McDonald had taken Mercy. It was silent. *What is taking the county sheriff so long to get here?*

Another minute and Owen wouldn't be able to keep Truman from breaking in on his own.

"He's trying to create a place where we make the rules. Someplace people can go and be heard."

"Bullshit. *The people* won't make the rules; he will."

Owen shuffled his feet. "Yeah, I see that now. He talks of a community of leadership, but all I've seen is that he makes the rules and—"

Owen clamped his mouth shut.

Truman waited. "What happened?" he finally asked. "What did he do?"

The sound of Owen swallowing was loud in the quiet forest. "He killed a guy. Shot him right in front of me."

"Why didn't you go to the police?" Truman nearly shouted as he fell back a step. *My God. McDonald truly is insane.*

Mercy.

I've got to get her away from him.

"It just happened today," Owen pleaded. "I knew then I had to get out and go to the police and tell them everything I know. I was trying to figure out how to leave . . . I didn't want McDonald coming after me and my family."

"Who'd he shoot?" Truman suspected he knew the answer.

"A Realtor. Jack Howell."

I knew it. "What else do you know about McDonald?" Truman could barely speak. Anger had dried out his mouth.

"He ordered Pence's death. Pence shot those deputies, and McDonald was furious that he'd acted without orders."

Truman's mind spun. "You saw this?"

"I wasn't there the night he ordered Pence's death, but I heard the story consistently from other men who were. They said Pence and

McDonald had a huge blowup over Pence taking things into his own hands. Supposedly Pence thought McDonald would be happy with the death of some cops, but he'd jumped the gun." He stopped and lowered his tone. "Striking back at the police wasn't to come until later. McDonald wanted to be more established first."

Truman pressed his palms against his eyes and bent at the waist, trying to fathom what Owen had just revealed.

McDonald was building a community to rule itself and kill cops.

Pence had killed the deputies on impulse, and McDonald had ordered his death. *This* was the type of community McDonald was putting together. One where he was king and took orders from no one. He was surrounding himself with a growing army of angry men who secretly hoped to be kings themselves one day and couldn't see that McDonald offered only a dictatorship.

A society formed by fear, paranoia, and isolation, not formed from freedom. "Why the fire at Pence's death?" Truman whispered.

Owen shrugged. "There'd been a lot of fires. McDonald figured you'd group them all together. Maybe even blame Pence for all of them."

I nearly did.

"How can you even be in the same room with him?" Truman asked, his mind spinning. "Most men would give him a wide berth . . . especially after hearing he ordered the murder of Joshua Pence."

Owen blew out a deep breath. "I was angry. Fuck, I was bitter and furious and looking to strike back after Levi's death. My brother *shouldn't be dead.*" His words shot through the air, forced out with anger and hate.

"I agree it shouldn't have happened."

"You were easy to blame," Owen said slowly. "Mercy was easy to blame. I was brought up to be wary of the government and law enforcement, and when my brother died, I needed someone to take responsibility. It was easier to hate the establishment than admit that Levi might have done something stupid."

"Levi was intentionally shot. Yes, Levi's actions up to that point weren't honorable, but he didn't pull the trigger. There's only one person to blame for that. Craig Rafferty."

"It's very unsatisfying to blame a dead man." Owen was broken, his voice barely a whisper.

He can't get past Levi's death.

"I hear sirens," Owen said in a tone of hope just as the far-off sounds reached Truman's ears.

"Yes!" Relief flooded Truman, and his breathing came easier. He checked for reception on his phone again, desperate to let the county deputies know what was happening inside the compound. No luck. "Dammit!"

The sirens stopped. Owen and Truman stared at each other in the dark, waiting for them to restart.

Perhaps they're coming in silently.

Rapid gunfire sounded. Even though it was far away, both men crouched and hunkered behind their trees.

"They stopped the law enforcement out on the road," Owen hissed. "I'm sure Tom sent out a crew to make certain no one gets into the compound."

Sounds of intermittent gunfire continued, cracking through the night. And then it stopped.

Truman held his breath. *Who won? Did more officers just die?*

He wanted to vomit.

"Your help isn't coming," Owen whispered.

"We don't know that." Truman's heart was somewhere around his feet. *What are we going to do?* The silence of the night air crushed his hope.

Shouts sounded from the direction of the mess hall. Both men spun to face it as Truman's heart rate spiked.

"You need to stay hidden," Owen stated. "If they spot you, I don't want to think about what they'd do, but I can go in and stall them.

Maybe I can get her out somehow." Owen started toward the hall. "McDonald is probably wondering where I am anyway. Try to get closer to the farmhouse. That's the best place to get a cell signal."

Truman grabbed his arm. "Be careful!"

Owen stopped and glanced back at Truman. "I should be fine. For some reason McDonald values my opinion."

Truman tightened his grip, needing to get the words out before Owen vanished. "Mercy loves you, you know. She's pissed as hell at how you've treated her, but she wants her brother back in her life more than anything."

Owen froze. His throat moved, and he opened his mouth. It took two tries to form hoarse words. "I know."

Truman let go of his arm and watched Owen vanish into the darkness. *Does he really understand? Does he see Mercy's pain?*

More shouts sounded from the mess hall, and Truman was alone in the cold night.

Do I have any backup?

"It's time for a trial!" McDonald shouted.

Cade blinked his one good eye in the bright light of the mess hall. Two men had untied his ankles, hauled him off the floor of the pantry, and dragged him onto a bench seat at the front of the room. His feet had been too numb to cooperate. The men of the ranch shouted their pleasure at McDonald's words.

Immediate sweat ran down his back.

They're bloodthirsty. And looking at me.

His eye was swollen shut, and he breathed heavily through his mouth, wondering how bad he looked. His nose ached unbearably, but at least the pain in his sides had diminished to simple discomfort. He turned his head to scan the room with his good eye.

What the hell?

On a bench ten feet away was Kaylie's aunt. She sat up straight, staring directly at him, her face expressionless. Her hands were fastened behind her back the same as his. She wore boots, dark jeans, and a half-zip sweatshirt, looking like any other woman he might see on the streets of Eagle's Nest, not like an FBI agent. He glanced at the crowd and felt a stab of fear at the way some of the men were staring at her.

His parents had taught him to respect everyone, and it wasn't respect he saw in the men's eyes.

He turned his good eye back to her. She hadn't moved a hair. If she'd been anyone else, he would have thought she was petrified. But the calm in her eyes told him she was in full control.

"I like 'em tall and lean," shouted one man from the audience. Mercy gave the crowd a brief glance and rolled her eyes, triggering bouts of laughter and more comments.

"She's not interested in you!"

"Which one you talkin' about?"

Louder laughter.

Cade ignored the crass comment as terror ripped through his heart.

"Settle down!" McDonald ordered. "Everyone take a seat! Now!"

The men in the room jumped to obey, pushing and shoving to get the seats closer to the front of the room. Cade looked at Mercy again. The two of them sat on identical benches, facing the crowd. McDonald stood between them.

Which one of us is on trial?

McDonald turned and smiled at him, his eyes nearly disappearing in the folds above his cheeks.

It's me.

McDonald's face stated he already knew the outcome of the trial. *He's stalling to create a show for his men.*

Mercy didn't hide her frown. Her gaze bounced from Cade to McDonald and then to the men. But still she wasn't scared. Cade was ready to shit his pants, but Mercy acted as if she were memorizing faces for execution later.

"As you know," McDonald began in an official tone, pacing between the two benches like a senior statesman, "Cade Pruitt is accused of leaking our secrets to the FBI and leading them to our doorstep."

"What secrets?" asked Mercy.

"Out of order!" McDonald pointed a fat finger at her face.

Mercy glanced at the audience. "Does Cade not have representation? Surely you'll allow someone to argue his case. Or are you afraid of what you'll hear?"

The audience was silent, but every man turned his gaze to McDonald. Frustration flitted across his face and vanished.

"This land is no longer part of the United States," McDonald intoned. "Things are run differently here."

"Where are we?" she asked.

No one answered.

"I bet your men would appreciate representation if *they* ever found themselves on trial," Mercy stated, raising a brow.

The audience shifted in their seats, and Cade felt the tension rise in the room.

"Owen." McDonald gestured. "Get up here and help this traitor defend himself."

Mercy's head turned with a jerk and froze as she spotted her brother. He slowly stood in the back of the room. Cade's lungs tightened. *Kaylie said he hates Mercy.*

Owen Kilpatrick took his time walking to the front. "May I have ten minutes to talk to the defendant?"

"You have one," McDonald snapped as anger flushed his face.

"You're talking about this boy's life," said Owen. "I think that deserves more than sixty seconds." He turned and looked over the room, holding his head high. "I know we're all new to this place, but I think we need to set a precedent of not making snap decisions when someone's life hangs in the balance. Who knows if it might be you sitting on this bench? How would you want it handled?"

Cade saw a few scattered nods and heard a few mutters. *Do they agree?* He couldn't tell if Owen had swayed the crowd. Owen took two steps closer to McDonald and whispered to him loud enough for Cade to hear. "Trying to make you look more objective."

McDonald's expression said he didn't believe that was the reason at all.

"Your time is up," McDonald stated. He looked at Cade. "What information did you tell the FBI about us?"

"He didn't tell us anything," said Mercy.

"Liar!" "Bullshit!" "Don't let her talk!" came from the audience.

Mercy looked to the group. "He never said a word," she shouted back. "I didn't know who he was until I came out here the other day. And I haven't seen him since then!"

The men didn't believe her.

Cade couldn't move, his limbs made of lead. He tuned out the audience's shouts, his focus on Mercy and Owen, the only two people in the room who seemed to want him to live. *Everyone else wants me dead.* He couldn't look at the men he'd worked alongside anymore; they'd become a pack of animals, any friendships he'd started forgotten in their need for blood.

McDonald jerked his head at the two men who'd dragged Cade out of the kitchen. They grabbed his arms and pulled him to his feet.

This is it. They're going to kill me.

His legs felt like pudding; his heartbeat was the loudest sound in the room.

"Do it in the woods," McDonald ordered.

The men faltered. Out of his good eye, Cade saw a questioning glance on the face of one of his handlers.

McDonald saw it too.

"Get it over with and you'll get the woman for your trouble."

The smile on his handler's face made Cade nearly vomit again. His legs gave way as the men yanked him toward the door, and a loud roar started in his ears. Beyond the noise in his head, he heard Mercy vehemently argue against his fate.

She's powerless.

The man on his right kicked open the door, and together the two of them hauled Cade out into the freezing night.

He started to scream.

THIRTY-ONE

He's still alive!

Truman silently jogged behind the two men, a sickening feeling in his stomach as they pulled Cade toward the woods. There were no other buildings in their path. Wherever they were taking the young man, it wasn't to make him comfortable. Cade shouted and fought, but the men handled him with ease, ignoring his cries. Truman crept closer, trying to see if either man was armed.

"When he said the woman, he meant the FBI agent," said the man on Cade's right.

"But he didn't say specifically *that* woman," argued the other. "For all we know he was talking about that bitch Shelly. I'm telling you, when McDonald isn't specific, it's for a reason."

"Well, I don't want anything to do with Shelly. Nearly every guy in this place has been between her legs."

"She's not so bad."

"I want a chance at that fed woman. She's hot, just like her blind sister. Too bad that blind bitch done got herself pregnant. But we made sure she paid for that."

"She had it coming," added the second man.

These two threw the rocks and mud at Rose? Fury fueled Truman.

"Please don't kill me." Cade's plea ripped at his heart. His shouting had been replaced with begging for his life.

"Sorry, kid. Boss's orders."

Fuck!

Both men had Cade's upper arms firmly in both hands. Cade thrashed with every step, fighting them as they drew deeper into the woods. *I've got to stop them.* Truman glanced around, looking for any witnesses.

It's now or never.

He took four running steps, sucked in a loud breath, and kicked the man on Cade's right in the side of the knee with his metal-toed boot, putting all his weight and momentum behind the kick.

The man made a sound like a strangled dog and let go of Cade as he collapsed in agony. Truman whirled on the second man and delivered a blow to his nose, appreciating the crunch of the cartilage as it was crushed under his fist.

He spun back to the first man on the ground and shot a swift kick to his abdomen. The first man gave another suffering-dog noise and curled in on himself. Broken Nose was doubled over with his hands over his face, so Truman administered a brutal kick to that one's knee, and then both men writhed in the dirt in pain. "That was for Rose."

Cade had fallen to his knees and dived out of the way.

Panting hard, Truman quickly checked each swearing man for weapons. He removed two knives, thankful neither had a gun.

He knelt behind Cade and struggled to untie his hands. He considered cutting the rope but knew that in the dim light he'd only cut the young man. After a minute of fumbling, he loosened the knots. Leaving Cade to massage feeling back into his hands, Truman turned to the two men in pain.

"Sit back to back," he ordered.

"Fuck off," said the one who'd sounded like an injured dog.

Truman stepped on his hurt knee and the shrieks hurt his eardrums. "Shut up," he ordered. "Or I'll silence you myself."

Broken Nose scooted over to press his back against the other man's. Truman quickly bound their wrists together behind their backs with the rope from Cade's hands. It wasn't a foolproof job, but he figured the knee injuries would slow them down more than anything, and they were too far away for anyone to hear their shouts for help.

"Where's the police?" Cade asked in a weak voice. He breathed hard through his mouth. The blood on his face looked black, and Truman realized he had one eye swollen shut.

"You okay?" he asked.

"Where's the police?" Cade repeated.

"It's just me," said Truman.

Dear Lord. There's no one else.

Mercy.

He turned away, stumbling a few steps, and dry heaved in the dark.

If Mercy breathed wrong, the entire room might explode.

Tempers were short and anger hung heavy in the air of the mess hall. Everywhere she looked, fury and impatience were written on the faces of McDonald's followers. There was also an eagerness, a need to see something dreadful shining in their eyes, reminiscent of the look of rabid fans watching a car race, hoping to see a crash. The tension had escalated as Cade left the room, and now their focus had returned to her.

A situation near boiling. A millimeter away from a trigger pull.

She breathed slowly and evenly, her mind considering and rejecting plans to safely escape.

Owen held up his hands to the audience. "Quiet down!" A hush fell over the crowd, and the abrupt silence did little to calm Mercy's nerves. *Don't let them see I'm scared.*

She briefly met Owen's gaze before he turned it on Tom McDonald. Something was different about her brother. When McDonald had called on him to defend Cade, there'd been a calm in his eyes she hadn't seen before. A different attitude. And just now she swore she'd seen a need to stop McDonald in his gaze. Had he finally seen the light?

"Did you just order Cade's murder?" he hissed at McDonald.

Anger flitted across the large man's face. "You're out of line, Kilpatrick."

They stared at each other as the rapt audience watched, and Mercy worried for her brother's life. *Be careful!*

Owen turned to the men. "Is *this* who you want for a leader? Someone who orders another man to be killed because he *thinks* he's a threat? Did we ever hear any concrete evidence against Cade Pruitt?" Conviction rocked his words as he made eye contact with several McDonald men. "That was no trial! That was an injustice. Another murder ordered by a man with too much power."

Restless murmurs sounded in the crowd.

Mercy saw eyes flicker and nervous feet shuffle.

"Stand down, Kilpatrick!" shouted a voice from the crowd. "We didn't sign on to follow you. We're with McDonald! The boy had it coming!"

Several voices chorused in agreement.

"Did Joshua Pence have it coming?" Owen asked.

Heads bobbed in agreement. "He didn't follow orders," said a man in the front row. "He could have brought the entire state's police forces down on our heads."

"*Fucking pigs!*" shouted a man from the back.

Mercy winced, feeling the room's anger refocus on her. She kept her head up, watching Owen and judging the temper of the crowd. They were a hair's breadth away from erupting.

"Did Jack Howell have it coming?" Owen asked. He pointed at one of the men. "You dealt with the Realtor in the past. Did he deserve to be shot in the head at McDonald's whim?"

Mercy caught her breath. *That's what happened to the Realtor?*

The room went silent, confusion crossing several faces.

McDonald gestured at Owen. "Get him out of here!" McDonald's face was the dark red of new bricks, and sweat beaded his temples. His chest heaved with each breath. "You're lying, Kilpatrick!"

A few men stepped forward to follow McDonald's orders, but hesitated to grab her brother.

"He shot Jack Howell right in front of me," Owen continued. "And then ordered me to take care of the body. I can see by your faces that you didn't—"

"Shut up!" McDonald roared. "Howell got sloppy and was about to ruin all our plans." He looked to the group. "Was I to let one man put asunder all that we've worked for?" His face darkened to a deeper shade. "Get Kilpatrick out of here before he does the same thing!"

Determination crossed the faces of the men who'd come forward to handle Owen. Two men grabbed his arms, and another removed her brother's gun, shoving it in the back of his jeans. "I'm not tearing this group apart," Owen yelled, attempting to jerk his arms away. "You're letting McDonald do it for you." His guards held firm and looked to McDonald for their next orders.

"No! This isn't right! He could do the same to any of us!" shouted a man Mercy recognized from her first visit to the ranch. "He's written off Cade and now Owen because they dared to have a different opinion!"

"That's not what we want in a leader," argued a second voice. Several men nodded emphatically.

The mob turned on one another, slowly dividing into two groups as they argued. Mercy held her breath, eyeing the high number of weapons on hips.

This could turn ugly very fast.

And then it did.

A man tried to pull away one of Owen's guards and got a fist in the jaw for his effort. Owen landed a blow on the mouth of his guard and the room erupted. Shoving, hitting, pulling, shouting. Mercy slowly stood and, with her wrists still bound, backed toward a door.

A hand grabbed her arm.

McDonald. His face was no longer red; it was gray, and sweat ran down both sides of his face. He looked ready to vomit.

"I'll get you out," he said in an unsteady voice, shocking her with his offer. "This way." He headed for the same door, towing her behind him. Mercy stumbled, trying to reverse direction.

I'm not going anywhere with him.

He held tight to her arm. "Mercy! This way!"

"Forget it," she grunted as she tried to jerk out of his grip. Her arm came loose and she planted her feet to regain her balance, planning to kick him in the groin.

An elbow from the brawl behind her nailed her in the back and she lurched forward. Back into McDonald's grasp.

Noooo!

He grabbed her upper arms and shook them, making her look at him. "Listen to me!"

"Like hell!" She twisted, trying to wrench out of his tight hold.

He swayed and grabbed at his chest with one hand and then fell to a knee, panting for breath, nearly pulling her to the floor. He looked up at her, his eyes terrified and his face radiating pain. Mercy suddenly understood.

"He's having a heart attack!" she yelled, scanning for anyone who would help. The melee was in full force, and her shout was swallowed up in the sounds of the fighting. McDonald yanked heavily on her arm as he fell completely to the floor, and she was forced to her knees beside him. "He needs CPR!"

Someone bent over beside her. The familiar man who'd just protested about Cade and Owen.

"Give him CPR!" she ordered. McDonald was gasping for breath, clawing at his chest with one hand, terror in his eyes. His hand had her upper arm in a death grip.

"I don't know how!" The man fished in McDonald's pocket and dug out the key to her cuffs, his hands shaking.

She bent close to McDonald, trying to give the helper easier access to her hands.

"You look like your mother," McDonald croaked, as the other man fumbled with her cuffs.

Mercy froze and met the dying man's eyes. "What?"

"I would never have let them do anything to you," he said in a hoarse voice, his eyes red and earnest. "My heart broke at the path you chose, but I'd hoped you'd come around."

Her arms fell to her sides as the cuffs came off. She pressed her fingers against the folds of flesh in McDonald's neck, searching for his pulse. She found a rapid fluttering beat, but he fought to breathe.

His heart is still beating, so I don't do compressions. He's still breathing, so I don't do rescue breaths.

Or do I?

Panic scrambled her brain.

"I wouldn't have let them hurt you," he repeated, holding her gaze. "Niece."

Niece? She searched his face, but it was unfamiliar. "Who are you?" she whispered.

Disappointment filled his eyes. "I'd hoped you'd know me. Did they let my memory go so easily?"

Confusion racked her. "I don't understand."

"I'm your uncle Aaron."

The sounds of the fights around her faded as a loud buzz clogged her ears. *My mother's younger brother? The Mount St. Helens eruption victim?* The high school portrait of a smiling teenager shot through her brain.

He looked nothing like the old picture. But she saw her other uncles around his eyes.

"You're dead," she whispered.

He gave a weak smile. "Only on paper."

Explosions and flashes of light filled the room, and Mercy covered her ears as she squeezed her eyes shut.

Flashbangs.

"THIS IS THE DESCHUTES COUNTY SHERIFF'S OFFICE," was announced on a bullhorn.

The cavalry made it.

THIRTY-TWO

Truman shoved his way through the throngs of deputies and McDonald followers. He'd been ordered to stay back as the SWAT team threw in flashbangs and then breached the mess hall. The abrupt attack, in conjunction with the confusion from the explosions, had brought the fighting inside to an immediate halt with no shots fired.

A success.

He spotted Mercy on her knees next to Tom McDonald's prone form at the front of the hall. Two deputies administered aid as Mercy watched.

She wasn't hurt.

Relief made his knees shake as he strode toward her, his gaze locked on the back of her dark head.

What would I have done if she hadn't . . .

He refused to let his mind go there.

"Mercy." He stopped beside her, and his heart double-skipped as she looked up at him. Relief and joy shone in her eyes. He helped her to her feet and pulled her to him, hiding his face in her hair.

"Dammit," he muttered.

"I know," she answered against his neck. "What happened?"

"The sheriff's department got stopped by McDonald's men at a roadblock on the property. A few men were injured, but none too badly. They backed off but had already sent a second group to enter the compound through the other road from the Brass property. When they showed up, I told them what was going on, and they immediately breached the hall."

"Come on, Tom!" hollered one of the deputies as he started CPR on the big man.

Mercy jerked out of Truman's arms and spun back to the frantic deputies.

"His breathing has stopped!"

"Get the oxygen mask!"

Truman grabbed her shoulders before she could kneel again at the man's side. McDonald's face was gray and his mouth slack. His eyes stared into space. "Let them work."

Mercy stopped struggling. "He's my uncle," she whispered.

"What?" Truman froze. *How can that be?*

"He's one of my mother's brothers. Everyone thought he was dead . . . Well, I thought he was dead." Her voice sharpened. "I wonder who knew he was still alive."

Truman was stunned. "You recognized him?"

"No. I've never met him, but he knew who I was." Her gaze was glued to the silent man on the floor. "He tried to get me out of here at the last second."

Truman tried to grasp what she'd just said. *McDonald tried to get her out?*

After all his bluster?

"He would have killed you if he needed to. Family or not," Truman stated slowly, not ready to accept any good intentions on McDonald's part. "No one was going to stand in his way. Especially cops."

She turned her head in Owen's direction. Her brother sat in a line with a dozen of McDonald's men, being questioned by deputies. Cade was receiving medical attention from a county deputy who'd covered his eye with gauze and requested an ambulance. Other than a few bloody noses and fat lips, McDonald's men seemed to have survived the brawl with few injuries. Except for the two men Truman had tied up outside.

They were currently being loaded into patrol vehicles by deputies. Neither could walk, and they had to be carried.

Truman spotted Eddie and Jeff Garrison among the interviewers, intently taking notes, and he gave a sigh of relief that they hadn't been injured in the shoot-out at the roadblock. The evening could have had a much deadlier outcome. For both sides.

Mercy's shoulders rose and lowered with her deep breaths under Truman's hands as she stared at her brother across the room.

"Who else has lied to me?" she quietly asked.

◆　◆　◆

The next morning Truman stared at an email on his department computer. He'd read it five times in the last few hours.

Would things have been different if I'd received this yesterday?

He didn't think so.

He picked up the yellowing fingerprints record he'd spent an hour searching for in his department's ancient storage. Even to his untrained eye, the prints clearly matched the scan of current prints that Deputy Chad Wheeler had sent from Idaho.

Tom McDonald used to be Aaron Belmonte. Mercy's youngest uncle reportedly killed in the Mount St. Helens eruption in 1980. His body had never been recovered, as was the case for many of the victims.

But now Aaron was truly dead. He'd never recovered from last night's heart attack.

The email was from the reserve officer whom Deputy Wheeler had asked to dig into Tom McDonald's background. There'd been no record of Tom McDonald's death in the past, but the officer had found an empty time slot between 1975 and 1980 where he'd vanished. No tax returns, no driver's license renewal, no legal paperwork anywhere. He was a loner, and no one had asked about his absence.

Then in 1980 he'd been issued a new license.

The officer couldn't find a copy of a license photo from earlier than 1980, but every photo after that was of the bearded Tom McDonald that Truman now knew was Mercy's uncle Aaron.

Digging deeper, the officer had found that in 1974, the real Tom McDonald had shared an address with Silas Campbell. The same Silas Campbell who'd had a falling-out with the new Tom McDonald last year. Truman figured Silas had helped Aaron take over Tom McDonald's identity in 1980 after the eruption.

Probably because Silas knew the original owner of the name was dead.

Truman was almost certain Silas had had a hand in the first Tom McDonald's disappearance. The Idaho militiaman had a ruthless reputation. A very clean reputation—he knew how to walk the legal line—but a ruthless one.

The old fingerprint card he held was from Aaron Belmonte's arrest in 1978. It'd never been digitized. No Idaho police department had called and requested a copy, so Aaron's prints had sat in a box for decades. Aaron Belmonte had a decent list of arrests in Eagle's Nest and in Deschutes County—DUI, speeding, theft. Nothing worth faking his death over. But investigating further, Truman suspected becoming a person of interest in the fire at the county courthouse in April of 1980 had made Aaron's palms sweat.

Someone had to have told Aaron's family he'd been camping near Mount St. Helens. Aaron hadn't had a crystal ball to predict the eruption and tell people he'd gone camping ahead of time. He needed to spread the camping story after the mountain blew. Something he couldn't do on his own.

Who was his accomplice?

No doubt it had been one of his four brothers. Happy to help get him off the federal government's radar for the courthouse fire.

Truman twisted his lips and gave Aaron a few props for the disappearing idea. Although he did remember others had tried to fake their deaths on 9/11, either to collect money or to escape from something in their lives. *Disgusting.*

The inability to see Aaron pay for his recent crimes gnawed at Truman's gut. But at least several of Aaron's men had been charged. The two men who'd talked about their assault on Rose and dragged Cade into the woods would be prosecuted, along with the half dozen men who'd formed the roadblock and fired on officers. Truman didn't know if there would be other arrests; for the most part, the rest of the men hadn't done anything but exhibit bad judgment by choosing to follow Tom McDonald.

Mercy would be arriving at the station at any minute. He'd already shared the email and his comparison of the fingerprints with her, and next they'd drive to her parents' home to break the news to her mother that the brother she'd believed was dead had just died again.

Or had her mother known he was alive?

◆ ◆ ◆

Mercy was numb.

When she wasn't pissed as hell.

As Truman parked in front of her parents' home, she alternated between the two emotions. Her uncle was dead; she should be grieving. But she'd believed he'd died before she was born, and the man she'd briefly known as Tom McDonald she hadn't liked. At all.

That's when the anger started to flare.

Who'd known her uncle was alive?

She was ready for some answers.

Owen had no explanations. She'd talked with him for an hour between police interviews, and he'd told her he'd thought it odd that Tom McDonald trusted him so rapidly, but swore he'd never dreamed the man was related to them. Like her, Owen was shell shocked over the revelation. He'd led the police to Jack Howell's body and told his story a half dozen times to different investigators. She didn't think he would be charged with Jack's death.

He'd apologized to Mercy. Their talk had been full of tears from both of them. He'd admitted he'd been full of rage after Levi's death and searching for someone to blame. She'd been an easy target. Seeing Owen break down as they gripped each other's hands, and hearing him admit he knew it wasn't her fault that Levi had died, started to heal the crack in her heart. A crack she'd feared would never be repaired.

Truman told her how Owen had kept him from rushing into a nest of McDonald men when she'd been grabbed at the farmhouse. And that Owen had gone into the mess hall with the intent to get her away from Tom McDonald.

She'd left her conversation with Owen feeling as if she was on the road to getting her brother back.

Kaylie was at the hospital with Cade. The teen had panicked over the condition of her boyfriend's injuries and refused to leave him. He had two broken ribs and was waiting to see a specialist about his eye. Some vision had already been restored, and the ER doctor was cautiously optimistic that it would fully heal. Two of Cade's friends were being charged with arson. Landon had shared names of accomplices, including a girl, explaining the female laughter that Clyde Jenkins had heard on his property.

Cade had stated he was ready for some new friends.

In private, Kaylie had told Mercy that she felt foolish for having doubted Cade's commitment. Mercy had given her a firm but gentle lecture on giving people the benefit of the doubt and not allowing her anxiety to screw with her emotions. Mercy had felt like an imposter as she gave her niece relationship advice.

It was easier to give advice than to apply it to her own life.

Now it was time to face her parents. They knew Mercy and Truman were coming. Mercy had called and told her mother about Aaron's new identity and asked if she'd known the truth.

The shock over the phone had sounded real.

But Mercy wasn't taking anything for granted. She needed to look her mother in the eye and ask again.

Her footsteps were heavy on her parents' stairs. Truman took her arm and gently pulled her to a stop, turning her to face him.

"Hey. No matter what we find out, nothing has changed."

"I agree," she said. "But it sure rattled me and everyone else. How could Aaron do that to his family?"

"You don't know what type of person he was," Truman stated. "I doubt your mother's happy memories of her brother reflect the man we dealt with. Someone who fakes their death and abandons their family has a lot going on in their head that we can never understand."

Deborah Kilpatrick opened the door before they could knock. Her mother looked as if she'd been awake for three days. Her eyes were red and swollen, and her skin was dull. She opened her arms to Mercy and Mercy stepped into them. "I'm so sorry, Mom."

Her mother squeezed her tighter.

Rose came to the door and joined the embrace. Mercy ran her hand over Rose's soft hair and felt Rose's flat stomach press against her side. Her pregnancy still didn't show. The gash on her cheek was healing rapidly, but the bruise around it had turned a horrendous purple.

A wave of love for Rose crashed through her, and she fought back the tears.

Lord, I'm an emotional wreck.

They moved into the living room, where her father stood behind a chair with his arms crossed. He nodded at Mercy and at Truman, but didn't move a step in their direction. Deborah led Mercy and Rose to the couch, and the three of them sat down together.

"I called your uncle John and uncle Mark in Washington," her mother started. "They were as shocked as I was."

"Are you sure they were telling the truth, Mom?" Mercy asked. "Someone helped Aaron with his plan way back after the volcano erupted. Do you remember who told the family that Aaron had gone camping?"

Her mother shook her head. "I have no idea. My mother told me over the phone. Neither Aaron nor I had lived at home for a long time, but one of my other two brothers could have told the family." Her voice caught.

And they took their secret to their graves.

"I don't think we'll ever know who helped him," said Mercy. "I can't believe the secret was kept for all these years." She glanced at her father, and her heart stopped.

He knew.

Karl Kilpatrick's face was stony and hard, and his eyes looked emotionally drained. *He's trying too hard to be expressionless.* Her father held her gaze for a brief second before looking away.

Damn you.

How could he keep that secret from her mother for decades? As her mother sobbed into her hands, Mercy became confident that she'd never known that Aaron had lived.

But her father was another story. Mercy glanced at Truman. He was studying her father with a knowing expression.

He sees it too.

Had her father helped Aaron start over, or had he heard about it from one of the brothers? Had he known Aaron was living outside of town and trying to build a militia? Her father hated militias. He viewed them as a crude attempt at government, a masquerade of representing the little guy, usually led by someone with a big ego who simply wanted power. Perhaps her father hadn't maintained contact with Aaron after he escaped to Idaho.

She doubted her father would ever tell her the truth.

Mercy needed to let it go. It no longer mattered.

But no one would stop her from getting to know her family again. She had everything to gain.

"What are you doing for Thanksgiving tomorrow?" Mercy asked her mother before she could talk herself out of the idea. "I think I need to spend some time with my family." A big smile crossed Rose's face, and she gave Mercy's hand an excited squeeze.

Her mother wiped the tears from her cheeks. "Please come over and eat with us." Deborah looked directly at Mercy, not her husband, as she made the request.

"I'd love to," said Mercy. "Truman is cooking a turkey. We'll bring that along with Kaylie and her pies. I've already made plans with Pearl for dessert, but I'll have her meet us here instead." Happiness unexpectedly bubbled in her stomach, and a warm feeling of contentment filled her limbs and made her smile. Her father could glower all he wanted. She wouldn't allow him to intimidate her away from her family.

I guess the holiday does mean something to me.

Mercy blew out a deep breath as they reached Truman's SUV in her parents' yard.

"Your father knew the truth about your uncle Aaron's death," Truman stated. He pulled her against him, and she took a moment to lean her head on his shoulder.

"I saw that," she said. "How can you hide a secret like that from your spouse for decades?"

"Your father is tough," Truman said. "He's got skin of steel. Sorta reminds me of you."

She gave him a side-eyed glance, not certain if that was a compliment.

Truman took a deep breath. "I was scared shitless when I saw them drag you inside the mess hall last night." He clamped his lips together as he held her gaze.

"I've got skin of steel, remember?" she joked, nervous about the intensity in his gaze. "I would have been fine."

His brows narrowed slightly, his brown eyes deadly serious.

Uh-oh.

"I've kept my mouth shut over the months we've been together," Truman said. "Because I didn't want you to feel pressured, but when I realized last night that you might die and I'd never told you I'd loved you, I swore I'd fix that immediately. I'm done holding back."

She couldn't move. *I'm not ready for this. Please, not now, Truman . . .*

"I love you, Mercy Kilpatrick. I've loved you since nearly the first moment I saw you. I knew immediately that you were someone who would challenge me and excite me and make me feel alive again. I was an idiot to not tell you sooner. I almost waited too long. So if you have a problem with the fact that I've told you I love you, that's too damned bad. Not long ago I told you that it's not a sign of weakness to allow yourself to be loved. Here's your chance to take the biggest risk of your life and allow my love to become a part of you. It's permanent and unconditional. It's never going to leave."

She held his brown gaze, feeling his words settle into her skin and deep into her bones. *How many women would love to hear their man say that?*

But I'm terrified.

But his dark eyes told her he meant every word. No one was more honest than Truman.

But what if he's wrong? He can't see the future.

"Come back, Mercy," he said softly. "I see you running away."

She lowered her gaze and spotted the healing burn on his neck inside his collar. *He could have been killed that day.*

She didn't ever want to experience his death. Never. The thought of losing him made every cell in her body hurt. *I've been so wrong.*

I have everything to gain and nothing to lose.

Her gaze returned to his. "I love you too." The words were awkward and stiff, but she knew they'd come easier with practice. "Please don't ever push me away," she whispered as her eyes filled. "And don't let me push you away. It's what I do, you know. I do it because I don't want to get hurt." Her voice trailed off.

He pulled her close. "Never, Mercy. Absolutely never. I'm here to stay whether you like it or not."

An extraordinary sense of calm filled her. One she'd never felt before. *I believe him.*

ACKNOWLEDGMENTS

Creating a book requires a firm foundation of wonderful people. I'm lucky that I have fabulous children, the best husband, and my closest writer-buddy, Melinda. My Montlake publishing team knows how to smoothly handle the curveballs I throw at them and the best ways to find new readership. Thank you, Jessica, Anh, and Meg, for your support and understanding, and thank you to Charlotte for making my books shine.

Thank you to my readers for loving Mercy's first book. I was nervous to start a new series while my fans were so enthusiastic about their enjoyment of my Bone Secrets and Callahan books. Thank you from the bottom of my heart for embracing this series too. You asked for a "colliding of worlds" between my series, so I gave Ava McLane a brief cameo. For the next two Mercy books, I will include more of your favorite characters from Bone Secrets and Callahan & McLane.

ABOUT THE AUTHOR

Photo © 2016 Rebekah Jule Photography

Inspired by classic female heroines such as Nancy Drew, Trixie Belden, and Laura Ingalls Wilder, Kendra Elliot has always been a voracious reader. Now a *Wall Street Journal* bestselling author, Kendra is a three-time winner of the Daphne du Maurier Award for Excellence in Romantic Mystery/Suspense. She was also an International Thriller Writers finalist for Best Paperback Original and a *Romantic Times* finalist for Best Romantic Suspense.

Kendra was born and raised in the rainy Pacific Northwest, where she still lives with her husband and three daughters, though she's looking forward to the day when she can live in flip-flops. To learn more about the author and her work and to connect with her, visit www.KendraElliot.com.